STAR WARS®

Kathy Tyers

THE TRUCE AT BAKURA

BANTAM BOOKS
NEW YORK   TORONTO   LONDON   SYDNEY   AUCKLAND

STAR WARS: THE TRUCE AT BAKURA
A Bantam Book / January 1994

Library of Congress Cataloging-in-Publication Data

Tyers, Kathy.
  The truce at Bakura / Kathy Tyers.
    p.   cm. — (Star wars ; v. 4)
  ISBN 0-553-09541-2
  I. Title.   II. Series: Tyers, Kathy.   Star wars; v. 4.
PS3570.Y4T78   1994
813'.54—dc20   93-11388
                                                                      CIP

Published simultaneously in the United States and Canada

Bantam Books are published by Bantam Books, a division of Bantam Doubleday Dell Publishing Group, Inc. Its trademark, consisting of the words "Bantam Books" and the portrayal of a rooster, is Registered in U.S. Patent and Trademark Office and in other countries. Marca Registrada. Bantam Books, 1540 Broadway, New York, New York 10036.

PRINTED IN THE UNITED STATES OF AMERICA

BVG   0 9 8 7 6 5 4 3 2 1

Dedication

I can't think of *Star Wars* without remembering the opening fanfare from its soundtrack. I can't imagine an Imperial Star Destroyer's long, triangular silhouette without hearing ominous triplet rhythms. And who can picture the Mos Eisley cantina without that inimitable jazz band?

It is with grateful admiration that I dedicate this novel to the man who composed the musical scores for the three *Star Wars* movies:

John Williams

CHAPTER

1

ABOVE A DEAD WORLD, ONE HABITABLE MOON HUNG SUSPENDED LIKE A cloud-veiled turquoise. The eternal hand that held the chain of its orbit had dusted its velvet backdrop with brilliant stars, and cosmic energies danced on the wrinkles of space-time, singing their timeless music, neither noticing nor caring for the Empire, the Rebel Alliance, or their brief, petty wars.

But on that petty human scale of perspective, a fleet of starships orbited the moon's primary. Carbon streaks scored the sides of several ships. Droids swarmed around some, performing repairs. Metal shards that had been critical spaceship components, and human and alien bodies, orbited with the ships. The battle to destroy Emperor Palpatine's second Death Star had cost the Rebel Alliance heavily.

Luke Skywalker hustled across one cruiser's landing bay, red-eyed but still suffused with victory after the Ewoks' celebration. Passing a huddle of droids, he caught a whiff of coolants and lubricants. He ached, a dull gnawing in all his bones from the longest day of his life. Today—no, it was yesterday—he had met the Emperor. Yesterday, he had almost paid with his life for his faith in his father. Yet a passenger sharing his shuttle up to the cruiser from the Ewok village had already asked if Luke really killed the Emperor—and Darth Vader—single-handed.

Luke wasn't ready to announce the fact that "Darth Vader" had been Anakin Skywalker, his father. Still, he'd answered firmly: *Vader* killed Emperor Palpatine. Vader had flung him into the second Death Star's core. Luke would be explaining that for weeks, he guessed. For now, he merely wanted to check on his X-wing fighter.

To his surprise, it was overrun by service crew. Behind and above it, a magnacrane lowered Artoo-Detoo into the cylindrical droid socket behind his cockpit. "What's up?" Luke asked, standing to catch his breath.

"Oh. Sir," answered a khaki-suited crewman, disengaging a collapsible fuel hose, "your relief pilot's going out. Captain Antilles came back on the first shuttle and went on patrol immediately. He intercepted an Imperial drone ship—one of those antiques they used for carrying messages back before the Clone Wars. Incoming from deep space."

Incoming. Someone had sent a message *to* the Emperor. Luke smiled. "Guess they haven't heard yet. Wedge wants company? I'm not that tired. I could go."

The crewman didn't smile back. "Unfortunately, Captain Antilles touched off a self-destruct cycle while trying to release its message codes. He is manually blocking a critical gap—"

"Cancel the relief pilot," Luke exclaimed. Wedge Antilles had been his friend since the days of the first Death Star, where they'd flown in the final attack together. Without waiting to hear more, Luke spun toward the ready-room. A minute later, he was hopping back and pulling up one leg of an orange pressure suit.

Crewers scattered. He sprang up the ladder and into his inclined, padded seat, yanked on his helmet, then touched on the ship's fusion generator. A familiar high-energy whine built around him.

The man who'd spoken climbed up behind him. "But, sir, I think Admiral Ackbar wanted to debrief you."

"I'll be right back." Luke closed his cockpit canopy and ran an Alliance-record speed check of his systems and instruments. Nothing flagged his attention.

He switched on his comlink. "Rogue Leader, ready for takeoff."

"Opening hatch, sir."

He punched in the drive. An instant later, the dull ache in his body turned to ferocious pain. All the stars in his field of vision split into binaries and spun around each other. Crewers' voices babbled in his ears. Dizzily, he reached down inside himself for the quiet center Master Yoda had taught him to touch . . .

To touch . . .

There.

Exhaling one trembling breath, he measured his mastery of the pain. Stars shrank into singular gleams again. Whatever had caused that, he'd deal with it later. Through the Force, he quested outward and found Wedge's presence. His hands moved on the X-wing's controls almost effortlessly as he steered toward that end of the Fleet.

On his way, he got his first good look at the battle damage, the swarming repair droids and tow vessels. Mon Calamari Star Cruisers were plated and shielded to withstand multiple direct hits, but he thought he remembered several more of the huge, lumpy crafts. Fighting for his life, his father, and his integrity in the Emperor's throne room, he hadn't even felt the gut-wrenching Force disturbances from all those deaths. He hoped he wasn't getting used to them.

"Wedge, do you copy?" Luke asked over the subspace radio. He vectored out among the big ships of the Fleet. Scanners indicated that the nearest heavy transport was cautiously moving away from something much smaller. Four A-wings swooped along behind Luke. "Wedge, are you out there?"

"Sorry," he heard faintly. "Almost out of range of my ship's pickup. You see, I've got to . . ." Wedge trailed off, grunting. "I've got to keep these two crystals apart. It's a self-destruct of some sort."

"Crystals?" Luke asked, to keep Wedge talking. There was pain under that voice.

"Electrite crystal leads. Leftovers from the old 'elegance' days. The mechanism's trying to push them together. Let 'em touch . . . poof. The whole fusion engine."

Tumbling slowly above the blue glimmer of Endor, Luke spotted Wedge's X-wing. Alongside it drifted a nine-meter-long cylinder bearing Imperial markings, fully as long as the X-wing and almost all engine, a type of drone ship the Alliance still couldn't afford. For some reason, the drone gave him an eerie foreboding. The Empire never used such antiques any more. Why hadn't the sender been able to use standard Imperial channels?

Luke whistled. "No, we don't want to blow that big of an engine." No wonder the transport was moving away.

"Right." Wedge clung to one end of the cylinder, wearing a pressure suit and connected to the X-wing by a life-support tether. He must have blown his cockpit air and dove for the cylinder's master control the moment he realized he'd accidentally armed it to detonate. In a space pilot's lightweight pressure suit and closed-face emergency helmet, he could survive vacuum for several minutes.

"How long've you been out here, Wedge?"

"I don't know. Doesn't matter. The view's terrific."

Closing in, Luke reversed engines with care. Wedge held one hand inside a hinged panel. His head swiveled to follow Luke's X-wing as Luke used short, delicate engine bursts to match his momentum with the cylinder.

"Sure could use another hand." Wedge's words sounded cocky but the tone betrayed his strain. That hand must be half crushed. "What are you doing out here?"

"Enjoying the view." Luke considered his options. The A-wing pilots decelerated and hung back, probably assuming Luke knew what he was doing. "Artoo," he called, "what's the reach on your manipulator arm? If I got in close enough, could you help him?"

No—2.76 meters short at optimum angle, appeared on his head-up display.

Luke frowned. Sweat trickled on his forehead. Anything small, solid, and disposable would help. If he didn't hurry, his friend was dead. Already Wedge's sense in the Force wobbled dizzily.

Luke glanced at his lightsaber. He wasn't about to dispose of *that.*

Not even to save Wedge's life? Besides, he'd be able to get it back. Cautiously he slipped the saber into the flare ejection port's feed tube. He launched it out, then extended a hand toward it across ten meters of vacuum. He sent it gliding toward Wedge. Once near the target, he twisted his wrist.

The green-white blade appeared, silent in the vacuum of space. Wedge's wide brown eyes blinked behind his faceplate.

"On my signal," Luke said, "jump free."

"Luke, I'll lose fingers."

"*Way* free," Luke repeated. "You'll lose more than fingers if you stay there."

"What's the chance you could Jedi me a little nerve blockage? This hurts like crazy." Wedge's voice sounded weaker. He pulled in his knees and braced to push off.

At moments like these, moisture farming for Uncle Owen back on Tatooine didn't sound too bad. "I'll try," said Luke. "Show me the crystals. Look at them closely."

"Ho-kay." Wedge pulled around to stare into the hatchway. Letting the lightsaber drift, Luke felt for Wedge's friendly presence. He trusted Wedge not to resist this, to let him . . .

Through Wedge's eyes, and fighting the excruciating pain in Wedge's hand, Luke glimpsed a pair of round, multifaceted jewels —one inside his palm, the other crushing inward at the end of a spring mechanism from the back of his hand. Fist-sized, they reflected pale golden sparks of saber light out the hatch onto

Wedge's orange suit. Luke didn't think the flight glove alone would keep them apart, or he'd've simply told Wedge to slip out of it. Brief depressurization didn't damage extremities much.

If Wedge jumped, Luke would have a second at most to slice one crystal free, and only a little longer before Wedge fainted. Wedge was tethered and he'd be able to keep breathing, but he could lose a lot of blood. The glimpse blurred at the edges.

Luke tweaked Wedge's pain perception.

Too much to juggle. Luke's own aches began to ooze up from under control. "Got it," he grunted.

"Got what?" Wedge asked dreamily.

"The view," Luke said. "Jump on the count of three. Jump *hard*. One." Wedge didn't object. Clenching his teeth, Luke eased into a closer accord with the saber. So long as he focused on the saber, he could maintain control. "Two." Keeping up a steady count, he felt the saber, the crystals, and the critical gap, all as parts of the universe's wholeness.

"Three." Nothing happened. "Jump, Wedge!" Luke cried.

Weakly, Wedge launched himself. Luke swept in. One crystal soared free, reflecting a whirling green kaleidoscope onto the X-wing's upper S-foil.

"Ooh," crooned Wedge's voice in his ear. "Pretty." He spun, clutching his right hand.

"Wedge, reel in!"

No response. Luke bit his lip. He stabilized the tumbling saber and deactivated its blade. Wedge's tether stretched taut, high above the other X-wing. His limbs wobbled randomly.

Luke slapped his distress beacon. "Rogue Leader to Home One. Explosives disarmed. Request medical pickup. Now!"

From behind the A-wings, hanging back out of the danger zone, a med runner swooped into sight.

Wedge's body rose and sank with each breath as he floated upright in the Fleet's clear tank of healing bacta fluid. Much to Luke's relief, they'd saved all his fingers. Surgical droid Too-Onebee set the control board and then swiveled to face Luke. Slender, jointed limbs waved in front of his gleaming midsection. "Now you, sir. Please step behind the scanner."

"I'm all right." Luke leaned his stool against the bulkhead. "Just tired." Artoo-Detoo bleeped softly beside him, sounding concerned.

"Please, sir. This will only take a moment."

Luke sighed and shuffled around a man-high rectangular panel. "Okay?" he called out through it. "May I go now?"

"One moment more," came the mechanical voice, then clicking sounds. "One moment," the droid repeated. "Have you experienced double vision recently?"

"Well . . ." Luke scratched his head. "Yes. But just for a minute." Surely that little spell wasn't significant.

As the diagnostic panel retracted into the bulkhead, a medical flotation bed extended itself from the wall beside Too-Onebee. Luke backstepped. "What's that for?"

"You're not well, sir."

"I'm just tired."

"Sir, my diagnosis is sudden and massive calcification of your skeletal structure, of the rare type brought on by severely conductive exposure to electrical and other energy fields."

Energy fields. Yesterday. Emperor Palpatine, leering as blue-white sparks leaped off his fingertips while Luke writhed on the deck. Luke broke a sweat, the memory was so fresh. He'd thought he was dying. He *was* dying.

"The abrupt drop in blood minerals is causing muscular microseizures all over your body, sir."

So that was why he ached. Until an hour ago, he hadn't had a chance to sit still and notice. Deflated, he stared up at Too-Onebee. "But it's not permanent damage, is it? You don't have to replace bones?" He shuddered at the thought.

"The condition will become chronic unless you rest and allow me to treat you," answered the mechanical voice. "The alternative is bacta immersion."

Luke glanced at the tank. *Not that, again.* He'd tasted bacta on his breath for a week afterward. Reluctantly he pulled off his boots and stretched out on the flotation bed.

He awakened, squirming, some time later.

Too-Onebee's metal-grate face appeared at his bedside. "Painkiller, sir?"

Luke had always read that humans had three bones in each ear. Now he believed it. He could count them. "I feel worse, not better," he complained. "Didn't you do anything?"

"Treatment is complete, sir. Now you must rest. May I offer you a painkiller?" he repeated patiently.

"No thanks," Luke grunted. As a Jedi Knight, he must learn to control sensations, and better sooner than later. Pain was an occupational hazard.

Artoo beeped a query.

Guessing at a translation, Luke said, "All right, Artoo. You stand watch. I'll take another nap." He rolled over. Slowly, his weight pushed a new furrow into the bed's flexible contour. This was the down side of being called a hero. It'd been worse when he lost his right hand.

Come to think of it, the bionic hand didn't ache.

One bright spot.

It was time to re-create the ancient Jedi art of self-healing. Yoda's sketchy lessons left much to be imagined.

"I'll leave you, sir." Too-Onebee swiveled away. "Please attempt to sleep. Call if you require assistance."

One last question brought Luke's head up. "How's Wedge?"

"Healing well, sir. He should be ready for release within a day."

Luke shut his eyes and tried to remember Yoda's lessons. Booted feet pounded rapidly past the open hatchway. Already focused deep into the Force, he felt an alarmed presence hurry up the hall. As carefully as he listened, he couldn't recognize the individual.

Yoda had said fine discernment—even of strangers—would come in time, as he learned the deep silence of self that let a Jedi distinguish others' ripples in the Force.

Luke rolled over, wanting to sleep. He was ordered to sleep.

And he was still Luke Skywalker, and he had to know what had alarmed that trooper. Cautiously he sat up and gingerly slipped down onto his feet. With the ache localized at one end of his body, he could diminish it by willing his feet not to exist . . . or something like that. The Force wasn't something you explained. It was something you used . . . when it let you. Not even Yoda had seen everything.

Artoo whistled an alarm. Too-Onebee rolled toward him, limbpipes flailing. "Sir, lie back down, please."

"In a minute." He poked his head out into the long corridor and shouted, "Stop!"

The Rebel trooper spun to a halt.

"Did they decode that drone ship's message yet?"

"Still working on it, sir."

Then the war room was the place to be. Luke backed into Artoo and steadied himself with a hand on the little droid's blue dome. "Sir," insisted the medical droid, "please lie down. The condition will rapidly become chronic unless you rest."

Imagining himself pain-racked for the rest of his life, and the alternative—another spell in the sticky tank—Luke sat down on the squishy edge of the flotation bed and fidgeted.

Then a thought struck him. "Too-Onebee, I bet you've got—"

Large enough to hold a hundred, the flagship's war room was almost empty. A service droid slid along the curve of an inner bench, passing between a light tube and glimmering white bulkheads. Down near the circular projection table that dominated the war room's center, near a single tech on duty, Mon Mothma—the woman who'd founded and who now led the Rebel Alliance—stood with General Crix Madine. Mon Mothma's presence gleamed visibly in her long white robes and invisibly through the Force, and the bearded Madine's confidence had grown since the Battle of Endor.

They both looked in Luke's direction and frowned. Luke smiled halfheartedly and gripped the handrests of the repulsor chair he'd commandeered out of the medical suite, steering it down over the steps toward them.

"You'll never learn, will you?" General Madine's frown got flatter. "You belong in sick bay. This time we'll have Too-Onebee knock you out."

Luke's cheek twitched. "What about that message? Some Imperial commander burned a quarter million credits on that antique drone."

Mon Mothma nodded, reprimanding Luke with her placid stare. A side console lit, this one a smaller light projection table. Above it appeared a miniature hologram of Admiral Ackbar, with huge eyes bulging at the sides of his high-domed, ruddy head. Although the Calamarian had commanded the Battle of Endor from a chair under the broad starry viewport on Luke's left, Ackbar felt more comfortable on his own cruiser. Life support there was fine-tuned to Calamarian standards. "Commander Skywalker," he wheezed. Whiskery tendrils wobbled under his jaw. "You need to consider the risks you take . . . more carefully."

"I will, Admiral. When I can." Luke reclined the floating repulsor chair and steadied it against the main light table's steel gray rim. An electronic whistle rang out from the hatchway behind him. Artoo-Detoo wasn't letting him out of photoreceptor range for thirty seconds. The blue-domed droid had to take the long way around. Eclipsing tiny blinking instrument lights, he rolled along the upper computer bank to a drop platform. There he downloaded himself, then rolled close to Luke's float chair before delivering a string of rebukes—probably from Too-Onebee. General Madine smirked behind his beard.

Luke hadn't understood a single whistle, but he could guess at this translation too. "All right, Artoo. Pull in your wheels. I'm sitting down. This should be interesting."

Young Lieutenant Matthews straightened up over the side console and turned his head. "Here it comes," he announced.

Madine and Mothma leaned toward the screen. Luke craned his neck for a better view.

Imperial governor Wilek Nereus of the Bakura system, to his most excellent Imperial Master Palpatine: Greetings in haste.

They hadn't heard. Months, maybe years, would pass before much of the galaxy realized that the Emperor's reign had ended. Luke himself was having a hard time believing it.

BAKURA IS UNDER ATTACK BY AN ALIEN INVASION FORCE FROM OUTSIDE YOUR DOMAIN. ESTIMATE FIVE CRUISERS, SEVERAL DOZEN SUPPORT SHIPS, OVER 1000 SMALL FIGHTERS. UNKNOWN TECHNOLOGY. WE HAVE LOST HALF OUR DEFENSE FORCE AND ALL OUTERSYSTEM OUTPOSTS. HOLONET TRANSMISSIONS TO IMPERIAL CENTER AND DEATH STAR TWO HAVE GONE UNANSWERED. URGENT, REPEAT URGENT, SEND STORMTROOPERS.

Madine reached past Lieutenant Matthews and poked a touch panel. "More data," he exclaimed. "We need more of this."

The voice of an intelligence droid filtered through the comlink. "There are corroborative visuals if you would care to see them, sir, as well as embedded data files coded for Imperial access."

"That's more like it." Madine touched the lieutenant's shoulder. "Give me the visuals."

Over the central light table, a projection unit whirred upright. A scene appeared that brought up a fresh rush of pain-deadening adrenaline. *Yoda would rap my knuckles*, Luke observed soberly.

Excitement . . . adventure . . . a Jedi craves not these things. He stretched toward Jedi calm. A terrified world needed help.

At the center of the tableau hovered the image of an Imperial system-patrol craft of a sort Luke had studied but never fought, projected as a three-dimensional network of lines that gleamed reddish orange. He leaned closer to examine its laser emplacements, but before he could get a good look, it silently spewed out an explosion of yellow escape pods. A larger orange image swung ominously into the viewfield, dominating the scene by its bulk: far larger than the patrol craft, stubbier than the Rebels' sleek Mon Cal cruisers—roughly ovoid, but covered with blisterlike projections.

"Run a check on that ship's design," ordered Madine.

After approximately three seconds, the intelligence droid's monotone answered, "This design is used neither by the Alliance nor the Empire."

Luke held his breath. The huge attack craft loomed larger over the table. Now he could make out half a hundred gun emplacements . . . or were they beam antennae? It held fire until six crimson TIE fighters vectored close, then the fighters lurched simultaneously and slowed. Fighters and escape pods began to accelerate steadily toward the alien ship, evidently caught in a tractor beam. The scene shrank. Whoever recorded those visuals had left in a hurry.

"Taking prisoners," Madine murmured, clearly concerned.

Mon Mothma turned to a shoulder-high droid that had stood silently nearby. "Access the embedded data files. Apply our most current Imperial codes. Locate this world, Bakura." Luke felt relieved that even the Alliance's knowledgeable leader had to ask for the system's location.

The droid rotated toward the light table and reconnected its socket arm. The battle scene faded. Star sparks appeared in a conformation Luke recognized as this end of the Rim region. "Here, Madam," the droid announced. One speck turned red. "According to this file, its economy is based on the export of repulsorlift components and an exotic fruit candy and liqueur. Settled by a speculative mining corporation during the final years of the Clone Wars, and taken over by the Empire approximately three years ago, to absorb and control its repulsorlift production capacity."

"Subjugated recently enough to remember independence well." Mon Mothma rested her slender hand on the edge of the light table. "Now show Endor. Relative position."

Another speck gleamed blue. Forgotten at Luke's shoulder, Artoo whistled softly. If Endor was a good bit out from the Core worlds, Bakura was still farther. "That's virtually the edge of the Rim worlds," Luke observed. "Even traveling in hyperspace, it would take days to get there. The Empire can't help them." It was strange to think of anyone turning to the Empire for help. Evidently the Rebels' decisive victory at Endor doomed the Bakurans to an unknown fate, because the nearest Imperial battle group couldn't help. Alliance forces had scattered it.

From a speaker at his left, Leia's voice projected clearly. "How large is the Imperial force at the system?"

Leia was down on Endor's surface, in the Ewok village. Luke hadn't known she was listening in, but he should've assumed it. He reached out through the Force and brushed his sister's warm presence, sensing justifiable tension. Leia was allegedly resting with Han Solo, recovering from that blaster burn on her shoulder, and helping the furry little Ewoks bury their dead—not watching for new trouble. Luke pursed his lips. He'd loved Leia all along, wishing . . .

Well, that was behind him. The intelligence droid answered her over a subspace radio comlink relay, "Bakura is defended by an Imperial garrison. The sender of this message has added subtext reminding Emperor Palpatine that what forces they have are antiquated, due to the system's remoteness."

"Evidently the Empire didn't anticipate any competition for

Bakura." Leia's voice sounded disdainful. "But now there's no Imperial Fleet to help there. It will take the Imperials weeks to reassemble, and by then this Bakura could fall to the invasion force —or it could be part of the Alliance," she added in a brighter tone. "If the Imperials can't help the Bakurans, we must."

Admiral Ackbar's image planted finny hands in the vicinity of its lower torso. "What do you mean, Your Highness?"

Leia leaned against the wattle-and-daub wall of an Ewok tree house and rolled her eyes toward the dome of its high, thatched roof. Han sprawled casually beside her seat, leaning on an elbow and twirling a twig between his fingers.

She raised a handheld comlink. "If we sent aid to Bakura," she answered Admiral Ackbar, "it's possible that Bakura would leave the Empire out of gratitude. We could help free its people."

"And get that repulsorlift technology," Han mumbled to the twig.

Leia had only paused. "That chance is worth investing a small task force. And you'll need a high-ranking negotiator."

Han lay back, crossed his arms behind his head, and murmured, "You step off onto an Imperial world, and you're an entry in somebody's credit register. You've got a price on your head."

She frowned.

"Can we afford to send troops, given the shape we're in?" Ackbar's voice wheezed out of the comlink. "We've lost twenty percent of our forces, battling only part of the Emperor's fleet. Any Imperial battle group could do a better job at Bakura."

"But then the Empire would remain in control there. We need Bakura just like we need Endor. Every world we can draw into the Alliance."

Surprising her, Han closed his hand on the comlink and pulled it toward him. "Admiral," he said, "I doubt we can afford *not* to go. An invasion force that big is trouble for this whole end of the galaxy. And she's right—it's us that ought to go. You'd just better send a ship that can make a fast getaway, in case the Imperials get ideas."

"What about the price on *your* head, laser brains?" Leia whispered.

Han covered the squelch. "You're not going without me, Highness-ness."

Luke studied Mon Mothma's expression and her sense in the Force. "It would have to be a small group," she said quietly, "but one ship is not enough. Admiral Ackbar, you may select a few fighters to support General Solo and Princess Leia."

Luke spread a hand. "What are the aliens doing? Why are they taking so many prisoners?"

"The message doesn't say," Madine pointed out.

"Then you'd better send someone who can find out. It could be important."

"Not you, Commander, and it doesn't look like we can wait until you've recovered." Madine rapped a white handrail. "This team should leave within a standard day."

Luke didn't want to be left behind . . . even though he had all faith that Han and Leia could take care of each other.

On the other hand, before he could pitch in, he must heal himself, and General Madine had suddenly become twins. His optic nerves were telling him to get horizontal soon, or risk a doubly humiliating faint in the war room. He eyed the handrail over the double row of white benches, wondering if the repulsor chair would lift over it. He ached to push the thing's envelope.

Artoo chattered, sounding motherly.

Luke fingered the float chair's controls and said, "I'll head back to my cabin. Keep me posted."

General Madine crossed his arms over the front of his khaki uniform.

"I doubt we'll be sending you to Bakura." Mon Mothma's robes rustled as she squared her shoulders. "Consider your importance to the Alliance."

"She's right, Commander," wheezed the small ruddy image of Admiral Ackbar.

"I'm not helping anyone if I'm just lying down." But he had to shake his reckless reputation, if he wanted the respect of the Rebel Fleet. Yoda had commissioned him to pass on what he had learned. To Luke's mind, that meant rebuilding the Jedi Order . . . as soon as he got the chance. Anyone else could pilot a fightership. No one else could recruit and train new Jedi.

Frowning, he steered to the lift platform, rotated his chair, and answered Mon Mothma and Admiral Ackbar as he rose. "I can at least help you put together the strike force."

CHAPTER

2

THE HIGHER-UPS CONTINUED TO CONFER AS LUKE FLOATED TOWARD A hatchway. The gray-furred guard, a Gotal, flinched as he saluted. Luke remembered that Gotal felt the Force as a vague buzzing in their cone-shaped perceptor horns, and he accelerated to keep from giving the loyal Gotal a headache.

Artoo shrieked behind him. Out in the corridor, Luke decelerated his float chair and let the little droid catch him. Artoo grappled the chair's left stabilizer bar and towed it along, spouting electronic static.

"Yes, Artoo." Luke leaned one hand on Artoo's blue dome. Gratefully he let himself be herded back to the medical suite. He pictured a thousand alien ships converging on . . . on a world he still couldn't imagine. He wanted to see it in his mind's eye.

And to know why the aliens took prisoners.

Once inside the ship's clinic, he pulled off his boots and sank back down on the flotation bed. Its "give" underneath him felt inexpressibly good. After a glance at Wedge's bacta tank, he shut his eyes and imagined he could hear all the way to the war room.

Let them worry. He was finished, for a while. Literally.

Artoo beeped something interrogative. "Say again?" asked Luke.

Artoo wheeled over to the open hatch and reached out a manipulator arm. The door slid closed.

"Oh. Thanks." Evidently Artoo thought he'd like to undress in privacy.

Evidently Artoo didn't know he was too tired to undress. He pulled his legs up onto the bed. "Artoo," he said, "get a portable data screen from Too-Onebee. Access those embedded data files from that message drone. I'll take a look while I rest."

Artoo's reply dropped disapprovingly in pitch as he wheeled away, but less than a minute later he rolled back, trailing a wheeled cart. He steered it to Luke's bedside and extended a connector into its input port.

"Bakura," Luke said. "Data files."

As the computer analyzed his voiceprint to confirm his security clearance, Luke stretched out and blinked. He'd never so appreciated normal, single vision.

A cloud-frosted blue world appeared on the screen. "Bakura," said a bland, mature female voice. "Imperial Study Survey six-oh-seven-seven-four." Cloud cover swirled closer. Luke's vision dropped through it to hover over a vast range of green mountains. Through a deep valley, two broad parallel rivers cut the mountains and wound down to a verdant delta. Luke imagined rich, damp smells, like on Endor. "Salis D'aar, capital city, is the seat of Imperial governorship. Bakuran contributions to Imperial security include a modest flow of strategic metals. . . ."

So green. So wet. Luke shut his eyes. His head sank.

. . . He sprawled on the deck of a strange spaceship. A huge reptilian alien, brown-scaled with a blunt, oversize head, tromped toward him waving a weapon. Luke ignited his lightsaber. Heavy with the Emperor's fingerprints, it slid through his grip. Then he recognized the big lizard's "weapon": a restraining-bolt Owner, used

to control droids. Laughing, he leaped into fighting stance. The lizard's Owner whirred. Luke froze in place.

"What?" Disbelieving, he looked down. He had a droid's stiff-jointed body. Again the alien raised its Owner device. . . .

Luke fought back to consciousness. He felt a powerful presence in the Force and sat up too quickly. Invisible hammers bashed both sides of his head.

The screen stood dark. On the foot of his flotation bed sat Ben Kenobi, robed as usual in unbleached homespun, shimmering under the cabin's faint night glims. "Obi-wan?" Luke murmured. "What's happening at Bakura?"

Ionized air danced around the figure. "You are going to Bakura," it answered.

"Is it that bad?" Luke asked bluntly, not really expecting an answer. Ben rarely gave them. He seemed to come mostly to reprimand Luke, like a teacher who could not give up hounding his student after graduation (not that Ben had stayed around to finish his training).

Obi-wan shifted on the bed, but the bed didn't shift with him. The manifestation wasn't literally physical. "Emperor Palpatine achieved first contact with the aliens attacking Bakura," said the apparition, "during one of his Force meditations. He offered them a deal, one that can no longer be honored."

"What kind of deal?" Luke asked quietly. "What danger are the Bakurans in?"

"You must go." Ben still didn't hear Luke's questions. "If you do not attend to the matter—personally, Luke—Bakura—and all worlds, both Allied and Imperial—will know a far greater disaster than you can imagine."

Then it was as serious as they feared. Luke shook his head. "I need to know more. I can't rush in blindly, and besides, I'm—"

Shimmering air brightened and rushed inward, stirring faint air currents as the image vanished.

Luke groaned. Somehow he'd have to persuade the medical committee to release him, and then convince Admiral Ackbar to give him the assignment. He would promise to rest and heal himself in hyperspace, if he could figure out how. Suddenly the notion of battle no longer excited him at all.

He shut his eyes and sighed. Master Yoda would be pleased.

"Artoo," he said, "call Admiral Ackbar."

Artoo burbled.

"I know it's late. Apologize for waking him. Tell him . . ." He glanced around. "Tell him if he doesn't care to come to the clinic lounge, we can set something up in the war room."

"So, you see . . ." Luke glanced up. The clinic lounge's door slid open. Han and Leia paused in the hatchway, then squeezed in between General Madine—who stood nearby—and Mon Mothma, seated on a stasis unit.

" 'Scuse us," Han grunted. Too-Onebee had approved the conference, provided Luke didn't leave the medical suite. This crowded little lounge, spotless white like the rest of the suite, doubled as interim storage for cold stasis units. Mon Mothma's "seat" held a mortally wounded Ewok, who rested in suspended animation until the Alliance transported him to a fully equipped medical facility.

Han backed up against the bulkhead. Leia sat down beside Mon Mothma.

"Go on." Admiral Ackbar's projected image (in miniature) shone on the floor beside Artoo, who stood at attention maintaining the projection. "General Obi-wan Kenobi has given you orders?"

"That's it, sir." Luke wished Leia and Han hadn't interrupted his explanation right at the most impressive moment.

Admiral Ackbar flicked chin tendrils with a webbed hand. "I have studied the Kenobi offensive. It was masterful. I have little faith in apparitions, but General Kenobi was one of the more powerful Jedi Knights, and Commander Skywalker's word is generally reliable."

General Madine frowned. "Captain Wedge Antilles should be fully recovered by the time any battle group could reach Bakura. I'd thought to put him in charge of the group—no offense, General," he added, smiling faintly at Han.

"None taken," Han drawled. "Separate me from the Ambassador there, and I'll resign my commission."

Luke covered a smile with one hand. Mon Mothma had already assigned Leia to represent the Alliance on Bakura, and to the Imperial presence there, and even requested that she attempt to contact the aliens. *Imagine how solidly the Alliance could challenge the Empire, if our ranks were swelled by that alien military force,* Mon Mothma had said cautiously.

"But Commander Skywalker is in considerably more serious condition," Ackbar declared.

"I won't be, by the time we can reach Bakura."

"We must plan for every contingency." Ackbar's ruddy head bobbed. "We must defend Endor now, and we've promised General Calrissian assistance with liberating Cloud City—"

"I talked to Lando on the comlink," Han cut in. "He says he's got ideas of his own, and thanks anyway." Imperial forces had taken over Cloud City when Lando Calrissian—its baron-administrator —fled with Leia and Chewie, chasing the bounty hunter who'd flown off with Han as his carbon-frozen prisoner. Lando had had to forget Cloud City while he led the attack on Endor. They had indeed promised him all the fighters they could spare.

But Lando had always been a gambler.

"Then we shall send Bakura a small but strong strike force," Ackbar declared, "to support Princess Leia in her role as chief negotiator. Most of your fighting will probably be in space, not groundside. Five Corellian Gunships and a Corvette will escort our smallest cruiser-carrier. Commander Skywalker, will that be enough?"

Luke started. "You're giving me command, sir?"

"I don't see that we have any choice," Mon Mothma said quietly.

"General Kenobi has spoken to you. Your record in battle is unmatched. Assist Bakura for us and then rejoin the Fleet immediately."

Elated by the honor, Luke saluted her.

Early the following day, Luke examined the status boards of the newly commissioned Rebel carrier *Flurry*. "She's ready to jump," he observed.

"Ready and eager, Commander." Captain Tessa Manchisco nudged his elbow. Fresh from the Virgillian Civil War, Captain Manchisco wore her black hair hanging in six thick braids down the back of her cream-colored uniform. She'd accepted the Bakura assignment with relish. Her *Flurry*, a small, unconventional cruiser-carrier retrofitted with all the stolen Imperial components that opportunistic Virgillians could cram on board, carried a Virgillian bridge crew: besides Manchisco, three humans and a noseless, red-eyed Duro navigator. Inside the *Flurry*'s hangar bays, Admiral Ackbar's crews had packed twenty X-wing fighters, three A-wings, and four cruiser-assault B-wing fighters, as many as the Alliance could spare.

Peering out the *Flurry*'s triangular viewport, Luke spotted two of his Corellian Gunships. Riding shotgun above the carrier—even in zero gravity they habitually established a "bottom" to every formation—drifted the hottest souped-up freighter in this quadrant of the galaxy, the *Millennium Falcon*. Han, Chewbacca, Leia, and See-Threepio had boarded the *Falcon* less than an hour ago.

Luke's initial elation over being given command had already faded. It was one thing to fly a fighter under someone else's orders, with the Force as his ally. Strategy was something else. He carried responsibility for every life and every ship.

Still, he'd been studying strategic and tactical texts. And now—well, to tell the truth, he was almost looking forward to it. . . .

Whoops. Abruptly his knuckles stung. He heard or remembered Yoda's soft laughter.

Frowning, he shut his eyes and relaxed. Everything still hurt, but he'd promised Too-Onebee that he'd rest and self-heal. He wished he felt better.

"Hyperdrive stations," called Manchisco. "Commander, you might want to strap down."

Luke glanced around the spartan hexagonal bridge: three stations besides his command seat, an array of battle boards now darkened for transit, and a single R2 droid socket occupied by the Virgillians' own unit. He buckled in, wondering what "disaster" waited at Bakura unless he dealt with it personally.

On an outer deck of a vast battle cruiser called the *Shriwirr*, Dev Sibwarra rested his slim brown hand on a prisoner's left shoulder. "It'll be all right," he said softly. The other human's fear beat at his mind like a three-tailed lash. "There's no pain. You have a wonderful surprise ahead of you." Wonderful indeed, a life without hunger, cold, or selfish desire.

The prisoner, an Imperial of much lighter complexion than Dev, slumped in the entchment chair. He'd given up protesting, and his breath came in gasps. Pliable bands secured his forelimbs, neck, and knees—but only for balance. With his nervous system deionized at the shoulders, he couldn't struggle. A slender intravenous tube dripped pale blue magnetizing solution into each of his carotid arteries while tiny servopumps hummed. It only took a few mils of magsol to attune the tiny, fluctuating electromagnetic fields of human brain waves to the Ssi-ruuvi entchment apparatus.

Behind Dev, Master Firwirrung trilled a question in Ssi-ruuvi. "Is it calmed yet?"

Dev sketched a bow to his master and switched from human speech to Ssi-ruuvi. "Calm enough," he sang back. "He's almost ready."

Sleek, russet scales protected Firwirrung's two-meter length from beaked muzzle to muscular tail tip, and a prominent black **V** crest marked his forehead. Not large for a Ssi-ruu, he was still growing, with only a few age-scores where scales had begun to separate on his handsome chest. Firwirrung swung a broad, glowing white metal catchment arc down to cover the prisoner from midchest to nose. Dev could just peer over it and watch the man's pupils dilate. At any moment . . .

"Now," Dev announced.

Firwirrung touched a control. His muscular tail twitched with pleasure. The fleet's capture had been good today. Alongside his master, Dev would work far into the night. Before entenchment, prisoners were noisy and dangerous. Afterward, their life energies powered droids of Ssi-ruuvi choosing.

The catchment arc hummed up to pitch. Dev backed away. Inside that round human skull, a magsol-drugged brain was losing control. Though Master Firwirrung assured him that the transfer of incorporeal energy was painless, every prisoner screamed.

As did this one, when Firwirrung threw the catchment arc switch. The arc boomed out a sympathetic vibration, as brain energy leaped to an electromagnet perfectly attuned to magsol. Through the Force rippled an ululation of indescribable anguish.

Dev staggered and clung to the knowledge his masters had given him: The prisoners only thought they felt pain. *He* only thought he sensed their pain. By the time the body screamed, all of a subject's energies had jumped to the catchment arc. The screaming body already was dead.

"Transferred." Firwirrung's fluting whistle carried an amused undercurrent. Such a paternal attitude made Dev feel awkward. He was inferior. Human. Soft and vulnerable, like a wriggling white larva before metamorphosis. He longed to sit for entenchment, and transfer his life energy to a powerful battle droid. Quietly he cursed the talents that sentenced him to go on waiting.

The catchment arc hummed louder, fully charged, more "alive" now than the limp body on the chair. Firwirrung faced a bulkhead stippled with hexagonal metal scales. "Ready down there?" His

question came out as a rising labial whistle, ending with a snap of
the toothed beak, then two sibilant whistles falling to throat-stop.
It had taken Dev years to master Ssi-ruuvi, and countless sessions
of hypnotic conditioning that also left him yearning to please
Firwirrung, head of entenchment.

Entenchment work never ended. Life energy, like any other,
could be stored in the right kind of battery. But brain wavelength
electrical activity, which accompanied life energy into the droid
charges, eventually set up destructive harmonics. The droids' vital
control circuits "died" of fatal psychosis.

Still, human energies lasted longer than any other species in
entenchment, whether slaved to shipboard circuits or motivating
battle droids.

Deck 16 of the huge battle cruiser finally whistled an answer.
Firwirrung pressed his three-fingered foreclaw against a button.
The catchment arc fell silent. The lucky human's life energy was
even now sparking in a reservoir coil behind one small pyramidal
battle droid's sensor clusters. Now he'd be able to see at additional
wavelengths and in all directions. He would never again need oxygen or temperature control, nourishment or sleep. Free from the
awkward necessity of will, of ever making his own decisions, his
new housing would respond to all Ssi-ruuvi orders.

Perfect obedience. Dev bowed his head, wishing it were him.
Droid ships suffered no sadness or pain. A glorious metamorphosis, until one day enemy laser fire destroyed the coil . . . or those
destructive psychotic harmonics unlinked it from control circuits.

Firwirrung retracted catchment arc, IVs, and restraints. Dev
pulled the body husk off the chair and slid it into a hexagonal deck
chute. It thumped away into blackness.

Tail-down relaxed, Firwirrung swept away from the table. He
poured a cup of red ksaa while Dev brought down a nozzle arm
and sprayed the chair several times. Biological byproducts flushed
harmlessly through drains in the center of the seat.

Dev raised the spray arm, locked it at standby, then waved at a switch for the chair to warm itself dry. "Ready," he whistled. Eagerly he turned to the hatchway.

Two small, young P'w'ecks brought in the next prisoner, a wrinkled human with eight closely spaced red and blue rectangles on the breast of his green-gray Imperial tunic, and a disarrayed shock of white hair. He struggled to wrench his arms out of his guards' foreclaws. The tunic provided pitifully little protection. Red human blood welled through his skin and torn sleeves.

If only he knew how unnecessary all this resistance was. Dev stepped forward. "It's all right." He held his paddle-shaped ion beamer—a medical instrument that could double as a safe shipboard weapon—in the blue-and-green side stripes of his long tunic. "It's not what you think, not at all."

The man's eyes opened so wide that obscene white sclerae showed all around the irises. "What do I think?" the man demanded, his feelings a Force-swirl of panic. "Who are you? What are you doing here? Wait—you're the one . . ."

"I'm your friend." Keeping his own eyes half closed to hide the sclerae (he had only two eyelids, unlike his masters' three), Dev rested his right hand on the man's shoulder. "And I'm here to help you. Don't be afraid." *Please,* he added silently. *It hurts when you fear me. And you're so lucky. We'll be quick.* He pressed his beamer to the back of the prisoner's neck. Still gripping the activator, he ran it swiftly down the man's spine.

The Imperial officer's muscles loosened. His servant-race guards let him fall to the tiled gray deck. "Clumsy!" Firwirrung sprang forward on massive hind legs, tail stiff as he railed at the smaller P'w'ecks. Other than size and drabness, they looked almost like the masterly Ssi-ruuk . . . from a distance. "Respect the prisoners," Firwirrung sang. He might be young for command rank duty, but he demanded deference.

Dev helped the three lift and position the smelly, perspiring human. Fully conscious—the catchment arc would not operate otherwise—the man wobbled off the chair. Dev caught him by both shoulders, wrenching his own back. "Relax," Dev murmured. "It's all right."

"Don't do this!" the prisoner cried. "I have powerful friends. They'll pay well for my release."

"We would love to meet them. But we won't deny you this joy." Dev let his spirit center float over the stranger's fear, then pressed it down like a comforting blanket. Once the P'w'ecks had securely anchored the restraint bands, Dev relaxed his grip and rubbed his back. Firwirrung's right foreclaw jabbed upward, placing one IV. He had not sterilized the needles. It was unnecessary.

At last, the prisoner sat helpless and ready. Clear liquid dripped out of one eye and a corner of his mouth. The servopump sent magnetizing fluid up the IVs.

Another liberated soul, another droid ship ready to help take the human Empire.

Trying to ignore the prisoner's wet face and enervating terror, Dev rested a slim brown hand on his left shoulder. "It'll be all right," he said softly. "There's no pain. You have a wonderful surprise ahead of you."

At last all the day's prisoners were safely enteched—except one female, who slipped free of the servant P'w'ecks and dashed her head against a bulkhead before Dev could catch her. After several minutes' effort at revival, Master Firwirrung's head and tail drooped. "No use," he whistled regretfully. "Sad waste. Recycle it."

Dev cleaned up. Entechment was noble work, and he keenly felt the honor of involvement, even if his role was merely that of a servant who could Force calm the subjects. He slipped his paddle-shaped beamer into the underside of an overhead storage shelf, with its flattened topside up, then pressed its pointed projection end into the sheath notch until it clicked. The knurled handle, specially made for his five-fingered hand, dangled beneath the flat paddle and behind its rounded handguard.

Firwirrung led Dev back up spacious corridors to their quarters and poured soothing ksaa for both of them. Dev drank gratefully, seated in the circular cabin's only chair. Ssi-ruuk needed no furniture. Hissing contentment, Firwirrung settled his broad tail and hindquarters comfortably onto the warm gray deck. "Are you happy, Dev?" he asked. Liquid black eyes blinked over the ksaa mug and reflected the bitter red tonic.

It was an offer of solace. Whenever life saddened Dev, whenever he missed the sense of wholeness he'd had when his mother Force linked with him, Firwirrung took him to blue-scaled Elder Sh'tk'ith for renewal therapy.

"Very happy," Dev answered truthfully. "A good day's work. Much kindness."

Firwirrung nodded sagely. "Much kindness," he whistled back. His scent tongues flicked out of his nostrils, taste-smelling Dev's presence. "Stretch out, Dev. What do you see tonight in the hidden universe?"

Dev smiled weakly. The master meant it as a compliment. All Ssi-ruuk were Force blind. Dev knew now that he was the only sensitive, human or otherwise, they'd ever met.

Through him, the Ssi-ruuk had learned of the Emperor's death moments after it happened. Because the Force existed in all life, he'd felt the shock wave of power ripple through spirit and space.

Months ago, His Potency the Shreeftut had responded immediately when Emperor Palpatine offered prisoners in exchange for tiny, two-meter droid fighters of his own. Palpatine couldn't have known how many dozen million Ssi-ruuk lived on Lwhekk, in their distant star cluster. Admiral Ivpikkis captured and questioned several Imperial citizens. This human Empire, he learned, stretched out for parsecs. Its star systems lay like nesting sands, fertile for the planting of Ssi-ruuvi life.

But then the Emperor died. There would be no bargain. The traitorous humans had abandoned them to get home as best they could, with the fleet's energy almost spent. Admiral Ivpikkis had come ahead with the battle cruiser *Shriwirr* and a small advance force, only half a dozen attack ships with supporting entenchment equipment. The main fleet hung back, waiting for news of success or failure.

If they could take a major human world, that entenchment equipment—Master Firwirrung's domain—would give them the human Empire. Bakura, when it fell, would provide the technology to construct dozens of entenchment chairs. Each enteched Bakuran would power or shield a battle droid fighter or vitalize some critical ship component on one of the large cruisers. With dozens of entenchment teams trained and equipped, the Ssi-ruuvi fleet could take the humans' populous Core worlds. There were a dozen thousand planets to liberate. So much kindness to accomplish.

Dev almost worshiped his masters' courage in coming so far and risking so much for the good of the Ssi-ruuvi Imperium and the liberation of other species. If a Ssi-ruu died away from a consecrated home world, his spirit roamed the galaxies alone forever.

Dev shook his head and answered, "Outside, I sense only the quiet winds of life itself. Aboard the *Shriwirr*, mourning and confusion in your new children."

Firwirrung stroked Dev's arm, his three opposable claws barely reddening the tender scaleless skin. Dev smiled, empathizing with his master. Firwirrung had no clutchmates on board, and the military life meant lonely hours and terrible risks. "Master," Dev said, "maybe—some day—might we return to Lwhekk?"

"You and I might never go home, Dev. But soon we will consecrate a new home world in your galaxy. Send for our families . . ." As Firwirrung glanced at the sleeping pit, a whiff of acrid reptilian breath trailed across Dev's face.

Dev didn't flinch. He was used to that smell. His own body

odors sickened the Ssi-ruuk, so he bathed in and drank special solvents four times daily. For special occasions, he shaved all his hair. "A clutch of your own kind," he murmured.

Firwirrung cocked his head and stared with one black eye. "Your work brings me closer to that clutch. But for now, I am weary."

"I'm keeping you awake," Dev said, instantly repentant. "Please get your rest. I'll come along soon."

Once Firwirrung lay nested in his cluster of pillows, with his body warmed by below-deck generators and triple eyelids sheltering the beautiful black eyes, Dev took his evening bath and drank his deodorizing medication. To take his mind off the abdominal cramps that always followed, he pulled his chair over to a long, curved desk/counter. He withdrew an unfinished book from the library and loaded it into his reader.

For months, he'd been working on a project that might serve humankind even better than he served it now (in fact, he feared that the Ssi-ruuk would entech him into circuits to complete this work rather than into the battle droid he hoped to earn).

He'd known how to read and write before the Ssi-ruuk adopted him, both letters and music. Combining those symbologies, he was devising a system to write Ssi-ruuvi for human usage. On the musical staff, he noted pitches. Symbols he'd invented signified labial, full-tongue, half-tongue, and guttural whistles. Letters showed vowels and final-click blendings. *Ssi-ruu* required a full line of data: The half-tongue whistle rose a perfect fifth while the mouth formed the letter *e*. Then a puckered labial whistle, down a minor third. *Ssi-ruu* was the singular form. The plural, *Ssi-ruuk*, ended with a throat-click. Ssi-ruuvi was complex but lovely, like birdsong from Dev's youth on the outpost planet G'rho.

Dev had a good ear, but the complicated task invariably overwhelmed him at the late hour of his free time. As soon as the cramping and nausea passed, he shut down his glowing reader and crawled in the dark toward the faint fetid smell of Firwirrung's bed pit. Too warm-blooded, he stacked a pile of pillows to insulate him from the quarters' below-deck heat. Then he curled up far from his master and thought of his home.

Dev's abilities had caught his mother's attention from a very early age, back on Chandrila. A Jedi apprentice who hadn't completed her training, she'd taught him a little about the Force. He'd even communicated with her over distances.

Then came the Empire. There'd been a purge of Jedi candidates. The family fled to isolated G'rho.

Barely had they settled in when the Ssi-ruuk arrived. Her Force sense vanished, leaving him far from home and bereft and terrified of the invading spaceships. Master Firwirrung had always said that his parents would've killed Dev if they could, rather than let the Ssi-ruuk adopt him. Terrifying thought—their own child!

But Dev had escaped death on both counts. The Ssi-ruuvi scouts found him huddling in an eroded ravine. Fascinated by the giant lizards with round black eyes, the undersize ten-year-old had taken their food and affection. They'd shipped him back to Lwhekk, where he had lived for five years. Eventually, he learned why they hadn't enteched him. His uncanny mental abilities would make him an ideal scout for approaching other human systems. They also allowed him to calm entechment subjects. He wished he remembered what he'd said or done that revealed his talent.

He'd taught the Ssi-ruuk all he knew about humankind, from mind-set and customs to clothing (including shoes, which amused them). Already he'd helped them take several human outposts. Bakura would be the key world . . . and they were winning! Soon, the Bakuran Imperials would run out of fighting ships and the Ssi-ruuk could approach Bakura's population centers. A dozen P'w'eck landing craft carried paralysis canisters, ready to drop.

Over a standard hailing frequency, Dev had already announced to Bakurans the good news of their impending release from human limitations. Master Firwirrung said it was only normal that they resisted. Unlike Ssi-ruuk, humans feared the unknown. Entechment was a change from which there was no returning to report.

Dev yawned mightily. His masters would protect him from the Empire, and some day reward him. Firwirrung had promised to stand beside him and lower the catchment arc himself.

Dreamily, Dev stroked his throat. The IVs would go . . . here. And here. Some day, some day.

He covered his head with his arms and slept.

CHAPTER

3

S TAR STREAKS SHRANK ON LUKE'S TRIANGULAR FORWARD VIEWSCREEN AS the *Flurry* and her seven escorts dropped out of hyperspace. Once he'd checked deflector shields, he swung his chair to get the master computer's insystem status report, while Captain Manchisco's communications officer scanned standard Imperial hailing frequencies. Luke felt better, so long as he moved slowly.

Scanners showed eight planets, none at the spot in its orbit where Alliance MasterNav had projected. Now he was glad Manchisco had overruled his impatience, planned cautiously, and dropped out of lightspeed in the outer system. She shot him a meaningful look. He touched one eyebrow in salute, then nodded at the Duro navigator, who blinked his huge red eyes and gargled unintelligibly.

"He says you're welcome," translated Manchisco.

Half a dozen blistered ovoids clustered around the system's third world, surrounded on his screens by a virtual sandstorm of small fighters. They all gleamed red for "threat," but they maneuvered crazily on the screen, breaking formation and regrouping, approaching and fleeing. Obviously they weren't all on the same side.

He glanced at General Dodonna's brainchild, the Battle Analysis Computer. He'd agreed to bring along a BAC prototype, and now he needed data to run it.

"Looks like a party, Junior," came Han's voice from the speaker at his elbow.

"I'm with you," Luke answered. "We're hailing the Imperials now. No sense—"

"Sir," interrupted the communications man.

"Hang on." Luke swiveled away from Han's speaker and got a leg cramp for his trouble. He was *almost* healed. "Did you raise some-one?"

The young, broad-shouldered Virgillian pointed at a blinking green light on his console. Someone had given the go-ahead to transmit. Luke cleared his throat. Before they left Endor, Leia had offered a list of things he might say. They just weren't his style.

Besides, he wouldn't be dealing with a diplomat or a politician. This was an embattled commander who could spare only seconds for each decision. "Imperial Navy," Luke said, "this is an Alliance battle group. We have the white flag out for you. Looks like you're in need. Would you accept our help, as between fellow humans?" Sure, there were aliens among the rebels besides Chewbacca and Manchisco's Duro navigator. One Gunship was crewed by seventeen Mon Calamari. But the human chauvinist Imperials didn't need to know yet.

The speaker crackled. Imagining some seasoned Imperial veteran frantically scrolling through a tutorial for standard Rebel-contacting procedures, Luke switched to an Alliance frequency. "All fighters, maintain defensive formation. Shields up. We don't know what they're going to do."

Musical fragments and garbled voices echoed across the *Flurry*'s bridge, and then: "Alliance battle group, this is Commander Pter Thanas of the Imperial Navy. Declare your purpose here." The brassy voice rang with authority.

For three days in hyperspace, Luke had vacillated between pretending ignorance and admitting the real situation. Captain Manchisco raised an eyebrow as if to ask, "Well?"

"We intercepted a message Governor Nereus sent to the Imperial Fleet, which is, ah, mostly in airdock at the moment. It sounded like serious trouble. As I said, we came to help you if possible."

Luke cut transmission and realized from spasms shooting down his calves that he'd stood up. Frustrated, he lowered himself onto the big chair again. He'd rested plenty in hyperspace. On his intergroup channel, the Gunships checked in. Their pips showed blue on the black status board. Outside his viewscreen, they formed up in pairs.

Near his elbow, Leia's voice spoke softly from over on the *Falcon*. "Luke, be subtle. You're dealing with Imperials. They're going to see us as hostiles and chase us away."

"They're not chasing anybody at the moment," Luke pointed out. "They're about to be wiped—"

"No wonder nobody picked up the standard distress transmissions," said the dry, crisp voice of Imperial Commander Thanas. "Alliance battle group, we would be grateful for assistance. I am coding a status report twenty cycles below this frequency."

"Well, all right," observed Han.

Only someone who already considered himself beaten would accept marginally identified reinforcements. Luke glanced at Communications Officer Delckis, who opened the channel Thanas indicated. Within moments, a small percentage of the swirling dots on the status board turned yellow-gold for the Imperials. Luke whistled softly. All six ovoids and most of the sandstorm still gleamed threat red.

The BAC started spitting information. Commander Thanas had less firepower than the invaders, and 80 percent of it was concentrated in a single *Carrack*-class cruiser. Not a big ship, with only a fifth of the crew that a Star Destroyer carried, but it outgunned the *Flurry* several times.

"You sure you want to do this?" muttered Manchisco.

Luke touched a call button that would send Rebel pilots scrambling up ladders. Fueled and pulled out into the bays during the last day in hyperspace, the fighters were launch ready.

"Reading your formation," Luke told his Imperial counterpart. He wasn't sure how to proceed. Calming, he reached inside himself for a leading from the Force. A hunch, as others called it . . .

Thanas said, "Can you—stand by—" A weird warbling whistle drowned out the Imperial commander.

Luke drummed his fingers against the console. When Thanas came back, his voice still sounded smooth and controlled. "Sorry. Jamming. If you could throw a cone of ships into the gap between the Ssi-ruuk's three central cruisers, it could inspire them to retreat. It would buy us time."

Ssi-ruuk. Luke filed the aliens' name at the back of his mind. Something underneath consciousness finally made a suggestion. "Commander Thanas, we're going to sweep down from solar north just spinward of those three cruisers.

"Set course," he murmured aside.

Captain Manchisco's navigator reached for his nav computer. "Valtis," the Duro gargled in Standard around thin, rubbery lips, "establish eight-seven norrrth, six spinwarrrd." The Virgillian pilot finger-hopped corrections onto his computer. Luke felt the *Flurry* break dormancy. Deck panels transferred engine vibrations to his feet and command chair. The access hatch, which they'd left open for ventilation, slid shut.

Thanas spoke again after another minute. "That's within our sphere of greatest need, Alliance group. Come in . . . and thanks. Just keep it away from the gravity well."

"What do you think, kid?" Han's voice filtered through the speaker at Luke's elbow. "Doesn't look good."

"I've got to get to Bakura," Leia insisted over the same speaker. "I have to convince this Governor Nereus to declare an official truce. Otherwise they have no reason to work with us. You can't end-run the entire Imperial Navy."

"Han," Luke answered, "did you read how we're going to move?"

"Oh, yeah." His friend sounded amused. "Good luck, hero. I'm afraid our only trained diplomat is going to wait this one out."

"Good idea," said Luke.

"What?" Luke heard exclamation points follow Leia's question. "What are you talking about?"

"Excuse us." He pictured Han turning aside, trying to reasonably explain an unpleasant truth to the more stubborn Skywalker twin. Maybe her brother ought to step in.

"Leia," he said, "look at the board. Bakura is blockaded. All communications out must be jammed—we haven't heard a peep except some scatter from entertainment bands. You're too valuable to risk in the battle zone."

"And you're not?" she retorted. "I have to talk with the governor. Our only hope is to persuade him that we're coming in as nonaggressors."

"I agree," answered Luke, "and we could use the *Falcon* in a sweep, but we're not risking you. Be thankful you're on your own gunship."

Stony silence. Luke called out more orders, maneuvering his carrier group into a loose carpet formation for the tricky intersystem jump.

"All right," Leia grumbled. "The sixth planet isn't far from this vector. We'll head in that direction. If it looks safe, we'll land and wait for a rendezvous."

"Planet Six sounds good, Leia." Luke could feel her indignation, and it wasn't directed only at him. She and Han must learn to resolve disagreements. Develop their own system.

He shut her sense out of his perception. "Be in touch, Han. Use standard Alliance frequencies, but monitor the Imperial ones."

"Affirmative, Junior."

Luke watched the light freighter swing out of formation through his viewscreen. The blue-white arc of its engines shrank in the black distance. According to his status board, his fighter pilots stood by, mounted and ready, with Wedge Antilles running squadron checks. He didn't belong up here. Today his cold X-wing would sit in a dark hangar bay, and Artoo in his quarters, linked through the *Flurry* into the Battle Analysis Computer. Maybe next time, he could rig Artoo to link him with the carrier's command deck and run things from a fighter . . . except where could he install control and status boards?

"Calculations are in," he announced. "Prepare to jump."

The blue picket ships' lights turned green.

Luke clutched the arms of his seat. "Now."

Han Solo kept an eye on the *Falcon*'s sensors as he swung the nimble freighter aside. Too experienced to get caught in the battle group's jump hyperwash, he couldn't resist watching until Luke's carrier—imagine the kid commanding a carrier group—winked out. Leia flinched.

Now he was back where he belonged, on board the *Falcon*. Alliance repair teams had wasted no time getting his beloved freighter back into service after Lando rattled her around inside the second Death Star (—*but no hard feelings, Lando. It was for a good cause*). He belonged in this cockpit, with good old Chewie in the copilot's seat.

But even that wasn't the same. Leia sat behind the huge Wookiee, wearing a gray combat coverall belted around her waist, leaning forward as if she thought she ought to be copilot instead.

Well. He'd give Leia everything he owned, the whole galaxy if he could swing it, but she wouldn't bump Chewie out of that chair. Yeah, she'd handled the *Falcon* just fine during a couple of emergencies. But even a smuggler drew the line somewhere.

Threepio occupied the other back chair, his golden head swiveling from side to side. "I am so thankful you reconsidered, Mistress

Leia. Although my expertise will be wasted more seriously than usual out here in the system's far reaches, our safety is of paramount importance. May I suggest—"

Han rolled his eyes and said mock-menacingly, "Leia?"

She hit the off switch at the back of Threepio's neck. He froze in position.

Han whooshed out a noisy sigh of relief. Chewbacca added a chuckling growl and shook his black-tipped cinnamon fur. Han reached for his control panel. "Seven minutes to close approach."

Leia unstrapped and pushed up to stand closer to the console, pressing her warm leg against his. "Imperials can't be far. Where are the scanners?"

Han shot a hand forward and turned them on. The sixth planet filled the scanner displays. Chewbacca barked several grunts and *rrowps*. "Dirt and ice," Han translated for Leia. "Bakura system's got only one gas giant and a whole flock of accreted-comet types trailing off behind it." He paused. "If the *Falcon*'s warm at all, she'll melt herself right to the surface."

"Look," said Leia. "Settlement of some kind near the terminator."

"I see it." Han held his course toward the cluster of regular shapes. "But there's no communication or defense satellites, and we're not picking up any transmissions." Chewie howled agreement.

Quickly, the domes swung into view. Han pulled them in on high resolution and spotted a double line of shattered walls between jagged new craters.

"What a mess," Leia said.

"Ten to one our mysterious aliens have already hit this place."

"Good." Leia flicked dust off Han's chair. Startled, he twisted around. "That means they probably won't be back," she explained.

"Checked it off the list," Han agreed.

"And they're out for bigger game now. I only hope Luke's careful."

"He will be. Okay Chewie, this looks like a nice quiet neighborhood. We're hidden better if we land . . . blend in with the rocks, you know. Let's get low and kill speed. Only enough to fight gravity. We're going in cold."

He didn't tell her how hard that would be. His sensors registered under 0.2 G on this ice ball, and no atmosphere to heat up incoming craft, but shedding temp was no simple job. Core heat was still up from the hyperspace jump, and friction was no small factor: even in the dead cold of outer-system space, they had already hit billions of ions and atoms. Han touched a control he rarely used, setting dorsal radiators on full. He wished he had chillers for the landing struts, but if wishes were fishes, Calamarians would be giving the orders at Alliance HQ.

Just beyond the terminator, he spotted a crater bottom long and broad enough to hold the *Falcon* snugly. He shut down the radiators, brought her low, and let her hover. Now, no braking rockets . . .

About to ease down, he spotted a dark shining pool spreading out on the crater bottom below him.

Not water ice, then, but ammonia or some other smelly volatile that melted at such a supercold temp that even hover jets puddled it.

Now what?

Chewie whuffled a suggestion.

"Yeah," he answered. "Synchronous orbit. Good idea."

"We're not going to land after all?" Leia relaxed into her high-backed seat as the *Falcon* swooped over the ruins and gained altitude.

Chewbacca howled, pointing out a small problem.

"It works well enough," Han said.

"What works well enough?" Leia demanded.

Han frowned at Chewie. *Thanks a lot, pal.* "The *Falcon*'s star tracker. For maintaining orbits on autopilot. It's slaved into a circuit that doesn't normally cover those things."

"Why?"

Han laughed shortly. "You don't make this many modifications on one freighter without slicing a few circuits. The tracker works well enough—but—Chewie, make sure we don't drift off course. So long as we stay close, no one'll spot us." Han jabbed a sensor. "Looks like Brother Luke's moving in on the Imperials' side. I suppose you want to stick around and watch."

Leia frowned. "With this scanner board, it's impossible to tell who's on which side. Anyway, I'm uncomfortable with the whole situation."

"Oh." Was that scanner-board comment another insult? "Oh," he added cheerfully. Maybe they'd finally have a quiet hour. Their so-called vacation after the big Ewok party had been worthless; Leia was bone tired. But during the jump, with all hands busy and Threepio bustling everywhere, he'd quietly had Chewie make a few modifications in the *Falcon*'s main hold that weren't in *Cracken's Field Guide*.

He only hoped Chewie had gotten it right. The big Wookiee was a master mechanic, but his aesthetic sense wasn't, well, human.

Han Solo hadn't exactly joined this picnic for the war effort.

Leia groped behind Threepio's neck and switched him back on, then followed Han aft. Once the Battle of Endor wound down, they'd talked for hours. Beneath that smuggler's cynical mask, this man hid ideals like hers. They'd simply been squashed harder. And she'd dreaded being alone ever since Luke gave her the terrible news: Darth Vader was her—

No.

Her mind dodged its own defenses and thrust again: As she'd watched Alderaan blasted from space aboard the Death Star, she'd thought she'd been watching her family die. In truth, her father had stood—

No! She would never accept *him* as her father. Not even if Luke did.

She ducked to miss a dangling hose. If she had to find a hiding place and pull her head in for a few hours, the time had better count for something. She'd already wasted too many days recuperating. She rubbed her right shoulder. Not even synthflesh completely countered the itch of a healing blaster burn. As she'd told Han, it wasn't bad . . . just hard to ignore.

He stopped near the entry ramp. She leaned against a bulkhead and stared up at him. "What's left to fix?" The *Falcon* was Han's first love. The sooner she accepted that, the less often he'd get his back up. Besides, it was foolish to feel jealous of a spaceship.

Han slid his hands off his hips and let them hang along his black pants' side stripes. "Things will probably stay quiet for a few hours. Chewie's on watch, too."

Abruptly Leia realized that was no combat glimmer in his eyes. "I thought something needed repairing." She tossed down the challenge. "Come on, isn't there some new modification that needs field testing?"

"Yeah. Back here, in the big cargo bay." He strode along the curving corridor, slapped the locking panel, and stepped down into the *Falcon*'s aft hold. He palmed open a bulkhead hatch into the closed starboard compartment. "Shield generators, back here."

The cargo bay smelled stuffy. She stepped down behind Han. "What are you smuggling this time?"

"Something I picked up on Endor."

"*We* picked up on Endor," she corrected him. Crates piled and braced with more crates walled off the back of the compartment. Han slid a crate aside and uncovered a locker she thought might be a refrigeration unit. He reached in, groped, and pulled out a glass bottle.

Straight-faced, she took it. Primitive glass sealed with a plug of tree bark, it looked less than sanitary. "What is it?"

"A present from that Ewok medicine man. You remember. The one who made us honorary members of the tribe?"

"Yes." Leia lounged against the stack of cargo crates and handed back the bottle. "You didn't answer my question."

Han yanked on the plug. "Berry . . . wine of some . . . sort," he grunted. The plug popped free. "Goldenrod about split a resistor translating, but the gist of what the fuzzy guy said was, 'To ignite the heart that's beginning to warm.'"

So that's what he was up to. "Hey, we're at war."

"We'll always be at war. When are you going to live?"

Leia felt her cheeks heat. She'd rather talk, argue, even fight with Han than hide out and sip . . . berry wine? . . . with a battle going on. As Bail Organa would've pointed out, this man wasn't even appropriate company for someone of her upbringing. He wanted to solve all his problems with a blaster. She was a princess by adoption, if not by birth.

Again the black-masked shadow fell across her thoughts: Vader. She had hated him so righteously.

Cloudy purple wine sloshed into stoneware. Probably not a palace-quality vintage. "Let's not . . ." she began, then she trailed off. She'd already decided she couldn't do Luke any good hanging around the subspace radio.

"Hey." Han handed her one cup. "What are you thinking? What are you afraid of?"

"Too much." She touched the rim of her cup to his. The pottery clinked softly.

"You? Afraid?"

Leia had to smile. It didn't make sense to be anything but brave and headlong. She sipped, then sniffed her cup and wrinkled her nose. "It's too sweet."

"I don't think they make anything else." Han set his cup on a pallet. "Look over here." He took her hand and tugged her around the freestanding divider of crates. She set her cup beside his. "I—" He stopped.

Leia looked down into a nest of self-inflating pillows.

"Chewie—" Han growled. He dropped her hand. "I guess that's a little blatant. I never should've trusted a Wookiee."

Leia laughed. "Chewie set this up?"

"Wait till I tell that big wet-nosed furball—"

Still laughing, she braced herself against a bulkhead and shoved him over backward. He caught her hand and went down flailing.

CHAPTER
4

CHEWBACCA HOPED HE'D GOTTEN IT RIGHT. HAN'S AESTHETIC SENSE wasn't, well, civilized. But his intentions were sterling. Leia ought to be able to figure that out. She seemed like a genteel female.

Threepio prattled behind him. Chewbacca fiddled with communications gear, checking occasionally on Luke's battle. He'd lost track of which blip in all that mayhem was the *Flurry*.

"And this is a rather precarious hiding place," Threepio added. "Planet Six is rightly denied the dignity of a proper name. Why, it's little more than a large boulder of ice. Not even a settlement, just the remains of a military outpost." Abruptly he paused. "What was that, Chewbacca? Tune back a few kilobits."

Chewie shrugged and suggested that Threepio butt out.

"I shall not 'butt out,' you ill-mannered fleabag," the droid squeaked. "The nerve of some creatures, discounting my expertise. I distinctly heard something back there."

Out here in the fringes of the system? Chewie considered tearing off a metal arm. It would serve Threepio right. But he'd just have to resolder all those connections again.

"I detected something that was not a naturally occurring phenomenon. Tune back a few kilobits."

Well, it was possible. Pressing his headset to one ear, Chewie hit the low-band scanner and had it repeat its sweep of near space. Something buzzed briefly, a signal too weak to key scanner-pause. Chewie spun a control to amplify. Several seconds of fine tuning brought up a low electronic hum.

Threepio cocked his golden head and posed authoritatively. "That's very strange, Chewbacca. It sounds like some kind of command code for communicating between droids. But what would active droids be doing in this vicinity? Perhaps it is a mechanical survivor from that abandoned Imperial outpost below or machinery still in operation. I suggest that you turn on the comlink and alert General Solo or Princess Leia."

Han had hinted that he'd better not be disturbed for anything short of catastrophic pressure loss. Chewie told Threepio as much.

"Well, I shall not relax until I have ascertained that signal's origin. We have, after all, entered a war zone. We could be in considerable danger. Wait—" Threepio leaned to the other side. "This is no code used in any Alliance or Imperial system."

The invaders? Without hesitating, Chewie swatted the comlink.

It beeped from Han's shirt pocket. "General Solo!" bleated Threepio's singsong voice. "General Solo!"

Leia wriggled in Han's arms. "I knew it," he muttered. Just when Leia'd been on the verge of relaxing. He pulled out the comlink. "What?" he sneered.

"Sir, I am picking up a transmission from near space. A droid control unit of some kind seems to be in operation very close by. I am not certain, but its source appears to be coming closer."

"Uh, oh," Leia said softly against his shoulder. She pushed up to her feet.

"Okay, Chewie, we'll be right there." Han made sure it sounded more like a threat than a promise.

Looking amused, Leia poured her syrupy wine back into the bottle and recorked it. Before sprinting up the corridor, she spread her hands and mournfully quoted Han's words back to him: "It's not my fault!"

Han had just swung into the cockpit when an electronic shriek rang out from the main console. "What's that?" Leia asked.

Great. Just great. Chewie was already powering up. "Not good, sweetheart," Han clipped. "We just got probed."

"By what?" Leia dropped into the seat behind him.

"Well?" Han tossed the question over his shoulder to Threepio.

"Sir," began Threepio, "I have not yet ascertained—"

"Okay," Leia interrupted, "shut up. There!" She pointed dead center on the viewscreen. "Look! What are they?"

From behind the dead icy bulk of Planet 6, eight or nine small shapes appeared in midstarfield, headed directly for the *Falcon*.

"I'm not sticking around to find out," Han growled. "Chewie, charge the main guns."

Chewbacca barked agreement full voice.

"We know the aliens take prisoners," Leia muttered. "I don't want to open negotiations from *that* position."

"You won't. C'mon, Chewie. You and me for the quad guns. We'll see what they're made of. Leia, take us someplace. Suddenly I don't trust Planet Six."

Leia slid into the pilot's seat. Hadn't he just vowed that she'd never take the *Falcon* away from him and Chewie?

Yeah. But this was different. As he rounded the bend, he heard Threepio's voice fade out: "The *Millennium Falcon* is better configured for running away than for engaging enemy fighters. . . ."

Han climbed up the turret and clambered into his seat, then

squeezed off a ranging burst. "They're closing fast," he told Leia via the pickup mike on his headset. "Is Goldenrod getting any data? What are they?"

Threepio's answer began, "Well, General Solo—" By then, Leia'd answered, "Deep-space droids. That's all he knows."

The droids swooped into close range. Three soared over the freighter's asymmetrical dish, firing energy bursts toward its main engine. "Analyze those beams, Goldenrod," Han shouted as he fired. "Are they laser cannons or what?"

Chewbacca snarled over his headphones. "Yeah," Han answered, "for ships of that size!"

"What?" Leia cried. "What, for ships of that—"

"Strong shields." Han poured firepower into a single droid, holding it steady in his sights for as long as it'd take to implode a full-size TIE fighter. The thing finally blew.

The *Falcon* rocked as another droid fired. Han relaxed into the gunner's power chair. This was just the old game. Another droid swooped along the freighter's rim, right at the edge of his sighting capability. "Smart droids," he muttered. "They learn fast."

Abruptly the starfield tilted, lining up the droid for a long, clean burst. "Better?" asked Leia's voice in his ears.

"Much." The thing finally exploded. Two more came in, still aiming for the engines, not the gunners' stations or the cockpit. *They want prisoners, all right.* So where was Big Mama, the boss ship? Or were these babies programmed to attack on their own?

As if she'd read his thoughts, Leia murmured, "What do you bet they're left over from the alien attack on this outpost?" Han finally overloaded the upper one's shields. A wave of debris sent its buddy spinning out of sight.

"Safe bet," he said tightly.

Silence.

"That everybody, Chewie?"

Affirmative roar.

Breathing heavily, he scrambled back down to the cockpit. "Where are we headed?" he asked Leia.

She stroked a control rod. "In system. There may be more of those out here. I don't know about you, but I'd feel *safer* with the rest of our battle group." As she stepped out of the captain's chair, the engine pitch fell off with a groan. Cabin lights darkened. "Now what?" Leia demanded. "I never know what to expect from this overmodified bucket."

Or its overconfident captain? Go ahead, Princess, say it. Han whacked a console. Ready lights blinked and the engines came back up. He swung into his seat with a flourish. "We're gone."

Leia crossed her arms and looked defiant. "For all the *protection* I've gotten, we might as well be doing Luke some good."

"Well, strap down, sweetheart. We're going to hustle."

Motionless but for his eyes, Luke glanced from viewscreen to BAC unit. Commander Thanas's Imperial ships were falling back.

Not because Luke was coming in. Evidently his battle group had dropped back out of hyperspace at the moment when the Ssiruuk meant to press their advantage to Bakura's surface. That meant the aliens had thinned their outer arc to push forward. One light cruiser was practically undefended, creating an area Luke's small force ought to be able to take easily.

"Delckis, give me squadron leaders."

His headset hissed. He adjusted it, pressing small hard components into his ears. "Okay, let's get their attention." He touched a BAC panel to transmit its evaluation into their targeting computers and highlight the solitary cruiser. "Gold Leader, Rogue One, that's yours."

"Got it, *Flurry*." Wedge Antilles sounded confident and experienced. "Rogue Group, lock S-foils in attack position."

Luke felt vulnerable, riding a target as obvious as this carrier. "Red Leader, split your squadron. Red One through Four, hold an escape cone open behind Rogue and Gold groups. We'll draw them away from the planet." Every byte of data his ships' sensors could feed into the BAC would help it analyze alien ships' capabilities.

He shook his head. The yellow-gold pips on his screen were Imperial fighters—and he was defending them.

"Red Five and the rest, stay with the *Flurry*," Luke finished.

Sitting beside him on the elevated captain's chair, Captain Manchisco swiveled away from the master computer. Three black braids swung on each side of her head. "Why, thank you, Commander." Her sense in the Force teased him. Eager for battle, she felt confident of her ship, her crew, and herself.

Gold and Rogue squadrons soared in, confounding the aliens' rearguard with a full-speed sweep. Luke stretched out with his feelings, barely aware of his body. Sensed through the Force, pilots swarmed like hive-minded insects. He tried reaching for alien presences, but couldn't find any. Unfamiliar minds were always difficult to touch.

As Wedge closed on a tiny enemy fighter—the BAC showed it a bare two meters across—he braced himself. Something that small might be just a remote, a drone. Or the aliens could be elfin-size. . . .

Wedge scored. Something weak and inexplicably putrid shrieked in momentary anguish, then fizzled away and died. Luke choked down his gag reflex. Had he felt two presences cry out? He drummed his fingers. The enemy fighters weren't true drone ships then, but piloted. Sort of. *Something* had died.

Almost before he finished that thought, another string of alien fighters winked out behind Gold Leader. This time, he deliberately opened himself. The cascading spiral of twisted misery was as faint as a whimper . . . but human.

Luke couldn't imagine human pilots on alien fighter ships of that size. Particularly not in pairs.

The BAC bleeped. Blinking away disquiet, Luke stared at the alien cruiser's red circle. It flashed: vulnerable.

"*Flurry* to Rogue One. Go for that cruiser. Now."

"I'm on it," Wedge crowed, barely audible over a weird two-tone whistle. X-wings soared past Luke's viewscreen.

Abruptly several more squadrons of tiny sparkling pyramids swarmed out of one end of the alien cruiser. "Abort, Wedge," Luke cried. "They've launched another wave."

"Yeah, I noticed." The whistle grew louder: jamming. Wedge didn't sound concerned. "BAC can't make up its mind, huh?" X-wings scattered in pairs, drawing out pyramidal ships to engage them.

He belonged out there. His best skills were useless on a bridge deck.

The BAC bleeped again, calling Luke's attention to a string of symbols. It had counted and plotted ships' positions, evaluating known and observed firepower, shield strength, speed, and other factors. The Imperials' retreat was transforming into a counterattack on the far underflank of the aliens' front. Pter Thanas was evidently a first-class strategist. Luke turned to his communications officer. A vaguely ominous stirring in the Force raised prickles at the back of his neck.

He bent closer to the BAC. Wedge was leading a sweep out and back toward that light cruiser. That looked good. The Imperials' position had just strengthened by fifteen percentage points. That looked excellent.

No, wait.

An alien gunship, far smaller than the cruiser but no doubt heavily armed, had left the main battle. It was closing on Wedge's squadron from six o'clock low, behind the light cruiser's cover, an angle and a proximity Wedge couldn't hope to see and evade. He guessed the gunship's captain had been waiting for Wedge and his boys to turn their backs. "Rogue One," snapped Luke, "Wedge, watch behind you. Big guns below." As an afterthought, he added, "Red Five and your group. Get out there and shoot those fighters off Wedge's tail."

"What was that?" He could barely hear Wedge for the jamming. X-wings scattered. Two vectored right into the picket ship's range. Luke's viewscreen flashed.

Two blasts of painfully familiar human anguish wrenched Luke's spine and stomach as Alliance pilots died. *Not Wedge*, he confirmed hastily, but they'd been people. *Someone else's friends. They'll be missed. Mourned.*

He regathered his wits and tried to shield himself better. He couldn't grieve yet. Flashing red on the BAC screen, the picket ship was still tailing Wedge's X-wing tightly.

Behind Luke, Captain Manchisco cleared her throat. " 'Scuse me, Commander, but you're leaving the *Flurry* wide open to—"

He was turning his head when the BAC board framed a crimson full alert: The *Flurry* itself was about to come under attack. Alien fighters whizzed past the viewscreen, reflecting crazy flashes of light. "Sure enough," Luke said. "They saw it too. Crew's yours."

Manchisco's black eyes brightened. She spun away and barked out a string of orders to her shipmates. The Duro gargled a question, waving long, knobby hands over his nav controls. Manchisco gargled back. The *Flurry* carried everything from gunners to shield operators. Luke concentrated on Wedge's danger and closed out his own.

Miniature alien fighters had almost surrounded Wedge and his squadron, trapping them inside an escape-proof globe of energy shields and firepower. Luke fought down panic and funneled his emotional energy into the Force around and inside him.

He stretched out his own point of presence toward the tiny alien ship dead ahead of Wedge's X-wing. Touching it, he clearly sensed two almost-human presences on board the small fighter. Shutting out the nauseating sense of twistedness, Luke brushed each presence. One controlled shields; the other, all remaining shipboard functions. Luke focused on the second, driving Force energy into its center. Though weak and faint, it resisted with tortured strength. Its misery goaded him toward despair: No one deserved to live free, its whole being declared. By its reckoning, Luke could do nothing for Wedge—and nothing to save himself—and nothing to save either human aboard the alien fighter. All were doomed.

Luke struggled to see through the stranger's vision. The entire sphere of space opened around him. It overloaded his senses. He had to narrow his field of view to find Wedge's X-wing. On either side of his projected presence, another pyramid hovered apparently motionless, flying in formation. From the center of each triangular face, a scanner/sensor cluster peered back like a compound eye. Laser cannon bristled at each corner.

Fear, anger, aggression: the dark side are they. Yoda had taught him that his methods were as critical as his motives. If he used dark power, even in self-defense, the cost to his soul might be disastrous.

He relaxed into the Force. Clinging to control for the sake of his soul and his sanity, he amplified the pitiful will. Its sense of humanity peaked, hopeless victory for a tortured spirit. It had lived, once—free. With all the intensity of the doomed, it longed to go on living.

Luke planted a suggestion in reply. *But a good death is better than life enslaved to hatred, and peace is better than anguish.*

With suddenness that startled him, the alien ship altered course directly for one of its squadron mates. It accelerated to ram. Luke wrenched free of the other human's will and sat gasping and swallowing. He wiped drenched hair off his face.

A whoop in Luke's headphones pierced his brain. It took him a second to refocus his mind on the carrier's battle bridge, another second to refocus his eyes and steady his stomach.

Wedge's X-wing shot out of danger through the gap created by two alien ships' destruction.

"Sir," clipped Captain Manchisco. Luke shook himself back to a localized awareness. "Are you all right?"

"I will be. Give me a minute."

"We may not have a minute, sir." The BAC still blinked red. The *Flurry* rocked under heavy bombardment. Manchisco's gunners had picked off a swarm of tiny fighters, but behind them came more—and three more alien picket ships. At one corner of the board, six red triangles flashed a shield erosion warning. He had the aliens' attention, all right. Despair melted out of him.

"Engineering can't give us any more power," she said. "Got any more tricks up your sleeve . . . sir?"

In other words, could the famous Jedi help them out of this pickle? Her sense was still cocky, but she, too, was peaking on adrenaline.

Her navigator gargled at her. "No," she ordered, sounding alarmed. "Stay on your station." He ran a long hand over his leathery gray head.

"All squadrons," Luke called. "*Flurry* needs reinforcements."

The ship rocked again. Bridge lights blinked. "That's it," announced a crewer from his sideboard. "Shields are gone. Now we'll see how strong the hull is."

Two-meter pyramids swirled past the viewscreen. Luke clenched a fist. He whirled with ideas, every one useless.

Something shimmered midbattle, the asymmetrical dish of a freighter dropping out of hyperspace amid the swarm of alien fighters. A picket ship strayed into its line of fire. No more picket ship.

"Figured you needed some help," said a familiar voice in his ears.

"Thanks, Han," he murmured. "Nice of you to drop by."

Fighter after enemy fighter fled past the *Flurry* for open space. Red warning lights turned amber. "How many d'you owe me now, Junior?"

"Several," he answered. Maybe he owed Leia. She might be learning to sense Force leadings too.

The swirl of battle gradually slowed. Numbers and figures shifted on the BAC, but Luke ignored them. Later, he might use that information to brief his pilots on alien ship capabilities. But for now, he stared out the light-splashed viewscreen and considered the situation. Surrender to the Force was reflective but not mindless.

"Red Squadron," ordered Luke, "ease into position beneath that cruiser. Come across its bow. Turn it insystem."

He rubbed a fingernail with his thumb and waited for the huge ship to turn, caught himself, and gripped his thigh with that hand. Slowly, the red enemy pip began to rotate on his board. It eased forward, as blind as he'd guessed to Red Squadron's presence. Just a little farther, and Red Squadron could . . .

"Red Leader?" Luke transmitted.

"Going in now," squeaked a young voice.

Luke had to clench his other hand against the edge of the board. Next time he'd let Ackbar send someone else to command. This was ridiculous. He hated command. First chance he got, he'd resign his commission.

Through the Force, he felt the cruiser's destruction. Milliseconds later brilliance lit his viewscreen. "Yes!" crowed Wedge's voice. "Good job, Red Leader!"

Luke imagined his youngest squadron leader grinning behind a blast-darkened canopy. "Well done," Luke echoed. "But don't close your eyes yet. There's still plenty out there."

"Right, *Flurry*." The cluster of blue X-wing pips did a four-way split swing, gathering data through each ship's scanners to add to the fleet's battle boards. *Nice try, Dodonna,* he thought at the BAC's inventor. Its sophisticated circuitry was as useful—and as limited —as the fighters' targeting computers.

"Sir," came Lieutenant Delckis's soft voice beside him. "Drink of water?"

"Thanks." Luke grasped a flat-bottomed drink bulb. A new pattern on the BAC intrigued him. Somebody on the other side had just given an important order, because red pips were disengaging all across the screen. "Squad leaders, they're getting ready to jump.

Stay out of their way, but pick off any that attack you." He had grown in the Force: Already his first choice was to intimidate, not to kill, particularly a battle group that might be turned against the crumbling Empire. He switched channels. "Do you see that, Commander Thanas?"

No answer, but Imperial Commander Thanas was busy too. Luke watched with relief as cluster after cluster vanished. "That's it," he said softly. "We're done, for now. Get the outer-system scanners up, Delckis. It's my guess they're not going far."

"Yes, sir."

Luke sipped bland, recycled water down his parched throat. He'd been breathing hard. *Better control next time,* he promised himself.

"Sir," said Delckis, "you were right. They're already coming up, barely outsystem."

"Mm-hmm." He liked being right, but he did wish they'd simply gone home.

He stretched. What next? He set the drink bulb on the BAC. It made a better table than strategy counselor. "Code a message to Admiral Ackbar, Delckis. We need more ships. Include BAC recordings for that battle. They'll show him what we're up against. Can you have it off in half an hour?"

"Easily, sir."

Thank the Force for contraband Imperial transceivers. "Do it." Next: refuel and rest. "Squad Leaders, this is *Flurry*. Good work. Come on home."

Manchisco exhaled, shook her braids, and whacked the Duro's shoulder.

Blue Alliance glitter-dots converged on the *Flurry*. Luke's radio crackled. "Alliance Commander, this is Commander Thanas. Do you have holonet capability?"

"Yes, but it's slow. Give us five minutes."

Lieutenant Delckis was already twisting levers and diverting power into recently patched-in components. Luke slid his chair into pick-up range. "Tell me when you're ready."

"Ready," Delckis said at last. "Two-way."

Over an instrument panel appeared the image of a man who looked about fifty, narrow faced with thinning brown hair cut almost short enough to hide its curl. "Thanks," said Commander Thanas, "and congratulations."

"They haven't gone far."

"I see that. We'll be on watch. You, ah, might want to move out of the battle zone. Those alien ships leave very hot debris."

"Hot?" Luke eyed a hull temp readout.

"Ssi-ruuvi drones burn heavy fusionables."

New term: *Ssi-ruuvi*. More important, if the aliens meant to invade Bakura, why scatter the system with radioactive cinders?

And why did Thanas go to all the trouble of using holonet for this minor exchange? Luke wondered as Thanas's image faded. Either Commander Thanas wanted to see his counterpart or—knowing the Rebels had holonet—Thanas might suspect they'd stolen other Imperial equipment.

Luke stared at the yellow-gold "allies" dots. "Analyze that," he directed the BAC. The reading came up quickly, and he moved his drink bulb to see it all. The Imperial cruiser drifted, manifestly crippled. Thanas's remaining forces had withdrawn from battle and established a defense web around that ship . . . and Bakura.

He guessed he wouldn't trust Imperials who claimed to want to help *him*, either. Making people trust each other would be Leia's job.

"Thanks again, *Falcon*," he said on their private channel. "Didn't things work out, at the sixth planet?"

"We'll tell you about it sometime," Leia's voice answered out of the speaker at his elbow.

CHAPTER

5

IMPERIAL BAKURAN SENATOR GAERIEL CAPTISON SAT WIGGLING HER TOES AND making patterns out of keys on her inset touchboard. Under a tiled ceiling that rose to a point above its center, the chamber of the Imperial Bakuran Senate lay silent—except for a soft trickle from four two-story, translucent rain pillars at its corners. Roof gutters channeled rain water into the pillars. Lit from below, they shimmered with the liquid pulse of Bakura's biosphere.

Gaeriel had stood in the rain this morning to watch it drum on dancing pokkta leaves, letting it soak her skin, hair, and clothing. She took a deep breath of damp, soothing Bakuran air and folded her hands on the table. Imperial Center was now the only world where a student could do postgraduate work in government—one of the Emperor's ways of ensuring that his philosophy trickled down to subject worlds. After a required year of indoctrination on Center, she'd returned last month. Confirmed now to the senatorial post she'd won as a youngster, she was here for her first emergency evening call.

Atop the stairs to Gaeriel's left, Governor Nereus's massive, purple-cushioned repulsor chair sat empty. The Senate, declining in power every year, awaited Nereus's convenience.

Down the steps from Governor Nereus's chair, a pair of tables lay on Gaeriel's long middle level; on a third, lowest level, two inner tables framed an open space. Orn Belden, senior senator, shook his finger across the low central table. "Don't you see?" Belden creaked at Senator Govia. "Compared to systems the Emperor truly wants to control, our ships and facilities are . . . well, the ships are older than I am, and the facilities are undermanned. As for staff, we're a dumping ground—"

"All rise," barked a voice near the chamber's door. A warden in ancient-style violet doublet and hose thumped a spear's butt on carpeted flooring. Gaeri slipped her shoes back on and stood with thirty-nine other senators. Only the Imperial Guards saluted. She hoped this session didn't mean more taxes. Not now, with the Ssiruuk threatening.

Imperial Governor Wilek Nereus strode in, flanked by four black-helmeted naval troopers. They reminded her of leggy beetles. Governor Nereus wore a specially designed uniform, heavy on braid and gold piping, its short coat cut to create an illusion of taper from his shoulders to his waist—and skintight black gloves that had given him a reputation for being fastidious. His features were heavy except for prissy lips, and he had the Imperial swagger down to a science. "Sit," he said.

Gaeri smoothed her long blue skirt and sat down. Governor Nereus remained standing near the entry. Taller than any of them, he used his height to intimidate. She'd always disliked him, but her year on Imperial Center had made him slightly more tolerable—by comparison.

"I won't keep you," he said, looking down his long nose. "I realize you are busy keeping your sectors pacified. Some of you are doing well. Some aren't."

Gaeri frowned. Her district's residents were abandoning their jobs to dig shelters, but at least bunker-blasting was productive.

She glanced at her uncle, Prime Minister Yeorg Captison. Here in Salis D'aar, Captison had been quelling riots, using Bakuran police to keep Nereus from sending out stormtroopers from the garrison.

Nereus raised a gloved hand to silence murmurers. Once he had their attention, he slowly turned his head and cleared his throat. "Rebel Alliance ships have arrived in the Bakura system."

That gave her a rain-cold shock. Rebels? The Empire allowed no dissent. After Bakura entered the Empire three years ago, two minor rebellions had been efficiently quashed. Gaeri remembered too much of that period. Both of her parents had died, caught in the wrong place during a running battle between insurgents and Imperial troops. That was when she'd gone to live with her uncle and aunt. She didn't hope to live to see another uprising, or any more of the bloody purges that followed.

Perhaps these troublemakers wanted the repulsorlift component factory in Belden's district. Could Nereus's forces protect Bakura from Rebel raiders *and* the Ssi-ruuk?

Nereus cleared his throat. "The *Dominant*, our only remaining cruiser, sustained heavy damages. On the advice of my staff, I have ordered our forces to withdraw from the main battle and protect Bakura itself. I request your confirmation of that order."

Belden straightened his back and fiddled with a voice amplifier on his chest. "Covering your tracks, Governor? So if anything else goes wrong, you can finger us? Who's keeping the Ssi-ruuk off, I wonder?"

It wasn't wise to attract an Imperial Governor's attention, but Belden seemed fearless. Maybe if Gaeri were 164, with a second prosthetic heart and one foot in the grave, she'd learn his kind of courage.

Abruptly distracted, she checked the time. She had promised Senator Belden that she'd visit his elderly wife this evening. Madam Belden's caregiver Clis left for the night at 2030, and Gaeri had offered to sit with her until Senator Belden finished a committee meeting. Fiery little Eppie's mind was eroding, at only 132.

(Eroding? It had washed out to sea three years ago.) Orn Belden's devotion, and the genuine affection of a few lifelong family friends such as Gaeriel, sustained her. Eppie had been Gaeriel's first real "grown-up" friend.

Governor Nereus ran a hand over his dark hair. He tried to mimic a classic Old Republic politician, using minimum threat of force to keep the population in line. Consequently, he'd built a new order suzerainty far from Imperial Core shipping lanes, with minimal open violence . . . after those bloody purges, three years back.

Nereus smiled blandly. "The action I have ordered merely ensures that Rebels will not strike at Bakura."

"Did Rebels disable the *Dominant,* or did the Ssi-ruuk?"

"I do not yet have full reports, Senator Belden. It appears that—for now—your factory is safe. I shall send over three defense squads from the garrison."

Belden wouldn't like that. Prime Minister Captison stood again. The deep green shoulders of his tunic seemed to float at the top of his perfectly straight back. Gaeriel had been stunned to find his hair white when she came back from the university. Captison's dignity shamed Nereus's posturing. He flicked two fingers against his trouser seam: placate. Apparently Belden saw it too. He sat down slowly, deferring to the P.M.

"Thank you, Senator Belden," said Prime Minister Captison. "Evidently, for the moment the Rebels are between us and the Ssi-ruuk. Perhaps that's the best place for them." He looked around the table. Forty senators, human except for two pale Kurtzen from the Kishh district, stared back. Like the senate, Prime Minister Captison had lost authority every time he crossed Imperial wishes. "Let us support Governor Nereus," he said without enthusiasm, "and confirm his withdrawal order."

He called the vote. Gaeri extended an open palm with the majority. Only Belden and two others closed their fists.

Gaeriel sighed to herself. Belden wasn't a follower of the Cosmic

Balance. He could not bring himself to believe that when he graciously allowed fate to diminish him, others were exalted. The wheel always turned, too, and those who humbled themselves for the present would one day reap rich rewards.

"Thank you for your support," purred Nereus. His beetlely escorts followed him out.

Gaeriel stared after him. Before the Empire arrived, Bakura had been governed by a prime minister and a senate—and no set of three individuals in the government could ever agree on a program. Schools had run half-year when Gaeri started attending, then shifted to "tumble month" schedule, two on and one off; then someone scrapped the entire curriculum. If the government couldn't agree on a school calendar, even a child knew it wouldn't agree on anything else. As a senator's daughter and the prime minister's niece, she'd overheard unending machinations and bickering about other subjects—social justice, repulsorlift exports, and taxation.

Most important, no two senators had ever agreed on a defensive strategy. Consequently Bakura fell quickly to the Empire.

She straightened her shoulders. Perhaps that easy conquest explained why Governor Nereus had left so much of the original government in place. Her experience on Imperial Center had taught her to keep her mouth shut about Bakura's senate. Other systems' residents reacted indignantly to its existence.

Imperial peace compensated Bakura for the autonomy it had lost, or so Gaeri's admittedly limited experience told her. It had ended the chaos and civil infighting, and brought Bakuran trade goods out onto stellar lanes.

Yet many older senators disagreed, and when they spoke quietly, Gaeri listened.

Speaking of dissidents, she'd better head for the Beldens' apartment. She slipped her shoes back on—again—and headed for the roof port.

•　　•　　•

Dev generally spent battle time in his master Firwirrung's quarters, working feverishly on his translation project to keep from feeling enemy fighters' fear when tractor beams caught them. Today, though, Master Firwirrung had asked him to carry food trays and a packet of drink bulbs from the galley up a brightly lit corridor to the command deck.

Busy defending the advance force, Admiral Ivpikkis had ordered the empowerment of additional battle droids instead of refilling the Shriwirr's normal complement of internal droid servants—except the security droids who guarded the bridge itself—so Dev filled a servant role different from his usual post. The Shriwirr's captain held back out of battle, protecting Ssi-ruuvi lives and holding open communication lines that stretched along a string of subspace beacons all the way back to the main fleet.

Whenever human prisoners were brought on board, Dev took secret comfort in their company . . . for a little while. They were always enteched so soon, their Force presences focused inside battle droids. He wouldn't deny them that joy for the sake of his own psychological comfort, but secretly—selfishly—it saddened him. Unbeknownst to his masters, he sometimes reached out through the Force during battles and fondled whole human presences. Feeling guilty but compelled, he stretched out now . . .

And touched power. Gripping the steering surfaces of his repulsor cart, he stood motionless. Someone—somewhere off the Shriwirr—had the deep, placid strength he'd always associated with his mother. His eyes flooded. Surely she hadn't come back for him? Could that be? He'd heard of visitations, but—

No. If this were the sense of a human—and the human was clearly not on Bakura, from its proximity—then this was the sense of an enemy. It was far stronger than his mother, too. He'd heard the admiral mention an incoming group in passing, almost as if it were beneath his notice, but this enemy made him think of . . . of home. The Outsider was concentrating on the combatants, too, but not with the same shade of passion Dev felt. Dev reached deeper. Their likeness beckoned and seduced him. The Outsider seemed not to notice his probe.

Dev gave the repulsor cart a push. He shouldn't think about it. He hoped the feeling wouldn't come back.

He paced onward. He had almost reached the bridge when a warbling whistle sounded over the general alarm system. Emergency: Harness for reorient.

Startled, Dev released his cart. He plunged through the nearest open hatchway and spotted several ceiling-to-deck emergency hammocks. Large russet Ssi-ruuk and small brown P'w'ecks struggled into the nearest harnesses. Dev spied one that hung limp. He dashed over, seized the red cord at its edge and held it against his breastbone, then twirled to surround himself. Now more than ever, he wished for a massive Ssi-ruuvi body. Slender and tailless, he had to twirl half a dozen times before the webbing enclosed him securely.

Then he had several seconds to think above the alarm trill. To try to remember if he'd netted the nest pillows this morning. He'd also left a laden cart in the corridor.

Worse, the invincible *Shriwirr* was accelerating unexpectedly for hyperspace. Surely this wasn't retreat. They'd been so close to victory. They'd—

The near bulkhead became deck, then ceiling. Dev's stomach protested violently. Acceleration smashed his face into six layers of netting. Unable to brace against the deck, he dug his fingers through the webbing and spun out of control. He clenched his eyes shut and begged it to end.

When gravity came from the deck again, the alarm whistle cut off. Dizzily, Dev struggled to unwind.

"What's going on?" one of his neighbors asked. "I don't remember an emergency reorient since Cattamascar."

The answer came in a disturbingly familiar voice. "We lost a cruiser. Nearly all the new drone fighters are gone. We're having to waste humans to protect our remaining ships. We must analyze the newcomers' tactics before going in again. This group is different. Different ship types, different command style."

Command style? Did the new group have a Force-strong commander? Perhaps a . . . a genuine Jedi, who'd finished the training his mother had only begun?

But the Empire had purged Jedi. Hunted them down.

Yes, and the Emperor was dead. A true Jedi might dare to show himself.

That was all supposition. Finally unwound, Dev stepped out of his hammock. Standing in front of him, staring down with liquid black eyes, stood the massive Ssi-ruu who performed his comforting "renewals": Sh'tk'ith, the elder they respectfully nicknamed Bluescale. Bluescale had sprung from a different Ssi-ruuvi race from Firwirrung's: brilliant tiny blue scales, narrower face, longer tail. Bluescale's race dominated on the home world as Firwirrung's dominated the military.

He should tell Bluescale what he'd sensed . . . but that would mean confessing his guilty secret habit. Dev blinked down at the deck. "I greet you, Elder—"

"What is amiss?" Bluescale demanded. His black scent tongues flickered, tasting the air. Of all Ssi-ruuk, he seemed most sensitive to subtle changes in human scent due to stress.

"Such . . . tragedy," Dev said cautiously, "that many battle droids lost. Those poor humans—their new lives, their new happiness, was cut so short. Let me mourn for my . . . for other humans, Elder. How sad for them. How sad." The boldness of his lie staggered him.

Triple eyelids blinked. Bluescale let out a guttural honk, the Ssi-ruuvi equivalent of a thoughtful "hmm." Tapping his foreclaws, Bluescale answered, "Later, then. After you have contemplated their deaths, return to me. I will renew you for happier service."

"Thank you, Elder." Dev's voice cracked as he backed away. "I must clean the corridor. Labor will give me time for thinking."

Bluescale waved a foreclaw and dismissed him.

Dev fled back out through the hatchway, feeling guiltier than ever. Had he endangered the advance force? Surely not. Admiral Ivpikkis would succeed. Dev's immediate problem was to hide that moment's touch in his memory, before Bluescale called him in and convinced him to confess.

Cold food splattered the bulkheads, and drink bulbs littered the gray-tiled deck. Dev hurried downship to a supply locker. Cleanup was P'w'eck work, but he felt responsible.

He had never been able to fool Bluescale. Wasn't hiding thoughts treasonous? His masters had saved him from starvation and death. He owed them so much.

Yet he'd never had so strong a reason before. His mind had touched a kindred soul. He couldn't betray it yet.

He flung open the supply locker, seized up a galleyvac and hurried upship toward the nearest dribbling glob.

CHAPTER

6

S AFE CONDUCT TO SALIS D'AAR, THE CAPITAL CITY. CONTROLLERS will talk you down," finished a spaceport flunky's voice on the *Falcon*'s transceiver.

"Thank you." Han cut the connection and leaned back.

Leia exhaled. "So. We can get to work."

Han arched an eyebrow. It seemed to him they'd been working already.

Leia didn't notice. "We have to decide what to do next." She smoothed one of the braids that circled her head.

"Right," he answered, glad to see her thinking sensibly. "Do we use this safe conduct and land on Bakura, or not? They're in better shape now. This might be a good time to take our troops and get out."

Leia stared at the *Falcon*'s deck. "That wasn't what I meant, but you're right. I can't help wondering if we'll be able to deal with Imperials directly."

On link from over at the *Flurry*, Luke spoke up. "Leia, aren't you feeling well?"

She cleared her throat and leaned toward the control board. "I'm uneasy, Luke. Maybe I'm starting to think like Han. I don't feel quite right about this situation. I'm more nervous than usual."

Han eyed Chewie, who whuffled softly. Yeah, maybe she was picking up a sense of self-preservation. Skywalkers seemed to be born without it.

"We're all nervous," answered Luke's voice. "Something's going on here besides what shows on the surface. I have to figure it out."

Han peered through the *Falcon*'s port at the *Flurry*. It hovered, looking lumpy and awkward, near the *Falcon* in a parking orbit outside the Imperial defense web. "You sure, kid?" he asked. "It'd be a good time to head home."

"I'm sure. Leia, you're in charge of negotiations. Do you want to shuttle over and make a dignified landing in the *Flurry*'s transport?"

"Wait a minute." Han straightened his back. "I'm not landing anything but the *Falcon*. I want this bucket planetside, in case we need to make another fast getaway."

"Another?" asked Luke. "What happened?"

"Later." Leia tapped her thumbs over clasped fingers. "What about the impression we'll create, landing in . . . well, think what the *Falcon* looks like if you don't know her."

Thanks a lot, Your Highness. "That's camouflage."

She spread her hands. "This will be the Bakuran Imperials' first impression of our group, Han. We want them as allies. Think in the long term."

"First we have to survive the short term."

Luke cleared his throat. "The *Falcon* won't fit in the *Flurry*'s hangar bay. It's full."

Leia glanced at the immaculate control panel, then over at one bulkhead wired together with leftover circuitry. She gave him a long, somber stare. At last she said, "Okay, Luke. Come on over. We'll land in the *Falcon* . . . but only if everybody dresses up."

Han clenched a fist on one hip. "Well, I'm not—"

"Except you, Captain." Her voice sounded sweet, but he saw an evil gleam in her eye. "It's your bucket. You'd better look the part."

Some time later, Leia stared out the viewport at cloud patterns on a stunning azure world. Chewie examined the boards and then stood, looking satisfied, to head up the corridor.

Luke appeared with damp, tousled hair. He'd taken her account of events at Planet 6 calmly, then said something about scrubbing down. "Feel better?" she asked.

"You bet." He plunked down in the oversize copilot's chair. "Let's see if we can raise Commander Thanas again."

"I still say it smells like a trap." Han slid back into the pilot's seat. "Maybe Thanas thinks he's being a nice guy, offering to let us into that defense web. But if we split our forces, we've got half tied up for some Imperial desk jockey and only half on alert where they ought to be."

Luke tapped a pattern onto the console. "Their ships are going to need longer repair breaks than ours. What I saw had been shot up pretty badly."

"And we still don't know what those aliens are up to," Leia said. She glanced sidelong at Luke. She could swear that he knew more than he was telling. "I have a very bad feeling about it."

"It's our necks in the noose, now," Han joined in, "along with the Bakurans."

"That was the idea," Leia agreed. "To prove we're with them by sharing their danger."

"Alliance Forces?" rumbled Commander Thanas's voice from the speaker.

Leia leaned over Luke's shoulder. Nearly dry already, his hair caught dim cabin lights like an aureole. "On frequency, Commander Thanas," Luke answered.

"I've cleared Alliance ships to join the defense web in the positions you requested, while your party conducts negotiations at Salis D'aar. I look forward to meeting you in person."

"It's mutual. Alliance out." Luke paused for a second after switching from the Imperial frequency to another. "Got all that?"

"Locked into the BAC," Captain Manchisco answered through the speaker. "Have fun down there."

Luke blew out a long breath.

"You're going to have to tell the Imperials who you are sooner or later, Luke." Han made a wry face.

Leia started. *No you're not!*

"I'd rather do it face to face," Luke said calmly.

Oh. They only meant revealing his name, not his ancestry. She hurried to agree. "He's got better control, better . . . discernment in person, Han. He can feel if they're covering up."

Han snorted softly. "It still smells like a trap. I don't like it." But he reached for the control panel. Luke relinquished Chewie's seat and took one in back.

"And Luke's a Jedi," Leia reminded him.

Luke nodded at her. "We'll keep our eyes open."

The *Falcon* vectored out of position in parking orbit toward an approach for the Bakuran capital city, Salis D'aar. Passing through the defense web, Leia spotted a huge repair station: saucer-shaped, not spherical, thank goodness. They'd had enough Death Stars. Han made a tight descent, all dive and no sightseeing. Leia peered between Han and Chewie's seats at the scanner display.

Between the twin rivers, an enormous outcrop of pure white rock sparkled in low-angle light. It dazzled her eyes.

Blinking, Han punched in a visual filter. "Better?"

"Look at that," Leia whispered. Where the outcrop took a southeastward bend, an entire city sat perched on its width. South of the city, she made out a double ring of large craters surrounding a tall metal tower. Civilian spaceport, she guessed.

She glanced north again, to the city. Radials and concentric circles of its road system gave it a web pattern, and considerable aircar traffic cruised on and off several sharp towers near its midpoint. "What's the local time?" she asked.

"Just after dawn." Han rubbed his chin. "Going to be a long day."

Irregular green blotches suggested that luxuriant parks had been created in pockets of soil on the rocky white outcrop.

"Look." Luke pointed a kilometer south of the spaceport. Inside a circle of barren black artificial surface, enormous turbolaser turrets guarded a hexagonal complex.

Leia folded her arms. "Standard design for an Imperial garrison."

"It's going to be crawling with stormtroopers down there," Han observed.

"What was that?" Threepio called from his usual station in the gaming area. "Did someone see stormtroopers?"

"Don't overload a circuit," said Han. "They're going to be everywhere."

Threepio's answering mutter had the rhythm of, "Oh dear, oh dear." Luke unharnessed and slipped out of the cockpit.

Chewbacca howled something. "Luke must be expecting a smooth touchdown," Han translated. "Don't know why not," he added.

Leia elected to stay in her seat and brush a wrinkle out of her white skirt. She'd ordered a copy sewn from her threadbare white senatorial gown. She still hoped to dispel the Rebels' ragtag reputation, if that was possible after landing in the *Falcon*.

Han flew the ship around the perimeter of Salis D'aar twice, swooping out over the river on each side of the stunning white outcrop that kept them from flowing together. "They're not firing on us," he said. "Guess we might as well go through with it."

Controllers directed Han toward a vacant multiship crater at the western end of the spaceport. The early morning shadows of several moveable repair gantries stretched out long on the rough white ground. "What's that surface?" Leia murmured as Han made his final descent.

Han glanced at a scanner. "Says here the outcrop's almost pure quartz. The crater looks like rock glass, but somebody roughed it up."

The *Falcon* touched down softly.

"There. See?" Han asked. "Nothing to worry about."

Chewie barked. Leia turned to look where he was pointing one hairy hand. About twenty people clustered around a long repulsor shuttle, near a gantry at the edge of their landing crater. "Hurry it up, Luke," Han shouted.

"Right." Luke's breathless voice echoed out in the corridor. Leia sprang off her seat and joined him.

Threepio stood nodding approval of Luke's white shipsuit without rank insignia. As Leia looked him up and down, he hooked on a silvery utility belt from which dangled a blaster, three trifle pouches, and his lightsaber. "Good enough?" He fixed his eyes on Leia. They looked so blue and innocent.

"I guess that's how a Jedi ought to dress," she said dubiously. *I wish you looked older.*

Luke glanced anxiously at Han. Han shrugged. Leia laughed. "What does it matter what he thinks?" she asked Luke.

"You look splendid, Master Luke," put in Threepio. "General Solo, you're rather untidy. Don't you think it would minimize our danger if—"

"Chewie," said Han. "You want to stay on board?"

It was a valid question. Chewbacca would represent the Alliance well if he came along. Imperials despised aliens on principle, but humans and Imperial-repressed aliens had founded the Alliance together.

Chewie roared. "Okay," Han said. "Guess we can use one more pair of eyes. Everybody look sharp."

Leia thought Threepio snickered, if such a thing were possible. Artoo chirped aloud.

"All right," Luke cut in. "Here we go."

Leia positioned herself in the center of the group with Luke on her right, Han on her left, and Chewie behind with Threepio and Artoo. Chewie dropped the entry ramp. She walked down slowly, sniffing cool wet air that seemed heavy with exotic plant odors. Her first breath on a new planet was always a treat.

As she stepped onto the pale spaceport surface, it crunched. She glanced back. The *Falcon* sat on a satiny bed of white rock and gray spaceport dust.

Enough exploring. Get to work. She strode to meet the Imperial group beside its shuttle.

"Ooh," Han said sarcastically. "All the pretty white armor."

"Cut it out," Leia muttered. "I'm wearing white too." She thought back to her days as an Imperial senator, the double game she'd played between the Emperor's coterie and the infant Alliance her father had died for.

Her *real* father, Bail Organa, who had raised and trained her and nurtured her sense of self-worth and self-sacrifice. Regardless of biology, she would never own another man by that title. Period. Enter data. End program.

The man at the center of the group had to be Imperial Governor Wilek Nereus. Tall and dark-haired with heavy features, he wore a khaki uniform that he might have borrowed from Grand Moff Tarkin, with the addition of a pair of thin black gloves. The other individuals in his group kept shifting positions to watch him. He was absolutely In Charge.

Relax, she told herself. *Flow with it. My strengths lie here, along a different path from Luke's.*

Governor Nereus's delegation made a semicircle around him. "Princess Leia of Alderaan." He sketched a half-bow. "It is an honor to receive you."

"Governor Nereus." She returned his bow, making sure hers dipped not a millimeter deeper. "It is our honor to be here."

"In the name of the emperor, welcome to Bakura."

She couldn't have hoped for a better opening than that protocol greeting. "Thank you for your welcome," she answered placidly. "You may think me terribly rude to correct your kind words, but it's no longer valid to welcome us in Emperor Palpatine's name. Emperor Palpatine died several days ago."

Nereus cocked a dark, heavy eyebrow and clasped his large hands behind him. "My dear Princess." He swaggered forward another step. "Have you come to Bakura spreading rumors and lies?"

"It gets better, Your Excellency. He was killed by his apprentice, Darth Vader."

"Vader." Nereus straightened several millimeters to loom over her. Distaste dripped through his pronunciation, a sentiment she understood perfectly. "Vader," he repeated. "His Imperial Majesty should never have trusted a Sith lord. I was prepared to disbelieve you, Your Highness. But Vader as an assassin, I believe."

"Lord Vader is dead as well, Your Excellency."

Luke's chin rose at the edge of her vision. She knew what he wanted her to add. Maybe Vader had died heroically, but ten minutes' contrition did not make up for years of atrocities.

The governor's people turned aside in pairs to whisper. Leia seized the initiative again. "Governor, may I present my escorts— first, General Solo." Han was supposed to bow, or at least shake hands. Instead, he stood aside with a flat disapproving expression. At this rate, he would never make a diplomat.

"His copilot, Chewbacca of Kashyyyk." Chewie grumbled as he bowed. Wookiees had been deeply betrayed by the Empire. She hoped Chewie didn't forget himself and start tearing arms off Imperials. The chilly morning breeze ruffled his fur.

She laid out her trump card with flair. "And Commander Skywalker of Tatooine, Jedi Knight."

Luke bowed beautifully—she'd coached him. Nereus squared his shoulders. After a moment, he returned the bow. "Jedi." His large nose twitched. "We'll have to watch ourselves."

Luke clasped his hands in front of him. *Good!* Leia praised him silently. He was letting her answer, just as she'd begged. Now she felt repaid for letting him take charge in battle. Maybe there was a future in this division of labor, so long as it didn't go too far. "Yes,

Excellency," she said. Governor Nereus turned his head toward her again. "We mean to reestablish the Old Republic, including the Order of Jedi Knights. Commander Skywalker is head of the order." Again she guessed what he wanted her to add: also the only member. *Don't look sheepish, Luke!*

"Commander Skywalker," Nereus repeated, and his tone became as oily as droid lubricant. "Ah. Now I recognize your name, Commander. Fortunately for you, Bakura has a good trade balance. You might know that for some years there has been a . . . an astronomical reward offered for your capture. Alive, only. That must be something of a distinction among Rebel forces."

"I'm aware," Luke answered quietly. This was nothing new, either. They were all on the most-wanted docket.

"And I see two droids," said the governor. "They'll have to be equipped with restraining bolts for the duration of their stay on Bakura."

Fitting droids with those bolts was standard procedure on most planets, compulsory on Imperial worlds and battle stations. "We'll see to it," Leia agreed. Now certain she had commanded Nereus's respect, she stepped out of her own protection. "Governor, Alliance forces intercepted your call for assistance. The Imperial Fleet is no longer a presence in this part of the galaxy. We are here to assist you in repelling the invaders. Once that is accomplished, we will leave you. Bakura must choose its own destiny. We will not attempt to impose ours upon your . . . on the Bakuran people," she corrected herself.

Governor Nereus showed her a chilling half-smile. The left side of his face contracted, pulling up that side of his mouth. The right side could've been cast in iron.

Luke stayed at attention. Just as Nereus's face wore two expressions, he was of palpably different minds. It would be difficult for such a man to accept Rebels as allies.

The gloved governor's savor in the Force licked and pushed at

him. Nereus had an uncontrollable compulsion to dominate people, and that kept his delegation at attention. Luke knew the type:
his ways were the only sensible ways. Anyone who countered him
would capture his attention only long enough to be squashed: the
quintessential Imperial governor.

Luke kept himself open to perceive intent all around. So many
nervous flickers tremored through the Force that simply looking
calm strained his control. He didn't intend to get fried by a trigger-
happy trooper before Leia talked out a treaty.

As Leia and Governor Nereus continued a guarded conversation,
he stretched deeper and opened himself toward them again. Leia:
calm and poised, not intimidated by Nereus. The governor: a
facade of trained manners, the compulsion to dominate, and—
underlying both—a gut-wrenching sense of terror. *Surely not of
us.* Again Luke thought of the despondent, not-quite-human
presences on that Ssi-ruuvi fightership. Had he contacted captive
Bakurans?

Obviously the governor meant to leap in any direction that offered protection. As hostile as he acted in front of his troopers, he
could easily jump into the Alliance camp.

Temporarily.

In a civilian shuttlecraft offered for their ride to the city, Luke
relayed that impression to Han.

"Yeah," Han muttered quietly. "He could jump into our camp, all
right. Or he could torpedo it. Want to place bets?"

Luke's formal trousers clung to his legs, clammy with the perva-
sive Bakuran dampness. Leia sat in front of him, lovely in her
hooded white senatorial gown. She stared out the window of the
plushly upholstered shuttlecraft. Sure enough, the Bakuran senate
had requested that they attend an immediate emergency session.

Abruptly Leia straightened. "Threepio, what do I need to know
about protocol?"

"I'm afraid that is not in my program." Threepio already wore his magneto-fixed restraining bolt, and his tone sounded whinier than ever. Artoo interrupted with an electronic whistle. "What? Master Luke downloaded the data files from that probe into your memory banks? Why didn't you say so, you overstuffed recycle cylinder?"

Artoo chattered back at length. Then Threepio answered Leia, "All I am able to ascertain is that Bakura was once governed by a prime minister and senate, but all real authority now rests in the Imperial governorship."

"Tell us something new," Han remarked aside.

A Bakuran pilot/guide brought them in low over a huge wedge-shaped building punctured by two wide greenwell arcs. "This is the Bakur complex," announced the pilot's assistant, linking one arm around a silver stabilizer bar. She stared at Chewbacca. Luke guessed she'd never seen a Wookiee.

The complex appeared to fill several hectares between two radial highways, and bordered the round city-center park along its south-western arc. "The complex includes guest and resident housing, Imperial offices, a major medical center, and the grand old park-side building that was our seat of government under the Bakur Corporation."

Leia looked down, as if she were watching huge, vine-covered trees flit across the complex's rooftop. Actually, Luke guessed, she was mentally reviewing Imperial protocol. Bakura's freedom rested on her ability to negotiate this truce. Han, beside her in the shuttle's front seat, fiddled with his blaster.

At a rooftop landing pad, they transferred to a repulsor tram for a rapid ride across the large complex. Their guide kept up the tour, concluding, "The corporation wing of the Bakur Memorial Building was built over a hundred years ago, overlooking Statuary Park at city center. Please remain seated until the car comes to a complete stop." The tram slid under a vine-draped arch and decelerated.

"Wait, Leia." Han sprang up.

Luke slipped out his own side of the tram. Leia kept her seat for a few seconds. "I believe this archway is suitably secure," Threepio's observation drifted through an open hatch. "Still, we must be certain of safety."

Leia poked her head out Luke's side. "Listen," she said, "if they mean to hurt us, the entire mission has already failed."

Han glanced over the tram. "Right. Okay on this side, Luke."

Luke swung around to the rear of the car and uncarted Artoo. The droid whistled jauntily and extended his tricycle wheels. Han and Chewie stepped out ahead of Leia and Threepio. Luke followed, trailed by Artoo. Door wardens in gold-trimmed violet doublets and hose admitted them to a spacious hallway carpeted in black. Gold traceries ran like veins of precious metal up a row of columns built in double-wedge style, then crisscrossed overhead on a vaulted ceiling. "Red marble," Leia murmured.

"Worth a fortune, if you could smuggle it out," Han answered over his shoulder. He followed one door warden. After a few mincing steps in imitation, he shifted back into his watchful stride with glances to left and right, behind every pillar, and toward each open door. Luke listened intently through the Force for flickers of aggression. He sensed nothing. Leia walked serenely ahead of him, at the center of the group beside her protocol droid.

The violet-legged warden stopped at an arch carved of glistening white stone. A rough wooden wall blocked most of it, with scanners hovering on silent repulsorlifts over each side and four Imperial stormtroopers standing guard. The sight of them gave Luke a fight-or-flight surge of adrenaline. "They're here illegally," Leia murmured. "We are the galaxy's rightful envoy to Bakura."

"Tell that to them." Han glowered at the stormtroopers. Luke stared up into one sensor's glossy round eye. Artoo's dome swiveled around and around as his own sensors scanned the hallway.

"Weapons check." A trooper bent over Leia and spoke in a metallic voice. "Leave all ordnance in a security locker." He gestured toward a bank of palm-keyed receptacles across the archway.

Leia spread her empty hands and then folded them mock-submissively. Luke crossed the arch, selected a cubicle, and then palmed its lock while pressing a button to key the locker to his hand print. He drew his blaster from its belt holster and laid it inside. "Come on, Han," he said softly.

Han had followed him, tailed slowly by Chewie and Leia. Han didn't seem happy about it, but he keyed a cubicle of his own and set his blaster inside.

Leia cleared her throat.

Han shot her a look that might've fried lead, then pulled out his boot knife, the pocket blaster from his wrist sheath, and his favorite vibroknife. Chewbacca was easing off the bandolier for his bowcaster when Luke's subconscious tossed up a suggestion. "Chewie," he said softly, "stay with the locker. Artoo, you too."

Chewie's lips drew back in pleasure, and he wrinkled his black nose. The big Wookiee had little use for politics and no trust for Imperials. He would love to stand guard.

Leia led the group back toward the arch.

"Stop right there," said the stormtrooper who'd spoken before. He pointed at Luke's lightsaber. "That's a weapon, too."

Luke extended a tendril of Force energy and answered soberly, "This is a symbol of honor. Not an offensive weapon. Let it pass."

"Let it pass," echoed the stormtrooper in the same sober tone. Recovering, he added, "I'd leave the droid at the door. Droid malfunctions nearly killed the first crew of Bakuran colonists."

"Sir," protested Threepio, "my function is—"

"Thank you," Leia said firmly. None of them were forgetting that restraining bolt. "Threepio will wait just inside."

A door warden announced, "Senator Princess Leia Organa, of Alderaan. And"—he waved a hand vaguely—"and escorts."

CHAPTER

7

LEIA LED THEM THROUGH THE ARCH AND MOUNTED FOUR BROAD STEPS
into a vast square chamber. Luke followed, matching Han
step for step, hoping he'd done the right thing by keeping his
lightsaber. He didn't want to offend the entire Bakuran senate by
carrying in a weapon, but they might not recognize it as dangerous. He also hoped Leia would've challenged him if she'd thought
it important.

The chamber was square under a tiled ceiling, and in each corner stood a tall, glassy pillar. Most of the senators were human,
with only two exceptions: tall, white-skinned individuals with corrugated scalp instead of hair. Luke opened himself to listen
through the Force. A babble surrounded him, the textures of forty
or fifty nervous minds. Narrowing his focus, he reached straight
across the chamber toward a massive repulsor chair, all gold and
purple except for two banks of controls on the armrests. Wilek
Nereus must have caught a faster shuttle. He sat there already, with
his double-mindedness coming through as strongly as ever.

Luke let his attention drift leftward, observing the senators' reactions to Leia. He sensed curiosity tinged with hostility, but a dark undercurrent of fear also pervaded the chamber. This world was under attack.

"Stay here, Threepio." Leia halted atop the stairs and faced Governor Nereus. "Good morning again, Governor."

His heavy eyebrows lowered. "Come in," he said. "Come down."

They stepped forward and down to the central rectangle. Floor seams showed where it could be slid aside. Luke had a disconcerting flash of memory that included a trapdoor and a huge, slavering Rancor that'd almost devoured him. Thrusting the image aside, he glanced around the chamber. The Bakuran senators displayed all common shades of human skin, a subtle blending of blood lines.

One trim, athletic-looking man with thick white hair, who sat below Governor Nereus at an inner table, extended a hand. "Welcome to Bakura," he said. "I am Prime Minister Yeorg Captison. Under normal circumstances, you would have had a protocol briefing, and I apologize for the haste with which this meeting was convened, but certainly you understand."

Leia—who'd barely acknowledged Governor Nereus—made a deep, deliberate curtsey to the older man. Luke scanned him. The prime minister's charisma made a glimmer in the Force only a shade dimmer than Mon Mothma's. Luke glanced back up at Nereus, wondering why the governor hadn't eradicated him. Captison must've been *very* careful. Or did he have Imperial connections?

"Please don't apologize," said Leia. "This is a desperate hour."

Another inner-table man stood up. "Blaine Harris, defense minister. You have no idea how desperate. All of our outposts on the other planets in the system have been destroyed. Our salvage crews that survived to report back found no bodies and no survivors." Harris's fear shot an answering shiver down Luke's back. Hastily he swept his focus leftward along that table, feeling echoes of fear, hope, and hostility. When he reached its end, he worked toward the right along the outer, upper table.

A sharp-chinned young woman sat third from the left. He paused, startled by the way she resonated the Force back to him. Like a deep, slow thrum, her presence echoed his probe with a rich overlay. It wasn't Force strength of her own—at least, he didn't think so—but a unique energizing effect on his awareness. He'd never experienced it before. Hurriedly, he slammed off all perception but his five senses. He mustn't let her distract him.

Nereus's strident voice carried distinctly across the chamber; he'd placed his throne at an acoustic focus point. "Princess Leia, do you understand what you are up against?"

Leia laid a hand on an inner tabletop. "No," she admitted. "We came to answer a distress call, to show that the Alliance has no grudges against Imperial-ruled peoples, only the Empire itself."

Nereus curled his lips. "I thought not. Ellsworth," he ordered into the air, "run the Sibwarra recording. Your Highness, come up here and stand with me. Bring your escorts."

Mounting the carpeted stairs behind Leia, Luke glanced left again. The young woman stared back, resting her chin on one open hand. Light brown hair swept around her face, framing pale flower-petal skin and an intent expression. Although she leaned forward, her slender shoulders set proudly straight. He didn't dare touch her with the Force again—not yet—but her very presence electrified him. Visually striking. Not blindingly beautiful, but striking. *Control!* he reminded himself sharply. *You're here to help Leia!*

Servomotors whirred behind him. Ahead, Leia drew even with Governor Nereus's chair, then she pivoted to look back. Luke stopped on the step below her and took the same position. Threepio gleamed on the other side of the room. Hovering over the place where they'd stood, a holographic projection appeared. It was a young human male with muddy-cream colored skin, short black hair, and a sweet face with prominent cheekbones. He wore a white robe with blue and green side stripes.

"Humans of Bakura, rejoice!" said the . . . boy? man? "I am Dev Sibwarra of G'rho. I bring you warm greetings of the Ssi-ruuvi Imperium, a culture of many worlds that stretches its hand out to you. Our flagship is the mighty *Shriwirr,* a Ssi-ruuvi word that means 'ripe with eggs.' We are approaching your galaxy at the behest of your own Emperor."

Luke glanced across at the young senator. When the invader's image had appeared, she'd withdrawn, clenching her hands on the tabletop and pushing straight-armed back into her chair. Cautiously he brushed her with the Force again. Fear and revulsion streamed out of her, but beneath those dark emotions hid a sensation as deep as a shifting pool full of jewel-toned colors. Bemused, he shook his head. *That* didn't make any sense. But that was how it felt.

He'd perceived all this in an instant. The holo image spoke on, "Bakurans, be glad! The joy that we bring goes beyond mere sensory happiness. Yours is the privilege of assisting the Ssi-ruuk to liberate "—the boy's grasping gesture looked more like taking than liberating—"the other worlds of the galaxy. You are the first, the spearhead! What an honor!

"As humans, you have inestimable value to my masters. From them, you will receive lives without pain, without need, without fear."

"Watch this," Nereus muttered.

The recording shifted. Several dull brown, saurian aliens clustered around a metallic pyramid that Luke recognized instantly. Antennae and laser cannon bristled at its four corners, swiveling thrusters filled its four faces, and scanner/sensor clusters surrounded each thruster. It lay on some kind of control console.

Full recognition blasted through Luke's mind. He recognized the creatures, too . . . from his disturbing dream back at Endor.

The boy's voice kept speaking. "Here you see the most beautiful fighting spacecraft in the galaxy. Even if you never dared to dream of flying the stars, we have one of these fighters for each of you. Your life energies will leap into one of these battle droids. You will soar between planets—"

Life energies. Luke recalled the human presences he'd touched, despairing and anguished. He leaned forward.

The robed boy reappeared. "To allay your fears, let me show you a bit of the entchment procedure. Then when the time comes, you may greet your destiny with joy." A smaller image appeared beside him. A man sat on a chair, anchored to it with clear binders, head lolling. Luke squinted. Were those tubes stuck into his throat? A smaller holographic image-within-an-image of the robed boy lowered a glowing white metal arc around the man. The small image froze.

"It is joy," said the larger image. "It is peace. It is freedom. It is our gift to you." He stretched out a pale palm.

Those *had* been humans they'd been fighting. Luke clenched his hands. The Ssi-ruuk weren't simple slavers, but robbers of souls. . . .

Senator Gaeriel Captison shuddered and pulled her warm blue shawl up on her shoulders. "Who does he think he's fooling?" she whispered.

"They got him young," answered the senator on her right. "Look at him. He acts just like a Flutie. He must even think like one."

Gaeri stopped watching. She'd seen this recording ten times, starting the afternoon it abruptly overrode all tri-D screens, vid monitors, and entertainment channels on the planet. The senate had studied and dissected it for nuances of meaning . . . of hope. The only possible conclusion had been to drive away these aliens or face a terrible fate.

So were the Rebels here to help, as they claimed? If they'd come hoping to steal repulsorlift coils, they'd fallen into the Ssi-ruuvi trap along with Bakura. They would have to help Bakura, now, simply to escape.

Gaeri eyed the delegates. Senator Princess Leia Organa, her own age, was known throughout the Empire as one of the Rebellion's chief perpetrators. She might be a deluded soul fighting for a lost cause, like Eppie Belden when she'd had her youth and her mind, but she had risen to leadership. Gaeri hoped to compare notes.

Princess Leia's dark-haired escort was no idealist, though. He watched everything and everyone, especially their escape route. According to the data files Governor Nereus had hastily sent Uncle Yeorg, this one—Solo—was a smuggler with a questionable past, a criminal record, and several blood prices.

But the fair-haired one hadn't been in any of those files. He had a deep calm about him that you could fall into. As the image of Dev Sibwarra warbled on about the joys of entechment, Escort number two leaned forward for a better view, although his upright posture did not appear to change.

Several trilling chirps drew Gaeri's attention back to the hologram. Here it came: the glimpse of the enemy. A massive upright lizard with a black **V** on its face shuffled into the field and stared with a calculating black eye. "My master, Firwirrung, has always treated me with the utmost of kindness, my friends."

The senator on Gaeri's right muttered, "Bloody-handed Fluties."

"Good-bye for now. I look forward to meeting each of you personally. Come to us soon." The image blinked off.

Now that the Rebels knew what Ssi-ruuk did to prisoners, Princess Leia's face matched her white dress. She touched the smuggler's arm, and he bent to listen to her whisper. Abruptly Gaeri guessed he was her Rebel consort. The younger man slowly stared his way around the tables.

Time to speak up. "You see?" Gaeri called without standing. "This is a threat against which we have no experience and no defense."

The young man nodded at her. He obviously understood their predicament.

"If I may be permitted to speak," called the gold-plated droid across the chamber. "I found that spectacle utterly appalling. Mechanicals of all kinds will be shocked by this perverse display of—"

Catcalls from around the chamber drowned it out. As projectors sank back under floor panels, the Rebels stayed on their step below the governor's chair. Princess Leia took another step downward. "Bakurans," she cried, "whatever you think about droids, listen to me now. Let me tell my own story."

Gaeri rested her chin on her hand. The Rebel princess extended one hand like a classical lecturer. "My father, Bail Organa, was viceroy and first chairman of the Alderaan system, a trusted official of the Republic from the days of the Clone Wars.

"When Senator Palpatine declared himself emperor, my father began to work toward reform. Change proved impossible. The Empire has never been interested in reform. It only wants power and wealth."

Gaeri's mouth twitched. True enough, if one-sided. The Imperial system discouraged change and built economic stability. She shifted on her repulsor chair.

"I was little more than a child when I began serving my father as a diplomatic courier and not much older when elected to the Imperial senate." She glanced sidelong at Governor Nereus. "The Rebellion was already active, and as the Emperor surely guessed, I was not the only young senator involved. My father had barely thrown in his open support when I was captured by the Emperor's henchman, Lord Darth Vader, and taken on board his first Death Star.

"The Emperor claims that Alderaan was destroyed as an example to other rebellious worlds. That is only partially true. I stood on board the Death Star. I saw the order given. It was given to terrify me into revealing information."

Governor Nereus rocked forward. "Princess Leia, that is enough —unless you wish to be arrested for your crimes here and now."

Princess Leia's chin tilted defiantly. "Governor, I have only strengthened your position. The Empire rules by fear. I have just given the Bakurans one more reason to fear you."

But not respect him. Gaeri crossed her ankles, willing for the moment to listen, if not to accept the Rebel point of view. That could have happened to Bakura, if the Rebels hadn't destroyed that Death Star. Two senators in Gaeri's field of vision shot covertly suspicious glances toward the governor.

"After the destruction of Alderaan," Princess Leia went on softly, "I fled to Alliance headquarters. I have lived with its leaders, moving frequently as the Empire continues to try to wipe us out. We mean to help you," she called. "The Alliance has sent one of its ablest military leaders, Commander Skywalker of the Jedi Order."

Jedi? Caught with her defenses down, Gaeri reached for a pendant on her necklace, the half-black, half-white enameled ring of the Cosmic Balance. According to her religion, Jedi had upset the universe by their very existence. For every height, there had to be a depth. She believed that every time an individual learned to wield so much power, that diminished a hapless counterpart somewhere in the galaxy. The power-greedy Jedi had puffed up their abilities without regard for the unknown others they destroyed. Their disappearance had become a morality tale, and the deaths of both her parents left her profoundly religious. At least in the Balance she'd found comfort.

But had some of the Jedi survived? Commander Skywalker looked so young, not at all like her idea of a Jedi, except his intensity. He'd stared right at her when she spoke. He might be listening to someone's thoughts.

Was a single Jedi so powerful that the Cosmos had brought in the Ssi-ruuk, reducing so many humans to droid-powering circuitry, to balance his rising powers?

He turned. Blue eyes probed her again.

She blinked and glared, and she didn't look away until he did, so she got the satisfaction of seeing his composure falter. He glanced at her again, then shifted his booted feet and stared at the ground.

With that threat dispelled for the moment, she stared a little longer. Something about him reminded her of Uncle Yeorg.

Chewbacca leaned against the bank of lockers, openly returning the stares of six stormtroopers. He thought he could guess their intention: to confiscate the group's weapons and leave them helpless. One trooper had started walking over a few minutes ago. A single teeth-bared growl had sent him back, but that wouldn't last. Luke's astromech droid stood near the arch with his antenna rotating. Artoo wouldn't be much good in a fight.

Chewbacca didn't mind the odds, though. One armed Wookiee against six stormtroopers should be just about even.

He heard bootsteps. Another Imperial strode up the red marble hallway. This one wore an officer's on-duty khaki. Stormtroopers gathered around him and spoke quietly.

Chewie fingered his bowcaster.

Leia hadn't missed the senators' whispers and sidelong glances at Luke. She guessed she'd seen how *she* would affect people if she were a trained Jedi. Luke had offered to teach her, but maybe it wasn't such a good idea. This was Vader's legacy: Even Luke's talents, used honorably to support justice and freedom, made people afraid.

She must recapture their attention. She sidestepped toward the governor's gilt repulsor chair. "Governor Nereus, don't you see? You must accept Rebel assistance or risk your entire population. We are your only hope. Allow us to help you turn the Ssi-ruuk back. We are not a large force, but we are well coordinated and equipped with better striking ships than the Empire has allotted you." Luke had shown her the BAC readouts.

Nereus pressed his effeminate lips flat, then said, "For the help you have given us, we will allow you to leave the Bakura system unmolested, and give you a head start back to Endor."

One senator jeered from the upper table, "If the Alliance is eager to assist, why didn't it send us more ships?"

Luke spread his hands. "We're doing all that we can without—"

"You see," Leia interrupted, anxious to smooth ruffled feathers, "our forces at Endor wish to return to their homes. Some may have already gone." Nereus grasped the armrests of his chair, smirking at their exchange.

"We have sent to Endor, though. For reinforcements," Luke insisted.

Leia didn't like the way Governor Nereus's frown firmed. "But our Endor troops are exhausted. Reinforcements could arrive within several days or not at all." *Don't work against me, Luke.*

Han extended one stiff hand. "The point is, we're here to help you. Seems like you ought to take advantage of the offer while it's open."

"Would you clear data files for our use?" Leia asked hastily. "On the Ssi-ruuk, of course, and any on Bakura itself that wouldn't compromise your security."

Governor Nereus covered his mouth with one meaty hand. Feeling like a bug on a laser dish, Leia held onto her poise and tried mentally to nudge him into cooperating. If this interview dragged on without a promise of mutual assistance, they were sunk.

A tall, elderly man stood up at one of the lower tables. "Nereus," he exclaimed, "take help where you can get it. Everyone on the planet knows why the Rebels are here. If you turn away their help, you're going to provoke an uprising."

"Thank you, Senator Belden." Governor Nereus narrowed his heavy-lidded eyes. "All right, Princess Leia. You have your data files. They will be keyed into the communications center in your apartment. Do you have any other requests for the moment, before I have your guide show you to temporary quarters?"

"Are you leaving the truce issue unsettled?" She bit back frustration.

"You've said your piece. We'll discuss it."

"Very well. Prime Minister Captison—" Leia hustled down to the inner table and extended a hand, which the trim gentleman clasped momentarily. "I hope we speak again." Leia led her party across the central rectangle, then up the steps on the other side.

"Move it, Goldenrod," Han whispered as they passed Threepio. "And keep your voice box turned off." He sprinted for the weapon locker. Chewbacca greeted him with a snarl and warned that the troopers had been eyeing their cache.

"Isn't that too bad?" Han plunged in for his blaster.

Luke stepped sideways. He held his deactivated saber one-handed, low in an ambiguous stance, not quite attack ready. Han watched his eyes widen. "It's all right," he said. "That officer has them under control."

"Who does?" Leia spun around. She stared hard at the conversing Imperials. "He's from Alderaan," she whispered low. "I can tell by the way he talks."

"Huh." That wasn't particularly comforting. Han settled his boot knife and his pocket blaster. "What's the chance he's got an Alderaanian conscience inside his Imperial uniform?"

"Not much," she said—but she said it to Luke.

Han straightened and stared. The black-haired officer looked like any other Imperial: like a target, with the kill zone marked by red and blue squares. He turned around and then strode toward them. Han kept a hand near his blaster.

Luke clipped his saber back to his belt and holstered his blaster, then walked to meet the tall officer. Leia followed Luke, leaving Chewie with the droids. "Cover us, Chewie," Han murmured, and he followed too.

"Your Highness," oozed the officer as he bore down on Leia, "what an honor to meet you at last. Captain Conn Doruggan, at your disposal."

Han wouldn't've minded disposing of him for good, but Leia had slipped into her senate manners again. "Captain Doruggan," she said with an elegant nod. "This is Commander Skywalker, Jedi Knight." Then she condescended to notice him. "And General Han Solo."

Luke shook the officer's hand, but Han kept his right hand low. He glanced over his shoulder at Chewie. The Wookiee stared back, watching (and covering) faithfully. Leia could take a few steadiness lessons from Chewie.

"We must be going," said Leia. "Thank you for introducing yourself."

The Imperial captain reached for her hand. Han pressed his palm to his blaster, barely keeping his trigger finger disengaged. She met the handshake and let him smooch her fingers. Immediately Luke glanced in Han's direction and flicked his hand. He must've done something with that Force of his: Han's jealousy cooled a hundred degrees, but it didn't go out. Leia led them up the echoing hall toward the roof port.

Following with Luke and Chewie, Han glared at Luke. "Don't do that to me," he said. "Don't ever do that." He'd been jealous before, of Luke. That'd been unnecessary. This probably was too.

"I'm sorry," Luke murmured, eyes ahead. "I had to. We couldn't afford what you wanted to do."

"I'll control *myself*, thanks."

Leia turned around and walked backward. "What's wrong, Luke?"

Not Han. Luke.

"Nothing." Luke shook his head. "I want to speak with . . . a couple of those senators. And Commander Thanas promised to make contact today. Let's go dig into our new data files."

CHAPTER
8

THEIR CONDUCTOR/GUIDE DROVE THEM BY TRAM BACK ACROSS THE Bakur complex, then took them to a second-floor apartment. The instant the suite's door slid shut behind Chewie, Han spun around. Leia guessed what he was going to say from the sour look on his face. It would've curdled Bantha milk.

"You told them too much." He waved one arm. "Especially about the Endor troops. Those Imperials don't need to know our people are exhausted. They'll gather up every fightership for parsecs and wipe out the Fleet."

"No, they won't. They can't *contact* anybody else. They've tried." Relieved, she laid her palms on his chest and looked up into his glittering dark eyes. She'd expected a lecture about that renegade Alderaanian. For one instant, the dead world had lived—bitter memories with the sweet. Imperial policies had never been approved on Alderaan. It was a rare and suspect individual who volunteered for Imperial service.

"Well, you did," he muttered. "Don't tell them so much."

"They'll assume—" Leia began.

"Hold it," said Luke. "Did anyone else hear the aliens' human say they came 'at the behest of your own Emperor'? These Bakurans are ignoring it."

"I caught it." Leia stepped away from Han. "I'm trying to figure out how to use it."

"Good."

"But did you—" Leia began again.

"Save it," said Han. He circled the apartment's main room, peering into all of its floor and ceiling corners. Paneled in pale yellow natural wood, the main room had a single long window looking out on one of the greenwells. A hexagonal lounge pit filled the room's center, cushioned in green with small blue pillows floating several centimeters above it. Han overturned every pillow, then started rapping walls. "I don't mind telling you I'd rather sleep on the *Falcon*."

"I wouldn't," sighed Leia.

Threepio stood by the door, one hand covering his restraining bolt as if he were self-conscious. Sometimes his pseudoemotive programming amused her. "Sir, droids require no rest. May I suggest that you humans sleep for a little while? Artoo will stand guard—"

From beneath a hanging lamp, Artoo cut him off with a derisive hoot.

Han paused in front of a long, curving wall that displayed a real-time forest mural. Its branches waved in an intangible wind. He peered at the detail work.

Leia shook her head. Of course the Imperials were bugging them. They probably had voice sensors trained on this suite from across the complex.

She said, "Obviously Nereus is the real power on Bakura. But he's trying to keep the Bakurans quiet by letting them play government games."

Han turned around and leaned on the mural. "You bet he is. And he's as bugged as a closet full of rat roaches about having armed Rebel ships in his system."

"But the *people* aren't," Leia insisted.

"No," rejoined Luke. "The people just want to survive. So does Nereus," he added drily.

"So once he's safe," said Han, "he turns on us and wipes us out—if we don't pay attention."

"We will." Luke glanced at the comm center. "We have a message," he added, sounding surprised. He walked over and touched a control.

Han peered past Luke's shoulder. Leia wedged between them. An Imperial officer's head and shoulders appeared on the tri-D screen: narrow face, thin curly hair. "Commander Skywalker, we need to talk, as agreed. How soon can you join me at my office?" The screen darkened.

"Commander Thanas," murmured Luke.

"Where's his office?" Han asked.

"Probably here at the complex. Let me find out."

Leia backed out of pickup range. "Come on, Han." She didn't want even a glimpse at another Imperial for a few minutes. This place was getting to her. Every time she turned around, she half expected to spot a swirling black cape. Vader was dead! Defeated! She mustn't let black memories distract her from her life work.

Luke told the recessed wall unit, "I believe Commander Thanas left a message—"

Silence. Then, "Yes, that would be fine. I'll be there in about an hour." He strolled back toward the lounge pit.

"Well?" asked Leia.

Luke clasped his hands behind his back. "We have Ssi-ruuvi ships in our backyard again. Thanas says it looks like a blockade, just out of the defense net's easy-kill zone. Approximately the orbital distance of Bakura's second moon. I, uh, also have an invitation to the Imperial garrison."

"Alone?" Leia exclaimed.

Luke nodded.

"Don't do it," said Han. "Make him meet you someplace neutral."

Luke shrugged. "Bakura isn't neutral. He's probably got better facilities up there for discussing tactics than we could find in the Bakur complex."

"Then take Chewie with you. This Thanas could arrest you just for being a Jedi. Never mind frying the Emperor."

"But I didn't—"

"They still don't believe the Emperor's dead," Leia interrupted. "But take Chewie anyway. Even disarmed, he's formidable."

Han fingered his blaster scope. "How fast could you call in some backup?"

"I've got a comlink. I could get an X-wing squadron off the *Flurry* in orbit in . . . oh, an hour."

"That could be too late," Leia insisted. The Wookiee roared agreement at both of them.

"I think I should stay here," Threepio suggested helpfully.

"Han—Leia—Chewie—I can take care of myself." Luke flopped onto a corner lounge, scattering small blue cushions. "The more we act as if we trust them, the more they'll go along with us. Leia made a lot of progress with the senate just now."

"Not enough." Leia pursed her lips. "An honest exchange is our only hope for a lasting treaty, one that could bring about the defection of many disillusioned Imperials."

"Go ahead." Han swept out one arm. "Tell me you feel good about working with these people, both of you. But look me in the eye when you say it."

"Well . . ." Leia glanced down at Luke for support. He raised one eyebrow. "No," she admitted.

"Mm, no," Luke answered. "I don't feel *good*. Alert."

"Right," said Leia. "And feeling uneasy can't interfere with our negotiations. We must make a start somewhere. We make it at Bakura."

Luke cleared his throat. "I'd rather take Artoo anyway."

From a corner where he stood, ignored, Artoo bee-dooped a query.

"For information sharing."

"Oh," Leia said. If Luke had come up with a plan, there'd be no changing his mind. "Tell me about the senators. What did you feel from them?" She sat down beside Luke and folded her legs up onto the lounge. Its repulsor field felt like unseen liquid holding them off the surface.

"They were hostile," said Luke. " 'Who are you, and what are you doing here, and what business is it of yours?'—at first. But that old fellow Belden was glad to see us. And there were others. Others . . ." He glanced toward Han, who had walked to the corner between windows. "Leia's story opened them up. It made the first real change in their attitudes."

"I'm so glad," called Threepio from his protocol post by the door. "I would prefer to return to our own people as soon as possible." Artoo burbled something Leia guessed was agreement.

"There, you see?" Leia stared at Han, willing him to turn around and give her some sign that he'd approved of her presentation. An invisible wall had dropped between them the moment that Alderaanian singled her out. "It has to be hard," she conceded, "after years of operating covertly, to be this open."

He finally swung around, thumbs hooked in his belt. "It's like showing your sabacc hand too early in the game. The cards can change faces on you. I don't like it. I don't like these people. I especially don't like Nereus."

Leia nodded firmly. "He's a perfectly normal Imperial bureaucrat. But Luke, what else did you sense? Their reaction to you . . ."

He frowned. "About what you'd expect, since they hadn't been warned. Why?"

She searched her feelings for the right words.

Luke found them first. "You've got Vader on your mind again, haven't you?"

Stung, she pointed a finger at him. "I want nothing to do with anything that came from Vader."

"I came from Vader, Leia—"

She clenched both fists at her sides. "Then leave me alone."

He shut his mouth without finishing the sentence she'd dreaded: *And so did you.* He could've said it, but he never chose to wound her with words. Already she regretted her outburst. It wasn't like her to lose her temper so quickly.

"Hey," cried Han. "Lighten up, Princess. He's only trying to help."

"What do you expect from me?" She jumped up and paced past him. "To take it calmly? To announce it to Mon Mothma?"

"Not again," muttered Han.

Leia planted her fists on her hips. Either she loved that man, or she was going to murder him.

"Again?" murmured Luke.

"Look," said Han. "Nobody's going to tell your secret. Not even Luke. Right, Luke?"

"We agreed." Luke shrugged. "For a while, at least, no one but us finds out that you're related to *anyone.*" He stretched out a hand.

Leia clasped it. Unexpectedly, Han pushed in and closed his hand around both of theirs.

There was a roar behind her. A huge hairy paw landed on her shoulder as Chewie continued to whuffle and shout. "What'd he say?" she asked Han. Chewie's other paw landed on Han's head.

"That we're his Honor Family." Han tried to duck. Black-tipped forearm fur trailed into his face. "That's the basic unit of Wookiee society. It's the best pledge of loyalty you'll get, Leia."

No nicknames this time, no teasing, just *Leia.*

That was the best pledge of loyalty she'd get from Han. "All right," she said quietly. "We have work to do. Let's use every moment until Luke has to leave or they call us back for another session."

Chewbacca growled. Luke dropped her hand and walked toward the comm center.

"Right." Han disentangled himself from his copilot. "We've also got to check on repairs. Our group has set up a temporary pit over at the spaceport. Pad Twelve. That's Chewie's."

"Ah." Luke was already punching keys. "There, I found our new data files. Artoo, run a check. See what you didn't already get from the drone ship."

Artoo whistled cheerily.

"Keep your eyes open, kid," said Han.

"And be careful!" Threepio exclaimed.

An Alliance shuttle picked Luke up at the Bakur complex's roof port. With Artoo loaded in its rear compartment, Luke watched the city sweep past, perched in its concentric circles on that incredible white rock vein.

He feared that his own nervous state had set Leia off, but he hadn't dared tell her or Han anything yet. He alone knew how desperately the enteched humans suffered, and therefore the danger they all faced if Bakura fell. And if that happened, Bakura's resources (and population) would help the aliens take another world, where they'd charge up more battle droids to take another, and another, in a chain reaction that could spread clear to the Core worlds.

Perhaps they intended to wipe out all humanity—or maintain prison worlds as breeding populations. It wouldn't surprise him if they had other kinds of droids that ran on human energy as well. He, Thanas, and even Nereus couldn't even be sure they faced the entire Ssi-ruuvi fleet.

In the light of this crisis, he'd had no business being distracted by Senator Gaeriel Captison.

Yet those sensations he'd felt, as her presence responded to his probe, made him tingle in memory. The sensations, that is, before her sudden reversal. He'd never felt so strong and sudden a change from attraction to disgust. Now he *had* to speak with her. If she opposed Jedi so vehemently, she could ruin Leia's chances for treaty talks. He'd rather have her honest opposition than be ignored. At first, anyway.

Sooner than Luke felt ready, his shuttle landed at the edge of the dark, artificial surface they'd picked out as the garrison. The nervous Alliance pilot helped Luke unload Artoo and then sped away north toward the spaceport. Luke stared up at the garrison's perimeter. Above and behind a fence that crackled with high voltage, stormtroopers paced catwalks between enormous observation towers. A shimmering, sparking force field blocked the opening between gatehouse towers. Patrol droids converged on him from three directions.

This was the Empire, all right. Luke strode boldly toward the gate. "Come on, Artoo."

A pair of black-helmeted naval troopers stepped out from behind one gatehouse. The force field snapped off. "Commander Skywalker?" asked one trooper, hand on his blaster.

I am peace. Luke pressed his palms together in front of his chest. "I'm here to speak with Commander Thanas."

"And the droid?"

"Information repository."

The trooper laughed shortly. "Espionage."

"I'll probably give Commander Thanas more information than I take away."

"Wait here." The trooper vanished into his gatehouse.

Luke stared through the fence. An AT-ST scout walker plodded past, looking like a huge gray metal head on legs. The main garrison loomed across a wide open area. "Standard" it might be, but from up close it looked suitably huge. Luke guessed it at eight stories tall. Turbolaser turrets gleamed on each upper level like guardians of a giant's castle. From this angle, he spotted two vast launch chutes aimed at the sky. He could only guess how many TIE fighters might be racked inside. He wouldn't've dared to go near this place with a squadron of X-wings. Alone, he was safer. He hoped.

The trooper reemerged with a restraining-bolt Owner and a repulsor disk with twin side struts. "The droid will come in on the disk," he said, "shut down. You may carry your personal Owner, but unauthorized reactivation will be construed as hostile."

Artoo beeped nervously.

"It's all right," Luke said. "Don't worry." He let the trooper deactivate Artoo's main power converter. Once they strapped the silenced droid to the repulsor disk, Luke checked the clasps to make sure his metallic friend wouldn't fall off. He touched his Owner, which dangled beside his lightsaber. It too reminded him of his dream back at Endor.

He'd never liked restraining bolts anyway. Governor Nereus's personnel probably had Owners, too, that would let them command Artoo and Threepio despite the droids' prior programming.

"Follow me," the trooper said. He led to an open skiff. Luke took a middle seat and hooked the repulsor disk's tow cable over one side. They sped over the base. The surface that had looked so dark on approach now seemed to be plain, dark gray permacrete. *But count on Imperial bureaucracy to cover up anything natural.*

The shuttle passed through huge blast doors between a pair of monstrous guard towers, and into a vehicle bay permeated with the familiar military odors of fuels and machinery.

At a speeder bike deck swarming with maintenance techs, the troopers parked their skiff. Luke felt curiosity prickle at him from all sides. *Sorry, I'm not a prisoner. Not yet.* As he disentangled Artoo, the curious became hostile. He lifted a finger and spun a line of the Force. Something toppled from one side of the speeder bike deck.

Techs dashed toward the noise. Ignored, Luke passed through, following the trooper who steered Artoo's repulsor disk. They passed down a narrow corridor with bare walls that sloped toward a narrower ceiling, then into a high-speed turbolift. Luke's stomach dropped as the turbolift rose.

He stepped off on another level at the end of a long straight hallway. Almost everything was gray—walls, floor, ceiling, furniture, faces—so he noticed the contrasts quickly. An officer in black hustled across from one door to another. Stormtroopers stood at every doorway, white-armored guardians. Luke strode past them, eyes forward but Jedi senses on 360-degree alert and one hand near his lightsaber.

In a circular reception area, Luke spotted a man approaching up the far hallway. His erect posture and measured stride gave him away. Narrow face and thin, curly hair confirmed Luke's guess. Luke walked to meet him. "Commander Thanas."

"Commander Skywalker." Thanas peered down an aquiline nose. "This way, please." He turned on one heel and sauntered back the way he had come. Tall and pike thin, he exuded an unthreatened self-assurance that warned Luke Imperial eyes surrounded them—as if he'd needed warning. Counting weapons visible in the corridor, Luke steered the repulsor disk after Thanas.

At the far end of the hallway, Thanas stepped into an office. Luke followed. Simply furnished except for a curious flooring like deep tangled moss, it looked like a place where business, not pleasure, was conducted. Even the clean-lined gray walls were bare of mementos, as if Thanas had no past. His plain rectangular desk had only one inset key panel that Luke could see.

"Sit down." Thanas waved at a repulsor chair. Leaving Artoo shut down, Luke took the seat. Thanas gestured toward a servo unit. "Something to drink? The local liqueur is astonishingly good."

Luke hesitated. Even if it weren't drugged, it might be strong enough to muddy his head. Anyway, it just didn't sound good. "Thank you, no."

Thanas sat without pouring for himself. He folded his hands

over bent elbows. "I will confess, Skywalker, I didn't expect you to come. I expected you to ask to meet me somewhere else."

Luke shrugged. "This seemed practical." He reached out for Thanas's sense. Watchful with a twinge of admiration, suspicious but free of deception: trustworthy for now, with tangible goodness underlying.

"True." Thanas touched a panel on his desk. Retracted projection antennae glided up through the desktop. Above them appeared a large blue-green globe. "Shall we observe the battle you so boldly interrupted?"

"That would be excellent. May I?" Luke gestured toward Artoo with the restraining-bolt Owner.

"By all means."

Luke switched the little droid back on. Artoo's dome spun once, then came to rest with the blue photoreceptor facing Thanas's hologram.

The battle had begun with a sweeping attack launched by the entire Ssi-ruuvi line. It was, as Luke had guessed, a final push against weakened adversaries toward planetary invasion. His forces had arrived barely in time.

"May I see that again?" Luke asked as blue Imperial pips regrouped for a counterattack.

Thanas shrugged and reran a few seconds of holo.

"Is that a standard maneuver?" Luke asked.

Thanas tapped fingers together. "Forgive me if I decline to answer."

Luke nodded and mentally filed the maneuver under Top Security.

"Tell me," Thanas said, "are my forces' scanners in error, or did one of your pilots bring a space freighter into the battle?"

Luke barely smiled. What Thanas didn't know about the *Falcon*, Luke wasn't telling. "You must remember that much of the Alliance's support is from the edge of legality."

"Smugglers?"

Luke shrugged.

"Probably modified beyond all legal standards."

"Stolen Imperial equipment is at a premium."

"Only after I asked did I realize the implications of your flagship having holonet capability."

Enough on that subject. "Are you aware of what's at stake here?" Luke told him most of what he'd concluded about the Ssi-ruuk's intentions. "Why did the Emperor contact them?"

Thanas scratched his neck, trying to look casual, but the stress lines around his eyes darkened. "If I knew, I would not be at liberty to tell you."

"But you don't know."

Thanas only stared back. This would be a touchy truce, if it held.

"We do need to discuss the current tactical situation," Luke suggested. "According to my data, between us we've got two cruisers, seven midsized gunships, and about forty one-man fighters, two thirds currently deployed in the defensive web, one third down for repairs. Do your figures line up?"

Thanas favored Luke with an amused curl of his lips. "Good data. You also have a rather irregular freighter."

"That, too." Luke shifted on the repulsor chair. "Have you been able to get any count on the Ssi-ruuk?"

Thanas nodded curtly. "Here insystem, three cruisers. Two midsize ships that've hung back, so far, near the orbit of Planet Four—our best guess is planetary assault ships. About fifteen large fighters or small picket ships, just outside the defense net. And no one knows how many of those little fighters—or which cruiser carries them. Maybe they all do."

Simply put, the situation looked bad. "Where do you get your information?" Luke asked, wondering what Thanas might tell him about in-system intelligence.

Thanas raised one eyebrow. "Standard sources," he said. "Where do you get yours?"

"Open eyes."

The exchange was punctuated by more frustrating dead ends, but when Luke stood up two hours later, he had a better grasp of the tactical situation, precise data on orbital defense-net vectors, and a few miscellaneous tidbits stored in his mind and Artoo's memory banks.

"Commander Skywalker," Thanas said softly, "I wonder if you wouldn't favor me with a demonstration of that lightsaber. I've heard about them."

"I think not." Luke kept his tone polite. "I don't want to alarm your troopers."

"They won't be alarmed." Thanas touched another key on his desk. The door slid open. Two white-armored stormtroopers stepped inside. "I'd like to keep your astromech droid here. You two: Take custody."

"I'd prefer to keep Artoo with me." Luke didn't think Thanas meant the threat seriously, but he unhooked, swept up, and activated the saber with a single motion. For all his willingness to talk, Thanas thought like an Imperial. He wanted a demonstration. He'd get it.

The troopers fired milliseconds apart. Luke pivoted into the blasts and deflected them. Tiny flames extinguished in Thanas's gray paneling.

"Hold your fire." Thanas lifted a hand. "Dismissed."

The troopers marched out.

"I don't understand." Luke stood at ready attention and kept the saber ignited. "You could have lost two of your men."

Thanas stared at the humming green blade. "I didn't think you would kill them. I'd have had to take you prisoner, if you did. I wonder if you'd care to fight your way out through the whole garrison."

Luke reached for his focus of control. "If I had to, I would." He sensed a trace of amusement in the older man. Perhaps Thanas was hostile more out of professional habit than out of real belief in the

Empire, but Luke didn't trust him yet. He closed down the saber. "I need to check on my forces' ship damages, Commander."

Thanas nodded. "You may go. Take your droid with you."

Luke tucked his thumbs into his utility belt. "My shuttle went back to the Bakur complex. I'd appreciate a lift over to Pad Twelve at the spaceport."

Thanas hesitated for a slow beat, then smiled back. "All right."

If Thanas meant to stop Luke and his party from leaving Bakura, he'd get plenty of chances.

A noncom drove Luke off in a repulsor craft. All the dull aches had come back. It was indeed turning out to be a very long day. He made a mental task list: check in with Leia and let her know he'd left the garrison safely, double-check that the *Falcon* was undisturbed, make sure the fighters were being serviced and the pilots were getting their rest . . .

Abruptly Luke realized he hadn't thought about that striking Bakuran senator for over an hour. He tried to dismiss her image again, and his memory of the way her Force aura had energized his own. Forgetting wasn't as easy without Imperials surrounding him. This wasn't the time or place to let personal urges distract him.

Yet the first Death Star hadn't been the time or place for romance either, and his desperate love for Leia had set so much in motion. If only Gaeriel Captison needed to be rescued. . . .

Shortly after Skywalker's shuttle left the garrison, Pter Thanas stopped tapping an Alzoc-pearl pocketknife against his desktop. He'd tracked the illegal freighter to Pad 12 at the civilian spaceport. Relevant information, but not yet vital.

He unfolded one knife blade and balanced it over his index finger. He never could have admitted to young Skywalker how long he'd wished to see a lightsaber in action. When Vader and the Emperor had wiped out the Jedi, he'd given up hope. Fascinating, the way it'd deflected laser fire. Its combat uses would be limited, but its very appearance was compelling.

As was the young man who carried it. Now he understood why the reward for his capture was so high.

Thanas imagined what he could do with so many credits. He'd been transferred to this dead-end position after refusing to wipe out a village of recalcitrant Talz slave miners back on Alzoc III.

He hadn't been trying to play hero. . . . He'd simply increased his miners' food allotment. Most sentients worked harder if better fed, and the storehouses had been full. Unbeknownst to him, the furry four-eyed Talz identified their benefactor. One day in the mines, he'd taken a step too close to the lip of an open shaft. Three Talz dove to save him. He owed them his life.

Six standard months later, a colonel with more greed than common sense reduced the food ration again. The Talz headman delivered a cautiously worded protest. The colonel ordered their village wiped out as an example. Thanas ignored the order. The colonel sent in stormtroopers himself, then ordered Thanas on board his own ship, "pending reassignment."

Thanas smiled bitterly. He'd been told to consider himself lucky —if he'd pulled that stunt in Lord Vader's presence, he'd have been dead of asphyxiation. Instead, here he sat on Bakura, an isolated, low-paying job with little hope for rotation out to the Core worlds.

Again he thought about that reward—and early retirement. He caressed the iridescent pearl handle. He could marry again and live quietly on some nonaligned world. The reward for Skywalker tempted him, but if anyone on Bakura claimed those credits, it would be Governor Wilek Nereus.

Thanas frowned, refolded the knife, and dropped it into his pocket. No early retirement for him. He hadn't even been able to repel alien invaders without reinforcements . . . from the Rebel Alliance. He'd never leave Bakura now.

Leia cleared Luke's message from her screen and keyed over to her next data file. A photographic memory would've been useful. This much raw data would take weeks to internalize. From Artoo, she'd already learned that Bakura had information-level technology, repulsor coil manufacturing and export (due to plentiful mineral deposits in the mountains north of Salis D'aar), and namana trees, a tropical cash crop that showed astonishing profit margins. New information was that descendants of the original Bakur Corporation ship's captain had always served as titular heads of government. Also new: the senate, not the smallish populace, elected senators to replace those who died or resigned.

Now, she reflected, it was an approval organ for Imperial Governor Wilek Nereus. She'd like quietly to interview a few private citizens and find out how much anti-Imperial sentiment the Rebels could hope to tap.

She yawned mightily, then stretched her arms and tipped her repulsor chair. Han's feet showed through the doorway of his bedroom—the suite had four private rooms, two with windows and two with real-time murals. If Han had fallen asleep on the floor, trying to study Artoo's data, she didn't care.

Looking at that much of him raised her blood pressure. The nerve of him, implying she wanted to dally with an ex-Alderaanian Imperial. A renegade, a quisling.

She didn't hear any sign of Chewbacca. Threepio probably stood where she'd left him, plugged into the main comm center near the doorway, and Luke—

Once Luke had left, she'd calmed down a bit. She shouldn't let the knowledge that Vader was their father infuriate her so. Even Han hadn't tossed a single snide comment when she'd swallowed her humiliation back on Endor and told him about Vader. He hadn't said anything, only held her. With all Darth Vader had done to him—sending the galaxy's lowest scum to chase him down, then using him as an experimental animal to test a carbon freeze unit, scorching and creasing his precious ship with TIE-fighter laser cannon—evidently Han wasn't going to hold any of it against Leia or Luke. So long as she avoided anything and anybody that reminded her of Vader or the Force, she'd be all right.

Fat chance, on this trip. *Get hold of yourself,* she ordered.

"Mistress Leia?" called Threepio's voice.

She walked to her bedroom door. "What is it?"

"A message for you. Prime Minister Captison."

"Put it on my bedroom terminal." She hurried back to the tri-D station. Her door slid shut on a frictionless channel. She'd never seen so many small-scale repulsors.

Leia sat down. She would have recognized the image even without Threepio's announcement. Collecting her composure, she greeted him respectfully. "I hope your senate decided in our favor, Prime Minister."

He smiled with the sad, authoritative dignity she remembered from Bail Organa. "Nothing was finalized," he said. "I hope you and your party are comfortable?"

"I'm delighted to be speaking at such length with your people, but we expect a little trouble convincing the Imperial military that we're here to do a job and then go home."

"Your Highness." The prime minister's tone reproached her gently. "That's not why you're here, is it?" Captison raised a hand. "That's all right. Our people need a distraction. They've had nothing but Ssi-ruuk on their minds for over a week."

"I understand," Leia murmured. "What can I do for you, Prime Minister?"

"You—and your party—could join me at my home this evening. Dinner will be at nineteen hundred."

She longed to put down her head and sleep, but . . . "That would be delightful," she said. It *could* be a wonderful distraction, a real breakthrough. "On behalf of General Solo and Commander Skywalker, I accept." What about Chewie? she thought suddenly. He wouldn't fit, not the way these people felt about aliens. Well, she hoped she could make him understand. *He* could get some sleep. "Thank you very much."

"I will send an escort for you shortly after eighteen thirty. Oh," he added, "I have invited Governor Nereus as well. A chance to open communication off the official records."

That would keep her awake. Guaranteed. "How thoughtful of you, Prime Minister. Thank you." Leia switched off. It *was* the perfect opportunity. High time to ask the Imperials what they thought about Emperor Palpatine's intentions, inviting the Ssi-ruuk in this direction.

She hoped Luke got back from the spaceport in time to clean up. She hoped Luke got back, period.

CHAPTER

9

BY THE TIME DEV HAD SCRAPED NAUSEATING BLOBS OF MIXED FOOD out of the galleyvac unit, an hour had passed. He must report to Elder Sh'tk'ith—Bluescale—before his midcycle bath. Not that he wanted renewal, but if Bluescale thought Dev had avoided him, he'd pry deeper. Bluescale was incredibly sensitive to changes in Dev's scent. Besides, the elder had a talent for hypnotic control, even though he was as Force blind as the rest of them. Dev ought to be able to resist him, for simple hypnosis was nothing next to the power of the Force.

But he couldn't control it well enough, and he had no one to teach him.

Dev had felt the presence of one of his own kind. What if it *were* a real Jedi out there? The Ssi-ruuk would be vitally interested, but Dev didn't want Bluescale to know yet.

On the other hand, maybe that wouldn't be so bad. They would seek out the other, and Dev would have a human friend—

No, the Outsider was stronger in the Force—a concept his mother had taught him long before that fateful invasion day. Dev would fall from his masters' attention. Still, they'd entech him at last. Walking lightly, he headed up the broad corridor. Ssi-ruuk passed him going both directions, stepping quickly with their massive heads bobbing. A few wore paddle beamers, for occasional P'w'ecks turned on their masters under the stress of battle.

On the other hand—he slowed again—they might try to entech the Outsider. Humans screamed on the entenchment chair. Someone that strong in the Force might kill Dev with his agony.

No, no. Only the body felt pain.

Yet what if this *were* a fully trained Jedi?

Dev dove into a turbolift and hurried to Bluescale's work station on the battle-droid deck. He wasn't there. Several small, brown P'w'eck workers bent over antenna-cornered pyramids recovered by tractor beam. This crew was made up of youngsters, short-tailed with jerky movements. As soon as they finished repairing these droids, the droids would stand ready for the next group of prisoners to be enteched.

Dev watched for a minute. Each P'w'eck did its own job without any sign of satisfaction. This dull-witted servant race only superficially resembled the glossy, muscular masters. Heavy eyes and sagging skin showed that even the young P'w'ecks didn't bother to eat well. Battle droids shone by comparison.

He hiked up to the bridge and sent one of the cylindrical ultimate security droids looking for Bluescale. He waited outside. A conductive net surrounded the bridge, strong enough to stabilize gravitics and repel energy surges during battle. Like a reactor, it could be overloaded, and a direct hit from a large enough ship would overcharge the net and make the bridge a deathtrap. Admiral Ivpikkis made certain no large hostile ship got the *Shriwirr* in firing range.

The droid couldn't find Bluescale either. Feeling increasingly urgent, Dev tried Master Firwirrung's entenchment hall.

Bluescale stood in the corridor, giving orders to a group of P'w'ecks. Dev stood back a respectful distance. Once the P'w'ecks scurried away, he stepped close. "You wished me to report, Elder."

Bluescale opened a hatchway. "Come in."

Once inside, Dev looked around cautiously. This wasn't one of Bluescale's usual work stations. In one corner, waist- and knee-high railings surrounded a meter-square sunken area. A gate hung open. Once Bluescale raised it, it would complete an enclosure. It almost looked like a cage built to hold a P'w'eck. They were led away for discipline sometimes. He'd never seen it done. He started to panic. "There?"

"Yes." Bluescale slid aside to a small table. Unable to do anything else, Dev stepped down into the enclosure.

Bluescale pressed something hard against his shoulder. "Lean on the railings, if you'd like."

Normally, Bluescale began renewals by having him lie down comfortably on the deck. At least, this didn't feel like discipline . . . so far. "What is it you wish?" Dev whistled uneasily. "What may I do to please you?"

"Talk with me." Bluescale settled his glistening mass alongside Dev. "How goes your project?"

Suddenly delighted by the elder's attention, Dev let his weight sag on the upper railing. "It goes very well. My latest effort is a translation of the announcement we delivered to Bakura, a few weeks—"

"Stop," said Bluescale. He bent his massive head closer to Dev and peered down with one eye.

Dev smiled back fondly.

"You are human," Bluescale said. "Think for a moment what that means."

Dev pushed up one sleeve and stared at his soft, fuzzy arm. "It means . . . inferior."

"Are you certain?"

Bewildered, Dev shut his eyes. From the deepest recesses of emotion, he released something controlled and repressed and stinking and hateful and—

The huge lizard loomed nearer. Dev howled and struck its fore-limb.

"Harder," it whistled. "You can do better than that, weakling."

Gritting his teeth, Dev plunged a fist into its upper arm. "You killed my world. My parents, my people. Every one of them gone, absorbed, murdered, mutilated. . . ." He trailed off, sobbing.

"Nothing new to be angry for?"

Dev raised his fists in front of his chest. What was the lizard doing, pumping him for information? It wouldn't get any this time.

It bent closer and blew lizard stench at him. "You'd like to poke at this eye, I'll guess."

Dev stared at the eye. It seemed to grow and surround him with blackness. It sucked him in. He fell into its depths, clutching the trailing edges of freedom.

He tumbled.

Horrified, he lay curled up on cold gray deck tiles. He had abused Bluescale. He could only guess his fate.

"Dev," Bluescale said softly, "you should never say things like that."

"I know," he said miserably.

Bluescale trilled, a soft throaty purr, "You owe us so much."

How could he ever think otherwise?

"Dev," Bluescale whistled.

He looked up.

"We forgive you."

He sighed deeply and pushed up to his knees, gripping the enclosure's lower railing.

"Here, Dev." Bluescale held out a hypospray. Gratefully, Dev leaned his shoulder into another sting. His shame melted magically away.

"I angered you deliberately, Dev. To show you how close to the surface your temper lies. You must never show anger."

"I won't again. Thank you. I'm sorry."

"What so disturbed you this afternoon, Dev?"

He vaguely remembered that he'd hoped not to tell, but he couldn't remember why. The Ssi-ruuk protected him and met all his needs. They gave him pleasure, even when he did not deserve it.

"It was remarkable," he began. "The sense of another Force user, close by."

"Force user?" Bluescale repeated.

"Someone like me. It's not that I'm lonely, but like seeks like. I wished I could seek him out, but I guessed he was an enemy of the fleet, since he arrived with the new ones. It made me sad."

"Him? It was male?"

Dev raised his head with an effort and smiled up at Bluescale. Whatever had been in the hypospray, it was making him so sleepy he could barely move.

"Perhaps I'll dream about him," he murmured, and he slid down off the railing.

Gaeriel lay resting in midair above a circular repulsor bed. A knitted fur coverlet wrapped her from shoulders to knees. The bed hovered over a slightly faded carpet. Yeorg and Tiree Captison's home was one of the finest on Bakura, so she'd heard, but as Imperial taxes increased, even the prime minister had to defer repairs and replacements. Gaeri's new salary helped with upkeep. She didn't care about "finest," but she did care about Uncle Yeorg and Aunt Tiree.

It'd been months since she'd needed a midafternoon rest, and the nap hadn't helped. She'd awakened in a cold fright that the repulsor bed only chilled. The Jedi Luke Skywalker had appeared in a disquieting dream, hovering over her head in a repulsor field he generated with his Jedi powers. Before she could wake herself up, his skin and hair darkened. He became the Ssi-ruuvi envoy, Dev Sibwarra. Sibwarra floated slowly downward into the repulsor field and through the coverlet, drawing life out of her—

Frustrated, she wriggled out of the coverlet and punched a wall control. The Imperial Symphony Orchestra struck up a soothing melody around and inside her ears. She'd returned from Center thrilled by the latest Imperial sound technology, a hydrodynamic music system. For her graduation gift, Uncle Yeorg had ordered a system built into the walls of this room. Each surface, even the long window, functioned as a huge speaker. Fluid slowly circulated between panels, carrying and amplifying sound. Workers had restructured her long, rectangular room into an oval for better acoustics.

However, Wilek Nereus owned the only hard-copy catalogs on Bakura to go with the system. Data, literary, and musical recordings had to come through his office. So far, all his dealings with her could be justified as "sponsorship." But Wilek Nereus did nothing for free.

Harmonies slowed overhead and muted brasses took up a melody. Maybe Bakura had a better chance of repelling the invasion with Rebel reinforcements. Idly, in this unguarded moment, she recalled the way she'd been drawn to the Jedi Skywalker before she learned what he was. If she'd been ten years younger, she reflected as she rolled over in the repulsor field, she'd have probably wished he were something else, and that he might stay for a while . . . or that she could go back in time and unlearn what she knew.

But the Cosmic Wheel rolled only forward, building tension and then balancing, building and balancing.

A bell rang. Gaeriel sat up as her door slowly slid aside. Aunt Tiree stepped through, looking elegant in a blue executive tunic and gold torc necklace. "Feeling better, Gaeriel? Headache gone?"

She felt obligated to tell the truth. "Yes, thanks."

"Good. We have invited guests for a late dinner tonight. This is very important. Please dress nicely."

"Who's coming?" Gaeriel turned down the sound system. This wasn't like Aunt Tiree. Generally, she used the intercom or sent a servant.

Tiree stood as still as a mannequin. Like Uncle Yeorg, she'd served Bakura for thirty standard years. Her poise had become a trademark. "The Rebel Alliance delegation and Governor Nereus need a chance to speak on neutral ground. It's our duty to provide the opportunity."

"Oh." Blast. Rebels *and* Nereus? For the second time in two minutes, Gaeri wished she were ten years younger. She could've begged off.

"We're counting on you to help us keep them from arguing, dear."

So she'd delivered the news herself to make sure Gaeri understood its importance. Bakura needed Rebel help to repel the Ssiruuk, but snubbing Governor Nereus might bring on fresh purges. "I understand." She swung her bare feet over the bedside. How long since she'd walked barefoot in Statuary Park? "I'll be there. Dressed."

To her surprise, Aunt Tiree sat down on the repulsor field beside her. "We are concerned about Nereus's attention to you, too," she said in a quiet, confidential tone. "He hasn't done much yet—not that you've told us, anyway—but this is the time to choke it off."

"I agree," Gaeri said, relieved to hear Aunt Tiree talk this way.

"I'm seating you with Princess Leia Organa, unless something disrupts my seating plan."

In other words, unless Uncle Yeorg had other ideas. "Maybe you could invite Senator Belden." One more friendly face, and one more comfortable voice, would make her job much easier.

"Good idea, dear. I'll see if he's free. You start dressing." Tiree patted her shoulder and hurried out.

Gaeri yawned and lay back down on the bed, but only for a moment. Bakura needed her. She was society's child, bound down with duties to the Empire and Bakura and the Captison family.

But not in that order, and she wouldn't want to live any other way. It was time to go back to work.

· · ·

"They're here, Luke."

"I'm hurrying!" Luke stuck his head under the water flow and scrubbed hard. Helping adjust engine brackets, he'd caught the edge of a lubricant shower. Would this day never end?

He told himself to stop whining like Threepio—but he *had* counted on a long, slow soak in an old-fashioned planetside tub. After growing up on desert Tatooine, he would never take rain for granted—or enough bath water to submerge in. Unfortunately Leia had met him at the door with news of their dinner engagement.

"I'll stall them," Leia clipped over the comlink.

Luke hustled to dress in his whites, then joined Han and Leia in the central room—Leia resplendent in a long red gown that left one shoulder bare, and Han dressed in an elegant, satiny black uniform with military-style silver trim. Luke wondered where, and on what pre-Alliance adventure, he'd found *that* outfit.

Then Leia brought her right hand out from behind her back. A massive bracelet made of long curling tendrils hung from her wrist, grooved and swirled to catch the light and shoot it in all directions.

She rotated her hand. "The Ewok chief gave me this. I tried to refuse it. They have so little metal—it was obviously a treasure of the tribe, and offworld. But they insisted."

Luke understood. Sometimes you had to accept an outrageous gift or else offend a sincere giver.

Chewie, immaculately brushed all over, emerged from the door beside Luke's. An Academy-age woman who stood waiting beside the main door stumbled backward. "Oh," she said. "Your . . . friend is welcome too, of course."

Luke glanced at Leia and Han. As he understood it, there'd been another disagreement over whether the invitation included Chewbacca. Evidently Han had won the battle but was losing the war, because Leia—whose hair lay tight to her scalp in the front

but flowed loosely down the middle of her back, like a living thing
freed—looked everywhere but at Han. Han's low-slung holster was
missing. *Carrying concealed,* Luke guessed. *Formal wear.*

"Let's go." Leia tossed her head. "We're late. Record any messages, Threepio."

Their escort took them down to ground level, instead of up to
the roof port. A closed white repulsor vehicle waited, running, in a
garage along the eastern radial highway. They climbed in. The
driver weight-stabilized the vehicle and then set off.

Luke glanced up and out as the vehicle purred along near
ground level. A pair of brilliant blue-white lights hovered in midair
over the street corner. The street seemed to be the same blue-white
shade. *But white stone would reflect any color.* At one spot between
tall towers, a steady stream of aircars whizzed overhead at right
angles to their boulevard. Immediately after they passed under the
aircar route, the escort turned left onto an avenue that curved to
follow the circles of the city.

Luke craned his neck. The lights here gleamed warm and yellow, not blue-white—but at the very moment he noticed their
color, the escort pulled into a short drive that arced to a portico
lined with softly glowing pillars. Luke stared. The massive stone
building behind that portico, built of white stone blocks, was
shorter than Salis D'aar's high-rises: a private midtown dwelling,
on a world where stacks seemed to be the norm. He wished he
could sneak away during dinner and see how anyone could fill so
many private rooms.

A man and a woman in dark green military jumpsuits—definitely not Imperial, maybe leftover from pre-Imperial Bakura—
opened the vehicle doors and then stood aside.

Luke sprang out first and looked around. Nothing seemed
amiss. He nodded over the top of the car at Han. By then, Leia and
Chewbacca had scooted out.

"There you are," exclaimed a feminine voice from between the
glistening porch columns. "Welcome."

He felt Leia panic. Reaching for his saber, he scanned the porch for a threat.

Prime Minister Captison, dressed in a dark green military tunic that was crisscrossed with gold braid from epaulets to cummerbund, bowed to Leia. "My wife, Tiree," he said. A spangled, black-caped figure stepped closer. Madam Captison wore a floor-length ebony hooded robe strewn with tiny gemlike beads, and she didn't even remotely resemble Darth Vader—despite the black cape. "Tiree, may I present . . ."

Leia curtsied to the woman, struggling palpably to control her panic. Luke frowned. This Vader preoccupation was really getting to her.

Captison's introductions made it obvious that Chewbacca's presence caught him unawares. Recovering, Leia glared at Han, but Madam Tiree Captison looked delighted. She reached up, laid a hand on one of Chewie's huge shaggy arms, and announced, "Let's go in. Everything is almost ready."

Leia ignored Han and took Prime Minister Captison's arm. Luke saw and felt Han bristle. "Easy," he murmured as they stepped into line behind Leia. "Show 'em your charm."

Han lifted his head. "Charm," he muttered. "Right."

Along both sides of this indoor hallway ran another line of glistening rain pillars, similar to those in the senate chamber and outdoors, but narrower. Behind the rain pillars, flowering vines covered irregular white stone walls.

Leia paused to touch a rain pillar, then smiled at Prime Minister Captison. "I haven't seen a home so lovely since I left Alderaan."

"This house was built by Captain Arden, the city's founder. Wait until you see the table my grandfather added." He raised a white eyebrow.

Luke held Han back a few paces. "It's only politics."

"I know. I don't like it. Give me an honest fight."

They caught up with Leia at the entrance to a dining hall surrounded by indoor trees with dangling, drifting branches. More vine-covered white stone walls enclosed the trees, and at their center he spotted a table that was roughly triangular, with its corners blunted for extra seating.

Then he looked down. Blue-green water rippled beneath the room's transparent flooring. Underwater lights cast small moving shadows of fish and an occasional long, snakelike creature.

Finally, amid the table stood a miniature mountain range delicately carved from some translucent mineral and lit from inside like one of the rain pillars. Tiny blue rivers trickled down its sides.

Ingrained habit reminded him to probe the room for hostile intent. Halfway down the table, he sensed . . .

Her—or else there were two women on this planet who could electrify him without even meeting his eyes. She already sat down, facing away from the door.

"Lovely," Leia murmured.

Madam Captison looked back over her shoulder. "Thank you, dear." She swept into the room, swirled off her cape, and handed it to a servant as she appeared to walk on water. Trees along the vine-covered walls raised their branches like arms. Luke wondered if her motion or some other cue signaled them, and if they were really flexible trees, some kind of primitive animal, or artificial.

Luke stepped forward, drawn almost against his will. Human servants scurried away from the table—he had yet to see a droid anywhere—probably having rearranged seating to accommodate Chewbacca. Captison escorted Leia to a spot next to himself along one side. Madam Captison took the other chair on that end. An elderly man wearing a voice box on his chest—Senior Senator Belden, Luke realized—already sat next to her on that corner. "Just beyond him, dear," she told Chewbacca.

Luke grinned despite his distraction. *Dear* wasn't a term he'd have applied to a Wookiee. Chewbacca ducked his head and chuckled softly. They'd left him almost an entire side of the table. No repulsor chairs here. The ambiance was antique and formal.

"Nice job of work yesterday," the elderly man told Luke. "My chance to thank you. We were ready to run for the hills when you arrived."

Han sat down next to Leia in the second corner spot. That left Luke only one chair, just left of that glimmer in the Force. He sat down, gathered himself, and glanced right.

Gaeriel Captison sat leaning away as hard as she could. Over her deep green dress, a sparkling gold shawl draped her slender shoulders.

"Our niece Gaeriel, Commander," declared the prime minister. "I'm not certain she was introduced in the senate chamber. Too much hurry."

"It's all right, Uncle Yeorg," she said. Before Luke could even say "Hello," she turned to Chewbacca. "If you'd prefer to sit with your party, I'd be glad to trade places."

Luke suggested subliminally to Chewie that he'd like to remain. Chewie snuffled.

"He says he likes it there," translated Han. "Look out, Madam Captison. Wookiees make friends for life."

"I'm honored." The older woman adjusted a triple strand of blue jewels on her pale gold bodice.

Luke made it a point not to look in Gaeriel's direction again until the matter of switching seats was settled. As conversations sprang up around the table, he turned toward her.

Caught by surprise, he looked closer. Senator Gaeriel Captison had one green eye and one gray eye. They narrowed. "How do you do, Commander Skywalker?"

"It's been a long day," he answered quietly, damping down his awareness of the Force to keep the seductive savor of her presence from monopolizing his attention. The entrance of another group robbed him of the chance to say more. Flanked by a pair of troopers in black dress uniform, Governor Nereus strode to the third corner of the table and sat down. His troopers stepped into position behind him in unison, then stood at alert parade rest.

Everything looked terribly formal . . . and something smelled delicious. Luke's stomach rumbled, making him feel more like a farm boy than ever. *Great,* he thought. *All I need is to make a fool out of myself in front of these people—and embarrass Leia.* He wished he had let her train him in diplomatic functions such as formal dinners. There was a truce at stake.

"Good evening, Captison. Your Highness. General. Commander." Governor Nereus's smile looked oily down the table. "Good evening, Gaeriel."

The arrival of a soup course made answering unnecessary. By the time Luke was free to speak again, Senator Belden had engaged Madam Captison, Leia, and the prime minister at their head of the table (good: Leia would cultivate Belden and the elder Captisons). Governor Nereus leaned aside to let one of his bodyguard/aides whisper something in his ear. Han's eyes tracked Leia.

Only Senator Gaeriel Captison was available for conversation. Luke took a deep breath—nothing risked, nothing gained: "You have some very strong preconceptions about Jedi," he said.

Her mysterious eyes blinked. Shallow creases furrowed her forehead.

"You see," he went on quickly, "this morning in the senate chamber, I was doing all I could to see who might be willing to work with the Alliance. I won't deny it."

"I am a trained Imperial diplomat, Commander." She touched a cloth napkin to her mouth and glanced up the table toward Belden. "It's possible some of the others are Rebellion sympathizers. And misled."

He definitely needed to talk with Senator Belden. "We want to help protect you from the Ssi-ruuk," he said softly. "I spent two hours at the garrison this morning, talking strategy with Commander Thanas. He has accepted our presence, temporarily. Can't you? For your people's sake?"

"We are grateful to the Alliance for help."

Deciding to stick with the direct approach, he laid down his spoon. "Perhaps you think I can read your mind, Senator Captison.

I can only sense your emotions, and only when I'm trying to. Most of the time, I live pretty much the way you do."

"It's not that," she admitted, but he felt something inside her relax. She fingered an enameled pendant that hung over her breast-bone on a short gold chain. "I have . . . religious difficulties with your kind."

That caught him like a kick to the stomach. Ben and Yoda had taught him that the Force embraced all religions. "And the Alliance?" he asked.

"You're right. At the moment, we need every bit of help we can get." She clenched a small hand on the tabletop. "Forgive me if I've seemed ungrateful. The Ssi-ruuk have us terrified, but in the long run, accepting your help could lead to unpleasant repercussions."

"Like what happened to Alderaan," he said softly. "I understand. The Empire rules by your fears."

She stared down at her soup dish. Stretching out, he felt a turmoil that had to be her struggle for a response.

"I'm sorry," he said. "You have to excuse my manners. I wasn't brought up to diplomacy."

"How refreshing." She flashed a subtle, enchanting smile. He flung self-control to the unseen winds of the Force and reached down deep to fully sense her presence. Layers and layers: the living depth of Endor's teeming forest, the all-enveloping warmth of a night on sandy Tatooine, and the hypnotic glitter of deep space came to mind. . . .

Small talk! he reminded himself. Servants brought in a main course of tiny green shellfish and buttery, unfamiliar vegetables, served with bowls full of pale blue-brown grain. Luke remarked on the greenery, the twin rivers, and the fishes underfoot, and tried complimenting her outfit. She remained polite but distant until he asked, as servants removed plates and bowls, "I like Senator Belden. Is he a friend of your family?"

"Yes. For years, despite his oddities." Evidently a very close friend. Abruptly, her stiff-upper-lip guard melted away. She grasped a carafe that stood beside the centerpiece and poured a few pale orange drops into the tiny goblet in front of him. "Try that."

Finally—a response. Curious, he swirled the goblet. The liquid clung to the glass like syrup.

"Go ahead." She raised an eyebrow. "It's not toxic. Our finest local product. You're insulting Bakura if you refuse." She poured herself an equal portion and drank it down.

He sipped. Liquid turned to fire and burned his mouth and throat. Then he caught its flavor, like intoxicating jungle flowers mingled with the sweetest fruit he'd ever tasted.

Her eyes sparkled. Obviously, she hadn't missed a nuance of his reaction. "What is it?" he whispered. He cooled his mouth with a sip of water.

"Namana nectar. One of our chief exports."

"I can understand why."

"More?" She reached for the carafe again.

"Thanks." He grinned. "But no. That's a little strong for my taste."

Gaeriel laughed and filled his goblet anyway. "There's likely to be a toast soon."

If Governor Nereus didn't pick a fight. "I hope so."

She passed him a transparent dish of yellow-orange candies. "Maybe you'd prefer tasting namana fruit this way."

He dropped one onto his tongue. Without the nectar's fire, its exotic flavor flowed smoothly down his throat. Tropical flowers . . . a hint of spice . . . he shut his eyes and studied the sensations it caused—

His eyes flew open.

"That was quick," she said, smiling. "Namana fruit, once processed, induces a faint sense of pleasure. Most people don't notice immediately. They just feel good without knowing why."

"Habit forming?"

She tucked a strand of hair behind her ear. "All the best sweets in the galaxy are habit forming. Be careful."

He decided to leave the candies alone—and he hoped his cheeks didn't look as warm as they suddenly felt. Still, Gaeriel seemed to have opened up. "I'm not . . . supposed to ask you about rumors," she said softly, bending her head closer, "but we've had no response from His Imperial Highness since we sent to him for aid, and what you said this morning went out over the media. Are you certain he is dead?"

Abrupt hostility grated at Luke from Gaeriel's right. Luke peered beyond her and saw Governor Nereus staring at him. *Jealous?* he wondered. Could Nereus have designs on Gaeriel?

He spoke quietly. "The Emperor was strong in the Force. For one thing, I felt his death." That was true, so far as it went.

To his surprise, she blanched deeply. "I hadn't . . . known that about His Majesty."

Governor Nereus turned aside toward Chewbacca. Luke relaxed his guard. "It's not just Jedi?" he murmured to Gaeriel. "Your religion condemns anyone with a strong Force ability?" What would she say if she knew how the Emperor had nearly killed him? *Later*, he told himself firmly. *Alone.* He imagined himself vindicating the Jedi and pointing the accusing finger squarely at her honored Emperor.

"Now, just a minute." Han's voice rose above the polite hum of dinner conversation.

Governor Nereus pressed his forearms to the table and said, "I am not accustomed to dining with aliens, General. Your Highness —*Senator* Organa—I question your good taste, bringing a Wookiee to table tonight when Bakura is fighting for its very existence against aliens."

Luke tensed.

Leia flushed. "If you—" she started.

"Do you think only humans—" Han began, but Chewie's interrupting series of bellows and howls stilled both of them. Luke relaxed, seeing Chewie's temper under control. The Wookiee could've upended the laden table, just to warm up. "Excuse me,"

Han said in a decidedly unrepentant voice. "My copilot doesn't want me to argue for his sake. But he said something you should all hear. It's humans your Ssi-ruuk are after, you know. So even if they invade, Chewie is at less risk than the rest of us." Han stirred the air with his spoon to take in the gathering. Chewie barked while Han paused, and Han grinned. "Yeah. The worst they could do to him is kill him, since they don't want Wookiees for their droid batteries."

Chewie growl-barked one more time. "He says," translated Han, "that if you needed somebody to carry messages out to their ships, he'd volunteer."

"Oh, yes." Nereus's tone scoffed. "What an excellent idea, General Solo. But Ssi-ruuvi speech has never been translated, and the Empire does not deal with . . . aliens."

Except as slaves, Luke added to himself.

"Never translated?" Han leaned over his scattered silverware. "*Never*'s a big word, Governor."

Gaeriel spoke up from Luke's right. "Not that we know of," she explained, "but if it's been translated elsewhere, that will do us little good here."

"And I doubt that the Wookiee could duplicate it," Nereus announced triumphantly, "since Wookiees have never even mastered human speech. Whistles, tweets—like a flock of birds. That's why we call them Fluties."

"Governor," Leia called from her end of the table. "Perhaps I might offer the service of my protocol droid, See-Threepio. He knows over six million languages."

Nereus laughed shortly. It sounded almost like a snarl. "Send a droid and an alien to represent an Imperial world? I think not."

Leia didn't answer. Chewie crossed his long arms and leaned back, the body language plainly conveying, "I'm not going anywhere." Han smiled at the centerpiece.

"One more thing," said Nereus. "Anyone who tries to talk

Bakurans into sedition—publicly or privately—will be arrested and expelled. Must I make myself clearer?"

"No, Governor," Leia said in an icy tone, "but I have a question for you. According to the recording you showed us in front of the senate, the Ssi-ruuk are here because your late Emperor invited them. How do you explain that?"

Nereus raised his head. "I do not presume to second-guess the Emperor, Your Highness."

"Maybe he thought he could conquer them," Belden suggested loudly.

Han rocked his ornate chair. "Maybe he had surplus prisoners to sell them."

Luke caught a flash of insight. "That's part of it," he guessed aloud. Faces turned toward him, some curious, some accusing. "What does any moisture farmer do with his produce?"

Gaeriel shrugged.

"He delivers it to a processor in return for a share of the processed goods." *Thanks, Uncle Owen.* "Palpatine wanted battle droids of his own. They're more maneuverable than your TIE fighters—and far better shielded for their size."

"True," Nereus admitted, "from what I hear."

"Well, we've seen them." Leia tilted her chin. "At close range."

No one spoke for several seconds. Gradually, separate conversations began to buzz again. Han leaned close to Leia. Luke barely caught, ". . . but this isn't getting us anywhere, Your Worship. Let's go back and get some sleep."

He only heard a few hissing words of her answer. "I *must* spend . . . Minister Captison."

A soft breath against his right ear startled him. "Is that man the princess's consort?" Gaeriel whispered.

They certainly fight like it. "I think so." Luke eyed Han. "He's a little rough at the edges, but he's the truest friend anyone could have. Didn't you ever know someone like that?"

"Well." She adjusted her sparkling shawl, which had slipped off one white shoulder. "Yes."

They were halfway into dessert, something cold in a bowl with six nut-flavored layers, when an Imperial trooper strode in. The soldier touched Governor Nereus's shoulder and led him out a vine-covered arch. "What do you think that's about?" Luke murmured to Gaeriel.

Her glance followed them. "We'll soon see."

The governor returned five minutes later, fairly blasting agitation and fear. Surely even Gaeriel saw it.

"Something's very wrong, Your Excellency." Luke spoke in a voice that carried throughout the dining room. All other conversation stilled.

Nereus drew a deep breath. Then he speared Luke with an angry expression. "That was a personal communiqué from Admiral Prittick of the Fleet. You all might as well hear it." His strident voice took on a knife edge. "His message confirms these Rebels' claims. The second Death Star has been destroyed, and Emperor Palpatine is presumed dead . . . as is Lord Vader. The Fleet is regrouping near Annaj."

Leia nodded. "Now do you believe us?" she asked. "Commander Skywalker saw him die."

Gaeriel recoiled. "I didn't kill him," Luke explained hastily, laying both palms on the table. "Lord Vader killed him—and died because of it. I was there as a prisoner."

"How'd you escape?" Grinning like an old war-horse eager to swap stories, Senator Belden leaned closer.

"It was chaos on the Death Star after Palpatine's death. It was under attack. I got to a shuttle bay." He glanced aside at Gaeriel. She buzzed with revulsion and awe and the effort to resolve them.

Prime Minister Captison tipped his chair over as he sprang up. "Then there will be no help from the Empire?"

Governor Nereus stared over the table at Luke. For once, Luke sensed no deceit. Despite his external composure, the man was frightened half to death.

"I think," said Luke, "that the Imperial Fleet is too busy patching ships back together to send troops out to Rim worlds."

"Which is one reason we came in the first place," said Leia.

"We tromped 'em," Han crowed. Hostility seethed up and down the table. Even Leia glared. A servant righted Captison's chair, and he sat back down.

But Governor Nereus shook his head. "Princess Leia," he said, standing up at his place, "if your troops are willing to cooperate with mine, under truce, we need your help."

Leia's shoulders straightened. "An official truce, Your Excellency?"

"As official as I can make it."

That sounded evasive to Luke, but evidently it satisfied Leia. She stood and extended her hand. The massive bracelet shimmered on her wrist; it seemed to add the weight of many star systems to her handclasp. This was a long stretch for both sides, literally and figuratively. For the first time—ever—Rebels and Imperials would fight a common enemy together.

Nereus engulfed her small hand in his gloved, meaty one. Then he lifted his goblet. "To strange alliances."

Leia raised her glass. Belden and Captison followed her. Luke braced himself and got a firm grip on his goblet. "Driving off the Ssi-ruuk won't be easy," he said. Neither would sipping that stuff again. "It will take all our forces in total cooperation."

"Right," Han rejoined. "Otherwise, we'll all end up motivating Ssi-ruuvi droids. Together."

Gaeriel shuddered and touched her glass to Luke's. The milliliter he tasted burned all the way down.

Around the table, people started farewell exchanges with their dinner partners. Reluctant to leave, Luke took a deep breath of Gaeriel's presence. *Worried?* "What's wrong?" he asked. Surely she didn't wish he could stay longer. That was too much to hope.

Staring at the centerpiece, she whispered, "If Governor Nereus can't count on a Death Star any more, he'll have to rely on threats closer to home."

A more realistic menace. Luke rubbed his chin. "If it weren't for the Ssi-ruuk, you'd be in for purges?"

Gaeriel's cheeks faded. "How do you know . . ." She didn't finish the sentence.

She didn't have to. "Standard Imperial procedure. We've seen it on several worlds."

Gaeriel seemed to withdraw momentarily. Across the table, Han and Leia sprang up and walked in opposite directions. Neither looked happy.

Just another tiff. "Are you sure you believe in the Empire?" Luke murmured.

She frowned. She blinked her mismatched eyes. She swallowed a last sip of namana nectar, and then stood up with him. "It's a balance. All things contain darkness and light. Even Jedi, I suppose."

"Yes," he whispered. If only the evening could last for a week. *Ask to see her again!*—Was the suggestion Ben's, or just his own impulsiveness? "Could we finish this conversation tomorrow?"

"I doubt there'll be time." Looking gracious but relieved, she offered her hand.

Hadn't he seen that Imperial officer kiss Leia's hand? Was that the proper gesture here?

Gambling, he raised it toward his face. She didn't snatch it away. It smelled like namana candy. Hurrying before his nerve failed him, he mashed her knuckles with his lips. He felt like a clod, but he didn't dare try it again.

She tightened her fingers on his hand, then pulled loose and walked toward Senior Senator Belden. Luke stood still, rubbing his hand and trying to visualize Gaeri as a part of his future.

By the Force, he'd *make* time to finish that conversation tomorrow.

CHAPTER
10

DEV TOTTERED TO HIS FEET. HE'D AWAKENED ON THE DECK OF A round, uncomfortably warm cabin full of lights and mechanical sounds. Above instrument panels, bulkheads curved inward to join the ceiling.

This had to be the bridge. He was rarely allowed up here. Bridge security was supreme priority. But the *Shriwirr*'s captain and Admiral Ivpikkis hunched beside Bluescale. All three slowly blinked at him.

Apparently the presence of another Force user mattered a great deal.

He'd known that and forgotten it. What games were they playing with his mind? Was he in his right mind now, or deluded by manipulation? Had his contact with the stranger, brief as it was, unsettled his mental patterns completely?

"Tell them what you told Elder Sh'tk'ith," Master Firwirrung urged from Dev's left side. "It felt like your mother's presence, but male?"

Barely able to recall the feathery touch of his mother, Dev studied metal deck tiles. He hadn't felt homesick like this since finding

Firwirrung. He had thought they *were* home. "Like," he said softly, "but different."

"How?" asked Firwirrung.

"This one has the . . . the shape, the sense of training that Mother had, but Mother . . . was not so strong."

Admiral Ivpikkis's left eye swiveled from Dev to the captain. The captain clicked his foreclaws and repeated, "Strong."

"Look at me." Bluescale thrust his head forward. The beautiful eye seemed to swirl. Up from a corner of Dev's mind bubbled a spring of excitement. *This* was his right mind. He *loved* them. "Why, if this one's trained," Dev exclaimed, "he could contact other humans. Even from a distance!"

Firwirrung's massive **V**-marked head turned toward him. "That is an interesting idea. How far, do you think?"

Dev felt freshly energized. "I don't know," he admitted, "but we were many light-years away when I felt the emperor's death for you."

"True," whistled Bluescale. He touched Firwirrung's shoulder scales. "With a strong enough direct contact, could you not conduct entechment from a distance?"

"Possibly." Firwirrung twitched his tail. "We might have to modify an apparatus . . . yes. Modify it to keep this strong one alive in a fully magnetized state, calling energies from outside."

Admiral Ivpikkis's tail quivered too. "A pipeline to humans. We could own all known space, not merely this empire."

Catching their excitement, Dev interlaced his fingers and squeezed hard.

"I observe," said Admiral Ivpikkis, "the need for another shift in strategy. First we secure the strong one. Then we test this theory. If in practice it works, we can call back to the main force of our fleet. . . ."

They spoke hurriedly among themselves. Ignored by Bluescale, Dev wilted. He could barely follow their speech. He had always been their special pet, their beloved human. Would they tail-sweep him aside?

He touched his throat. He might get his battle droid at last, but at what cost? His anticipation curdled like the slop he'd cleaned off the bulkheads. Entchment was to have been his reward, not . . .

They might entech him simply because they no longer needed him. He wanted his battle droid, but he craved their love.

They turned around simultaneously. Firwirrung stroked Dev's arm, lovingly raising red welts. "Help us now. Stretch out to the unseen universe. Give us a name, a place. Help us find him."

"Master," Dev whispered. "Will you always put me first?"

Firwirrung stroked harder, bringing tears to Dev's eyes. "We have never doubted your devotion. Surely you don't mean to make us question it."

"No, no." Dev felt his face go pale. He had made Firwirrung his family, Firwirrung's cabin his home. He had given up his humanity. If Firwirrung replaced him, what was left?

Bluescale lurched forward. "Dev Sibwarra, we need your service as never before."

Dev couldn't tear his eyes off Firwirrung. The entchment chief had always implied that he loved Dev, but had he ever actually sang the word, *love*? Shaken, Dev took a step backward.

A P'w'eck wrapped brown foreclaws around Dev's shoulders and held him toward Bluescale. The elder lifted a hypospray.

They couldn't be doing this. The hypospray wouldn't hurt much, but he remembered now what would follow. How could they be so unkind, after all he had done? Didn't they love him? Didn't Firwirrung? Recognition filtered up out of Dev's memory. They'd been unkind before, and before that too.

This was his right mind. *This* was Dev Sibwarra, human, restored by touching the Outsider . . . but he couldn't beat his masters' drugs or Bluescale's direct domination. He was slipping.

The hypospray relaxed him as before, though he fought it for the sake of his secret. Firwirrung bent close. "Look outward, Dev. Serve us now. Where is this one? What is his name? How can we find him?"

Firwirrung's head blurred. Dev squeezed a salty river out of each eye. Then he closed out his grief and his awareness of the *Shriwirr*'s deck, and escaped into the Force. He let the swirling universe carry him past his masters' dim auras.

The Outsider felt as strong and as close as before, undeniably masculine and kindred, though a second, diffuse feminine presence hung close by. The first one's sharply focused light almost washed out the second: an echo, perhaps? He didn't understand. All that he knew was that love and security came from Firwirrung. He avoided touching the Outsider's Force presence. "In the capital city," he murmured, half-conscious. "Salis D'aar. The man's name is Skywalker. Luke Skywalker." Distracted by the effort of speaking, he opened his eyes again. Firwirrung's shallow happy breathing tore at his heart. The master didn't care—maybe didn't even know!—how jealous their attention to the Outsider made him. Perhaps Ssi-ruuk never were jealous.

"Skywalker," repeated Bluescale. "An auspicious name. Well done, Dev."

Dev relaxed into the Force. Their glee and greed vibrated around him. With an unlimited supply of enteched humans, Admiral Ivpikkis could rapidly conquer known space. Dev would be part of it.

Yet he felt humiliated. As much as he resented the Outsider, he opened himself to a bare touch, almost a Force caress, of farewell.

Firwirrung bent close and sang, "Are you unhappy, Dev?"

His sentiments had seesawed so many times in the last few minutes that he was sure of only one thing: if they manipulated him once more, he might lose his sanity. He shut his eyes and nodded. "I am content, Master." *I hate you I hate you I hate you.* They would not twist his humanity. No more games with his mind.

Yet he could not hate Firwirrung, the only family he had known for five years. The emotion softened. He dared to reopen his eyes. "Master," he whispered, "my highest pleasure is to help those who love me." He forced himself to gaze fondly at Firwirrung.

Firwirrung honked thoughtfully. Plainly the entchment chief's pleasure was not compassion this time, but control. He touched Bluescale with one foreclaw. "Elder, Dev has grown close to having true love for our kind. Let him stretch a little. Let the decision to serve me be of his own free will. That is higher affection."

Dev shuddered. Firwirrung had already enslaved him, spirit and soul. Now he wanted Dev willingly to tighten the cords of his own bondage. That might be Firwirrung's mistake.

Dev laid a hand on Firwirrung's upper forelimb, making the gesture as Ssi-ruuvi as he could. "This is my master," he crooned. At any moment, Bluescale might look into his eyes or smell the deception.

"You see?" said Firwirrung. "Our relationship broadens."

"Take your pet and go," said Admiral Ivpikkis. "Abuse it as you will. We have work to do, as do you. Busy your mind with the modifications . . . for Skywalker."

Firwirrung rocked his head gravely and swept a foreclaw toward the hatch.

Every step away from Bluescale took him that much farther from enslavement. Dev reached the hatchway, then the corridor. The hatch slid shut behind Firwirrung.

An hour later, forgotten as Firwirrung busied himself with schematic drawings, Dev curled up in the sleeping pit's warm center. How had his mother taught him to open contact? It had been five years. His ordeal had exhausted him. He wanted to lie still and fondle sweet memories.

But he must try before Bluescale renewed him again, and there wasn't much time. The Ssi-ruuk would catch him eventually. They "renewed" him every ten or fifteen days, even if he didn't feel needy. He'd pay for this with the deepest renewal of his life, but he owed humankind one effort.

He closed his eyes and emptied himself of hope, repentance, and bitterness. Fear wouldn't leave. It tinged his control, but he touched the Force through it.

Almost instantly, he felt that brilliance again. He flicked at its edge for attention, then formed an urgent warning in his mind.

Luke flung thermal covers away into darkness. One slithered off the edge of his bed's repulsor field. For a cold, sleepy instant, he couldn't remember what had awakened him. Then he recalled a dark, urgent sense of fear and warning. Humanity was in peril because of him. The aliens meant to take him prisoner, and . . .

Whoa.

Exhaling, he lay back down. Artoo burbled at him from the foot of the bed. "I'm all right," he insisted. What a dream. He had to guard against inflating his ego. He might be the last—and first—Jedi, but he was no focal point for humanity's enslavement.

Yet the memory didn't fade as a dream would. Perhaps someone had honestly warned him of something.

Ben? he called. *Obi-wan? Why is this happening?*

Forget questions, he commanded himself. There is no *why.* Search your feelings.

He cast aside fear and false humility and reconsidered the warning in light of the Ssi-ruuk's known intentions and methods. In that context, the concept felt chillingly real.

What kind of terrible mistake had Ben Kenobi made, sending him here? Jedi masters weren't perfect. Yoda had believed Luke would die at Cloud City. Ben had thought he could train Anakin Skywalker.

He curled his arms around his knees. If Yoda and Ben could make mistakes, Luke Skywalker could too. Fatal ones.

If the warning were real, some trace would show in the future.

Like ship sightings from a distance, visions of the future sometimes conflicted, but any hint that he could help the Ssi-ruuvi war effort would confirm the eerie warning.

He calmed himself, steadied his breathing and heartbeat, and reached forward to scan the future in his mind. Some things were hidden from him, and some possibilities he glimpsed looked ludicrously unlikely. Seconds, minutes, months later, he spotted the possibility: a map of the future showing the Ssi-ruuvi Imperium stretching into the Core worlds. As Han feared, they had blundered into a trap—but it was worse than they'd anticipated.

And the Ssi-ruuk were about to invade Bakura.

Dev rolled over, clutching cushions. It *was* a Jedi out there. This time he'd felt the unmistakable, trained control—even when barely awakened.

Firwirrung's cabin gleamed under brilliant lights, but he didn't feel rested. "Master?" he murmured. "Is it time to get up?"

Firwirrung climbed out of the pit. "Hatch alarm," he whistled. "It's for me. Go back to sleep."

Dev curled up tighter but kept one eye open. When the hatch slid aside, a massive blue shape appeared. "Come in." Firwirrung's greeting warbled with surprise. "Welcome."

Bluescale marched toward the bed pit. Dev tried to uncurl, but his muscles stayed taut. He guessed what was coming: The elder had changed his mind and doomed him. The rounded rim guard of a paddle beamer protruded from his shoulder bag.

"Admiral Ivpikkis has conceived a new mission for our young human ally," Bluescale sang. "He must be freshly renewed before it begins."

Panicking, Dev wanted to spring up and run away. But where would he run?

Firwirrung blinked slowly. "Then it is my honor to submit Dev to you."

Bluescale closed a massive foreclaw around Dev's right arm and yanked him upright. Dev kicked and tried to settle his feet on the firm deck.

Bluescale released him. "Precede me," he whistled. "Firwirrung shall follow."

Dev plodded out the hatch and up the dim, nightshift-lit corridor. He could fight this. He could survive a little longer, free to think if not to act . . . but for only a few minutes. And if Bluescale bullied, cajoled, or hypnotized him into confessing what he'd just done, the Ssi-ruuk might kill him outright. Waste his life energy in their justifiable anger. He'd seen them beat a P'w'eck to death, just using their broad muscular tails.

Worse, if the Ssi-ruuk knew Skywalker expected them, they'd find a way to take him anyway: more force, greater numbers, inventive technology. Even a Jedi didn't stand a chance. The galaxy would fall.

Dev could think of only one escape. Using what little he knew of the Force, he could plunge willingly into the renewal trance, bypassing Bluescale's hypnotic awareness.

He recoiled from the idea. Renewal would mean the death of Dev Sibwarra, human. He would forget all that had made him free.

Free for how long? Hanging his head, he grimaced. He had thrown down his life countless times already, for no purpose. This time, he could save dozens of millions of humans . . . including one Jedi. His was a small, poor unsung sacrifice to buy so many lives. But he'd help them if he could. He'd honor his mother's memory.

Standing straighter than he had stood in five years, Dev led Bluescale through a too-familiar hatchway.

"Are you awake, small thing?"

Dev blinked. He lay on a warm, nubbly deck near a pair of massive, clawed hind feet. He knew that whistling song and the scent of that breath. A narrow-faced blue head bent close to him. He felt pristine and fresh, like a hatchling emerged from its egg.

"I have healed you," said . . . ? Dev struggled to remember the name. "Welcome back to full joy."

Dev reached up and wrapped his arms around . . . around . . . Bluescale! . . . and squeezed embarrassing moisture out of his eyes. "Thank you," he whispered.

"You have only the thoughts, emotions, and memories that will strengthen you. None of the overburdening clutter that complicates life for your masters." Bluescale crossed slender forearms over his chest.

Dev inhaled deeply and gladly. "I feel so clean." He couldn't remember how Bluescale did this. He *never* could remember. Obviously, then, that memory wouldn't have helped him continue his life of selfless service. Anything that gave someone this much peace had to be right. Anyone who gave it must be wholly good. It must be long, hard work.

Master Firwirrung waited outside Bluescale's chamber, muscular tail flicking anxiously. Dev cringed at the concern narrowing his warm black eyes. Evidently Firwirrung had worried for him. That made him guess something evil had been cleansed away. "I'm much better, Master," Dev volunteered. "I've thanked our dear Elder. Thank you, too."

Firwirrung touched his left shoulder with his right foreclaw and bobbed his great head, scent tongues extended. "You are welcome," he answered.

"Now we will go to Admiral Ivpikkis," sang Bluescale.

Yes, the mission! He remembered that, now, too: a supreme privilege for the sake of the Ssi-ruuvi Imperium. Dev walked between the elder and his master with his head bowed and clawless hands clasped. He had white eyes, furred skin, and a small stinking tailless body. Who was he to deserve such effort on their part, such happiness in service, such important life work?

Jangling noises jostled Luke out of a fitful doze. A light blinked at his bedside, but other than that the room remained dark.

"What?" he asked drowsily. There'd been a macabre nightmare . . . no, a warning. "What is it?"

"Commander Skywalker?" spoke a male voice out of his bedside console. "Are you awake?"

"Getting there," he answered. "What's wrong?"

"This is Salis D'aar Spaceport Authority. There's been a disturbance with some of your, uh, troops. We have several speeders at the Bakur complex for official use. How quickly could you get to the roof port?"

Could this be a trap? Did it have anything to do with the dream warning? He jumped out of the warm, comfortable bed. At least he felt rested, and his aches had left him. "I'm on my way."

He dressed hastily and decided to wake Chewbacca and take him along. Chewie wouldn't need to waste time getting dressed, and he'd be extra eyes, brain, and especially muscle. Han had to stay with Leia, though. She'd said something about a breakfast appointment with Gaeriel's uncle.

A disturbance. He couldn't imagine Rebel troops making trouble—

Well, yes. He could. He clipped on his lightsaber.

He dashed out his bedroom door and around the corner into Chewie's, then stepped back from the bed. He didn't want to tangle with a suddenly roused Wookiee. "Chewie," he whispered, "wake up. We've got trouble."

"Slow down, Chewie."

Chewbacca steered the landspeeder around the spaceport's outer-arc access road. Luke peered ahead and to the right. Pad 12, the temporary Alliance ground base, lay just beyond the next radial road outward from the control tower. Spaceport lights gleamed on this side of the radial, but on the other side, dark night was lit only by occasional flashes that looked like blaster fire. Either someone had shot out Pad 12's lights, or someone had shut them down. Where was Spaceport Security?

They swooped left, past Pad 12, then onto its access road through an open gate in its high metal-chain fence. *Unguarded*, Luke observed. Maybe the guards had gone in to settle the disturbance. He pulled down the hitched-up back of his parka. Out here in the night, between two rivers, damp air wasn't so pleasant.

Four multiship launching/landing pads lay in a cluster between these radial roads and the spaceport boundary, and in the middle of that cluster sat a small, unattractive cantina that looked like two bungalows joined at right angles. Someone standing next to it waved them down.

Chewie grounded the speeder in the angle between bungalows. With the repulsor engine shut down, eerie silence rang for about ten seconds. Then another whizz of blaster fire brought up the hair on the back of Luke's neck and lit the silhouette of a tall repair gantry. The dark-haired person sprinted toward them. "Manchisco!" Luke exclaimed. "What's happening?"

The *Flurry*'s captain shook her black braids. "Our *allies*—right over there—insist they've got a pair of Ssi-ruuk trapped behind one of our ships. I can't get in close enough to confirm it. They're shooting everything that moves."

"Nobody has any macrobinoculars?" Han had a pair on the *Falcon*, a quarter of a kilometer away.

Manchisco shook her head.

"Well, c'mon. You too, Chewie!" Luke ran toward the gantry, unhooking his saber.

Before they reached it, a voice shouted, "You! Get down! Get back, if you're unarmed—the aliens have landed! They've killed two of us!"

Manchisco ducked into the pitiful cover of an Artoo-size recharge unit. Chewie edged closer to the gantry.

"Ssi-ruuk wouldn't kill people," Luke muttered. "They'd take prisoners. Chewie, cover me." If the Ssi-ruuk were here, he'd rather deal with them himself—despite that eerie warning.

But he had an unsettling hunch. He drew and ignited his lightsaber. By its glimmer, he spotted Chewbacca aiming his bowcaster into the darkness. "Stay there," Luke said softly. "That's close enough."

Eerie silence had fallen again. "Everybody hold your fire," Luke shouted. Step by step he advanced, holding the saber upright in front of him. Although its light was dim compared with the spaceport beacons, it was all the light in Pad 12.

He rounded an Alliance gunship. Two human bodies lay sprawled on that odd, rough glassy surface. He paced past them, listening hard for hostile intent. All he felt was panicked fright.

Geometric forms sparkled ahead, metallic surfaces of another repair gantry reflecting the light of his saber. "Who's there?" Luke shouted. "Show yourselves!"

A domed Calamarian head appeared behind the gantry. Then another.

Luke groaned and sprinted toward them. "What are you doing down here?" he demanded.

"Shore leave," wheezed the nearer one, straightening his stiff, high round collar.

"Authorized?" Luke asked. Surely their commanding officer had more sense than to—

The Calamarian waved a finny hand. "Of course, Commander. Our rotation came up. We're as tired as anyone else. But these strangers spotted us."

"So you killed two of them?"

"Commander, they were charging us! Ten of them! They fired first, Commander."

Luke wanted to go back to Endor. "One of you come with me."

"Sir?" The Calamarian backstepped, clenching his blaster.

"That's an order," Luke said quietly. "Follow close, so I can cover you."

Slowly the tall alien wormed out of his hiding spot in the gantry. A blaster bolt zinged in from across the way. Luke whirled and deflected it, then shouted, "Hold your fire! Chewie, beat their heads together if you have to!"

A Wookiee roar echoed across the empty area between ship and gantry.

"All right," said Luke. "Come on."

Walking a little more slowly, this time—the Calamarian wouldn't move any faster—Luke retraced his steps toward the gunship. He avoided the spot where the bodies lay. "Chewie, where are you?"

Another burst of blaster fire flashed in, then another. Luke leaped and spun, parrying without thought.

Just as suddenly, the firing stopped. A weird creaking groan came from the gantry ahead . . . and the unmistakable roar of a furious Wookiee. Luke held up his saber to get a better look. The metal tower rocked violently. High overhead, several dark forms clung to struts in the black night. Blasters clattered to the ground.

"Good work, Chewie," Luke called. He adjusted his grip on the saber. "Okay," he shouted, "everybody down. Get a good look. This is a Mon Calamari. Not a Ssi-ruu. Look at him!" He heard scuffling noises, but no faces appeared in the green-lit circle. "Come on," he called, losing patience.

After three seconds of silence, he heard Chewbacca whuffle.

Then out they came, ten humans—eight males and two females —dressed in an assortment of loose, bulky coats and warm hats. None appeared to be armed, now. One male, shorter and thinner than the others, pointed at the Calamarian. "He's right—it's not a Flutie," he said. Luke recognized the voice. This was the man who'd tried to warn him away.

A larger man pushed forward, squinting. Green light flattered nobody, but Luke guessed this character wore dark circles under his bulging eyes in any light. "Quiet, Vane."

The thin man shut his mouth but shuffled closer to Luke and

the Calamarian. Tessa Manchisco stepped into the circle of light. Her eyes reflected green anger.

"This pad is blocked off for the use of Alliance crews," Luke said sternly. "Why are you here?"

Dark-circles crossed his beefy arms. "This is our planet, sword boy. We'll thank you to keep critters like that fish—and that hairy one—off of it."

Chewbacca edged toward that side of the gang.

Luke needed information, and he needed it quickly. Had these ruffians been sent in by the Empire, or were they acting alone? The thin Bakuran stood close enough for Luke to attempt probing his mind, briefly. Luke felt certain his motives were good enough that he didn't risk drifting toward the dark side.

Still, he hesitated before focusing his attention tightly toward the thin man, opening himself to listen for the man's feelings (*confusion, fear, embarrassment, suspicion . . .*). He thrust past them into memory.

He didn't have to search very deeply. "A little something, direct from the governor's office," had been promised if they hung out close to Pad 12 and made certain the Ssi-ruuk didn't infiltrate Bakura by way of that closed-off Alliance landing area.

Luke broke off the contact and lowered his lightsaber. "Go home." He hoped his voice sounded as disgusted as he felt. "Tell Governor Nereus that we'll police Pad Twelve ourselves."

No one moved.

A deep, throaty rumble started from Chewbacca's direction. Picking up the cue, Luke added, "Go on. You still haven't seen a Wookiee get really mad."

The thin man slunk out of the green-lit circle toward the bodies. One by one, the others followed. Soon a bedraggled little group shambled toward Pad 12's main gate, carrying their comrades.

No sooner had they passed through the gate than the main bank of lights lit up again.

Someone must be watching from the Imperial garrison, only a

few kilometers south. And Spaceport Security was unquestionably busy at Pad 2, or 6, or 9. On Imperial business.

He exhaled hard. "Let's go make sure the *Falcon's* okay, Chewie."

When Threepio wakened Leia early, she found a message from Luke: He'd taken Chewbacca to the spaceport to oversee ship repairs. She dressed hurriedly in the bathroom and braided up her hair. Scurrying back out, she caught sight of a tall human standing against the mural wall. She gasped and stopped in midstep. By dim room light, he glimmered faintly and washed out the real-time image of a sparkling city.

Luke had said he sometimes saw Ben Kenobi like this. Backing away, she squinted. This man didn't look like the old general, nor anyone else she'd met before.

Whoever he was, he didn't belong in her apartment. She eyed her blaster, just out of reach on the repulsor bed. It probably lacked a certain threat against apparitions, if this was one. "Who are you?" she demanded. "State your business."

"Do not fear me," the figure said softly. "Tell Luke to remember that fear is of the dark side."

Who was this person, bringing messages for Luke into her allegedly private quarters? A Bakuran? An Imperial? "Who are you?"

The stranger stepped sideways into a darker spot, where his glow brightened. He was tall, with a broad pleasant face and dark hair. "I am your father, Leia."

Vader. A chill started at her feet and shivered its way to her scalp. His very presence stirred every dark emotion she owned: fear, hatred—

"Leia," the figure repeated, "do not fear me. I am forgiven, but I have much that I wish to atone for. I must clear your heart and your mind of anger. Anger is the dark side, too."

Her blaster definitely wouldn't help. Even when he'd lived, he'd deflected blaster bolts bare-handed. She'd seen him do it at Cloud

City. "I want you to leave." The dark chill froze her voice. "Disincorporate. Fade out, or whatever you do."

"Wait." He did not move away from the wall. If anything, he seemed to shrink in size and proximity. "I am no longer the man that you feared. Can you not see me as a stranger, not an old enemy?"

She'd lived too long with the fear of Darth Vader. "You can't restore Alderaan. You can't bring back the people you murdered, or comfort their widows and orphans. You can't undo what you did to the Alliance." Old pain jabbed her like a fresh wound.

"I strengthened the Alliance, although that was not my intent." He extended a glimmering arm. The mellow voice sounded wrong. The mild, naked face didn't look as if it'd hidden for decades behind a black breath mask. "Leia, things are changing. I may never be able to return to you."

She glanced away. Maybe she couldn't harm him with her blaster, but it would feel good in her hands. If she stretched, she could almost reach it. "Good."

"There is no justifying . . . my actions. Yet your brother saved me from darkness. You must believe me."

"I heard Luke." She crossed her arms and clenched her hands around her elbows. "But I'm not Luke. Or your teacher. Or your confessor. I'm only your daughter by a cruel trick of fate."

"Of the Force," he insisted. "Even that served a purpose. I am proud of your strengths. I do not ask for absolution. Only your forgiveness."

She set her chin and kept her arms crossed. "How about what you did to Han? Are you going to beg him for his forgiveness?"

"Only through you. My time here is short."

She swallowed. Her throat felt dry. "I can almost forgive you torturing me." He bowed his head. "And the evils you did to other people—because those drove so many worlds into the Alliance. But cruelty to Han . . . no. If you want to go through me, you won't get his forgiveness. Never."

The figure shrank farther away. "*Never* is too large a word, my child."

Darth Vader, lecturing her about virtue and eternity? "I will never forgive you. Dematerialize. Go away."

"Leia, I may not speak to you again, but I'll hear if you call me. If you change your mind, I will be watching."

She stared. How dare he, after all his cruelties and perversities? Let Luke deal with him. She would not.

How did Luke stand knowing this was their father?

She rushed out of the bedroom. Morning light streamed through the main room's long window, lighting yellow walls and dark flooring. Han pushed up out of the closest corner lounge. "You're going to be late, Highness-ness."

Threepio waddled toward her. "Are you ready, Mistress L—?"

She had seized up the Owner and shut off Threepio. Now she turned to watch the bedroom door. No one emerged. "He can't do this to me," she muttered. "To my life. He can't do it!"

Han glanced at the comically frozen droid, then crinkled his mouth. "He who? Did you get a call from that captain guy?"

Flinging out her arms, she paced past the windows. "Oh, fine. That's all you can think of, your petty"—she grabbed a couch pillow—"lousy"—she twisted it between her hands—"jealousy! Vader's been here, and all you can think of is . . . acch!"

"Whoa, Princess." He showed her his palms. "Vader's dead. Luke burned him. I took a speeder bike out and saw the ash pile."

Leia's stomach hurt. "You saw his body. I just saw the . . . rest of him."

"You're seeing things too, now?" He stood hip-hitched, hands in his pockets, eyebrows raised. "Either you're getting stronger in this Force stuff or Luke's a bad influence."

"Maybe both," she said bitterly. "If I had to see ghosts, I could've put up with that Yoda of his. I would've enjoyed talking to General Kenobi. Who do I get?" Dropping the pillow, she struck the yellow wall with a fist.

"Easy," he murmured. "It's not my fault."

"I know it isn't." Now her knuckles hurt, too. Frustrated, she pivoted to lean against the wall. She glared back across the lounge pit's blue and green cushions toward her bedroom.

"What did he want?"

"You're gonna love this. To apologize."

Han gave a short, disbelieving laugh and ran a hand over his eyes.

"Yeah," she said. "My sentiments exactly."

"You know, you've been jumping at everything that reminded you of him. Now you've faced him down. Maybe the worst is over."

"It's not." She let her shoulders sink. "Han, he's still here. I'm . . ." Unable to finish the sentence, she shut her eyes.

"So what?" Han stepped closer and laid a hand on her shoulder. "Hey, nobody gets to be as big a deal with the Empire as he was without a lot of strengths and abilities. You got 'em. You're just using 'em differently."

How could he be so insensitive? "Thanks a lot, Han." She considered taking a swing at him.

"Leia?" He spread his arms. "I'm sorry too. I guess. Sorry I made a stink about that Alderaanian guy, anyway."

She drew a long, slow breath and stayed against the wall. "Go away."

"All right," Han exclaimed abruptly, "okay! I can take a hint." Glaring, he stalked around the lounge pit.

"Han, wait!" What had she done, venting her anger on the one person she shouldn't hurt? He passed Threepio, then the darkened comm station, almost reaching the main door. "Han, it's . . . it's the Vader in me. I can't help what I am."

As the impact of what she'd said flooded through her, Han stopped beside the black console. He turned slowly. "No," he said. "It's the Skywalker in you."

That name—Luke's name—didn't raise her hackles the same

way. A fleeting thought flashed through her mind: What had Vader been like . . . before he was Vader?

"I'll tell you one thing." Han walked up to the edge of the lounge pit. "Governments need each other. Yeah. Planets do, species do. But so do people."

Governments. She was going to be late for breakfast with the prime minister—"Yeah." She paced back to his side. "Right. Anyway, he's gone. He didn't hurt me. Maybe he can't hurt me any more."

"That'd be good." Han ran a finger around the tight braids pinned to her head.

She yanked out the pins and pulled off the end clasps. Han stood with his eyebrows at attention as she ran her fingers from scalp to ends and tossed her head. Her hair swung loose. "But I'm not going to forgive him," she said softly.

"Are you sure you're all right?" He fingered the dark cascade, then wrapped an arm around her waist.

His shoulder made a firm, warm pillow. "I love you, Nerf Herder."

"I know that."

"Do you?"

He stroked the back of her head. "What makes you think I don't?"

"I'm sorry," she whispered, straightening her neck. She held her lips near his chin.

Accepting the invitation, he bent and kissed her. She felt her life energy draw up into the kiss until nothing existed but barely perceptible movements of Han's mouth. She flattened her hands on his shoulders. His legs shifted toward her. All perception vanished but the taste of his breath. Her pulse quickened in her ears.

The comm center blatted behind him.

"Mmmf!" Han cried before she could disengage. Once he pulled free, he shouted, "No! It's not fair!"

Laughing at her own despair, Leia pushed her hair behind her shoulders. "Want to get it? Or shall I?"

"Well, you're—" He looked her up and down and smiled crookedly. "Lovely."

"But I'm not presentable."

"It isn't your usual image," he agreed with a sad head shake. "I'll get it."

Leia backed aside. Han touched a control and then blinked. "Luke!" he exclaimed. "What's up?"

"There's been a little trouble," said Luke's voice.

Leia whisked back to Han's side. Luke looked calm. She tried stretching out with the Force to feel his presence, but she couldn't. She must still be too agitated. "I thought you were going to check on ship repairs," she said.

"I didn't think the comm center was secure enough to leave messages. Our Mon Calamari crew came downside for an authorized shore leave. Some Bakurans on the wrong side of the spaceport—at Nereus's suggestion—spotted them and thought the Ssi-ruuk had landed. By the time I got here, the Calamari had blasted two in self-defense."

"Oh, no." Treaty papers burned in Leia's imagination.

"Sorry I missed it." Han grinned. "Looks like you made out all right."

Luke nodded. "It was still dark enough that one lightsaber lit up the whole pad area. Once Chewie and I had both sides' attention, and the Bakurans got a good look at our people, they declared a cease fire."

Han raised one eyebrow. "Not bad, farm boy."

"But, Luke." Leia pushed hair behind her shoulder again. "What about the injured Bakurans?"

He pressed his lips together and shook his head. "Did I say injured? Sorry. Dead. Their families need formal apologies. Could you do it for me? You're better at that kind of thing."

Leia didn't relish the idea, but he was right—she wanted it done correctly. "I will." She tried stretching out for him again. What she touched frosted her blood. The crisis might be over, but in his deeper sense hid a dark disquiet. "Luke, what's wrong?"

His cheeks colored. "Come on, Leia. This isn't a secure channel."

Luke was deeply afraid. What else had happened in the night? Han cocked an eyebrow at her. She shook her head. "Later, then," she said. "Han and I will go straight from here to the prime minister. I'll apologize to him first. I'm also taking him Threepio and Artoo, to try translating."

"Good. Artoo's probably still in my bedroom, plugged in. Han, I'm leaving Chewie here to keep things calm. I'll try to talk to Belden next, if I can find him."

"Belden?"

"The senior senator. I have a feeling," he said softly.

"About the shooting?" asked Han.

"Right. See you two later." The image faded.

Han folded his arms. "I suppose the sooner we get on with it, the sooner we can get away from this planet with our skins."

Leia stretched a hand toward the comm board. "I'll send Prime Minister Captison a message that we'll be late." Good thing they'd been late. Otherwise, they'd've missed Luke's transmission.

Frowning, she punched in Prime Minister Captison's code. Maybe some day she would wish she'd accepted Vader's apology. Anakin's. Whoever he was. He had been polite.

Watching her, was he? Freshly furious, she shook her fist at thin air.

CHAPTER

11

LUKE STEPPED OUT OF THE COMM BOOTH CLOSEST TO PAD 12, GLAD HE hadn't settled for the cantina's nonvisual comm net. From watching Han and Leia's faces, he felt sure they'd be all right. Better than all right. While he was on line, he'd also filed an incident report on the mainframe and looked up an address.

Chewie stood on watch. Luke grabbed a handful of arm fur and said, "Thanks, pal." The Wookiee slapped Luke's shoulder in reply, then stalked past the shabby cantina back toward the *Falcon*. A thorough investigation had assured them that nobody'd messed with it.

Captain Manchisco lounged against the cantina's corrugated wall. "Heading out, Commander?" She must've cleaned up for shore leave, but gray spaceport dust had smudged her cream-colored shipsuit during the fracas. Three black braids still dangled jauntily on each side of her head, dusted with leaf fragments and twigs.

On board the *Falcon*, she'd declared that she (sensibly) offered her Duro navigator triple overtime to stay shipboard. Luke wished the Mon Calamari captain had thought of that. Credit-poor the

Alliance might be, but its leadership would rather pay triple over-time than provoke incidents that cost Bakuran lives. "Say, how's the *Flurry*?" he asked.

Manchisco frowned. "Small problem with her starboard shield. It's fixed, but I had to let an Imperial maintenance team on board. All her specs are probably on Thanas's computer now." She thrust her hand into a deep pocket.

"Did they do good work, though?"

"Looks all right." She shrugged. "I don't know if I told you it's been a pleasure making your acquaintance."

"I like working with you, too. And I'm sure we're not finished here."

Her battle-hard face lost a few smug lines. "You're the one who knows about these things, but I've got this odd feeling we won't meet again."

Another warning. Or had Manchisco experienced a premonition of her own? "I don't know," he answered honestly. "The future is always in motion."

She waggled her left hand. "Doesn't matter. We do what we can, for as long as we can. Eh, Commander?"

"Exactly." A two-seat speeder cruised through the gate to Pad 12, overloaded with four Alliance crewers. Just what he needed. Spaceport Authority had reclaimed the speeder he arrived in.

"Hot night downside," Manchisco observed. "Let's hope there wasn't any more trouble."

The crewers looked bleary-eyed but nonviolent. "I think they're all right. Force be with you, Captain." Luke commandeered the speeder and drove it out the perimeter road.

Five minutes later, he parked atop a residential tower. He found Senior Senator Belden's apartment near the drop shaft, ran a hand over his hair and straightened his gray shipsuit, then touched the alarm panel.

While he waited for an answer, he glanced up the hall in both directions. This musty corridor, with plating peeled off several door frames, was a far cry from the Captison mansion. Perhaps the Belden family owned a finer home elsewhere, or maybe Governor Nereus made sure that the dissidents' credit balances stayed slim.

The door slid aside. He stepped back. *Gaeriel, here too?* "I—" he stammered, "uh, hello. I was hoping to speak with Senator Belden."

"He's out." She was sliding through the doorway into the hall when a cracked voice behind her called, "Let him in, Gaeri. Let him in."

"That's Madam Belden," Gaeri whispered, "and she's not well." She touched her forehead. "Come in for a moment. Clis—her caregiver—had a family crisis, so I'm having tea this morning."

"I'll just say hello," he murmured. "I didn't mean to bother you."

A wizened woman sat propped up on cushions in a brocade chair with wing-shaped armrests. She wore yellow-orange, almost the color of namana candy, and she'd dyed her sparse hair auburn. "You're back, Roviden. Why did you stay away so long?"

Luke shot Gaeri a puzzled glance. "She thinks you're their son," Gaeri whispered against his ear. "He was killed in the purges, three years ago. She thinks every young man is their son. Don't argue. It's better."

Was there an escape route? Luke saw spindly wooden furniture that was probably antique, a gray box that was probably electronic, and Gaeriel's bare feet beneath her space-blue skirt and vest . . . but no way of gracefully evading a filial masquerade. Hesitantly he took Madam Belden's hand. "I'm sorry," he murmured. "So much work to do. For the Rebellion, you know," he added on a gamble: *Son killed in the purges.*

She squeezed his hand. "I knew you were working undercover somewhere, Roviden. They told me—oh, but it doesn't matter. Gaeriel's missing, you see, and—"

"No, she's—" he began.

"I'm here, Eppie." Gaeri sat down on a furry repulsor footstool.

"You're—?" Madam Belden stared from Luke to Gaeri, shaking her head helplessly. "I'm—?" She shut her eyes and set her chin.

Gaeriel shrugged. "You're fine, Eppie. Would a nap feel good?"

"Nap," repeated the woman in a tired voice.

Luke followed Gaeriel back toward the door. "Tell me about Madam Belden. How long has she been like this?"

"Three years." Gaeri shook her head sadly. "Unfortunately, she was deeply involved in resistance to the Empire. She broke down when Roviden died. It . . . destroyed her."

"Maybe that's why they let her live," he guessed.

Gaeri's sharp chin tilted angrily. "You can't—"

Madam Belden thrashed in her chair. "Don't leave without saying good-bye," she cried.

Wedged too tightly into the awkwardness to run away, Luke hurried back and knelt beside Madam Belden. He cleansed his mind of concern and desires and focused inward, examining Madam Belden's deep presence. It pulsed too powerfully for someone who needed full-time care. The mind remained, affecting the Force . . . creating a life pulse so strong that Luke guessed she had untrained strength of her own. But some of the links connecting mind to senses and communication didn't operate. They'd been severed. *The Empire did this,* he guessed.

He blinked up into sad, watery eyes. Gaeriel was watching him from behind. If he used the Force, she might throw him out. Or she might begin to respect his abilities.

Regardless of what Gaeriel wanted, Eppie Belden needed healing. Luke stroked the spotted, bony hand. Should he go on pretending to be her son? That seemed like a dangerous dishonesty, using the Force. "I want to show you something," he murmured, ignoring Gaeriel. That was hard. "If you can do this, you may be able to heal yourself."

Her sense brightened and became eager.

"No," he directed. "Be calm and still. Listen deep." He pressed into her awareness and showed her how he had healed himself, traveling in hyperspace . . . the silence, the focus, the strength . . . and he made certain she saw, even if she didn't understand, that he hadn't been able to do it perfectly. Then he turned her focus inward. *Something has been damaged,* he told her. *I think the Empire did it. Find it. Heal it. Fight back, Eppie. May the Force be with you.* Yoda would've called her "too old for training," but this wasn't training. Not exactly. *And, Yoda, she's not going to go off chasing trouble like I did.*

A wave of her gratitude washed him out of her mind. He inhaled deeply and pushed up off his knees. Eppie Belden rested against her cushions, eyes closed, breathing tranquilly.

"What did you do?" Gaeriel stood in an unconscious fighting stance.

Luke studied her eyes. Somehow the gray one calculated while the green one looked angry. "There's still a very sharp awareness in there," he murmured. "I don't think her problem is natural. I really think she was harmed."

Gaeriel hesitated. "Deliberately?"

Luke nodded. Feeling her hostility swing away from him, he stayed silent a moment longer and let her process the implications. Someone had harmed her. Who but the Empire? Then he elaborated, "I know a little about self-healing. I showed her something she might try. That's all."

"Is that so little for you?" she asked bitterly.

A non-Jedi couldn't do that much. "I did nothing *to* her. My word as a . . . as an honorable man."

At last she shrugged, dismissing the matter. "Come out here. Sit down." She strode through a door arch into a white-tiled dining room, both hands brushing her long vest as she walked. She motioned him past a fragrant, simmering tea warmer toward a seat at a transparent table. "If you can do so much with the Force," she said, "why don't you simply get into a fighter, blast your way onto the Ssi-ruuvi flagship, and get rid of them?"

I might try it, if you told me to. He sighed away the impulse and explained, "If I used my powers in anger or aggression instead of for knowledge and defense, the dark side would take me. It took . . ." He strangled a terrible temptation. Some day, he must admit his ancestry. He almost wished he had it over with, but the time hadn't arrived when his humbling, provocative revelation would count for something. Telling Gaeriel would be disastrous. "It took many Jedi. They became agents of evil, and had to be hunted down."

"I should've guessed." Gaeriel looked him up and down, then cocked an ear toward the open door.

He might yet win her, through Eppie. "If she tries what I showed her, she might seem to sleep for . . . well, days."

"That might be a blessing." Relaxing, Gaeri crossed her ankles under the table. "What did you need to talk with Orn about?"

Oh, blast. Commanding the *Flurry* was easier than admitting this. "Some of your people attacked some of mine at the spaceport this morning. Mine had Alliance aliens with them, and yours thought they were Ssi-ruuk. I suspect Governor Nereus found some Bakurans who like trouble, and tried to make some for them."

He felt her suspicion. "Were there casualties?"

"Two Bakurans. Princess Leia is making formal apology," he added hastily. "I wish we could do more. It shouldn't've happened." He glanced out a broad window. The morning sun was turning brilliant, but he felt chilly. He'd been warned. Somewhere out there, the Ssi-ruuk would soon be looking for him. He didn't think he was in any serious danger, but he still wasn't certain why they wanted him. What was he doing here, endangering Gaeriel and Madam Belden? "If Senator Belden has any thoughts on the incident, please have him contact me." He stood up. "I hope Madam Belden improves. What I sensed underneath her troubles . . ." He searched for words. "I think I would have liked her. She was a fighter, wasn't she?"

Gaeriel's left eyebrow arched.

Great. He'd reminded her of his Jedi abilities again. Staring at the floor didn't help either, because her bare feet suggested a light-hearted spirit. *Except when I'm around.* "Thanks. I'd better leave."

He glanced at Madam Belden on his way to the door. She hadn't moved. Gaeriel slipped out into the drab hallway behind him. "Luke," she murmured, "thank you for trying."

"Luke"—she finally used my name. He hurried to the roof port with a lighter heart.

Leia caught herself bustling as she led Threepio through a guarded door arch in the Bakur complex's old Corporation Wing. Artoo wheeled silently behind, and Han followed at rear guard. Reddish wood paneled Prime Minister Captison's inner office. His massive desk had been sawed freeform out of the weathered burl of some rain forest giant. He sat near its center, where a flat space had been carved and polished, and he was frowning.

Was she that late? Abruptly she realized he was frowning at Threepio and Artoo, not at her. She brandished the restraining-bolt Owner to show Captison she had both droids under control. She'd also programmed Threepio not to speak until she rescinded the command. Asking him to keep quiet on his own just hadn't seemed kind—or plausible. "I'm sorry to have been delayed," she said.

Captison wasn't a large man, but like Luke, he radiated assurance. "I hope you were able to take care of your personal problem."

"Yes, thank you."

He extended his hands toward two repulsor chairs. Han pushed one toward her, then took the other one. Sideways. *I love you, Nerf Herder,* Leia silently repeated as she sat down on the gently bobbing seat. "I must make a formal apology for the deaths this morning. May I contact the families of the fighters who were killed?"

One corner of Captison's mouth twitched up as he watched Han. "I think that would be appreciated. Yes, I'll arrange it for you.

There has also been a reconfiguration of Ssi-ruuvi ships outside our defense web," Captison added. "The web reconfigured to compensate. So much I hear from Commander Thanas, at any rate."

Leia caught Han's sidelong glance. "Does he report to you *and* Governor Nereus?" Han asked.

Captison shrugged. "I've asked him to. Seems the least he could do."

Leia puffed out a breath. "Maybe you don't know how unusual it is for an Imperial officer to pay the slightest attention to the people he's allegedly defending."

"Really."

Maybe Captison did know. Maybe he'd cultivated Commander Pter Thanas. "At any rate, here are the droids I offered. May we try translating whatever you have?"

"I'm not fond of droids," Captison said drily. "But at this point I'm willing to use them, if there's a chance they could help."

She shot at Threepio with the Owner. It whirred softly.

As if he'd never been silenced, Threepio chimed in. "I am fluent in over six million forms of communication, sir."

Leia had heard that sentence so many times she'd forgotten how impressive it was. Captison's sudden interest reminded her. "That's right, Your Highness said so over dinner." He touched a panel on his desktop console. "Zilpha, key in those ship-to-ship recordings we picked up from the Fluties." He leaned back in his chair and explained, "We've got plenty of their chatter. Sounds like a flock of birds—great big ugly ones, with deep voices."

"Well, if anyone's good at talking, it's our Goldenrod." Han rapped Threepio's metal shoulder.

Threepio's head whipped toward him. "Thank you, General Solo!"

A light changed color beside Captison's elbow. "Here we go. Have your droid listen to this."

"You can talk to him directly," Leia put in. "His full designation is See-Three-Pee-Oh, and he answers to Threepio."

"All right," said Captison. "Listen, Threepio. Tell me what they're saying."

The console emitted a series of whistles, clicks, and grunts, some as high as an alto voice, and others eerily basslike. The "Flutie" played a very large instrument. As Leia listened, she stared around Captison's office. His dual windows looked down on a round park scattered with stone figures. Bordering the clear window panels, tall leafy trees with straight trunks had been executed in three-dimensional colored glass. Namana trees, she guessed.

Threepio's head cocked. He shook it. "I am sorry, Prime Minister, but I can make nothing of it. It is entirely outside my comprehension. I have been in service for many years, and I can communicate in every language ever used within Republican or Imperial space."

"Our Fluties are from outside Republican and Imperial space," Captison declared. "I believe that was mentioned."

Han rubbed his chin. Leia couldn't think what to say.

From behind her came a whistling echo. Startled, she spun around. Artoo stood his place in a wood-paneled corner, warbling what seemed to be a perfect imitation of Prime Minister Captison's recording.

"Threepio," she said when Artoo finished, "wasn't that exactly how the Ssi-ruuk sounded?"

"No," Threepio answered firmly. "He missed one note by a full four vibrations."

Artoo honked.

"Soak your own transistors," Threepio retorted. "I won't stand for that language."

Captison raised a white eyebrow. "It can duplicate them that closely?"

"I wouldn't doubt Artoo, though it never occurred to me that he'd be able to do that," Leia admitted. "Sir, I'm certain that given enough time and recordings, Threepio could make a solid effort at decoding that language."

"If he can," Captison said, pointing at the little blue-domed droid, "we've got a native speaker if we need one. Take your metal friends to my aide's office. Zilpha will set them up with enough recordings to keep them busy well into tomorrow night."

Governor Wilek Nereus bit the end off a namana twist and chewed thoughtfully. In this cool greenway lined with tall fern trees and passion-bud vines, he could momentarily ignore the menace surrounding Bakura and ponder his own career. With both Palpatine and Vader dead, the Rebel Alliance—downtalked so disdainfully on all official communiqués—became rather more of a threat.

Still, all odds favored the Empire, and he had two high Rebel leaders within striking distance. He could weaken the Alliance substantially.

He thrust the distraction aside. Strolling down the greenway, he returned to his original thought path. Someone new would undoubtedly spring onto the Imperial throne. Nereus would've cautiously evaluated the risk of attempting that leap himself, except that this far out on the Rim, he didn't stand a chance . . . and anyone who jumped and failed was ruined or dead. So he must watch for a new emperor to emerge, flatter and praise him, and meanwhile make Bakura a shining example of pacified, profitable enterprise.

If the Ssi-ruuk didn't take it away. He despised them on principle, even without the entechment complication. As a youth, he'd pursued two hobbies: alien parasitology and alien dentition. The Empire had quietly used both talents. Aliens were creatures to dissect or fight—not to ally with.

His aide snapped to attention several paces away from the southeast greenway's central fountain. Nereus had issued strict orders that he was not to be disturbed, and he let the messenger wait. He'd come here to enjoy a few minutes' peace, and by all the forces and balances that those idiots worshiped, he was going to have it.

He took another fruity bite and stared into the fountain's heart, measuring the pleasant glow the candy gave him. He controlled his namana habit: nectar in the evenings only, and only two candy breaks a day, usually here by the fountain. Water leaped from a hundred sonic motivators in gravity-defying swirls, finally captured by Bakura and pulled into the turbulent blue pool.

The Empire could weather turbulence too. Nereus's Imperial colleagues had made the galactic bureaucracy self-perpetuating; and employed by the Empire, Wilek Nereus would rise farther, grasp more authority, and wield more power than in any other system of government. Therefore, he would sell anyone and anything to keep the Empire on Bakura. The loss of another Death Star peeved him. Fear was his ultimate tool for keeping Bakura subdued.

Well, the natives were afraid now. Sighing, he turned to the aide. "It's important, I trust."

"Sir." The aide saluted. "You have a personal message waiting on holo from the Ssi-ruuvi fleet."

The Fluties had captured several Imperial ships since sending the Sibwarra recording, so now they had access to Imperial holonet. "Idiot," Nereus snapped, "why didn't you speak up? I'll take it at my desk."

The aide pulled a communicator from his belt to relay the reception order. Nereus marched up the greenway's mossy path. Two uniformed guards held glass doors open at the corner of a long, artificially lit tunnel connecting this greenway with the other. Nereus strode sharply left, then left again through his personal staff's station and into his broad-windowed private office.

On the holonet reception pad alongside his desk, a green light blinked. He straightened his collar and whisked one hand over the rank insignia on his chest to make sure they hadn't picked up any passion-bud pollen, then swiveled his repulsor chair to face the transmission pickup. "Receive," he told his desk. He curled his hands around his armrests. What did the Fluties want now?

A meter-high, translucent figure appeared over the reception grid: human, in striped white robes. "Governor Nereus." The figure bowed at its waist. "Perhaps you remember me, I'm—"

"Dev Sibwarra," Nereus growled. Now *that* was an alien parasite. "I know you as well as I want to. What joyful news do you have this time?"

Sibwarra shook his head. "Less joyful than before, I fear, but perhaps in the short run it will please you better. The mighty Ssi-ruuk, seeing your hesitancy to join the Imperium's quest for galactic unity, to experience freedom from physical limitations—"

Nereus snatched a long ivory Llwelkyn tooth off a pile of flimsies. "Make your point."

Sibwarra extended one palm. "Admiral Ivpikkis is willing to move our fleet out of your system, if you'll grant us one boon."

"Keep talking." Nereus fingered the tooth's serrated slashing edge. If the holo had been flesh, he could've sliced it just . . . so. . . .

"Among the new visitors in your system is a man named Skywalker. If you can hand him over to a special Ssi-ruuvi delegation, we will leave immediately."

Nereus made a deprecating sound. "What do they want him for?"

Sibwarra cocked his head and squinted, looking reptilian. "We simply mean to rid you of an unpleasant presence."

"I don't believe that for an instant." Still, if the aliens went elsewhere for human droid-charges—he might suggest Endor—then Bakura returned to status quo, he remained in power, and he could alert the Empire to oncoming danger.

Sibwarra said, "I'm told to admit that he would be useful in certain experiments."

"Oh. Certainly." *Hah.* Whatever they really wanted Skywalker for, it had to have something to do with entchment. He trusted neither Sibwarra nor his reptilian hosts. If they wanted Skywalker, they mustn't get him.

Yet surely he could work this proposition to his advantage. "I will need time to arrange things." Killing Skywalker outright was one option. Or . . . yes, he could help the Ssi-ruuk take the young Jedi, but ensure that he died before they made use of him, killing two dangerous birds with one carefully planned strike.

But would Rebel officers serve Thanas, if their Commander vanished with the alien fleet? He tapped the long tooth. They would, if it were their only hope of survival.

Still squinting, Sibwarra pressed his palms together and touched his fingers to his chin. "Would a day be sufficient to make your arrangements?"

Nereus despised him. "I believe so. Contact me again tomorrow noon, local time."

Three quick raps on Gaeriel's office door interrupted her effort to regain a lost morning's work. Luke Skywalker's intimation that the Imperials took Eppie Belden's mind had preyed on her all the way back to the complex. Immediately on arriving, she'd checked Eppie's criminal record. Every rabble-rouser arrested during the takeover or the purges had one, even including Uncle Yeorg (a very minor offense).

But not Eppie. Either it had vanished or it was under an extremely high-level security seal. Why would the Empire bother covering up?

She put her revenue-revue program on "hold, security" and called, "Come in."

A slim woman in a dark green jumpsuit glanced over her shoulder and then slipped through the glide door.

Gaeriel sat straighter. "Aari. What is it?"

"Monitor," Aari mouthed. "Nereus's office."

Gaeriel motioned Aari closer. Her aides had broken several of Governor Nereus's security systems, but surely his aides had ears in her office as well. "What did you hear?"

Aari's lips brushed Gaeriel's ear as she whispered, "The Ssi-ruuk just made Nereus an offer if he'd turn Commander Skywalker over to them."

A lump of ice formed in Gaeri's stomach. Luke Skywalker had seen the Emperor die. Obviously he was not simply a new Jedi. He had to be one of the pivotal individuals in the Alliance . . . in the changing galaxy.

So what did *they* want him for? Gaeri curled her toes tightly inside her shoes. Luke had deliberately risked her goodwill by using his powers to help Eppie, and frankly she admired his decision. If Jedi were self-serving at heart, why had he acted on his conscience despite her disapproval, when he so obviously—and frighteningly—hoped to befriend her?

Evidently the Ssi-ruuk thought they could handle him. If so, any human—even Wilek Nereus—ought to know to keep Luke away from them. Either Nereus didn't understand what surrendering Skywalker could mean to humankind or he was obsessed with getting Alliance people off his world, or . . .

Or he'd try to kill Luke before they could abduct him. The third possibility meant Luke Skywalker, whatever he was, had no time left.

Should she warn him? To do nothing would give weight to Governor Nereus's side of the Balance. To aid Skywalker might unweight the rest of the universe.

But it was hard to think in universal terms when danger threatened the Bakuran people. Luke had finally convinced her that he'd do everything in his power to help Bakura repel the Ssi-ruuk. "Thank you, Aari." She stood up and checked her chrono. Sensible people would already be eating dinner. "I'll take care of this."

CHAPTER
12

L UKE TRUDGED DOWN THE WHITE STONE CORRIDOR TOWARD THEIR apartment suite. After talking to Gaeriel and Madam Belden, he'd spent the rest of the morning and half the afternoon reasoning with shop supervisors. His reputation as a Jedi was obviously getting around. They'd given him grudging respect for getting his hands greasy with them—that had been the highlight— then let him sandwich all the remaining A-wings onto that day's service schedule. Luke suspected that Bakura's best repair teams had been shuttled up to the Imperial cruiser *Dominant.*

Then, without a chance to clean up, he'd had to help his quartermaster provision the battle group, spending the nonexistent collateral of a maybe-someday government. He'd've given a lot for Leia's help on that one. All this while watching over his shoulder for the Ssi-ruuk and pondering what the dream-warning really meant. No wonder his barely healed body ached.

A pair of Imperial stormtroopers stood guard in the broad lobby outside the suite, blast rifles slung across their chests. Weary as he was, his adrenaline surged. Quicker than thought, he went for his lightsaber.

Then thought caught up. He dropped his hands to his sides, fingers spread. "Sorry," he murmured to the near guard. "Not used to this."

"Understood, sir." The Imperial stood back. Luke slipped inside, then spun through the common room to his bedroom and fell onto the repulsor bed, laughing off his tension. He'd never heard of such a preposterous situation. His apartment, guarded by "friendly" stormtroopers?

He stared across the room and through a huge window, wondering what his Uncle Owen would've given for a rain shower like the one that'd just started. Early summer on Bakura would've been heaven on Tatooine.

A message light blinked on his personal console. Sighing, he called it up. Senior Senator Belden requested his presence at an early dinner.

Luke groaned. Gaeriel must've relayed his message, but he was too late. He'd barely have time to rush over if he didn't clean up. He needed to speak with the elderly senator—if nothing else, to discuss his wife's medical history.

Luke keyed in a polite request to see him tomorrow, sent it, then bent over to pull off his boots. The door chime rang. "No!" he whispered irritably. Their guide had shown him how to use the bedroom console to scrutinize callers. He poked several buttons but couldn't make it work. Wishing he didn't feel so greasy, he hustled through the common room and answered it himself.

Gaeriel stood half turned away from the door as if she'd rather keep walking than speak with him. She carried a tightly woven string satchel against her blue skirt, and as before, her very presence made his Force sense tingle. "Commander?" she asked tentatively. "May I speak with you for a few moments?"

Luke back stepped away from the Imperial guards' inquisitive eyes. "Please."

Once the door shut, she cupped her hands around her mouth and whispered, "You're monitored. We're about to disappear." She lifted the satchel and held it open. Inside was a gray box like the one at the Beldens' apartment. She toggled a large switch, then said aloud—but softly, "Disruption bubble generator. I can't leave it on for more than a few seconds at once. You're in danger."

"What's wrong?"

"The Ssi-ruuk have approached Governor Nereus." She slid her hand back into the satchel. "Is your party comfortable here, Commander?" she asked full-voice.

He had to think quickly. "The situation's a little awkward," he answered. "I have an allergic reaction to stormtrooper armor."

Good, she mouthed. She raised her right eyebrow, over the green eye, then twisted her wrist again and softly said, "They've asked Governor Nereus to surrender you and offered to leave Bakura if he does."

The dream-warning rushed back into his mind. So, they meant to move through Nereus. "Naturally, he's tempted."

"I don't think so. He's not stupid. If they want you alive, he's going to make sure they don't get you that way." She glanced down and moved her hand again. "We all have to deal with our automatic reactions, I suppose," she announced.

So much for Leia's assurance that Nereus wouldn't harm them. *Now the fun begins.* "The accommodations are excellent, though." He motioned toward a corner lounge. "I've been on my feet all day. Please. Sit down, so I can."

"I don't think I should."

He overlaid his voice with a calming veneer of Force overtones. "I wish you would trust me."

She slid her hand back into the string bag. "I suppose my reaction to Jedi is like yours to stormtroopers."

"I'm learning to suppress mine."

"So am I. Eppie was still sleeping when I went back." She glanced away, then mumbled, "Thank you. Now . . . my aide and I intercepted a transmission from the Ssi-ruuk. Governor Nereus asked for one day to arrange things."

"One day." Luke nodded. "Thank you."

Shift. "Is there anything your alien requires? What did you say he was, a Wook?"

"Wookiee. Nothing special, just twice as much food as the rest of us."

"I understand." She worked the generator again. "They wouldn't come after you the way they'd grab one of us plain folks, you know. Neither will Governor Nereus. Watch your back. Watch your guards. Watch what you eat and drink and breathe."

"What do the Ssi-ruuk want me for?"

She shrugged.

"I'll be careful," he said quietly. Nereus would probably try to play all angles, convincing the Ssi-ruuk he meant to cooperate.

Maybe he did.

"Have you eaten this evening?" Gaeriel asked. "I can have a light dinner sent to my suite and then diverted here."

Touched, Luke brushed at a grease stain on his coverall, then hid it under one hand. "Would you?"

Once she'd called over the comm center for something he couldn't remember, let alone pronounce, awkward silence fell. Luke held his peace, wondering what she would say if he waited. At last she stopped pacing around the room, looking out the long window into the greenwell, and up at the ceiling. She glanced over at him. "Are you listening to me think?" she asked boldly.

Her string bag lay on the repulsor lounge. "I can't do that," he said carefully. "Some of your feelings come through the Force, but that's all." *Not really all.*

"That's still not fair. I can't tell what *you're* feeling."

Luke slid out the gray box and found the control. "Would you like to know what I'm feeling?"

"Yes."

He drew a deep breath. Honesty was one thing, stupidity another. He wished he had Leia's gift for turning a phrase. "I already know you on a deeper level than anyone else does. Of course, that makes it worse, because all you know about me is what you think you believe." Had he said that right? He plowed on. "Your feelings are strong for me. Strongly ambivalent."

She walked toward the lounger. "It's not that I'm afraid of you, Commander—"

"Luke," he insisted.

"I have a religious objection to what you are. What you've become. You weren't born a Jedi. And you'd better turn that back off for a few seconds, or we'll both be in trouble." Then he caught it: through the Force, a swirl of intense attraction that had *not* come from him. Five years ago, he might have seized her hand and sworn away everything—the Fleet, the Alliance, and the Force.

But those five years had molded his destiny. Perhaps he could change her mind.

He caught himself. What right did he have to chip at her beliefs? She drew on the Force like anyone else, though she couldn't accept it.

Quickly, he switched the field off. "How long have you been a senator?" he asked. Surely that could be considered casual conversation.

"The senate elected me five years ago. I've been in school ever since, either here or at Imperial Center. And don't be too impressed with the position." She tapped her thumbs together. "It mostly involves finding creative ways to drain tax credit out of Bakurans. Now we've got an influx of Imperial data flow and culture to support, too. Some of it's very good," she added, "but some of it only appeals to a few people who think like Governor Nereus."

In every subjugated culture, there'd be a few people who welcomed the Empire because they were already Imperials at heart. "I don't think you're one of them."

She glanced at the generator. Perhaps the conversation was getting too personal for comfort. "Does it always rain this much?" he asked. "I was raised on a desert world."

After a few more noncommittal comments on the weather, he turned the generator back on. "I will respect your fears," he said. "And your beliefs."

The door chimed.

Gaeri sprang up and opened it, grateful for the distraction. She had no business flirting with destiny this way, and no hope of bringing Luke Skywalker to understand the universe as she saw it.

One of her personal staff pushed a hover cart through the door. Gaeri motioned for the staffer to park it between their chairs. Once he had gone, she uncovered the single plate. "I hope you like seafood." *Raised on a desert world—and this is twice in two days.*

"Would you stay?"

"Forgive my cowardice, Luke, but . . ."

Wordlessly he unhooked a cylindrical silvery object from his belt and laid it on the repulsor cart. Long enough to grip two-handed, it looked like half of a weapon.

"Is that what I think it is?" she asked softly.

"You may be safer here than at home." His face colored. "Sorry," he added. "I sound like a swaggering stormtrooper."

At least he could laugh at himself. She hesitated. For a few minutes, she'd probably be safe. "There are two of them out in that corridor," she reminded him, "and if I were you, I wouldn't trust them any more. Still—this smells very fresh. I'll join you."

Evidently he did like seafood, because he ate like a starving man. She blunted her hunger with a few delicately seasoned bites. In a few minutes, he reached for the projector, which now lay on the cart beside his lightsaber. "Do most Bakurans share your beliefs?" he asked.

Relieved that he'd brought up the subject, she answered, "Many are stricter. My sister is an ascetic. She lives with almost nothing in order to free up more for everyone else. I'm less . . . devoted. We're a minority, but the weight of the universe could balance on one rightly placed atom."

"I can feel through the Force that you're a woman of depth. Of deep feelings."

"I thought I'd convinced everyone that I'm a career politician."

"Everyone else seems convinced."

"Good," she said lightly. *Mustn't look at his eyes—but they're such a delicate blue.*

"The Ssi-ruuk are out there." He gestured with his fork. "I have a day, at most, to get ready for them."

"Less."

"Once I settle with them, I'll come back—to talk with you, Gaeriel—if there's any hope that you'd reconsider about me. About Jedi. You were only partially right when you said I wasn't born a Jedi. The Force is strong in my family."

Startled, she sipped from the water glass. Part of her head had guessed he might say something like this, and part of her heart had longed to hear it. *Why not admit it?* she asked herself. *See how he reacts.* "Thank you for being . . . honest. We have no time to be socially correct. And I'm drawn to you, which is dangerous."

He shook his head. "I wouldn't—"

"Yes, you would. If I encouraged you." She stared down at her clasped fingers. "You could manipulate people easily if you chose to."

"I wouldn't," he repeated, blushing. "That would be dishonest. There's no future in it."

She fingered her pendant. "What are you, Luke Skywalker? What gives you the right to these powers?"

"I'm a . . ." He faltered. "A farm boy, I guess."

"A family of Force-strong farm boys?" she asked sarcastically.

The high color drained from his face. She must've struck a nerve. "Think of it this way," he murmured, scraping the last morsel off his plate. "There will always be people who are strong for evil. If the only way to protect others is for a few of us to become strong in the Force for good, isn't that important? Even if your beliefs are correct, and that means bringing someone else low?

People constantly sacrifice themselves for good causes. I didn't ask anyone to die for me."

Almost persuaded, she resisted his seeming genuineness. "The Cosmos must balance."

"I agree. The dark side calls constantly for aggression, revenge, betrayal. The stronger you become, the more you're tempted."

That made her hand tremble. "Then if you, you loved someone, you could easily hate them."

He glanced down at the generator and raised an eyebrow.

She forced herself to ignore the hurt in his eyes. "No need for the generator," she said. "We could easily be eating in silence."

"Here's another balance." He pressed a hand to his dirt-streaked forehead. "The mountaintops in my life are balanced by canyons. I've lost friends, family, teachers. The Empire killed most of them. If I'd never even begun my Jedi training, they'd still be dead." He frowned. "Actually, I'd be dead too. The day I met my first teacher, the Empire struck our farm. They butchered my Uncle Owen and Aunt Beru while I was away. Everyone who was home died. Haven't they done that here too? Do you approve of the Empire?"

"That's a loaded question."

"Do you?" he pressed.

Of course she did. Didn't she? "The Empire has seized more power than any government needs," she admitted. "Yet it balances submission with privilege. One advantage to living under the Empire is a wonderful range of educational opportunities. Bright children may study right at Imperial Center."

He made a wry face. "I've heard that the brightest don't get to go home."

How did he know that? Some stayed on, offered lucrative employment. Some vanished. She'd preferred to go home. "Let's say we learned to hold back a little. Imperial leadership has been good for Bakura, anyway. It restored order when we were close to civil war. It has drawbacks, but I'm sure your people would tell you that the Alliance has problems."

"They're the problems of freedom."

That stung. "You frightened us when your battle group arrived. The Rebel Alliance's reputation is destructive, not constructive."

"I guess from an Imperial point of view, it could be. But we're not. Honest."

He's no diplomat. "Thank you for talking this through," she said. "I feel better—"

"I wish I did."

"—And more certain of myself," she lied firmly. She reached into the satchel, twisted her wrist, then slipped the bag over one shoulder. "We will work together against the Ssi-ruuk."

He made a hand-twisting motion. She switched on the generator one last time. "Is there a chance we—I—could buy a few of those?" He pointed inside the string bag.

She shook her head. "This is Eppie's. There are only a few of them left on Bakura, property of the original families. We've kept them secret from Governor Nereus."

"That's too bad."

"Yes, it is," Gaeri agreed. "I'll take the hover cart out."

He clipped his lightsaber back onto his belt.

Luke walked her to the door. He wanted to stroke her hand, reason with her, erode her defenses with the Force. Even begging seemed reasonable. Instead, he palmed the door open and then thrust his thumbs through his belt.

"Thank you," she said. The stormtrooper guards watched as she pushed the hover cart out and strode down the hall without looking back. Once she vanished around a corner, Luke dropped his hands. He clenched them, loosened them, and clenched them again. His abilities had always opened doors. Doors into danger, both in space and in the brighter, darker, wider spaces of his own soul, but he'd always had the freedom to walk through.

Gaeriel had tried to slam this door in his face, but she hadn't succeeded. He'd felt the conflict within her. She might not fight him forever.

Then again, she might. Exhausted, he shut the apartment door behind him and strode up the hall in the opposite direction. A roof access door opened on his left. He pushed through and rode the lift up.

By night, the roof garden could have been primitive, isolated forest. Still air cooled his face. Clusters of white tree trunks branched out of protruding root wads, then swept up and ended in bright yellow-orange twigs, damp but no longer dripping. Two small round moons and several dozen bright stars shone overhead, and night glims edged a stone path between dark, mossy banks.

As he paced away from the lift shaft, the path branched. Several meters down the narrow spur toward the complex's edge, he knelt on a bench, rested his elbows on the restraining wall, and looked down. The circles of the city stretched out around him, lit by hovering blue-white street lamps at the center, then pale yellow, fading to reddish—

Like a diagram of star types. The comparison leaped into his mind. Salis D'aar's founders must have laid out the city for navigation by star colors, with the finest homes—like the Captisons' mansion—in the zone that represented warm, hospitable yellow suns.

The moment of insight cheered him. It *wasn't* wrong for a human to learn to use natural talents. If Gaeriel's religion were carried to its logical end, everyone would have to be equal—even identical—in all respects, for fear of diminishing anyone else.

And his life was no longer his own.

He thought he could make out slow-moving pinpricks of light overhead that would be ships in the orbiting defense web. Locked in position with other ships, joined by common orders and a common enemy.

Many of those pilots had life mates to return to—or, at the last need, to grieve them. The stronger he became in the Force, the harder it might become to find a woman who'd have him.

He opened his empty hands. "Ben?" he whispered. "Ben, please come. I need to talk with someone."

Not even a breeze answered. Along the wall's surface, a black creature the size of his smallest finger humped on twenty legs. He concentrated on the rhythms of those legs, focusing his spirit. After it vanished into a crack, he called again. "Master Yoda? Are you near?"

Foolish question. Yoda was with the Force and therefore everywhere. But he did not answer.

"Father?" he called hesitantly, then repeated, "Father," wondering if Anakin understood. He tried to imagine himself in Gaeri's place. With her home world threatened and her life in peril, into the crisis came a man who frightened her. A Jedi.

He felt someone approach. *Ben?* he thought, but the intensity wasn't that of a master, and it carried the restless striving of a living person. Light footfalls hurried down the path. Leia hesitated at the branching, her white gown glimmering between vine-shadowed white trees.

"I'm over here," he called softly.

She hurried up beside him. "Are you all right?" She pulled a blue Bakuran knit shawl around her shoulders. "I heard—well, I thought I heard you call out through the Force."

She'd tracked him this way at Cloud City, too. He sank down onto the bench. "It's been a long, rough day. How was yours?"

"Uh," she answered, "good. I left Artoo and Threepio with Prime Minister Captison." A self-conscious excitement begged him not to notice. She tingled with eagerness.

Envious, he said, "Let it flow, Leia. He loves you."

She glared. "No use hiding anything from you, is there? We went walking. We talked. We . . . it's been hard to find time alone."

Luke smiled, feeling bashful. "So this is what I missed. Growing up without siblings, I mean."

Leia flicked the ends of her shawl. "It's good to have a brother. Someone to talk to."

"You also have Han. Someone ought to pass on the family strengths," he added glumly. "It doesn't look like I'll get the chance any time soon."

She laid a hand on his shoulder. "What's wrong, Luke? Is it that senator?"

"A Jedi feels no passion." Anyone who could manipulate his emotions could endanger him, making him unable to calm himself —unable to control. "But sometimes the Force obviously controls me, rather than the other way around. It favors life."

"It *is* her. I was beginning to worry about you, Luke. You've been so . . . detached."

Her insight made him squirm. The easiest way to distract her was to rile her. "You and Han," he said. "Let me ask you something I've no right to ask. You're not . . . opposed to having children some day, are you?"

"Hey!" She snatched back her hand. "That isn't an issue."

"Sorry. It's just that I've thought so much about it lately." He had? Amazing, what his subconscious would tell somebody else before it informed him. For a moment, he pictured himself as head of a clan of young Jedi apprentices with mismatched green, blue, and gray eyes. "But a child who's strong in the Force will have a great potential for evil too."

"Of course." Leia sat down and flipped the ends of her shawl into her lap, then plucked a purple trumpet flower off a vine and sniffed it. "That's a risk humans have always had to take. It's perilous to bring an intelligence into existence."

"Doesn't it make you wonder how our mother dared it?"

Her anger flared faintly, startling him. "Oh," she said lightly. "That reminds me, I'm supposed to deliver a message. I've seen Vader."

"Vader?" Luke's mind went blank. "You saw . . . Father? Anakin Skywalker? Vader doesn't exist any more."

"Have it your way, then. Anakin. But I saw him."

A sense of loss wrenched him. Why had his father appeared to Leia, and not him? "What did he say?"

She stared past him over the complex's edge. "I'm supposed to remind you that fear is of the dark side. He apologized to me, or tried to."

Luke stared out over the city. "I only saw him once—just for a moment. He didn't speak."

"Well, I don't claim any part of him, and I don't want him popping in on me."

Luke mulled over his father's message. *Fear is of the dark side.* Gaeriel's fear of him: It came from the dark side, too. "Hatred is also the dark side, Leia."

"It's not wrong to hate evil."

"Did his, um, did anything he said, well, have anything to do with . . . ah." He stumbled to a halt. "Oh. I interrupted something when I called this morning, didn't I?"

Even by dim starlight, he saw her cheeks flush. "It's been hard to find time alone," she repeated.

"I'm sorry. But maybe Father accomplished something good, if he sent you to Han for comfort."

"You can't say that. When I saw him, looking normal like that, I . . . I realized that a normal person became . . . what he was. That I could, too."

"For the good side," he insisted. He brush-kissed her cheek. He'd loved her, long ago it seemed, before they learned what she refused to acknowledge. "I'll see you in the morning."

"Hold on!" She straightened. "You're not sending me away."

"Only for a while, Leia. Go to Han," he murmured. "I'll leave you alone."

She stared into his eyes and took several breaths, plainly irritated. Finally she sprang up and hurried off.

Luke glanced down at the circles of the city and up at a passing repulsor bus's lights, then clasped his hands in his lap and bent forward. "Father?" he whispered. The thought crossed his mind that he'd made his peace with Anakin. That would explain why he'd appeared to Leia instead.

He started one of Yoda's meditations, concentrating his will deeper than himself. Personal troubles vanished in perspective, and the strength of the universe flowed through him. He had a sister; he wasn't alone. Some day, as he grew in the Force, real love would unite him with someone else of his own kind. Every emotion of either partner, every ripple of pleasure or pain, would bounce back from the other, resonating until sweet echoes faded.

He opened his eyes and unclasped his hands. He hadn't lost Gaeriel yet. He would help her as he could, and if she rejected him, he'd leave Bakura with only faint regrets.

Laughing unmatched eyes and swirling skirts danced in his mind. Who was he kidding?

And what was he doing up here alone? He stood up and walked to a drop shaft.

Dev stroked the sleek new entenchment chair . . . or should he call this something else? Three dozen new chairs were under construction, to supplement the energy flow Skywalker would give them, but this one was special. More of an upright bed than a chair, a motor reclined it from zero to thirty degrees. Instead of a catchment arc it had in-built energy-attracting circuitry that would lie under Skywalker's back. Larger restraints stood open along its sides and near its foot, and other medical attachments enhanced its obvious design for the long-term survival of an occupant (they'd tested those parts yesterday). All silver and black, it glistened under brilliant cabin lights. "It's beautiful, Master Firwirrung."

"I'm sorry, Dev," Firwirrung sang low. "I know this will hurt your feelings—"

"I wish it were real, Master. But I know you need to test it. Let's begin."

Firwirrung nodded his huge **V**-crested head.

Dev had suggested most of the design features for initial installation and restraint. No catchment arc covered the bed, and it leaned back a few degrees from vertical. Cautiously he backed up to it. His left foot brushed an open binder. It snapped shut around his ankle. "It works!" Dev exclaimed.

"Try the other," crooned Firwirrung.

Dev watched this time. Out of a groove in the bed protruded a flexible black arch. He eased his right ankle toward it—

Snap. That second catch activated another cycle he'd suggested. This one tipped the bed back twelve degrees. He relaxed and rode with it, arms crossed over his chest. As his torso touched another trip panel, a thicker restraint circled his waist. It held him down far more securely than the restraints on the old entenchment chair.

"Beautiful." Firwirrung swept closer and stroked the waistband with a foreclaw. "Is it firmly coupled?"

Dev tried to twist his body. "Yes. But loose enough that I've no trouble breathing."

"The human form is so odd," Firwirrung whistled merrily. Dev laughed with him. "Are you comfortable, Dev? We can only guess at *his* size."

"Oh, yes."

"Left hand, now."

He laid out his left arm. Another broad restraint swung rapidly and firmly into place. Embedded in this one was a tangle of life-function sensor relays that his thin scaleless skin would not obstruct. Behind Firwirrung on a black bulkhead panel, pale lights started blinking. Firwirrung pivoted around and examined them. "Leave the right free," he instructed.

How Dev wished he would really be entenched today. He envisioned the moment when he sparked to life behind eyes that would never close, but saw everything. Inside a new body that could do anything—and chose only to please its masters. Yesterday, they'd begun entenching immature and overage P'w'ecks off the other ships, preparing for the assault. Enteched P'w'ecks wouldn't last as long as humans, but numbers were needed—briefly.

Firwirrung touched a red panel. Something stung the small of Dev's back. "That works, too," he called. That mechanism was also critical for long-term confinement, as was the upper-spine beamer. Now the procedure would not depend on disabling Skywalker's nervous system first.

"Can you move your feet?"

Dev peered down. The angle of tilt held them off the gray deck tiles. "I can't even feel them," he announced happily.

"Good." Firwirrung swept closer. "Ah, Dev." He unhooked a clear tube from the bedside beside Dev's left shoulder. "I know how badly you wish this were real. I am sorry to tease you this way."

"My time will come." Dev shut his eyes. He felt a little pressure at his throat, then a thrust that barely stung. He relaxed against the bed, savoring the sensation, while Firwirrung moved to the other side and repeated the motion. He wished, oh he wished . . .

Yet an undercurrent of fear lurked behind his longing. His right hand trembled against his chest.

Hearing a whoosh, he opened his eyes to see Bluescale and Admiral Ivpikkis stride in, followed by two P'w'ecks who dragged a limp human prisoner by his head and arms. Following Firwirrung's new procedure, they had already prepared him with a paddle beamer. *That* was the one who'd actually be enteched. Dev tried again to wiggle his toes and felt nothing. Perfect. For that poor frightened human's sake, he hoped he could do his part.

"Review for me," demanded the admiral. "How will this differ from standard entechment?"

Firwirrung pressed foreclaws together in front of his chest. "We believe that a Force-talented individual will be able to draw energy from a distance—a short distance, in Dev's case. If Dev is properly linked to catchment circuitry, the other subject's energies will flow through him, but Dev will remain unenteched and will be able to repeat the procedure indefinitely."

"Not like the . . . chair, then." Ivpikkis glanced at it. Dev recalled how amused they'd been when he first described human furniture. P'w'ecks were enteched lying flat on the deck.

"No," agreed Firwirrung. "The actual subject need not be caught. With Skywalker's involvement, the subject will not even need to be within the range of a tractor beam—or so we hope."

"But for convenience's sake, we have caught and prepared this one. Is everything ready?" Bluescale's scent tongues flicked out of his nostrils toward the prisoner. The poor human was probably unclean.

"It is." Firwirrung turned his **V**-crest toward Bluescale, his right eye toward Dev, and his left toward the P'w'ecks and their prisoner. Then he pulled down the main switch.

Dev's throat burned. This time the servopumps injected not simple magsol but a solution of magsol and other factors. It should orient the entire nervous system toward the bed's in-built catchment circuit, drawing energy toward it. This eliminated the necessity of a catchment arc. First his neck, then his head, then his chest and his limbs felt the pull, rapidly becoming heavier as if gravity had shifted or the *Shriwirr* had reoriented. Abruptly he felt as if his upright bed had tipped. Firwirrung and the others looked for all the worlds as if they stood on the nearest bulkhead. The biogravity illusion virtually convinced his eyes. "I feel," he said, "as if every nerve in my body were being tugged toward the focus point. It hurts a little," he admitted.

"That should not affect the catchment function. Are you ready to try funneling this human's energies into a battle droid?"

"I'll try." The next best thing to entechment might be granting that gift to someone else. Dev shut his eyes and reached down past the discomfort for his center of control. Deeply and humbly aware of his limitations, he flailed through the Force toward the other human presence. It seemed like forever before he touched and embraced it. Letting the catchment circuitry pull through him, he used the Force to suck its energy into himself. For an instant, he felt huge and heavy. Twice as much pain pulsated in his nerves. Then the extra weight vanished. Panting, he opened his eyes wide. The prisoner lay limp on the deck.

Admiral Ivpikkis stroked one foreclaw with the other. "Deck Sixteen?" he called.

From the bulkhead came the words Dev longed to hear. "It works." Ssi-ruuk, P'w'ecks, and Dev cheered with equal enthusiasm.

"The next test," Firwirrung sang softly, "is whether we can force Skywalker to do our will, not his own. He is a far stronger Force user than our Dev, if Dev is correct in his reckoning."

"He'd better be." Bluescale appeared to climb down the bulkhead/deck toward him. Dev's right hand clenched involuntarily as the huge blue head bent close. The eye swirled. He fell in.

Then, to his surprise, Bluescale stepped back. "Try it," he whistled.

Firwirrung climbed down the bulkhead and held out a three-pronged knife used to declaw the small meat lizards they called Fft. He pressed its handle into Dev's free right hand.

"Yes?" Dev felt no fear, only curiosity.

"Stab it through your other palm."

What could be more reasonable? He struggled to twist his body against the waist restraint, positioned the Fft knife, and drove it as deeply as he could. Bone crunched. Red human blood welled out along the blade. There was pain.

"Leave it there," said Firwirrung.

Dev rolled back into the ready position and waited for his next command.

"Right arm."

Dev snapped his free hand into place.

Firwirrung pulled the knife out of Dev's palm, wiped it clean on Dev's robe, then slapped a piece of synthflesh—probably from a captured Imperial medpack—against each side of Dev's wounded hand. Then he swiveled his head back uphill to Admiral Ivpikkis. "Do you think it will work on Skywalker?" asked Ivpikkis.

"We have no reason to believe otherwise. The will for self-preservation is strong in all humans, and you saw how completely we overrode Dev's. The final test and most vital, of course, is how long a subject can remain alive in this state. We have only time for a brief simulation, but several hours should be sufficient for any degradation of life signs to begin."

Admiral Ivpikkis twitched his tail and peered across at the bulkhead panel, then down at Dev. Dev managed a smile. Bluescale followed the admiral out. Firwirrung ordered one P'w'eck to remove the human corpse and the other to remain with Dev. "Alert me if any numbers change." He rapped the bulkhead panel with his curled foreclaw.

Then he swept out.

Several hours. Lying here, so close to genuine entchment.

So uncomfortable. His nose itched, and he couldn't scratch it. No one had told him to. His hand throbbed hard enough to help him ignore the deep ache throughout his body. To pass time, he recited poetry he'd learned as a child. Mentally he translated it into Ssi-ruuvi, then pictured it in his special Ssi-ruuvi alphabet.

Too soon, he ran out of poetry. His eyes felt as if they would fall through his brain and his skull into the catchment circuitry. Poor Skywalker: doomed, like Dev, to survive without winning his own battle droid. Doomed by the same abilities.

Dev sighed and started counting pulse beats by the throbs in his left hand.

He lost track between four and five thousand. More time passed. The discomfort had long ago intensified to pain, and Firwirrung had not returned to check on him. Hurt and bewildered, he started counting again.

He still couldn't scratch his nose. No one had told him to—

Do it yourself, bonehead! Now that he could try, the inability to reach it maddened him. Why hadn't Firwirrung stayed? This was cruelty. Maybe if he held his breath long enough, he'd pass out and the dull-witted P'w'eck would notice a change in life signs. He inhaled until the waist restraint cut into him, then trickled it out. Empty, he closed his throat and held on.

An intense electric shock jabbed across the arc between left and right wristbinders. He inhaled involuntarily.

He'd *suggested* that mechanism. Irritated, he tried to pull his right hand free. He pressed his thumb against his smallest finger and wrenched his palm into the soft binder. Not far enough. He kept pulling. Three hundred heartbeats later, he gave up. He rested. He tried again.

The hatch whooshed. Startled, Dev thrust his wrist back through the three millimeters he'd managed. Firwirrung entered first. Without even glancing at Dev, he stalked past the P'w'eck guard toward the bulkhead panel. Bluescale led another P'w'eck, who dragged a second prisoner.

"Excellent." Firwirrung turned around. "All life signs steady. Describe the sensation now, Dev."

"I hurt," he said thickly.

Bluescale blinked and stomped close enough that Dev smelled him. "Legs, too?"

He pulled his ankles deeper into their bonds. "They move again. But they hurt. They're too heavy."

"Ah." Firwirrung examined a readout and hissed contentment. "Neuromuscular control returned in two and seven-twelfths hours, precisely on schedule. This is excellent."

Dev swallowed hard. "It hurts," he repeated in a cracking voice.

"That should not affect the catchment function. Entech this woman for us, Dev."

"You're not listening." Dev compressed his lips. "It hurts."

"Hurts?" mocked Bluescale. The alien turned slightly. Abruptly recognizing the posture, Dev winced and braced himself. A muscular tail slapped his legs so hard Dev saw stars. "Good," Bluescale sang. "We need you unwilling, human."

Firwirrung moved toward him, carrying an oddly shaped hypospray. "You're right," he sang back to Bluescale. "Surely the Jedi will not cooperate. Now that our war effort depends on fail-safes for controlling Skywalker, we'll try this . . . instead of your talents. Then the victory of our people will not depend on the survival of any one of us."

"It could kill him." The tip of Bluescale's tail twitched threateningly.

"It will either kill him or force him to obey. How much better to maintain professional objectivity on this less valuable subject."

Less valuable? Master, what are you saying? Panic-stricken, Dev tried to writhe away from the hypospray. It burned his thigh for a moment. He waited. Then—

"Entech that woman," ordered Firwirrung.

Dev blinked. What else were humans good for? He stretched out for her. As her essence plunged through him, there was more pain. He heard a scream. A male scream that hurt his throat. Then he opened his eyes again, awaiting orders.

Bluescale pulled the Fft knife from his shoulder pouch. Firwirrung honked. "Not necessary," he said. "I'd like to leave him there for several days, to test the other life-support functions—"

"But you heard the admiral," Bluescale sang wryly through his nose. "They want to begin on Skywalker immediately."

Several days? Dev trembled and clenched his hands. The left one felt seared. He'd probably chipped bones and sliced tendons.

Firwirrung's scent tongues flicked. "How they stink when they're afraid."

"They almost behave intelligently at times. Wouldn't it be odd if they had souls, when our P'w'ecks do not?"

"Not a chance." Firwirrung's callousness appalled Dev. "Finish it."

"Look at me," ordered Bluescale. The eye was black and lovely and rounded, and it swirled. . . .

His hand ached unbelievably. As his foggy brain recognized the sensations of a fresh but partial renewal, Master Firwirrung released the last wrist restraint on the shining new bed. Blinking, Dev tried to stand upright. He tottered between two P'w'ecks, fighting a strange inexplicable weakness. Something smelled bad. Human. He sniffed himself. Phew.

"Did it go well?" he asked Firwirrung. Talking hurt his throat. "Why . . . renewal, why now?"

"Ah, Dev." Firwirrung stroked his arm with an open foreclaw. "It would make you too sad, to remember coming so close to entechment and being denied the joy."

Their kindness and forethought overwhelmed him. "But it worked? Did I give him his battle droid?"

Firwirrung wrapped a foreclaw around Dev's head and pulled it against his scaly chest. "It worked. Now we lack only one thing."

"Skywalker," Dev whispered.

Firwirrung shoved him away affectionately. "Please go bathe, human."

CHAPTER

13

GOVERNOR WILEK NEREUS MARCHED INTO THE OPERATIONS ROOM OF his suite, firmly controlling a sense of anticipation. Ceiling, bare walls, flooring and furniture were black in the Ops Room for the easier viewing of projections. At the short black conference table, standing across from Commander Thanas and beside the fraudulent "General" Solo, he found Commander Luke Skywalker, Jedi Knight, self-assured in his invulnerability.

"Is everything going well, gentlemen?" Nereus took the repulsor chair at the table's head and waved his bodyguards back. The others sat down.

Commander Thanas looked appropriately serious for a man whose career rested on Nereus's next biannual report. He was probably eager to redeem himself from the Alzoc blot on his record. "All fighters are repaired," said Thanas. "The crews stand ready for our signal."

That attack would not come, if the Ssi-ruuk kept their word— not that Nereus expected them to. If they took Skywalker and attacked anyway, he and Commander Thanas had brought onto line a new weapon that should take a heavy toll on battle droids. "What about that new ship-mounted, ah . . ."

"DEMP gun," Thanas prompted him. Obviously caught unaware, Skywalker glanced over at Thanas and then down to his smuggler friend. "It disables droids at some distance using electromagnetic pulse," Thanas explained. "We've installed two prototype super-DEMPs on system patrol craft, but they're untested."

Solo immediately requested DEMP guns for Rebel gunboats. Nereus stroked his chin and let Commander Thanas explain that no others existed. While they sparred, he slid a miniature medisensor out of his belt pocket, laid it on the glossy tabletop, and aimed it at Skywalker.

Concern, not remorse, made him frown. All readings indicated near-perfect health. The man had allegedly ingested a five-year-old egg pod without knowing it. Nereus needed to make certain the eggs had been viable, and quickly—but a complete medical scan would rouse Skywalker's suspicion, and the Jedi's ignorance was a critical factor to success.

A holographic projector whirred up to table level, creating an image midtable between Skywalker and Thanas. Surrounding a pale blue sphere, silver and gold ship dots mapped out Bakura's defensive web. Farther out, the red Ssi-ruuk glimmered.

"You people use red for *threat,* too," Solo observed.

"Probably standard wherever people bleed red," Skywalker said softly.

Oh yes, they bleed red. Nereus smiled beneficence and leaned back, quietly touching keys on his recessed board and contacting his medical department.

Fifteen minutes later, the others were still talking strategy when his medtechs patched the complex medstation's powerful main sensors to his handheld model, which still lay on the table. He used directional keys on his touchboard to focus a smaller zone between Skywalker's belt and collarbone. . . .

Two minuscule fourteen-hour larvae squirmed in the left

bronchial passage. Primitive circulatory systems pumped for dear life.

There'd been three eggs in the pod, but one Olabrian Trichoid larva was deadly. Any good alien parasitologist knew that.

Solo, who'd pitched insults at both sides for two hours, finally objected with a straight face. "Commander Thanas, there's one thing about this I don't like. Look." He waved at the projected complete maneuver. "Go back three steps," he ordered the programming circuit. Ship dots swirled backward. "There," he said. "Stop. Do you see? You've—"

Nereus cleared his private screen. Solo paused. Skywalker nudged him to continue.

"You've got Alliance fighting pairs at every point of maximum risk," Solo insisted. "Your projection isn't showing losses by subgroup. If you fed those in, there'd be a lot less silver dots in the 'completion' frame. I don't like that."

Perhaps the smuggler had some grasp of tactics after all, Nereus observed. Commander Thanas, who'd been fidgeting with his souvenir pocket knife, dropped it into a breast pocket and said, "Commander Skywalker suggested I consider your forces my own. If those were my fighters, that's how I'd deploy them to minimize overall losses." He keyed his console. "Show phase four, with projected losses." The pattern changed. "Now I'll program a switch of squadrons to replace half of those key positions with regulars. Fair enough, General?"

Solo spread his hands.

"There." Commander Thanas touched a key. "Phase four, projected losses, with squadrons switched."

A significant number of specks extinguished, both Imperial and Alliance.

Skywalker exhaled easily. The cough would probably come in four to six hours, depending on his general physical condition— about two hours before massive thoracic hemorrhaging. "Convinced, General Solo?"

"I suppose."

Skywalker folded his hands on the table. "I think we can confirm it. Alliance forces will spearhead each thrust. We'll break the blockade and cut off that cruiser for you to englobe. Destroy one cruiser and we might change their minds. Destroy two. . ." He trailed off. "Well, we'll see what they actually throw at us.

"One more question." Skywalker addressed Commander Thanas. "If the Ssi-ruuk go on waiting for us, how long do we keep them waiting?"

Nereus cleared his throat for attention. "Tomorrow evening," he said. *By then, young Jedi, you'll be dead.*

"I'd like to move sooner," Thanas said carefully. "The element of surprise will work in favor of the attacking—"

"Tomorrow evening," Nereus repeated. Commander Thanas would have to redeem himself according to Nereus's plan, not his own wishes. The *whole* plan . . . or become a slave miner himself. Nereus would make that clear when they met privately tonight.

"Very well," said Thanas. "Commander Skywalker. General Solo. Until tomorrow."

Nereus shook hands all around, keeping his gloves on. Larvae weren't transmissible at this stage, but the very idea nauseated him. Olabrian Trichoids used almost all higher animals as breeding hosts. He'd tried infecting the Ssi-ruuk already, but apparently they destroyed enteched prisoners' bodies immediately. Skywalker, he guessed, might be kept around long enough to nurse a brood of the large, voracious adults—which emerged from a brief pupation already fertile. If the Ssi-ruuk didn't take Skywalker offplanet, of course, he'd have to be destroyed tonight. He might even volunteer, to head off a planetwide infestation. Young idealism sacrificed itself so nobly.

But Skywalker would almost certainly pass through Pad 12 at least once in the next eight hours.

.   .   .

Luke felt Governor Nereus's stare follow as he and Han strode out of the Ops Room. Nereus expected never to see him again.

Once they passed the first corner, Han muttered, "You have got to be kidding, trusting those people."

Luke answered out one side of his mouth. "Reconsider Commander Thanas."

"Oh?" Han raised one eyebrow, then turned his head aside to stare down a corridor.

Good. They'd both better stay jumpy. "Straightforward," said Luke. "Wants to do a good job and is glad for help. He's not Nereus's man."

"Empire's man."

"Mm."

"Do you like Thanas because he complimented you in there?" Han suggested.

Luke smiled. "No. But that was refreshing."

"Compliments from an Imperial. Right."

They slowed at the edge of a wide lobby. Luke reached out through the Force. No one waited there. Han kept one hand near his blaster as they hurried across.

Once they left the Imperial Offices corridor, Han frowned. "Is it my imagination," he asked, "or are you being just a little more careful than yesterday?"

"I had word from an inside source that Governor Nereus plans to hand me to the Ssi-ruuk. Did you notice that he got a message or something during that session?"

"Yeah," said Han. "Finally going to be careful, uh?"

"I've *been* careful." Luke's exasperation didn't distract him from watching shadows. "And is it my imagination," he came back, "or are you just a little more pleased with yourself?"

Han paused in midstep. "What is this? I suppose you're going to ask my intentions toward your sister."

Luke took a careful look around, then dropped his guard and

smiled at Han. "I know what your intentions are, friend. She needs you. Just don't let her down."

Han's crooked smile shone like an asteroid beacon. "Not on your life."

Luke clapped his shoulder. All they'd been through had already bonded them like brothers. Now, this—

Following footsteps snapped him back to attention. He slipped behind a pillar and unhooked his saber. Han slid in beside him.

Three sets of footfalls approached. Luke stayed in his cover. Han raised an eyebrow. Luke shook his head. He moved around the pillar, staying behind it as the trio passed: Nereus, followed by a pair of stormtrooper bodyguards.

He'd felt so controlled, back in his office. But something in his walk, and the faintest hint in his Force-sense, nudged Luke to an unexpected conclusion. "He's starting to panic," Luke observed in a whisper.

"Panic?" Han wrinkled his forehead. "Him?"

"It's just setting in." The trio's backs receded up the corridor. "We'd better watch him."

"That's nothing new." Han's hands relaxed at his sides.

Once they reached the apartment, Han disappeared into his room. Luke hastily encoded a message to Wedge Antilles, out in the orbital net. *Attack coordinated for tomorrow night. Work with Governor Nereus's forces, follow Thanas's orders, but keep your deflector shields up.* Smiling grimly, he sent it. Han and Leia were headed for the *Falcon* as soon as he located her. She'd gone off alone after breakfast, but with the attack this imminent, it was time to stand ready. Luke would catch the next shuttle to orbit and reboard the *Flurry.* He would enjoy proving Manchisco's premonition wrong.

His stomach grumbled a more immediate message. He ought to catch lunch, but not here. The food at Pad 12's cantina should be nontoxic. "You ready, Han?" Luke called.

Han stepped back out. "Leia's not answering."

"Maybe she and Captison went someplace where the Imperials couldn't listen to them."

"Possible," said Han. "Let's get you to the troops. Then I'm going looking for her."

Prime Minister Captison had suggested a drive, and to Leia's surprise, Senior Senator Orn Belden climbed aboard with a bulging breast pocket. She assumed it contained his voice amplifier. This time, the Bakurans wouldn't be distracted by droids or Chewbacca.

Captison's liveried chauffeur steered a closed-cockpit government speeder off the roof port. Belden laid a finger across his lips.

Leia nodded understanding: *Not yet.* "It's a lovely city," she observed lightly. "In many ways, Bakura reminds me of Alderaan." She glanced up at a layer of broken clouds. "Some of its wetter regions, anyway. Have you explored this quartz outcrop for metals?"

Sitting beside her in the center seat, Captison folded his hands with a knowing smile. "Thoroughly. Why do you think they planted the city here?"

"Ah," said Leia.

Captison leaned back, looking relaxed. "After a few boom years, the veins began to narrow and the Bakur Corporation factioned. My father's element wanted to prospect other sites. Another faction lobbied to develop Bakura's other resources. Still another—mostly second-generation—wanted to bring in settlers at exorbitant fares, or establish a set of luxury resorts."

"Once the galaxy learns about a newly opened habitable world, it often becomes . . . stylish."

"Which brings in a certain undesirable element."

Perhaps he meant rebels and smugglers, or gamblers and trinket sellers. "It can."

Captison laughed. "In many ways, Leia, you remind me of my niece."

"I wish my life had been as simple as Gaeriel's."

"She has been a good child," Belden wheezed from the back seat beside Captison's bodyguard. "It remains to be seen if she'll be a good senator."

Prime Minister Captison tapped a window absently. "She has abruptly reached the disillusionment phase of new adulthood."

"I understand," said Leia. "I reached it rather young." Captison's chauffeur kept the speeder between two others in a crosstown lane. Salis D'aar, like many sizable cities, funneled air traffic along established routes.

"Oh," interjected Senator Belden, "please thank Commander Skywalker for trying to help Eppie. He'll know what I mean." Then he started talking about mountain soil, namana fruit harvest, and juice extraction.

Leia waited, wondering when the men would feel safe enough to really talk. This could be her only chance to gain headway for the Alliance.

Five minutes later, Captison's chauffeur landed the speeder at a small dome surrounded by gaudy repulsor signs that hovered several meters overhead. Leia reached for the entry hatch. Captison laid a hand over hers. "Wait," he said softly.

Ten minutes after that, Captison's chauffeur and bodyguard took off again in the government speeder while Leia stepped into the front passenger's seat of a smaller rental craft, Hoth-white with ice-blue cushions and console. "Do you do this often?" she asked, amused but pleased by their subterfuge.

"Never done it before." Captison steered out into traffic. "It was Belden's idea."

"It's safe to assume that the speeder pool's not secured for talking." The senior senator leaned forward between them and patted his bulging breast pocket. "This will help, too. We are now inaudible."

Captison frowned and switched on a music channel. Tuned percussion filled the cabin. "You must understand we're taking some risk speaking with you at all. In public, we're even forbidden to console you on the loss of Alderaan. However, in private . . ."

Not his voice amplifier, then. "What do you have, Senator?"

Belden covered his pocket with one hand. "A relic from pre-Imperial Bakura. Corporate infighting crippled our government, but it made our ancestors into survivors. This creates a bubble impenetrable by sonic scanners. Under the Empire, no faction has dared to manufacture more of them."

Mentally Leia calculated the instrument's value at somewhere near the *Falcon*'s. "Better not lose it, then. Gentlemen," she said, clearing her throat, "I'd be intrigued to know why the Empire hasn't pushed Bakura into the Rebellion camp."

"Nereus has been subtle, I suppose," guessed Captison. "Applying pressure slowly. Like boiling a butter newt."

"Beg your pardon?" asked Leia.

"They're too primitive to react to slow stimuli," creaked Belden. "Put one in a pot of cold water, bring up the heat slowly, and he'll boil to death before he thinks of jumping out. And that's what'll happen here, unless—" He poked Captison's shoulder.

"Easy, Orn."

Leia glanced starboard and down into a hilly park. "What would it take to push you, Prime Minister?"

"Not much," Belden interjected. "He's smarter than he lets on."

"Is there an underground, Senator Belden?"

"Officially, no."

"A hundred members? Ten cells?"

Belden cackled. "Close enough."

"Are they ready to rise?"

Captison smiled sidelong and thumbed a steering rod to turn right. He seemed to be circling just inside city limits. "Lovely Leia, this isn't the time. We have Ssi-ruuk on our minds. We're hoping that the Empire will save us, not subdue us."

"But it *is* time," Leia insisted over the background music. "The

Ssi-ruuk have united your people. They're ready to follow a leader to freedom."

"Actually," said Belden, "three years of the Empire have united our people. Nowadays they know what they lost when they lay down too quickly, and that they'll have to cooperate to get it back and keep it."

"They believe in you, Prime Minister," Leia urged him.

Captison stared ahead. "And you, Princess Leia? What is your true goal here?"

"To bring Bakura into the Alliance, of course."

"Not to defend us against the Ssi-ruuk?"

"That's Luke's goal."

Captison smiled slightly. "Ah. The mission's defined objective depends on who defines it. The Alliance begins to mature."

One more round for division of labor. "Prime Minister, how much power do you and the senate truly have?"

Captison shook his head.

"If you could choose freely and without risk to your people," she pressed, "which side would you wish Bakura to support?"

"The Alliance," he admitted. "We are displeased with Imperial taxation, with offworld rule and sending our young men and women into Imperial service. But we are afraid. Belden's right: We've learned to appreciate each other, now that we've seen what it's like to be subjugated—to lose our identity because we couldn't stand together."

"Isn't that worth fighting for? Isn't it worth spending the lives of free persons? Prime Minister, I don't expect to see . . . fifty," she said, guessing at his age. "But I would rather lay down my life for others' freedom than die quietly in slavery."

Captison sighed. "You're exceptional."

"All free people are exceptional. Let me talk to your cell leaders, Senator Belden. Give your people a chance to fight for their freedom, and they'll—" Out of long habit, Leia glanced over her shoulder. A double-podded local patrol craft followed ten lengths back. "Those are Imperials behind us, I think," she said quietly.

Captison checked a sensor screen and pushed his throttle forward.

Leia searched the instrument panel for communications equipment. Han would be on his way to the *Falcon* by now, en route and unreachable. "They're still on us. Head for the spaceport."

"One more, coming up from below. I can't turn south from this lane."

"Looks like an escort," Leia observed. Captison swung the speeder northwest in a long arc. Then the escorts let him straighten out again. "Where are they herding us?"

"Back across town." Captison frowned. "Complex, I think."

"Are either of you armed?" she asked quietly.

Captison slid one hand under his jacket, showed her a hold-out blaster, then concealed it again. "But that's going to be useless if we're outnumbered. Belden, can you lose the generator?"

"Under a seat, maybe." Belden's voice came muffled.

Leia thought quickly. "It might be safer to wrap it in . . . here, in my shawl . . . and drop it, rather than be caught with it."

"No," Belden said stiffly. "It's too delicate. Too fragile. People are used to seeing me carry a voice amplifier. I'll keep it in my pocket."

The modal percussion pounded on.

Cloistered in a bare, tiny windowless room lined with recording banks and communication setups, Threepio expelled a dramatic sigh. "Every time I feel certain they've come up with one last way of making us suffer, they invent another. They're so difficult to fathom."

Artoo-Detoo squalled disdainfully.

"I am not stalling, you mismated collection of crosswired nanochips. There was nothing in that last recording that was not in any of the others. Six million forms of communication, and they find a new one. Nonmechanicals are quite impossible."

Artoo stretched a manipulator arm toward the playback machine.

"I'll do it," blustered Threepio. "You can't reach high enough."

Artoo *thbb*'d like a seven-year-old human with his tongue out.

Threepio removed one recording rod and inserted another, carefully replacing the old one in the prime minister's array case. "Even Prime Minister Captison, an admitted droid hater, simply has to agree that we serve a useful purpose now. We've been on the job for seven hours without so much as a break for lubricants." The speaker twittered and chirped. Threepio leaned his head closer. "Quiet, Artoo."

Artoo, who *was* being quiet, *thbb*'d a little softer.

"There's something different on top of this one." At a human-inaudible whine, a series of electronic bursts followed the Ssi-ruuvi birdsong. His automatic scanners compared the code with millions of others. Before the recording ended, "That's it!" he exclaimed. "Artoo, run that one again."

Artoo chirped wryly.

"Of course I can reach it better than you can. Don't blame me for your shortcomings." Threepio turned his upper body, pressed a repeat key, then held the awkward position. Automatic programming preset his left auditory sensor to follow the Ssi-ruuvi language, his right auditory sensor to record the electronic code, and a central processing unit to compare the two. It noted a decisecond delay, repeated tonal patterns, and inhuman labial/guttural modifiers.

The recording ended. Threepio ran it again. Another circuit, programmed to deduce logical variables out of context, supplied alternate readings and compared them with similar statements he had recorded during the years since his last memory wipe—a long, long time ago.

"Excellent!" Threepio exclaimed. "Now, Artoo. We must begin at the beginning and listen through *all* the recordings. They'll provide Princess Leia with all kinds of useful information."

Artoo whistled.

"Yes, Prime Minister Captison too. Don't get impatient." Threepio tapped Artoo's dome. "I realize this isn't your specialty. Think of the hours I spent shipboard, functionless."

Artoo tweaked his memory.

"That's not funny." Threepio pressed the play key. "Be quiet and listen. I'll translate for you."

The recordings began again, all seven hours at high speed. Threepio listened, and Artoo listened to Threepio. Most of what was said was inconsequential: *Realign your ship with the squadron* and suchlike.

But abruptly Threepio exclaimed, "Oh, *no*. Artoo, you must call Master Luke at once. This is dreadful—"

Artoo was already rolling toward a communications interlock.

Leia slid out of the rented aircar into a cool, gusty breeze and stared around the Bakur complex's roof port, mentally counting stormtroopers. Eighteen, with weapons drawn. This was no friendly welcome committee. Now she wished she'd been able to bring Chewie—even though she wouldn't have, to please the Bakurans. Belden bumped her and mumbled, "Be sure you give Commander Skywalker that message, Your Highness."

"Get ready to move," she mumbled back. She reached up one sleeve for her little blaster. She could probably take three or four before they stunned her. Flinging herself onto the permacrete rooftop, she started shooting.

Five stormtroopers toppled before someone seized her right elbow from behind. She wriggled violently and almost won free before a white gauntlet pried her blaster from her hand.

Half the battle is knowing when you're beaten. Where had she heard that? Alderaan, she guessed, slowly getting to her feet with both hands clasped over her head. She wasn't beaten yet. But it was important that they think so.

Governor Wilek Nereus strode out of the lift shaft, followed by four naval troopers in black helmets. "Prime Minister Captison," he said smoothly, "Senator Belden. Going for a little drive?" He pointed at the aircar, and two stormtroopers climbed aboard.

The trooper who'd confiscated her blaster took something away from Prime Minister Captison. Another seized his arms and locked on a pair of wristbinders. "You have just run out of good sense," Belden wheezed, red-faced and already cuffed. "This is a preposterous maneuver."

"Why so much effort to escape observation, if you're doing nothing wrong?"

Leia stepped in. "There is such a thing as a right to privacy, Governor."

"Not when it endangers an Imperial world's security, my dear princess."

One trooper emerged from the aircar. "Negative, sir."

"Take it apart. You. You, and you." He pointed at three other troopers. "Search them."

Leia stoically endured scanning and then a thorough physical frisking. The trooper took her empty wrist holster and pocket comlink, then cuffed her hands. Another walked swiftly from Belden to Governor Nereus, carrying the small gray box. "What have we here, Senator?"

Belden raised his bound hands and shook a finger at Governor Nereus. "My voice amplifier is a personal item. Give it back."

"Ah. Righteousness, maligned." Nereus smiled. "I've suspected for some time that you or your wife had possessed illegal devices, Belden . . . but since you're so certainly innocent of wrongdoing, I'm sure you won't mind our detaining you until my people ascertain the nature of this instrument."

Leia groaned. Belden's forehead shone wetly over scarlet cheeks, and his breathing had become shallow. He looked as if he might keel over. At his age, these were danger signals.

Yet this incident could set Bakura aflame. *Butter newt,* she re-

minded herself. Prime Minister Captison hurried to Belden's side,
reaching him just before one naval trooper. "Governor Nereus, you
have overstepped—"

"Guards," Nereus called, "these three are under arrest. Suspicion
of subversion will do. Put them in separate parts of the complex."

Leia stepped toward Nereus, deliberately drawing attention.
"This was a pleasure drive, Governor."

Nereus lowered his stare. "I made you a promise over dinner
that concerned subverting Imperial peoples, my dear. Believe me, I
keep my promises. When a speeder full of people goes silent on
sensor fields, it rouses curiosity." A stormtrooper stuck his blast
rifle in Belden's back. "No talking," Nereus ordered. "Interview
each one separately."

Leia had to prove to Captison that she'd meant every word about
sacrificing herself. She lowered her head and took a run at Governor Nereus. She caught him right at his generous midsection.

With a puff of surprise, he went down. Leia climbed onto his
chest, wedged his head between her knees, and pushed her
wristbinders onto his nose. "Get back, all of you, or we'll see
whose head is harder." Stormtroopers backed away, but she didn't
spot the one who stunned her from behind.

CHAPTER

14

HAN BRAKED HIS SPEEDER JUST LONG ENOUGH FOR LUKE TO VAULT OUT at the spaceport gate, then he spun it around, raising a black cloud of dust. He disliked leaving Luke out here alone, but Luke had insisted he'd be fine. The *Flurry*'s shuttle was due any minute, and meanwhile, Luke should have plenty of cover at the spaceport cantina. Probably reinforcements, too: Alliance pilots bunking in temporary scramble shelters. They'd sure outnumber the crew of a single Imperial shuttle grounded close to the cantina, just outside Pad 12. Anyway, Luke was Luke, lightsaber and all.

Speeding north, he spotted smoke near the Bakur complex. Several seconds later, a glimmering face appeared in midair over his head-up city map. "Alert, all residents. A curfew has just been imposed. Leave the streets and the air. Security forces will shoot to kill leaders and stun their followers to incarcerate them. The curfew will take effect immediately."

What was this? A second face appeared. "This follows the arrests of Prime Minister Captison and Senior Senator Orn Belden on suspicion of subversion, along with Rebel ringleader Leia Organa.

Imperial leadership demands full cooperation. Ssi-ruuvi invaders could attack at any moment. Any collaboration with outside forces will be punished severely and immediately."

Leia, under arrest? Han ignored the rest of the disembodied heads' messages about shortened business hours and prohibited districts. Obviously the Imperials were worried about causing an uproar.

But he had an uproar of his own to start. He accelerated to full throttle, muttering, "I'll get you for this, Nereus."

But how? He didn't even know where Leia was.

Although filtered through the speeder's intake, the air smelled smoky. He streaked to a landing on the Bakur complex's roof port, then took the nearest drop shaft down. As before, two storm-troopers stood guard outside his apartment. Their helmets swiveled as he strode inside past them. They probably didn't mean to let him back out.

Threepio stood inside, waiting with infinite mechanical patience. "General Solo," he exclaimed. "Thank goodness you've come. Senator Captison returned me here, but she took Artoo to her office. His restraining bolt—"

"Not now. Find Leia."

"But, General, the Ssi-ruuk are coming for Master Luke—and then attacking—immediately!"

"We know that. He'll be all right—" Han skidded to a halt halfway across the common room. "Wait, did you say, 'attacking'?"

"Within an hour. We must—"

"How do you—no. It'll keep. Where's Leia?"

The tall droid straightened. "She left us in Prime Minister Captison's office, translating—"

"I know where she left you." Han paced across the lounge pit, bouncing off repulsor fields all the way. "She and Captison have been arrested. Have you warned Luke about the attack?"

"I've been trying, sir—"

"I left him at the cantina next to Pad Twelve. Tap into the central computer. Find out where they've got Leia—now!"

"General Solo, Artoo is equipped for direct interfacing. I am not."

Han's cheeks heated. "Then stand there and punch the panels like a human. That's why they built you like one."

Threepio waddled to the main terminal. Han watched over his shoulder for a few moments, but Threepio worked too quickly to follow. Han checked the charge on each of his blasters and examined his vibroknife. He glanced out the window, then peered into Leia's bedroom. No sign of disarray. She hadn't been abducted from there.

"General Solo." Threepio's call rang out across the common room.

"What?" Han rushed the droid. "Did you find her? Did you find Luke?"

"I left Master Luke a message with cantina staff, but they were quite rude, and I have doubts as to whether it will be delivered. But Mistress Leia—"

"Which detention area? Where?"

"It appears that she was flown to a small installation in nearby mountains. Some kind of private retreat, I believe."

"Where is it from here? Show me."

Threepio brought up a map. Han noted the location—about twenty minutes northwest of town, in a hot speeder. "Okay. Focus close now." Threepio changed the display. A security fence surrounded one large **T**-shaped building with a long central hallway and a broad recreation area. Ten woodburning chimneys: Real nostalgia stuff, except for speeder parking near the northeast corner of the fenced grounds. "Yeah," Han said. "Hunting lodge and party house, I'll bet. Can you get me inside its security system?"

Threepio tapped more keys. "I believe I have it."

"Shut it down."

Threepio posed with one hand touching his chin. "If I may say so, General Solo, shutting it down will put the entire establishment on alert."

"All right. Shut down anything that'll let 'em see me coming from the air. And find out how many guards he's got out there."

"Ten." Threepio worked more keys. "It looks like rather minimal security. If I may be allowed to speculate, I would guess Governor Nereus is keeping most of his guards around himself for the duration of the crisis."

"Smells like another trap." On the other hand, maybe Nereus simply didn't want to bring the Alliance down his throat. Maybe he only wanted to space Captison, and he'd just as soon wash Leia off his hands. Off the planet, in fact.

Or maybe Threepio was correct, and he was just scared. Sometimes it took a coward to spot a coward.

He drew his blaster and stalked toward the door. "Let's go, Goldenrod. We've got to get past two stormtroopers."

"Sir! Take a minute to plan, this once! Minimize your risks!"

Han hesitated. "Minimize? How?"

"Instead of blasting your way out, you might attempt a deception of some sort."

"What did you have in mind?"

Threepio's metal fingertips pinged against his waist. "I do not have the imaginative bent. Your creative faculties might be brought to bear on—"

"All right, shut up. Let me think about this."

He counted his resources. Two blasters, a vibroknife, and Threepio.

Yeah. Threepio. Assuming they got past the door guards, there *was* one thing Han really could use: a master coder, to override palmprint, retinal, and voice-ID security circuits. They were as illegal as Lowickan Firegems, and impossible to make on most worlds, because most worlds' master circuits were encoded against droids. "You're absolutely right," he told Threepio. He hustled to the nearest repulsor couch, dug into its control circuit, and levered out its master chip. "Here," he said. "Wipe that, then imprint it with an Imperial override code off the mainframe."

"Sir!" Threepio screeched like a horrified soprano. "They'll melt us *all* down if I counterfeit . . ."

"Do it," Han growled. "This place doesn't have droids, so they won't have antidroid security. Should be a piece of cake."

Still, he stood tapping one foot until Threepio handed over the reimprinted chip. He fingered it. That smooth, six-centimeter strip of plastic and metal would get him into almost anything—including very deep soup, if they caught him with it. He slid it into his shirt pocket.

"General Solo, shouldn't we warn the populace about the imminent attack?"

"You say Senator Captison brought you back here?"

"Yes, but—"

"You told her, didn't you?"

"Yes, but—"

"Then she'll take care of it. Trust me." Han set his blaster for "stun" (only out of respect for Leia's wishes, he told himself). "Come on. Here's the next step."

Less than a minute later, he sent the glide door open and stood back. Threepio fled into the lobby, screeching gibberish, waving both arms and swaying violently back and forth. Mentally Han counted to three, giving the stormtroopers time to wonder if they ought to shoot him down or hit him with their Owner. Then, he crouched low and crept to the door. He could only see one trooper, but that Imperial's attention was riveted to the droid. Threepio spun in circles, babbling in yet another language. Han aimed carefully for a weak spot in the body armor, fired, then sprang to the other side of his doorway. The other trooper fired back at a sensible chest level, but the bolt zipped over Han's head. He dropped the other trooper.

"Okay, Threepio. Help, and hustle it." Han seized one guard by the boots and dragged him into the apartment. Threepio grabbed both troopers' blast rifles while Han maneuvered the second one just inside the door. "Hurry up." He relieved one trooper of a utility cable and tied the pair together. "It's a cinch we're not coming back here," he muttered. Bakurans or no Bakurans, he pried off Threepio's restraining bolt. "There. It's time to split up. I'll get Leia. You make sure Luke got that message."

"But, sir—how will I get there? Even on Alliance worlds, droids aren't allowed to pilot speeders unaccompanied."

Han thought that over. Should he drop Threepio at the *Falcon*? Ask Chewie to abandon ship and come get him? Too much time. Too dangerous.

Hah. "Okay, Sunshine, you're about to play hero." He untied one still-stunned trooper and yanked off his helmet. "Help me with the rest of this stuff."

Threepio shuffled closer. "Now, what—Oh, no. Sir, *please* don't order me to—"

"They won't shoot at you wearing this. I want you back at the *Falcon*."

Soon Threepio stood arrayed in full stormtrooper gear, and his bewildered voice filtered through a lumpy white helmet. "But, sir, where am I to find a speeder?"

"Follow me. And set that blast rifle just under 'stun.' You're gonna be shooting at *me*."

"One more thing?" Threepio pleaded. "Please let me have your comlink. I must contact Master Luke."

Han tossed it. Threepio caught it. Then Han nodded. "Go," he commanded.

He dashed up the hall toward the nearest lift shaft. A backward glance showed Threepio struggling to keep up, firing stun bursts as he came. Han gave the droid time to close up, then sprang into the lift shaft.

After he emerged on the rooftop, things moved faster. Smoke roiled up over one edge. The Bakurans were really riled about those arrests. Several harried-looking people, walking toward the nearest drop shaft, scattered as he leaped into an open speeder. He waved the code chip over its owner-recognition panel, and its engine came to life. Meanwhile, the clumsiest Imperial stormtrooper ever seen shuffled out of the lift shaft, firing his blast rifle at anything and missing everything. Bakurans dove and flattened.

Han waited until Threepio levered himself into another speeder, then he took off headed north, glancing back only once to make sure Threepio didn't crash on takeoff. Then he concentrated dead ahead, squinting while the wind whipped his hair.

The cantina adjoining Pad 12 smelled like smoke and old grease. Everything inside looked cheap, from stippled black floor to ceiling panels. Several of those flickered as if their power supplies were giving out. No automation, nothing even remotely modern. Tour hawkers would no doubt call it "quaint."

Luke glanced down at an open commnet hookup that lay at a central table, then toward a corner table that hunkered behind a tottering divider. A hefty service-crew type sat back there, hunched over a more private commnet terminal. Luke had spotted only these two terminals in the building, and the outdoor comm booth, while it had visual capabilities, wouldn't access an uplink to orbit.

So he'd rather use the semiprivate hookup than sit out in the open at a greasy orange tabletop, even if that meant waiting a few minutes. He was stuck until the shuttle to orbit arrived, anyway. He wanted to check in with Wedge, and find out how the defense web was holding—and why his shuttle was overdue. More of Nereus's maneuvering? He glanced out the cantina's west window. The *Falcon* was only a quarter kilometer away, but he couldn't see it for gantries and other parked ships.

Something scraped the grubby floor behind him—not one of Bakura's ubiquitous repulsor chairs, but a plain, cheap, metal-and-cushion affair. Luke turned around. The corner table stood empty.

Luke sat down facing out into the room, pecked in his clearance code, and requested contact with Wedge Antilles: vocal/keyboard interface, if possible.

Black letters appeared beneath the ones he'd punched in.

Capt. Antilles unavailable, sir. This is Lieutenant Riemann. May I help?

Luke recognized the name, a young artist of interplanetary stature who'd been forced by the Empire first into hiding and then into fighting back. "What's the status of the defensive net?" he asked softly. "Have you monitored anything unusual during the last few hours?" This would've been so much more convenient with Artoo to relay. He wondered if the droids had finished translating for Prime Minister Captison.

His answer appeared.

The net's still holding, everyone's in his assigned orbit. We've monitored a lot of chatter on the Flutie bands in the last hour, but those close-in gunships and that cruiser haven't shifted.

Something was afoot, even if the Ssi-ruuk weren't moving yet. He asked about that next shuttle up to orbit.

On its way down, sir. Should land in about 30 minutes.

Luke thanked the lieutenant and signed off.

What could he accomplish in thirty minutes—here? At the back of his mind he heard Ben Kenobi telling Master Yoda, "He will *learn* patience." Determined to prove Ben correct, he made himself calm down. Soon he'd be back aboard the *Flurry,* and once Han located Leia and picked up the droids, they'd join Chewbacca on the *Falcon.* He pushed away from the corner table.

As he was about to pass a booth clustered with strangers, his comlink squeaked in his breast pocket. He spun around and headed back to the corner, where he pulled out the comlink. "What is it, Han?" he asked quietly.

"Master Luke," Threepio's voice exclaimed, "I'm so glad that I reached you. Mistress Leia has been arrested. General Solo has gone to rescue her—"

Luke slumped behind the booth divider and kept his voice low. By interrupting and repeating hasty questions, he found out where Han had headed. "And sir," Threepio added, "the Ssi-ruuk mean to attack within less than an hour. You must hurry. Notify Chewbacca that I'm on my way to the *Falcon*, but I'm disguised as a stormtrooper. He mustn't shoot me."

Less than an hour? With his shuttle overdue? "Where's Artoo?"

"Senator Captison took him, sir. We'll have to return later for him. Sir, if you think I could be more useful here on the ground during the next few hours, instead of in space—"

"Head for the *Falcon*. We'll talk later." Luke stuffed the comlink into his pocket, then reached for the commnet board. Should he send Chewie with the *Falcon* up into the hills to help Han? No, sometimes Han moved faster than anyone expected. They might miss him on their way back.

But sometimes Han blundered into situations that were too complicated to handle with a blaster. Luke bit his lip. He had to help Han and Leia, but he had to alert the *Flurry*—to get aboard— before the aliens attacked. That was his responsibility, as commander.

Abruptly he straightened in the shabby seat. Command? Wait a minute!

He reopened the line to Lieutenant Riemann.

For a city under curfew, Salis D'aar looked good and lively to Han. Small groups dashed from building to building, avoiding platoons of stormtroopers. A double-podded security craft swooped toward him. He dove out of the traffic lane, into a canyon between tall buildings and groundcar ramps. His pursuer followed, firing erratically. Han braked, swooped into a narrow alley, then jinked an Immelmann up-and-over back out into the canyon. Security sped into the alley, passing beneath him. Han didn't see him fly back out.

As soon as he regained his bearings, he streaked out of the city and dropped low over the western river. Keeping low enough to catch fish, and spitting distance from the huge white cliff on his right—hoping to evade surveillance—he waited until the foothills looked tall enough to offer some cover. Then he zipped across the river and up a small tributary stream.

Once he located the right valley, it didn't take him long to spot his target, an ancient **T**-shaped log building with a dark green stone roof, huddled inside a rock wall. Planning two minutes ahead—Threepio would be proud—he unlatched safety restraints and loosed his feet on the control surfaces, getting ready to go overboard. Nobody fired as he approached. He decelerated low over dark treetops. The instant that he judged he'd shed enough speed, he passed the outwall. He jumped for a clump of low bushes. The speeder exploded with a resounding *boom* and a roil of flaming smoke against the grounds' opposite wall. By the time four naval troopers converged on it, Han was slinking through a temporarily unguarded door that hung from huge black hinges.

Only one door stood closed on the main hallway, with a skinny security droid sitting beside it like an extra doorpost. Obviously, the Imperials didn't bother to humor Bakuran antidroid sentiments here at their private installation. Han leveled his blaster at the droid's midsection and fired once. Blue lightning whipped around it and sparked off four rodlike appendages at the top. Han slunk closer. It spluttered and smoked.

Minimum security, he observed, waving his chip key at the lock panel. *A little too convenient.* If this was another trap . . .

They'd deal with it. Threepio ought to be back at the *Falcon* by now. He wished he had his comlink, but stray electronic signals would've brought down every trooper on the grounds.

"Leia?" he called softly into the darkened suite. "It's me."

Lights came on. "Hey," said her voice high above him. She stood perched on the seat of a repulsor chair directly over the doorway. "Good thing you spoke up. I almost flattened you." She landed the repulsor chair at the foot of an old-fashioned, nonrepulsor bed. He'd never seen a repulsor chair do that before. She must've somehow reprogrammed its circuitry.

"Have they hurt you?" He muscled the burned-out droid inside before he slid the door shut. If nobody saw it, maybe they wouldn't notice it was damaged.

"Not really. As I understand it, Governor Nereus meant to make me a present to the next emperor. He has insisted that I will enjoy his hospitality. Lunch was delicious. I've even got a fireplace." She swept one arm around the rustic bedroom. Rough, pale wood covered its walls and ceiling.

"So you're just the guest who's not allowed to leave?"

"I won't be here long. Let's get out of here." She balled her fists on her hips. "You, ah, found your way in. I don't suppose you've thought of a way of getting back out."

"Not yet."

She rolled her eyes. "Not again."

"Look, sweetheart," he said thoughtfully, sitting down on the edge of the bed. "I jimmied the black box of a speeder and crashed it into their wall. As far as they can tell, I bailed out a long way back. Let's lie low for an hour, let them check it out and look the grounds over—"

Heavy footsteps approached outside the hall door. Han sprang off the bed. "Can I get out up there?" He dashed toward the fireplace.

"Of course not. Too narrow."

Too late. The door whooshed. Han seized a metal rod inside the blackened chimney, jumped as high as he could, and pulled up his legs.

"Have you seen anything suspicious out this window?" asked a helmet-filtered voice. Han wedged himself between two scratchy black stone walls. He wanted to gain more altitude, but didn't dare attract attention by knocking down soot. Smoky residue made his nose and throat itch. At the thought of that guard droid sitting right inside the door, his hands got clammy.

"I haven't tried." Leia's voice defied the intruder.

"Right. Stand aside." He heard slow steps—two pair—and imagined a scanner team checking for life-forms. He wondered if stone blocked their equipment. He couldn't reach his blaster. At any second, they'd notice that droid. . . .

"All right, you've run your check. Now get out of here," Leia said. As if in tribute to the icy menace in her voice, the troopers' bootsteps beat a hasty retreat. After a few seconds, she called from beneath him, "They're gone."

"Stand back," he said. Cautiously he got a grip on both walls, then he straightened his legs and dropped. For an instant, he saw her standing with a horrified expression. Then carbon dumped like a downpour, obscuring his vision.

"Some rescue," her voice observed.

"Suppose they'll be back?" he asked, stepping sideways on the stone platform around the fireplace. Once the soot settled, he could see again. What a mess. The guard droid stood in a corner beside the door, artfully draped with articles of clothing to look like furniture. Leia'd moved fast, too.

"Yes," she answered. "I think lying low is out of the question." She ducked through a small door and reemerged carrying a large white towel. "Stand still. I'll do what I can."

One minute later, she dropped a black towel onto the floor. "You're clean enough for now."

Han had been staring at her repulsor chair. "Hey," he said, "I've got an idea."

CHAPTER

15

GAERIEL STOOD OUTSIDE EPPIE BELDEN'S DOOR AND STRAIGHTENED HER freshly pruned bundle of cloudberry spikes. Each fragrant blossom could have produced a succulent fruit, but too many spikes on a vine made the fruit tiny and sour. The symbolism—some blossoms, some lives cut off to allow a few to grow stronger—gave her small comfort. Would Eppie understand that her husband for over a century had died in Governor Nereus's custody? Or would he return again and again in her perception, like Roviden?

Eppie's caregiver opened the door. "Good morning, Clis."

"Hello, Gaeriel." Clis stepped aside with a queer expression on her round face. "Come in. Quickly."

"Something wrong?" Gaeriel walked past Clis toward Eppie's favorite wing chair. No one sat in it. "Where is she?" Gaeriel asked, alarmed.

"In the study."

"The study?"

"See for yourself."

Gaeriel strode through the dining area to Orn Belden's office. A work screen silhouetted a small, hunched figure. "Eppie?" Gaeri cried.

The figure turned around. Eppie Belden's wrinkled face glowed with the intensity of a small bird's. "You know anyone else who's likely to be here?"

"She's been like that all morning," murmured Clis. "Go on in. She's been asking for you."

"And for that young man." Eppie paddled her repulsor chair away from the work screen. "Who was he? Where did he come from?"

Stunned almost beyond the ability to articulate, Gaeri sat down on top of a packing crate. There weren't any other chairs in the office. "He's a . . . Rebel, but a . . . dangerous one. A Jedi. One of *them*."

"Oh, ho." Eppie's feet swung under her chair. "Our teachers have taught us a lot of wisdom down the years, but also a load of guff." She pointed a bony finger. "You should judge that Jedi by what he does, not by rumors or morality tales. Tell him to come back and see me again, in any case." Her head turned. "Go make a nice arrangement out of Gaeri's flowers, Clis."

The portly caregiver left the door. Eppie slapped a control that shut it.

"Eppie, you're . . . you're well!"

"You're here to tell me about Orn, aren't you?" The wall of her preoccupation thinned, and Gaeri glimpsed her fresh grief. Full realization hadn't set in. Eppie was working while she could, the better to grieve later. "Thank you anyway, love. I heard. No one else thought to notify me, but I've been plugged in all morning."

"But—"

"I haven't watched the news for years, so you assumed I hadn't heard? Be careful of your assumptions, Gaeriel."

"But he . . . Orn . . ."

Eppie's shoulders slumped, transforming her into a wizened old woman. "I'll miss him, Gaeri. Bakura will miss him. Let the Imperials call it a cerebral hemorrhage, but I know he died for Bakura, as I should've."

"Should've?"

"Confession is good for the soul, child. But I'm not ready to tell you everything. Some of it's not for young Imperial ears." She spun her repulsor chair and touched a work station control. A screen full of symbols translated itself into a news media picture. "Fires, and strikes, and running street battles in Salis D'aar. I wish I were eighty again."

"Eppie, what did you do?"

"Only what that young man—excuse me, that terribly dangerous young Jedi—showed me to do. You're a lot of good things, Gaeri, but reconsider your intolerance."

Gaeriel gaped. "Then something *was* done to you?"

"I won't burden you with my past. Let's get on with the future."

"Your past may be my future."

Eppie's keen blue eyes blinked at her. "I hope so. And I hope not."

Gaeri reached out a hand. "You're going to wear yourself out. Shouldn't you lie down for a bit?"

Eppie shook her head. "I've missed years. Can't waste minutes now. Bakura's rising. I want to be in on it."

Gaeriel steadied her hands against a tremor. "Rising?"

"Against Nereus, of course."

"But we *need* Governor Nereus and his forces. We're going to be invaded any minute. The Alliance talks about freedom, but Bakura was . . . was crippled by chaos. The Empire saved us from tragedy."

"We will never be free from tragedy, Gaeriel. Each of us must be free to pursue her own tragedy."

Gaeri crossed her ankles and stared. How could this lucid philosopher be the mind-sick woman she'd helped nurse since before she went off to Center?

"Even after a defeat," Eppie murmured, "it's possible to have a full and happy life. I wish Orn and I had realized . . .

"Anyway," she exclaimed, drawing herself up, "there's work to be done. Are you for me or against me?"

"What—what are you doing at that work station, Eppie?"

"Are you going to turn me in? Look at this!" She swiveled back around and tapped controls beneath the screen. One key brought up an image of flames rising near the Bakur complex. Another showed stormtroopers chasing down armed civilians. Automation, claimed another screen, had gone haywire at the repulsorlift coil production plant. "Salis D'aar is furious. Orn's dead, your uncle arrested, the Rebel princess in custody. What are you going to do about it?"

"If we fight each other now, the Ssi-ruuk will have us piece-meal!"

"That's why it can't be done wrong. Those people on the streets are only the distraction. You and I, and a few others on the inside, will run the real rebellion. We could accomplish plenty before the aliens actually attacked."

"They're attacking in less than an hour. I've warned Governor Nereus. There's no time."

"No one ever told you that I used to be a circuitry guerrilla, did they?"

Gaeri gaped at the thought. How could she even consider collaborating with Eppie and the Rebels? The Alliance was impractical. Naively idealistic.

Her own tragedy. If fate guaranteed her life an ending, what tragedy did she choose?

A triumphant one. Gingerly she handled the fragile new thought. She couldn't deliver Eppie Belden to Wilek Nereus. *And there's your answer,* she told herself. There wasn't a single Imperial officer, bureaucrat, or professor that she'd ever admired the way she loved Eppie.

Then this was her decision. She loved Bakura, not the Empire. "I'm with you," she said softly.

Eppie seized her hand and squeezed it. "I knew you had more sense than you were letting on. It's a hard decision, girl, and it'll cost you . . . but congratulations. Now let's see what else we can do at that repulsorlift coil plant."

"*You* sent the automation haywire?"

Eppie's smile smoothed half of her wrinkles and deepened the rest of them. "That plant's worth all the rest of Bakura to the Imperials. If production shuts down, even during wartime, they'll send every trooper left in Salis D'aar to restore order. That leaves the Bakur complex for me—and a few friends."

Gaeri's blood tingled. "I can help you better from my office. I've got one of the Rebels' droids stashed away there."

"Wait." Eppie rummaged in a drawer and drew out a tiny bit of metal and plastic. "You know about that allegedly secure stormtrooper channel?"

Gaeri nodded.

"Orn wanted you to have this a long time ago, but he couldn't trust you. Use it now. It'll let you give the stormtroopers a few commands before they come for you."

Gaeri closed her hand around it.

"Well, go! Run!" Eppie slapped her shoulder.

Gaeri flew her aircar back to the complex, dodging security patrols and steering between trouble spots and firefighting crews. The Rebels' droid, Artoo Detoo, stood right where she'd left it, beside her desk, spinning its dome and beeping unintelligibly. Gaeri groaned. "You must be trying to tell me something. But I can't understand any of that. Aari?"

"Here," exclaimed her aide.

"Dump all the information you can get from Nereus's office net, even if it means compromising our security. Everything's about to break apart."

"Will do." To Gaeri's amusement, the droid rolled to a terminal and plugged in, too. Evidently it had a good deal of perception and volition programmed into it.

"Here, Senator." Aari had delivered a screenful. Nereus had ordered stormtroopers across the city to quell three demonstrations, and sent his top intelligence man to the coil production plant in Belden's district. Intell officers shot first and interrogated survivors.

Gaeri clenched a fist. She must try to free Uncle Yeorg, and that Rebel princess as well. But first, no Captison had ever dallied when turmoil wrenched Bakura. She handed Aari the chip. "Install that. It'll give us the stormtrooper frequency."

Aari raised one black eyebrow. Artoo Detoo beeped and trilled. Even to Gaeri, it sounded excited.

Her own hands shook. They'd catch any unauthorized user online and change all security codes within minutes, but this would be her memorial to a brave old man.

"You've got it," Aari announced a moment later from her adjoining desk. Working her main bank, Gaeriel accessed factory data for the namana juice extraction plant fifteen kilometers down the seacoast—a safely irrelevant, nonmilitary distraction—and then she dumped it onto the troopers' information banks, replacing their data for repulsorlift coil production. When they tried to move in on Belden's factory, they would possess all the wrong information. They'd be totally lost, and that might give Belden's people enough time to . . . well, she wasn't sure what Eppie was up to, and she didn't want to know.

But she did call the repulsorlift plant supervisor on a conventional frequency. She warned him he had troopers on the way—and that Bakura's resistance had begun. It might not be wildly revolutionary action, but it would confuse the Empire for a few minutes longer.

"All right, Aari. Pull the chip."

Aari dove for her tool kit and removed the illicit Imperial chip. "I'd better melt this."

"Right." Now that she could think of trying to free Uncle Yeorg, she realized that she knew only one person who could possibly help. She cleared her terminal, then bent close to the droid. She felt ludicrous talking to it. "Artoo Detoo, can you help me locate Commander Skywalker?"

Chewbacca stalked slowly around the *Falcon*, on watch. She was ready to take off, all systems operational—for the moment—and looking good from the outside, which was to say that she hunkered close to the rough-glass white surface, so battered and streaked that a casual observer would doubt that she'd ever lift again. He eyed each ship and gantry, every parked landspeeder and building he could see. There was no sign of Luke.

Finally the whine of an open-top speeder approached. Chewie slipped around the hull and took up a position from which he could fire without being seen. Seconds later, the speeder landed within range. A stormtrooper climbed out clumsily.

That looked like trouble. The trooper didn't challenge him, but shuffled forward with his arms hanging oddly. Either he couldn't call out, or he chose not to.

Chewie had just gotten the *Falcon* lift ready. He wasn't taking chances on some high-handed Imperial slapping a lock on her hatch. He pulled his blaster, set it for "stun," and fired off a shot.

The stormtrooper came on, tottering. Chewie fired again. This time, the trooper fell. Tempted to let the intruder lie, he decided the armor might be useful. He dragged the surprisingly heavy body up the *Falcon*'s ramp. The main hatch slid down into position with a hiss. Crouching, he gripped one side of the white helmet with each massive paw and lifted it off.

A golden head gleamed inside, repeating in a tinny, high-speed voice, "uke! Master . . . uke! Master . . ."

Threepio!

Now he'd have to run all those diagnostics again. Disgusted, Chewie kept peeling off armor.

Luke glanced one last time at the cantina's cracked chrono. In five minutes, if his shuttle hadn't arrived, he'd join Chewie on the *Falcon*.

He eyed a slab of unevenly cooked, greasy, mysterious meat. "I guess I'll have one of those, with whatever you can put on it," he said. "To go." He would eat with Chewie. . . . "Oh. You'd better make it three." The sooty orange countertop—unoccupied—suggested Pad 12's nearest cantina was often empty this close to noon. Isolated clusters of Bakurans sat at scattered tables, murmuring and glancing around. "Arrest," he'd heard from one, and "dead" from another. "Belden" and "Captison" buzzed from table to table. He'd also heard "Jedi."

The sooner he left, the better.

Quick footsteps approached along the wall outside. Alarmed, he reached out through the Force, so he felt Gaeriel before the main door swung open. His senses came alive, focusing tightly on her presence. She hurried through, followed by an Artoo unit . . . *his*, he realized, remembering Threepio's message. Artoo beeped and whistled incoherently, and Gaeriel's sense buzzed with shocked excitement. She hurried over, skirt whisking the dirty floor. Luke pushed away from the orange countertop. "What's going on? How did you find me?"

"Your droid brought me to the commnet terminal you'd used most recently. Haven't you heard? They're about to attack. Uncle Yeorg's been arrested." Her eyes stayed wide. "Your princess, too."

"Yes, I've heard. I'm trying to get to my carrier—"

Artoo's insistent warbles rocked the little droid from side to side. "Artoo, wait. I'm not getting any of that." Closing out Gaeriel for the moment, he reached into the distance for his sister's feelings. Farther, farther . . .

"There's a curfew in effect," insisted Gaeriel, "and—" A server strolled past, obviously listening. She continued more softly, "Orn Belden keeled over when they tried to lock him up, and died half an hour later. The city's in turmoil."

"Poor old Belden," he murmured. In that instant, he found Leia. Very busy, very excited. Han had obviously found her.

Artoo pushed closer to him, extended a probe . . . and shocked his left calf, still beeping. "Artoo!" he exclaimed.

Gaeri looked both ways and whispered, "This is your moment, Luke. Bakura's with you."

He glanced up at her, a new hope striking wildfire in his imagination. "Why were they arrested?"

"Governor Nereus found a DB projector," said Gaeriel. "Sedition carries the death penalty, Luke. The city's going crazy. You've got to get Princess Leia and Uncle Yeorg free." She glanced around as if finally noticing her surroundings. "But what are you doing here alone? Didn't I warn you?"

"Yes. I didn't want to endanger anybody. I can protect myself, but you'd better not stay more than a few minutes." He glanced around, half-expecting stormtrooper helmets at the windows. "Let's have Artoo try to find your uncle. Can you interface the governmental mainframe from a public commnet?"

"I should be able to."

Luke grabbed a bread knife off the nearest table. After two seconds of prying, Artoo's restraining bolt popped free.

Gaeriel's wide eyes looked scandalized. Trying to pacify her, he said, "Artoo, put Gaeriel on your recognize-and-obey program. And her friend Eppie Belden," he added on impulse. "Okay?" Artoo tweeted up the scale, approving. "Good. Now see if you can find Prime Minister Captison."

Artoo rolled toward the corner table.

"Not much good without translators, are they?" Gaeriel asked.

Luke followed Artoo. "I understood some of that. He's an astromech droid—a pilot's aide, I guess you'd call him—but you'd be surprised what he can handle groundside." Luke glanced at the kitchen doors. The cooks were taking an awfully long time. "Han's already gone looking for Leia," he said.

"Luke . . ." Gaeriel clasped his arm just above the elbow. Warmth and determination flowed through that touch. "Come back when it's over. Talk to me. There's no time now, but we've got to—"

Luke tugged free. A vague sense of aggression arose in the kitchens. Almost instantly, it resolved into three distinctly alien presences and one that mystified him—human, but alien-scented. He covered his lightsaber with his right hand. What was that about not endangering other people?

And hadn't he wished Gaeriel needed rescuing? He drew his blaster left-handed and flipped the grip toward her. "Can you shoot?" he murmured. "There are Ssi-ruuk in the building. I'm sorry I can't help your uncle now. Take it," he urged. She closed her hand around it uncertainly. "Have Artoo get word to the *Flurry,* up in orbit, and tell them what's happening. Then find your uncle. Get out of here. Now."

Fear throbbed out of her. "I'm not hiding behind Jedi abilities. I want to help the Rebellion."

Exasperated, he stretched out a hand and steadied himself to use the Force on her. "No one else has any trouble letting me—"

The front and side doors blew open simultaneously. The muzzle of a heavy blaster rifle appeared through each one. Then a white-armored stormtrooper.

This time, Luke guessed they weren't on his side. He seized Gaeriel's shoulders and swept her behind him. The handful of Bakuran customers dove under tables.

Three Ssi-ruuk pushed through the kitchen door, large smooth-scaled creatures with long, muscular tails to balance massive upper bodies. Two of different sizes were glossy brown, one intense blue. The heads looked birdlike, with huge toothy beaks and all-black eyes. Each wore a shoulder bag slung across its body under one forelimb. They towered over the frightened service staff. Artoo froze in position beside the corner table.

Luke had to narrow his perception to keep Gaeriel's revulsion from pulling him under. Cautiously, he stretched toward the aliens. Their feelings leaked into the Force, strengthening the dark side. He'd felt less hostility in Jabba the Hutt's ravenous Rancor.

He held his lightsaber down at his side. "What do you want?" he asked, sweeping the Force against that hostility, probing for weaknesses.

A human in striped robes stepped around the counter after the aliens. "Fortunate one!" he hailed Luke, squinting. "You are the Jedi, Skywalker. I will translate for you."

Luke recognized Dev Sibwarra from the hologram recording. He focused deep into the Force, drawing on all Yoda had taught him. He was at peace. He *was* peace. "I am Skywalker," he said. "How did you get down here?"

"Quietly. Subtly." The young man whistled to the aliens, then flattened long brown hands in front of his chest. The left hand moved stiffly. "Governor Nereus dispatched a shuttle to us, then ordered the orbital net to allow it through on official business . . . which is to receive you. You are to be the guest of Admiral Ivpikkis, as you begin a new kind of life you have only dreamed of before. Give my companions your weapon, and come gladly with me."

In person Dev Sibwarra looked younger, perhaps fifteen. Luke reached out with the Force—

And recognized him a second time. This boy had also sent the dream warning. Luke felt his strength in the Force, twisted and bent backward. He'd been brainwashed or hypnotized, altered so deeply that his thoughts were no longer his own. Luke couldn't hate him. He must try not to kill him in self-defense, either, because the boy was young enough to apprentice—if Luke could win him and heal him.

"Thank you for your invitation," Luke said quietly. "I would rather stay here. Ask your masters to sit down. We will talk."

"They do not sit, my friend. We would be honored to accept your companion too, as our guest. But you must hurry." Gaeri's cheeks whitened as the blue Ssi-ruu stomped forward, but she stood her ground. It reached a clawed forelimb toward her shoulder. Something black slithered out of its nostrils. She gasped and brought up Luke's blaster.

"Back," Luke ordered. The alien's head turned. A deep black eye focused in his direction, and the nose-tongues flicked toward him. He channeled Force energy into his words. "Get away from her." The eye seemed to swirl like a dark storm, beckoning for attention, sucking at his will. Unquestionably this one, or another like him, kept Dev Sibwarra leashed.

Dev whistled at the blue alien, sounding surprisingly like Artoo. The big blue Ssi-ruu's forelimb dropped from Gaeri's shoulder. He clicked and whistled in a deeper, more flutelike voice than Dev's, with greater range and a more resonant tone. "He says that a female's companionship will doubtless bring you comfort," Dev translated, "and I sense that your feelings are strong for her. Please ask her to cooperate. We must hurry."

Artoo rocked back and forth, chirping electronic fury. Luke wondered what he was telling the Ssi-ruuk. Two stormtroopers eased forward, blocking Artoo's path to the door.

Luke called to the troopers, "You have no business with this woman. It's me they want. Let her leave."

"The Fluties want her," answered a trooper's filtered voice. "This time, the Fluties get what they want."

Luke ignited his lightsaber and got a solid, two-handed fighting grip. "Not necessarily."

Dev backed away. "Stun them!" he cried to the stormtroopers.

Four blast rifles leveled at him, black holes framed by white helmets. Luke crouched and turned his body sideways, presenting a smaller target. "Get *down!*" Gaeri dropped prone. She hadn't used his blaster. Just as well: From all signs, she'd lose a firefight. Apparently she knew it, too. This wasn't her element.

Standing ninety degrees apart, the troopers opened fire. Luke stretched deeper into the Force, willingly dependent on the energy that surrounded him. He felt his body whirl and his saber leap, and vaguely sensed energy bolts splashing on gritty cantina walls. He eased closer, dodging tables, toward a point between his attackers. Suddenly the blasts stopped coming, as the Imperials realized they were sighting past Luke at each other.

He stretched out with the Force, touched two hostile minds, and leaped.

Blue-white stun bolts crackled through the air beneath him. Troopers dropped on both sides. Luke spun back toward the aliens. He felt slow, still slightly sluggish from the Emperor's attack. He coughed, then caught his breath. "Artoo," he shouted, "get her out of here. Get help."

Artoo rolled toward Gaeriel. She lurched up to her hands and knees and then edged toward the front door.

Dev Sibwarra spread his hands. "Friend Skywalker, you rob her of incomparable joy."

"She prefers her freedom."

"Freedom?" Dev arched his eyebrows. "We offer you freedom from hunger." He waved a hand over a stack of abandoned plates, raising a cloud of flying insects. "From disease, from—" Luke felt a whiskery swirl of the Force brush his body. "Ah," Dev exclaimed, and his voice sounded genuinely friendly. "Is it true that your entchment has already begun?"

Luke stepped backward. "What?"

"Your hand. The right one."

Luke glanced down. Repaired back at Endor, the prosthetic hand looked entirely lifelike again. "This was not my choice."

"Is it not better than the biological hand? Stronger, less apt to pain? See how you hope to rob so many humans of real life. Real happiness." Dev sidled toward the wall. The Ssi-ruuk had pulled off their shoulder bags. Each held a paddlelike object that had hung outside. What had appeared to be handles projected forward, while the aliens grasped rim-guarded grips.

Luke stepped sideways. "Dev, warn them I can't stun them with a lightsaber. I'll have to kill them if they come at me."

"You mustn't!" Dev cried. "If they die here, away from a consecrated world, it is eternal tragedy. They certainly will not kill you if they defeat you. Swear that you won't kill them."

"No," Luke insisted. "Warn them."

Dev whistled frantically.

The aliens sighted on him. Gaeri had crawled closer to the door, but not close enough. They'd get her unless he attacked first.

Then it was time to use the Force for defense. Hers.

CHAPTER

16

ONE ALIEN RAISED A PADDLE. A THIN SILVER BEAM SHOT OUT OF ITS narrow point. Confidently Luke stepped toward the beam and swung his saber into it.

It didn't deflect. It only bent slightly. Before he could react, the beam swept through him. It left his midsection tingling. Relieved that it didn't do worse, he adjusted his grip on the lightsaber. The second alien moved out from behind the first and added his beam, aiming low, shooting for his legs. The first shot hadn't injured him noticeably, but a second might. He pivoted aside, setting one brown Ssi-ruu in front of the other. One beam snapped off. The other tracked him, closing.

Big Blue stepped to one side and projected a beam down the room's central aisle, halving Luke's space.

"No!" Gaeri raised up onto her elbows and shot at the blue alien. Her blaster bolt missed. The alien trained its beamer at her. Silver light illumined the hollow of her throat. She gave a little cry, crumpled, and lay still.

Luke charged the small, **V**-crested brown and swung his saber at its mysterious weapon. The Ssi-ruu lost a foreclaw with his paddle-beamer. Fluting wildly, he spun away from Luke.

"Don't!" Dev wrung his hands. "Don't harm them!"

"What has he done to Gaeriel?"

"She's not harmed. She'll recover."

But she wasn't moving. Unless Luke killed or disarmed them all, they'd abduct her. The larger brown stomped toward him, muscular legs pumping like pistons. Even if he destroyed its weapon, it could physically crush him or Gaeri. Luke flung the saber in a long spinning arc. The big brown Ssi-ruu fell headless as the saber spun back into Luke's hand. "Stop!" Weeping, Dev dashed toward the fallen alien.

Big Blue projected his beam through Luke again . . . or, rather, where Luke had been. Luke somersaulted over the beam, thrust out a hand, and tried to wrest the weapon away.

That pulled the Ssi-ruu's forelimb toward him. The beam focused at the top of Luke's right leg.

It collapsed, nerveless. Staggering, Luke tried to jump backward. He struggled to balance, to regain full control of the Force. The weapon scrambled nerve centers, then. Gaeriel was probably conscious. "Artoo, drag her out of here!" he cried.

As the little droid rolled toward her, both aliens pressed their advantage. They swept forward, backing him between beams against an upturned table. He caught a whiff of their weird acrid odor.

He leaped left-legged almost into one alien's arms and swept up the saber. As he did, he relaxed deep into the Force and spun without thought. The hum of his saber didn't change pitch as it sliced through the blue giant's weapon. Big Blue dropped both halves and backed away, whistling energetically.

One more weapon down. Artoo reached Gaeri, seized her by the leather waistband of her belt, and dragged her toward the front door. Luke hopped crookedly onto the nearest orange tabletop. His numb right leg twisted as his full weight landed on it. *That'll probably hurt, later.* He had to use the Force to stay upright.

Artoo's shrill whistle spun Luke around. Dev aimed an Imperial blaster upward at his body, a classic stun shot.

Luke loosened one hand from his saber and Force-yanked the blaster from Dev's hand. It sailed to him with slow grace. Easily he spun and sliced. Two halves of the weapon clattered onto the table. *Now*, urged his inner sense. He reached deep into the Force and felt for the hypnotic control that twisted Dev Sibwarra to the aliens' will. The shadow of something enormous darkened most of Dev's memories.

The boy had tremendous strength in the Force, though. Luke wrapped his will around the dark, roiling blockage and blasted it with Light.

Dev tottered backward against another table. In an instant, his mind had flooded with horrific recollections. His anger coalesced, small and stunted but as fierce as a P'w'eck invasion army. Disoriented, he blinked. The monstrous Skywalker had suddenly become fellow human. He didn't feel depressed, just furious. He couldn't need renewal . . . unless . . .

He stared up at Skywalker, who still stood on the tabletop, and caught a glint of keen eyes and the grim set of his chin.

Dev stroked his throbbing, clumsy left hand, remembering how he'd injured it. Firwirrung! His master had bound him with tender loyalty over years of abusive manipulation. Dev opened his eyes wide to the world, forsaking his squint. He'd never felt such agony or regret, yet so glad to be human. Despite everything they had done . . . had done . . . he was battered but whole.

"Are you all right?" whistled Bluescale.

A shiver shook him. He remembered everything now, including the speech habits he'd picked up during his imprisonment. "I'm all right. Are you, Elder?"

"Tell the Jedi to hurry along with us. Promise anything."

Realization flashed through him: The Ssi-ruuk meant to reduce humankind to breeding animals and energy sources. They would lie, kill, torture, and maim to achieve domination. They deserved nothing but hatred.

Luke Skywalker called down from the tabletop, "Hate is the dark side. Don't give in to it."

Had the Jedi plunged him through depression into total release?

"What?" asked Master Firwirrung. "What is he saying to you?"

Confused, Dev answered automatically. "He apologized for killing one of our kind, Master."

"Tell him to precede us outside. He must hurry."

Dev looked back up. In human speech, he said, "They want you to—"

A piercing siren echoed through the cantina. Abruptly Dev remembered the most terrible moment of his childhood, a civil defense scramble alarm. Invasion under way.

He snapped back to the present and stared at his masters, stricken. Had Admiral Ivpikkis attacked the orbiting ships after all? He'd promised that the Ssi-ruuk would withdraw if Skywalker came with them. One more link in their twisted chain of lies!

Luke glanced out the far window, thoughts roiling. The Ssi-ruuk had probably hit that big saucer-shaped orbital station. That would've been his first strike, if he were invading. Beyond the fence surrounding Pad 12, the gantries hadn't rolled away, so he still couldn't see the *Millennium Falcon*. Chewie probably waited on board. Han would be trying to spring Leia from custody (or by now, Leia might be trying to free Han).

Artoo rolled back in without Gaeriel. He hoped Artoo had left her somewhere safe. And how badly had he wrenched his numbed leg?

Dev's confusion also worried him. This young potential apprentice carried deep scars on his psyche. Yet he'd proved his strength.

His sufferings under the darkness might make him more loyal to the light. Luke glanced down at Dev again.

Abruptly the room tilted. He flailed and fell.

Caught up in his own thoughts, Dev almost missed the swift sweep of Bluescale's tail. Struck on the head, the Jedi collapsed. His lightsaber flew loose, sliced through the table, and into black flooring. There it hung diagonally for an instant. Then the pommel dropped. The green blade sliced back up and lay hiss-humming.

He stood motionless, maintaining the masquerade of obedience, but his mind shrieked, *Skywalker! Can you hear me?*

Bluescale stalked forward, pointing his beamer at Skywalker's upper spinal cord. Dev forced himself to hurry close and simper, "Well done, Masters. What can I do? Is he stunned?"

"Mild concussion, I think," whistled Bluescale. "The human skull is surprisingly fragile. You may carry him. He seems subdued."

"Oh, thank you." Dev guessed at the right amount of enthusiasm to pump into his voice. He knelt and pulled Skywalker's arms over his shoulder. *Skywalker,* he projected again, *are you all right?*

The Jedi did not answer. The buzz of his thoughts had shut off. He must be truly unconscious, then. The aliens had won . . . for the moment. Dev struggled to his feet. His anger boiled every time he remembered another abuse. They popped to the surface of his memory like foul bubbles. He couldn't let the Ssi-ruuk win—and not just for the sake of the galaxy. They owed him a life. A personality. A soul.

"Good," said Bluescale. "Now help Firwirrung."

Staggering already, Dev let the smaller alien lean on his shoulder. Firwirrung wobbled forward, covering his wounded forelimb with the intact foreclaw. The double weight sent new spasms down Dev's weakened back. He bit his tongue. He was supposed to be brainwashed. The Ssi-ruuk saw humankind, like P'w'ecks, as livestock . . . experimental animals . . . soulless.

Bluescale bent and seized the lightsaber. *What about the female?* Dev guessed Bluescale wouldn't want to carry her. Skywalker's resistance had saved her, at least. With only Dev able to carry, the Ssi-ruuk wouldn't go looking for her. They must even leave their beheaded comrade behind.

Bluescale led toward the kitchen doors, letting them swing back and bump Dev. He lost his balance and almost dropped his burden against a hot cooking surface. The ends of Skywalker's hair shriveled over its intense heat. By the time Dev had recovered his balance, the hissing green blade had vanished. Bluescale dropped the silent saber handgrip into his shoulder pouch, clipped the pouch around his body again, and proceeded between kitchen machines with his beamer drawn. Firwirrung stumbled against Dev. Dev racked his memory for an appropriate reaction. "Are you in pain, Master?" he asked softly.

The alien grunted.

Bluescale held the rear door for Firwirrung. Outside under a pall of spaceport dust stood the Imperial shuttle. Those now-stunned stormtroopers had flown it to the *Shriwirr,* then ferried the party planetside. The sirens had taken effect; Pad 12 and the others clustered around this cantina looked almost deserted. Two P'w'eck guards still stood beside the shuttle, hidden from observers by its drooping wings.

"Help Dev secure the prisoner," Bluescale whistled. Dev limped up the ramp. The Jedi's cylindrical droid attempted to roll up after him, railing at them in Ssi-ruuvi. Two P'w'ecks shoved it over the ramp's edge. It landed with a crash and a final impotent threat. Dev pulled Skywalker into a rear seat, insisting to himself that he had not given up hope. The P'w'ecks snapped wristbinders onto the Jedi and then drew a flight harness around him. Unwatched for the moment, Dev checked again through the Force for life presence. Even unconscious, Skywalker's mind seemed warmer, brighter, louder than other humans'.

What to do? If the Ssi-ruuk worked their will on Skywalker, humankind was doomed.

Dev clenched his hands. That shot a paroxysm of pain up his left forearm. Was he strong enough to strangle the Jedi, while Firwir-rung and Bluescale tried to fly the human shuttle?

Perhaps he could, but he recoiled. That would be a Ssi-ruuvi trick. Skywalker was all Dev might have wished to be, if his mother had survived to apprentice him to a master. He couldn't kill Skywalker—except at the last moment, to keep the Ssi-ruuk from absorbing him.

If that happened, Dev wouldn't have long to grieve for Skywalker. The Ssi-ruuk would kill him instantly.

Yet humankind would live free if he and Skywalker died. Agonizing, he buckled into his own seat.

"How's it going up there?" Leia called softly.

"Almost through." Han perched on her reprogrammed repulsor chair directly over the bed. Delicately holding his vibroknife in one hand, he cut a broad oval in the wooden ceiling panel. A pale stream of sweet-smelling sawdust fell glittering onto the white bedcover. "There!" he exclaimed. He struck the ellipse with the palms of both hands, and it popped upward, showering him with more dust.

"You're sure you can fit?" she asked.

The chair rose. His head and shoulders vanished, then the rest of him. A moment later, his head and arms reappeared. "Looks good up here," he said. "Stand back." He touched the chair's controls.

It crashed onto the bed. Leia gripped the blaster she'd stuck into her belt and waited for a guard to open the hall door, but none did. She climbed onto the bed, muscled the chair upright again, then switched it on. She rose in stately grace toward the hole Han had cut, then seized his arms and let him pull her through. They left the chair hovering.

A crawl space crossed the building from end to end, its low sloping roof tapering to both sides. Dim daylight cast hazy rays in a large dusty room at one end. "Vents at each side," Han murmured. "Speeders are parked outside, around the corner to the right." He pointed toward the light. "Walk softly. They'll hear you."

"No. Seriously?" she asked, loading her voice with sarcasm. She led forward on hands and knees, careful to set her weight silently on beams and joists. This attic felt more ancient than any human habitation she'd ever been in. She made the right turn around a thick wooden pillar, then crawled up to the vent. "Knife?" she whispered over her shoulder.

Han drew the vibroknife and sliced cautiously through the large vent's snap bolts. "You take that end," he directed. "Pull it toward you."

She pried inward with her fingernails until it jutted out far enough to grip, then together they pulled it free and set it silently in the dust beside a desiccated pile of insectoid exoskeletons. Han crouched, peering out the new hole, almost invisible in his sooty camouflage. She crouched closer.

Several speeders sat halfway between the lodge and the outwall, with five troopers lounging around them. She eased sideways so she could see and point a blaster out the hole at the same time. He did the same. "Ready?" she asked.

"Now," he whispered. She squeezed her trigger. Got one. Got two. Another fell. The fourth and fifth dove behind a grounded speeder.

"Here goes nothin'." Han plunged through. Blaster bolts whined. Leia spotted the trooper shooting at Han and dropped him. The other kept his head down. Han jumped up and ran for the near speeder. A flash of light clipped his left foot.

She leaped, rolled to break her fall, and then sprang to one side. Another blaster bolt scorched the ground where she'd landed. She whirled around and shot back, but the trooper ducked.

The roar of a speeder caught her attention. She zigzagged toward it and scrambled on board, then grabbed an acceleration rail. Something stank like burnt boot leather. Instantly, Han wrenched the throttle and lifters. They soared over the compound's walls.

"Did they get you?" she shouted over wind noise as moody green forest passed underneath. The view south stretched over foothills, city, and emerald plains toward a hint of blue ocean. Smoke rose from several sources midcity.

"Don't think it burned through the sole," he answered tightly. She eyed his sooty, wind-whipped face and recognized pain.

She could do nothing till they reached the *Falcon*. He was obviously functioning. "Life with you's never dull." She stroked his scratchy chin.

He managed a smile. "Couldn't have that," he called. The wind blew his words back at the forest.

Leia glanced away. The speeder's roar seemed to change pitch. No, it was another one. "Han—"

"We've got company," Han interrupted. "Over there."

"There's one on my side, too—no, three of them!"

They were surrounded. "So it *was* a trap." Han grimaced. "They can shoot us down and get rid of us for good."

"Escaping arrest," Leia agreed aloud.

"Hang on!" Han spun the speeder in a tight arc back up into the foothills. Two more Imperial craft appeared in front of them. Han pulled back on the altitude control, climbing and turning simultaneously. Leia twisted around in her seat and fired at one speeder. She felt like a trapped animal with the pack closing in, and nothing to fight with but her teeth and fingernails.

Her stomach swooped up through her midsection as Han flipped the speeder through the top of the arc. "No good," he shouted. "They've got hot military models." Something bright and noisy, a streak of laser-cannon energy, passed beside them on the starboard side.

Shedding altitude at a dizzying pace, Han steered for the treetops. "When I say jump, jump. Hide behind some rocks or—"

"Han!" she exclaimed. "Reinforcements!" A pair of tiny X-winged silhouettes dropped out of the cloudy blue sky. X-wing space fighters had twice the speed and firepower of those landbased speeders. . . .

Instantly Han pulled the speeder up again and pushed for altitude. "The minute they spot 'em—"

Sure enough, the Imperials scattered. "Wish we had a comlink," Leia muttered. "They almost act like somebody *sent* them here. Maybe Luke?"

"Wouldn't surprise me," Han muttered. He steered down the drainage toward the wide river. An X-wing swept into position at his three o'clock, and the other came in at nine o'clock high.

Leia waved. Inside the slanting cockpit, a slim black-gloved hand waved back.

Their escort looked incongruous this close to a green planetary surface. Leia recalled Yavin, and the hidden groundside Rebel base where she'd waited for the first Death Star to attack.

Where the river curved southeast, just north of Salis D'aar, both fighters soared again toward space. "They don't want to be seen this close to the city," Leia observed. "It'd alarm the Bakurans."

"Glad somebody's thinking," answered Han.

Thanks, Luke. It was still just a guess, but Leia felt confident about it.

"Shortest route to the *Falcon* is right through downtown," Han observed. "If the locals try to stop us for violating curfew, they're going to have a rough time."

Salis D'aar's ground routes, including a high bridge connecting the white cliff with the western side of the broad river, teemed with slow vehicles—probably families moving their worldly goods north into the mountains, curfew or no curfew. Leia wished momentarily that they could stop by the complex. She hated leaving the Ewoks' bracelet behind, but it wasn't worth risking her life.

They met little air traffic. "Anybody who could fly out already did," Han guessed.

"Where are the droids?"

"Artoo's probably still in Captison's office." Then he explained what he'd done with Threepio.

She laughed, picturing his arrival at the *Falcon*. "I only hope Chewie didn't blast him before he spoke up."

"He's got my comlink. I'm sure he took care of himself."

Shreds of dusty smoke covered the spaceport from hundreds of blastoffs. Han steered down into the murk and landed practically on top of the *Falcon*. It wasn't guarded, except by one lone Wookiee. "Where's Threepio?" Leia exclaimed.

Chewbacca snorted and snarled. "You *what*?" Han answered. "Chewie, we've got to dump his Flutie-talk program onto the *Falcon*'s computer!"

Chewbacca howled, sounding apologetic.

"Yeah, I should've. Well, fix him up."

Chewie *had* blasted him. Too late for regrets. Leia dashed up the ramp behind Chewbacca. "I hope it's fueled," she exclaimed as she dropped into her high-backed seat.

Chewbacca bellowed. "Topped up and ready for a trip to the Core," Han translated as he hobbled into the cockpit. "Do what you can for Threepio, Chewie. Leia, strap down."

Leia's seat began to vibrate. The engines' roar mounted.

"Chewie, wait! Any new modifications?" Han shouted.

His partner woo-woofed from behind her.

"Oh." Han sounded appreciative. "That should come in handy. Where did you patch it in?"

Chewie reappeared in the corridor, rolled his eyes at the overhead panels, then answered.

"You sliced out *what*?"

"Now what?" Leia asked.

"Ah, he got a Bakuran tech to give us more power to energy

shields, but that increased the hyperdrive multiplier. As soon as we're out of here," he insisted, leveling a finger at Chewie, "that goes back to specs. My specs."

All Leia wanted now was speed insystem. "*Falcon*'s coming up," she snapped. "Let's move it."

CHAPTER

17

"Now the left leg."

Obediently Gaeriel wiggled her toes.

The Imperial medic frowned, pressed Gaeri's head back with inexorable professional gentleness, and reexamined the faint burn across the hollow of her throat. "Some kind of nervous-system ionization, I suppose. That's what I'll put on the report."

She coughed. "May I go now?"

"I'm sorry. We've been asked to keep you here a little longer, under observation."

"What's going on? I heard a siren."

"They've struck at the orbital station."

Then it had begun. She gazed around the bare room. Four white walls and a distant ceiling, no windows, one door. The emergency patrol had brought her back to the complex on a repulsor stretcher. Before that, her most vivid memory was of Luke advancing toward four armored stormtroopers. Then the civil defense alarm. Then the droid dragged her outdoors to safety, and she'd lain alone for a long, long time, until the emergency patrol reached the cantina. By then, Skywalker and the Ssi-ruuk had vanished in the Imperial shuttle . . . and she could almost move again.

But it was over, humankind doomed. They'd taken Luke. She couldn't imagine even a Jedi with enough power to singlehandedly resist . . . whatever they hoped to do with him. Would they try to make him a superdroid? Maybe they would fail.

But even if they didn't, she'd rather die here on Bakura than a Ssi-ruuvi prisoner. Her depression hardened to resolve. Nothing and no one could threaten her now.

The medic slipped out. Gaeri slid down from the bed and limped to the door. All her muscles seemed functional again, but her movements lagged behind her intentions. She touched the door's sensor panel.

Locked.

They couldn't mean to hold her here long. The room didn't even have . . . Now that she'd thought about comfort facilities, she wished she hadn't. She considered Eppie, running a revolt from a keyboard in a shabby apartment. Would she have time? The Bakur complex sprawled across the heart of Salis D'aar, with dozens of entrances: How did she mean to get control of it— or did she? She only needed control of Wilek Nereus. Commander Thanas and the space forces were already offplanet, defending Bakura—

Her thoughts spun to a dejected halt. There'd be no defense against the Ssi-ruuk now.

The door opened. Two naval troopers stepped through. "Come," ordered one.

Gaeriel followed him past a medical station and up a hallway. Soon she realized where they were taking her, and she resisted the temptation to bolt. She'd always managed to avoid Governor Nereus's private office. She'd heard disturbing rumors. And then there were Nereus's subtle attentions. . . .

The lead trooper opened the governor's door and motioned her inside. She walked in calmly. Better to die on Bakura, but die fighting.

Governor Nereus sat at a desk with a polished, off-white surface. Faint brownish veins on it made concentric circles, like tree rings, but it didn't look like wood. He silently motioned her to a chair and watched the troopers leave.

A framed tri-D on the nearest wall caught her attention first: a huge, snarling carnivore. Its four long white fangs looked eerily substantial.

"The Ketrann," said Nereus. "Of Alk'lellish III."

"The teeth. Are they . . . real?"

"Yes. Look around you."

Above and beyond the tri-D hung others like it, with here and there a simply arrayed full set of teeth. "This is your collection, then?"

"Predator species. I have seventeen worlds, including the Bakuran Cratsch." He tapped a clear cube at one corner of his desk. "On that wall—" He pointed left at another set of tri-D images. "Intelligent aliens." She thought of the Wookiee Chewbacca's huge canines and frowned. "And the most dangerous predator." He tossed her a multifaceted crystal. Inside gleamed two pair of human incisors.

She wanted to throw it at him, but resisted. She might cause more effective damage later. "I hope you can add a set of Ssi-ruu teeth soon." She tried to sound cool.

"Yes, interesting that they have beaks with teeth." He cleared his throat. "I prefer taking specimens from individuals I have hunted down myself, of course. The Rebel princess seems to have left my hospitality for the moment. She must be punished for defying orders. My dental specialist is not gentle."

Fiend, she thought at him. She'd play along, and she'd be the snake in his picnic basket for now, but Wilek Nereus would pay for his crimes. She swallowed hard to choke down a cough. This was the wrong time to catch a virus. He opened his hand, and she tossed back the crystal.

"Admirable diplomacy, Senator. Outstanding reserve under pressure. Did you get a good look at the weapon they shot you with?"

Gaeriel described it while Nereus passed the crystal from hand to hand. As she finished, she thought of Eppie Belden again. If this Ssi-ruuk attack failed, Eppie would need another opportunity. "Governor, please reconsider allowing a public funeral for Senator Belden. Bakura needs—"

"It does not need any more public gatherings. No. The curfew stands." He stared, abruptly giving her the impression he was waiting for something.

"What did the Empire do to Madam Belden?" she asked, to distract him.

He arched a thick eyebrow. "Did the Empire do something to her? Let me check my records." His fingers skated over an inset desktop panel. Gaeri leaned forward. "What do you think of my desk?" he asked. "A single slab of tooth ivory."

That was a tooth? A meter and a half in diameter, it implied a monstrous mouth. "Sea-going creature?" she asked at a guess. The urge to cough was getting stronger.

Nereus nodded. "Now extinct. Here we are. Ah." He smiled slowly. "Madam Belden was scheduled for termination. Her husband agreed to permanent incapacitation as the price of keeping her companionship."

Gaeriel clenched her hands. Orn Belden had . . . *agreed* . . . to let the Empire . . . ? She didn't want to believe it. She was suddenly thankful Orn Belden had died, so she couldn't ask him if it were true.

"And evidently she submitted to protect *him*. Oh, yes," he added, studying his screen. "I had forgotten specifics. We used a tiny creature native to the Jospro sector, which parasitizes the neocortex of the brain. It scars the region, suppressing long-term memory to a comfortably moderate extent. Easy and painless to introduce, and she and her husband could go on keeping company. Quite the loving couple, for their age. Go ahead and cough, my dear. Your forehead is turning pink."

"I don't need to." She gulped.

He folded his hands on the ivory desktop. "How much of that meal did you share with Commander Skywalker?"

The pit of her stomach turned to lead. That meal . . . "What do you mean?" she asked.

He flipped one hand. The gesture looked careless and calculating, but his fingers quivered. "When Skywalker's apartment guards reported that you'd gone inside, I naturally began tracing signals attributed to your ID number. I intercepted your request for a meal, sent to your quarters . . . good try, my dear, but you failed. I had the main dish inoculated at the kitchens. Your actions, like your questions, mark you as a Rebel collaborator."

What had Nereus done? Was she going to die? Was Luke? Surely he wouldn't have told her what he'd done, if he simply meant to kill her. Once she'd steadied herself, she asked numbly, "What is it? Another parasite?"

He smiled slowly. "The Olabrian Trichoid lays pods of three eggs in ripening fruit. Larvae hatch in a host's stomach, then migrate to the lungs while the host sleeps. They remain there for a day or two, while they grow and the mouthparts develop. Then they start nibbling toward the heart. That takes a varying length of time, depending on the host's size and physical condition. They pupate in a nice, large pool of slowly clotting blood—You're pale, my dear. Would you like to put your head down?"

She seemed to feel something growing inside her.

"Don't worry. The larva is extremely susceptible to pure oxygen. You're almost instantly curable—for about the next hour." He touched a key on his desktop. "Medic. Bring kit cee-dee twelve."

"So I got it instead of Skywalker?" At least Luke stood a chance, up there.

"No," he said mildly. "Remember, three eggs in each pod. He

definitely carries two. I had wondered about the third egg. Be proud of your friend, Gaeriel. Through him, the Ssi-ruuk fleet may become infested. I can almost guarantee that no natural predators of Olabrian Trichoids travel with the Ssi-ruuvi. If we can hold them off for one day, we have won."

The door slid open. Her medic hurried through, carrying a breath mask, a pony bottle, and a specimen jar. "This will only take a minute, Gaeriel." Nereus folded his hands on his desktop. "Cooperate with the medic."

She eyed the bottle, wondering what it held besides oxygen. "Only if you breathe it first."

Nereus shrugged. "I'll take some of that, if you don't mind," he told the medic. After he'd drawn two deep breaths, he smiled toothily. "Your turn, Gaeriel."

She waited until the medic sterilized the mask before she let him press it to her face. The gas had no odor. She inhaled again, then stared up at the medic's eyes. "Keep it up," he said, "until you—"

Abruptly she gagged. The medic held the mask down firmly. She choked, shut her eyes, and spit out something awful. Then she staggered backward to her seat as the medic dumped something out of the mask into the jar. She felt queasy. *Luke*, she moaned silently. Just as she'd feared, he might die before the Ssi-ruuk could use him. Perhaps Nereus had saved humankind, after all—but at what cost? Now that he was doomed, she regretted every harsh word.

"Bravely done." Nereus clapped his fingertips. "Naturally, it is inconvenient that you know what happened to Madam Belden."

Gaeriel concentrated on swallowing. "Perhaps not, Governor. Some kinds of knowledge need to be disseminated, if you mean to frighten people with them."

"Well played, indeed! I like you better and better. Once we defeat the Rebels, I may pardon you. I may go so far as to make room for you on my personal staff. But you've known that I'd like that all along. Haven't you?" He rested his chin on one hand.

Repulsed, she gripped her knees. "May I have a drink of water?"

He called for one. Once she'd sipped it, and the medic had left carrying his specimen jar, she said, "I understand there's going to be a battle. May I observe from your war room?"

"No need to go anywhere." He fiddled with his desk console. A small but detailed hologram of near space appeared over his desk. He bent down, reached into a desk compartment, and raised a sealed bottle of namana nectar. "To celebrate the Imperial victory," he said with a flourish.

Celebrate, she echoed bitterly, vowing not to taste it. Her throat burned already.

Dev's heart rate accelerated as they approached the orbiting Imperial defense web. This time, no Imperial troopers on board would guide them through it. Peering out the shuttle's main viewport, Dev could see slower shuttles docking with orbiting ships. Humans were scrambling for battle. Directly in front of him, Bluescale, Firwirrung, and the others warbled among themselves. They sat on the shuttle's deck, curled around the front seats.

If human fighterships blasted this shuttle, that would settle the matter of Skywalker. Still, he doubted it would happen below the defense web. All the defenders would be looking outward, trying to keep Ssi-ruuvi gunships from breaking through to the planet's surface. Besides, this craft looked like any other Imperial ship, shuttling its crew to an orbiting cruiser.

Something flashed in front of them. An instant later, pieces of one human fighter blasted out of the flash zone. It must've been maneuvering to attack them. Through the new gap in the defense web poured squadron after squadron of battle droids, opening an alley to the *Shriwirr.* Human fighters swooped in and started picking them off, but the battle droids kept coming. Dev guessed that Admiral Ivpikkis would have launched simultaneous strikes at several points, to direct the defenders' attention away from this shuttle.

Once Skywalker lay helpless and Firwirrung pulled the main switch, they could entech humans from nearby ships, and even planetside, and energize all the battle droids they could need to complete the invasion. Through his inner vision stabbed the agonizing memory of lying on that table himself. He glanced at the motionless Jedi.

"Dev?" Firwirrung's huge black eye appeared over the back of his seat. "Are you all right? You don't look happy."

"Oh," Dev exclaimed hastily, wishing Ssi-ruuvi faces showed readable expressions. "I'm concerned for your wound, Master. He had no right to do that to you."

Firwirrung blinked triple eyelids. "It is a wound of honor. But our prisoner does not seem to please you."

Dev's fingers twitched. If he betrayed his state of mind, they'd renew him instantly. Worse, they'd separate him from Skywalker. The perfect answer sprang late into his mind. "He hurt you, Master."

Firwirrung slowly nodded. "I see." He turned and whistled something too softly to understand.

The Jedi gave every impression of unconsciousness, slumped with his mouth hanging open. Dev ran a hand over his head. From warmth in the Force he found where Bluescale had struck him. It was healing already. Again doubt clamored at him.

Skywalker? Dev thought tentatively. *Are you aware? Can I help you? What can I do?* His only answer was the pulse of the galaxy.

Dev bit off a fingernail. A flight of battle droids flashed upward past the shuttle. Defending it, he realized. He could almost picture Admiral Ivpikkis stroking one thumbclaw with the other.

Entechment circuitry worked only on conscious individuals. There would be a few seconds, at least. *You'll have to move quickly,* he thought hard at the helpless Jedi. *They're not going to create any openings.*

Entechment. He shuddered. He'd longed to escape his own will.

He'd cooperated with his own enslavement. He'd hoped to share it with all humankind. He glared at the back of Bluescale's head.

The *Shriwirr's* underside swept across the viewport. The idea of licking Ssi-ruuvi footclaws again, for any length of time, made him bristle—but it wouldn't last long. Soon he'd be free or dead, or both.

Metal blast doors closed behind them. Seconds later, the shuttle landed roughly on the deck of a docking bay. Skywalker did not flinch.

Dev stayed in his seat while medics helped Firwirrung out the nose ramp. He caught himself drumming his fingers, and pressed his palms flat to make himself stop it. A brainwashed slave showed no anxiety.

The medic's scaly head peered back up the ramp. "Unconscious?" he whistled.

"Minor head injury," answered Dev. "It has kept him immobile."

The medic made a disgusted clacking noise. "Our knowledge of human anatomy is limited. We'll need you to stay with him."

Chilled, Dev realized they might cut him apart to see how Skywalker was built. "Here, Master," he said. "Let me carry him."

"Good," grunted the Ssi-ruu. "We only brought one stretcher."

Dev unharnessed himself, then Skywalker, then cautiously ran a hand over the injured spot. At least, he thought it was the spot. All evidence had faded. It took him several minutes of fumbling in a crouched position, battling fettered arms and dangling legs and the weight of the Jedi's compact, muscular body, before he reached the open hatch.

Clustered around the shuttle in an immense landing bay, a dozen Ssi-ruuk stood waiting. Dev forced a grin, expecting a cheer. Silent instead, they watched him struggle. His deck shoes clicked down the ramp. They probably enjoyed the spectacle of one human slave, bearing the fate of humankind on his shoulders.

Staggering under his load, Dev followed the medic across the landing bay, then between the bulkheads of a cargo airlock, and then up a long, bright corridor. He heard a clack-clack behind him and wondered how many followed. Things looked more and more hopeless. He almost wished he had strangled the Jedi while he had the opportunity.

No, he didn't. Not while there was one chance of saving him. He'd found a friend, after all these years living with enemies. For reawakening his humanity, he owed the Jedi a chance to fight.

Up a lift, around several corners, toward the entenchment lab. It ought to be nightshift-dim by now, but the yellow overhead light tubes burned at full brilliance. Dev stumbled and almost dropped his burden. "Carefully!" snapped a voice behind him.

"Yes, Master." It wasn't difficult to sound exhausted and repentant. "I didn't mean to. He's all right." Dev's back might not be, though. He took penitential satisfaction in that pain.

He followed the medic inside the spacious lab. The new entenchment platform bed stood against a bulkhead near the old, standard chair. Now he dared to turn around. Two others followed in. The rest would stand guard.

Firwirrung already waited beside the control panel, assisted by another medic and by two P'w'ecks. That made five Ssi-ruuk and two servants against Dev and one unconscious Jedi. "Ah. Dev," whistled Firwirrung. "You are strong. Well done."

Manipulative praise: Now he recognized it. Clinging to the hope Skywalker was conscious, Dev let him slide to the ground. "No," exclaimed Firwirrung. "The new apparatus will hold him upright. Here, I shall help you."

Dev crouched and raised Skywalker over his shoulder again. *Now's the time!* he exclaimed. *They'll have you trapped, if you don't move now!* Skywalker did not respond. Sorrowing, Dev steadied the Jedi. A medic released his wristbinders and Firwirrung pressed him against the table. Restraints snapped around his ankles and waist, but his arms dangled away from the trip panels. Firwirrung pushed them into place. The bed tipped backward with its captive.

The hatch slid open. Dev turned, then froze in place. Bluescale swept in, shut the hatchway behind him, and then marched to Dev's side. "The Jedi human will be unconscious for some time, you guess?"

Dev spread his hands. Ssi-ruuk used the empty-claw gesture for confusion, too. "It will be difficult to wait, Elder."

Bluescale turned his massive head to fix Dev with one hypnotic black eye, then whistled what Dev had dreaded to hear. "You are in desperate need." Two other aliens slithered toward him, beamers drawn.

"Wait," exclaimed Firwirrung. "Dev has served us well. Let us reward him." He stroked the old entenchment chair. "Sit down, Dev. There is time. I will place the IVs and lower the catchment arc myself, exactly as I promised."

Dev's tongue swelled like pillow stuffing. His fawning hadn't convinced any of them. How hideously had he acted all these years?

"Don't you smell yourself?" Bluescale sang softly.

So that was how they'd caught him. Seizing his last free moment, he jumped for Skywalker. His good hand and his aching one closed on the helpless Jedi's throat. "I need nothing," he cried. "You'll never—"

Lights went out in the chamber. Words died on his tongue.

CHAPTER

18

T HE WEAK-MINDED LITTLE P'W'ECK LUKE HAD BEEN CONTROLLING honked confusion with the rest of them, not realizing its tail had crushed the control board and extinguished cabin lights. Luke only hoped that he'd also disabled the abominable alien machines. He could tell the aliens from Dev by their presences, even in the dark. One potent individual tramped toward a power-locked hatchway.

Luke had already unlatched his bonds with the Force. Easily throwing off Dev, he leaped down. His head no longer hurt, but his right leg had no feeling. He leaned left. "Dev," he cried, "get under something. They'll trample you."

"Right!" Dev's voice sounded giddy with elation.

Feeling Dev shift between determination and fear had been the hardest part of staying still for the last several minutes. He wished he hadn't given up his blaster—or else that he had another, to arm Dev.

From a safe spot near the bulkhead, Luke stretched out his right hand and visualized his lightsaber. It had to be close. Less than a second later, its satisfying weight arrived. "Are you down, Dev?" he cried over the cacophony of deep Ssi-ruuvi whistles.

Muffled answer: "Yes."

"Good." Luke extended the saber's blade. The chamber lit eerie green, and the aliens' alarmed whistles rose to shrieks. Two black eyes reflected the saber a moment before it sliced below them. Another alien bellowed. Luke spun and decapitated it.

Big Blue—it was him, at the hatch—finally kicked it in and escaped. Another followed him into the bright corridor.

"Now what?" Dev shouted.

"Stay low!" Three mechanical shapes that resembled Artoo appeared in the hatchway. The first droid rushed him. He sliced it diagonally with the saber and reached for the others with the Force. They weren't true droids, but marginally alive. One fired a pair of stun bolts at him. He deflected one bolt back toward his attacker and the other at its partner. Both overloaded and switched off—but the weird stench in the Force, like the presence of a soul half decayed, only faded slightly. He'd caught the same stench from the battle droids, and the ship itself. The cruiser reeked in his senses, permeated with stolen human energies. It might burn heavy fusionables for ordnance and thrust, but its control systems had to be powered in the hideous Ssi-ruuvi way.

Dev crept out from behind the grim chair. Glimmers of dark side energy lingered around it from thousands of victims' terrorized agony. "You all right?" Luke asked.

Dev's pale brown skin looked olive green by the saber's light, and he gripped a paddle beamer with both hands. "That was wonderful."

It wasn't too soon to launch Dev's apprenticeship. "Two of your Ssi-ruuk died."

"I know," he groaned, "but how else—"

"Exactly. You have to fight, but you mustn't like it." He hoped Yoda didn't laugh aloud, hearing him say that.

Dev chewed his upper lip. "Now what?"

"Stand back." Luke spun on his strong leg and sliced once, twice, three times through the chair and its dangling machinery, then again through the upright table. Pieces crashed to the deck, denting its tiles. He returned the saber to rest salute position. "Are there more labs like this?"

He felt Dev wilt, eyes haunted and wide. "They've nearly completed another thirty."

Thirty! "It'd take us too long to ruin that many. No more operational?"

"Not that I know of. And I assisted with . . ."

"We'll assume this is the only one, then." Perspiration ran down Luke's face, even with his mind relaxed into the Force. "Are onboard control systems powered by human energies too?"

Dev's frown deepened. "I don't know. I'd never thought about it. It's possible."

"I can feel it. Can you take me to the engineering sector?"

"Yes."

Holding the saber low, Luke sidestepped toward the outer bulkhead. He slid along it and peered into the corridor. "There are six more droids active out there, but no Ssi-ruuk."

"They're scared to death of you."

"Why?"

"They don't want to die off one of their home worlds. That's why they force slaves and P'w'ecks to do all their fighting." Dev edged up behind him and whispered, "Be careful."

"Just stay behind me." About to relax into full control, Luke realized he was already there. He stepped into the hatchway, holding his saber ready. An energy bolt sizzled toward him. Dev cried out and jumped back. Luke's saber swept up and returned the energy. The droid sputtered dead.

One down. The other five were undoubtedly programmed to fire . . . *simultaneously!* came the blasts. Luke's saber whirled. The droids dropped, smoking and throwing sparks.

Dev whistled soft admiration.

"I'll teach you to do that." Luke's right leg tingled and ached. He must've wrenched it worse than he thought when he jumped onto that table.

"Do it soon," Dev said earnestly. "I want what you have."

"Engineering deck first," Luke murmured, satisfied. Dev's apprenticeship looked official. "Stay close behind me."

They crept up a bright corridor. "Left," Dev whispered. Luke whirled across the passage to draw the fire of anyone guarding it. Unchallenged, he pressed on, calmly listening in front and behind, using the Force to refresh tiring muscles and take the bite off increasing pain in his right leg.

"Now right," Dev whispered. "Drop shaft."

Luke shook his head. "We'd be helpless inside. That big blue one's probably still on board. Are the decks connected by stairs?"

"Ssi-ruuk can't use stairs," Dev murmured. "Neither can P'w'ecks, the smaller ones."

"More slaves?" His voice caught, and he cleared his throat.

"Yes."

The Ssi-ruuk would probably never accept other races as equals. "Any other links between decks?"

"I don't know," Dev admitted. "I've only used power lifts."

Luke stretched out into the invisible world again. A web of weak living energy surrounded them, punctuated here and there by the brighter Force-gleams of sentient beings. He found a vertically sizeable empty area ahead. "Come on," he murmured. Unable to find a hatchway, he cut a way in through the bulkhead. A spiral ramp, cramped for humans—obviously designed for P'w'eck or droid use—led up and down. It sounded and felt empty.

"Go ahead," Luke whispered. Dev pushed one leg through, then his head, then he vanished into the rampway. Luke followed. Dev pointed downward, so Luke led down into the spiral ramp. His right leg didn't bend easily. The muscles tightened and stayed tight. Behind him, Dev's pain sense echoed: He'd injured his back and left hand.

Dozens, maybe hundreds, of souls must be slaved to the *Shriwirr's* circuitry. He couldn't bring even one back to life . . . but perhaps he could release a few of them to rest peacefully.

After a long hunched walk, Luke asked through gritted teeth, "How far down is Engineering?"

"Eighteenth deck." Dev indicated a symbol on the bulkhead beside a narrow hatchway. "We're at the seventeenth, now."

Luke led around several more turns of the shaft, then paused at a hatchway. "Here?"

"This is it."

Luke felt inside the circuits on the other side of the hatch. Again he found a center of life energy set to power nonliving circuitry. He sent a pulse of excitement into shreds of human will.

The hatch slid open.

He stumbled out, saber ready, into another empty corridor. As Dev sprinted past him, he spun around and sliced into the power center. The tortured sense of tethered presence winked out.

One more freed.

Dev examined writing on a bulkhead. "I think this is it," he said softly.

"You haven't been down here before?"

Dev shrugged. "No."

"All right." From behind another bulkhead, the half-dead Force stench wafted out. Luke was about to step under an illuminated arch when he caught a glimmer above it. He leaped backward.

"What is it?" Dev asked.

Luke traced power flow up a bulkhead, overhead, then down the other side. "I don't know," he answered, "but the life power is linked to a strong amplifier." He sliced a flap off the breast of his tunic, dropped it onto the deck, then blew on it. It skittered forward.

Sizzling blue energy burned it to charcoal.

·   ·   ·

Sh'tk'ith's blue foreclaws framed the security board. "There," he exclaimed to the P'w'ecks behind him. "We've found them. Stun trap outside Engineering."

He flipped a coil. "Progress?" he asked Firwirrung, who was working frantically in a second lab.

"Finished," answered his colleague. "It won't keep the Jedi alive as long as the original would have, but I'll make another, better, before he deteriorates too far."

Although wounded, Firwirrung seemed determined to atone for his disaster. He and his P'w'eck aides had completed a secondary table from one nearly finished chair and spare parts, a fresh means to start harvesting immediately—if Sh'tk'ith could subdue the Jedi. Victory still beckoned.

Sh'tk'ith called Admiral Ivpikkis's lifeboat over an outside coil. "We're about to close in on them. I left three gangs of P'w'ecks under full compulsion on Deck Sixteen. I predict we can start launching battle droids the moment we succeed."

"Good," came his answer. Ssi-ruuvi picket ships still surrounded the *Shriwirr,* protecting it under Admiral Ivpikkis's command. "All our other cruisers have launched their full complement," Ivpikkis sang.

"Firwirrung thinks he may be able to combine Sibwarra's energies with the Jedi's."

"Hold both of them alive. You may exact a pride price on Sibwarra once we take Bakura."

Sh'tk'ith yanked off his shoulder pouch. Hefting his beamer, he whistled at his cowering P'w'ecks. "Follow!"

Han had his hands full getting the *Millennium Falcon* where Commander Thanas wanted her, and the Ssi-ruuk had moved nine picket ships into engagement vectors. The *Falcon* dipped and dove while he chased down droid fighters and poured energy into their miserably strong shields. They came at him so thickly that he managed to fry a few with the *Falcon*'s engine blast. Chewbacca was trying to fix Threepio, and Leia kept the lower turret hot. But where was Luke? "Somewhere in space," Leia had insisted. "But not on board the *Flurry*," they'd heard from Tessa Manchisco.

Three TIE fighters swooped overhead. Han balled his fists. Those TIEs might be on his side, but he didn't trust Commander Thanas one minute longer than the Fluties lasted. Caught in the middle of an invasion maneuver, the aliens weren't even using their trooper scooper—no sign of tractor beams anywhere. One big Ssi-ruuvi vessel had already launched a dozen landing craft. Sluggish and underpowered, those had made a poor first ring of offense. He couldn't tell if the Imperials' new DEMP guns were working, but he wanted one.

His vector took him close to a big Flutie cruiser, one of three slowly moving in on Bakura. Eerie two-tone jamming momentarily drowned out offship communications. "Any progress?" he asked Chewie over the private comlink. Chewie howled an affirmative. "Good. Hurry it up. Leia, where's Luke?"

"Right there! On board that big cruiser." Leia's voice, carried on both of Han's headphone channels, seemed to sound between his ears. "Quick—put out word to our forces that it's not to be attacked."

The cruiser they'd just passed under? Han switched extra power into rear deflectors and dodged fire from its picket ships, then blasted one picket to atoms. "What's he doing there?"

"I can't tell," Leia answered.

"Lookit that," someone exclaimed, once he could hear the intersquad frequency again. Shuttles and escape pods popped off the Ssi-ruuvi cruiser like snap rivets from a stressed coolant vane.

"You were right," Han observed to Leia. "Luke's in there."

Luke eyed the charred shred of fabric. "They're none too sure of security."

"Stun trap," said Dev. "It'll put down a Ssi-ruu, right through that hide. I think it'd kill you or me."

Luke located the power link at shoulder height on a gray bulkhead, just out of saber reach beyond the arch. Because life created the Force, every circuit that used this unclean energy was easy to find and control—and he was getting better at it as he went. He touched this one gingerly with his mind and found a weak, exhausted will supplying power. Tired as he was, his first impulse was pity. Quickly and cautiously he showed it what he needed. Then he offered release. The will seemed to blink. . . .

"Quick, Dev!" Luke jumped through the arch. Brandishing his paddle beamer, Dev followed. Blue energies singed his flapping hem.

Luke hesitated. "Just a minute." He must keep his promise. Carefully he flicked his lightsaber into circuitry. The pitiful will touched his mind, leaving gratitude as it fled.

The stun traps occurred at six-meter intervals. Luke chafed at each delay, and each energy required a different persuasion. As he tired, his sense of urgency grew stronger.

They reached a junction. Their corridor went forward, slowly curving to the right, but another narrower opening branched right sharply. A yellow light rod gleamed down the center of its arched ceiling. Across the main corridor from that junction, a wide metal hatchway loomed shut.

Ambush, Luke's senses shouted. Cautiously he stepped around the corner to the right, pressed against the bulkhead, then turned to listen behind the broad metal hatch. He thought he felt someone—

Dev's choked cry whirled Luke around in time to see the broad hatch shoot up into the ceiling. A P'w'eck leaped through, seized the boy from behind, and brandished a claw at his throat. Dev ducked and fired his paddle beamer over one shoulder. The P'w'eck collapsed, leaving a thin trail of red blood across Dev's neck.

Guided by his subconscious, Luke whirled and slashed behind him. Two more P'w'ecks had appeared as if from thin air. They fell wounded and shrieking, but others lurked in an opening where he'd seen no hatchway. They pelted him with diffuse blue blaster bolts. They were still shooting to stun. His saber deflected bolts onto bulkheads and alien flesh. Dev cried out and fell to the deck. Luke hadn't seen—or felt—anything hit him. "Dev?" he shouted.

The massive blue Ssi-ruu dove toward Luke through the broad hatch, warbling and whistling. It fired a steady silver beam. Dodging, Luke raised his saber and bent the beam toward a P'w'eck in the narrow hatchway. It collapsed, forelimbs flailing. The blue one came on across the junction, watching Luke but not the deck. From up the curving corridor, Dev crawled on elbows and knees toward the blue giant. Luke dove across the yellow-lit hall and ducked the silver beam. The blue's will daunted him, even from a distance. It might not perceive the Force, but in Luke's senses it cast a huge dark shape with the same savor that tainted Dev's memory-crippling shadow.

Dev lunged up from the deck. From behind Big Blue, he fired his paddle beamer into the base of its tail. The alien twisted its upper body toward Dev and fell limp legged. Luke dashed forward, brandishing his saber. Ducking the silvery beam, Dev pressed his paddle to Blue's head and fired. The creature honked, then screamed. The scream ended in a gurgle. Dev zigzagged his beamer across its head. Clattering noises retreated up both curving corridors. Luke relaxed, coughing a little. Deep in his throat, something tickled.

Dev sat down on Big Blue's flank and kicked it. When it didn't move, he cradled his left hand under one arm and let his beamer dangle. "I faked that hit. It seemed safer to play dead than to go on fighting," he rasped, panting. "I didn't seem to be helping you at all." The trickle across his throat was darkening. Luke touched the wound. "It's not deep," Dev insisted. "Just a claw mark."

Big Blue lay still except for a narrow black tongue that drooped, quivering, from one nostril. "Is he stunned?" Luke asked.

"Dead." Dev stared up into his eyes.

Luke saw pain, guilt, and triumph. "Who was that?"

"He . . . controlled me." Dev stared at the gray deck tiles. "But Firwirrung was my master—the small brown with the **V** on his head, the one whose foreclaw you cut off. Firwirrung is the really dangerous one. We're all dead if he catches you. Everyone. Everywhere."

"Why? He didn't seem to be in charge."

"No, but he runs the entechments."

"Have they always . . . enteched . . . to power their droids?"

"They've enteched older P'w'ecks for centuries. But humans last longer," Dev explained. "He means to force you to entech other humans from a distance. The Ssi-ruuk want to enslave the whole galaxy. There are . . . I don't know how many more ships, waiting out there to hear when Bakura falls."

"This is just a scout force?" Luke asked, alarmed.

Dev nodded, and Luke sensed his shame. "Believe me, Firwirrung's ready for you."

He'd helped. . . . So that was the story, at last. Luke shut his eyes. No wonder Dev had tried to strangle him, rather than let the Ssi-ruuk have their way. "Well." Luke choked another cough. "Let's get the job done before more of them show up."

"Are you all right?"

Luke coughed again. That reptilian odor irritated his nostrils and throat. "Something I'm breathing must bother me. I guess you're used to it. Come on, let's go."

Engineering was a jumble of controls and conduits, but Luke had no trouble finding the master display panel. This locus created a gargoyle imitation of life so powerful, so abominably twisted, that he flinched. A hundred intermingled energies seethed at his subliminal senses. Freshly enteched energies writhed frantically within the numb, frayed ribbons of others' nearly spent volition.

Luke swung his saber through the console with a deep sweep of his shoulders, then shifted his body and reversed the stroke. The gargoyle cacophony fell silent.

He took a long slow look around, breathing deeply and cautiously. The chamber and the ship felt clean at last.

Had he just stranded himself onboard?

Light rods gleamed behind gray conduits along the ceiling, so emergency power existed. Now he had to trace energy flow on the boards like anyone else. "Dev? Can you read any of this?"

After a hurried consultation, they decided that the ion drive and hyperdrive still operated—but he'd blown the linkage between Bridge and Engineering. "That's amazing," murmured Dev.

Luke stared around at glowing displays. Not stranded in a dead hulk, then, but the *Shriwirr* was crippled. He coughed again. They had life support, weapons, and communication. No medpacks, though. Nothing for strained leg muscles, and no breath mask to filter out whatever was irritating his lungs. He'd have to tough it out till he could get off the *Shriwirr*. Again the thought crossed his mind that he'd just as soon not be stranded here, especially if the Ssi-ruuk lost. "Let's get to a shuttle," he said, pushing off from the control panel.

Dev led him to three giant shuttle bays in turn. Every flyer port and escape pod crane lay empty. They couldn't even find the hijacked Imperial craft they'd ridden up from Salis D'aar spaceport. "Abandon ship," Luke muttered. "Escape the terrible Jedi and his mighty apprentice."

Dev swept out his arms. "Then *this* is our lifeboat. I'll take you to the bridge."

Luke's cough rattled phlegm in his chest. "It'll have to do," he said reluctantly.

"Sorry about the DEMP guns," Han crowed at Commander Thanas. Both had misfired, disabling the patrol craft, and he wasn't sorry at all. Good thing he hadn't gotten one for the *Falcon*.

"Casualties of war," Thanas answered over the command channel in Han's left ear. "As is Commander Skywalker, it seems. I am sorry. I admired his capabilities."

"What's going on?" Leia's voice demanded.

"Governor Nereus just sent word. The aliens kidnapped him."

"Don't count Luke out," Leia said tightly.

Han sniffed the air. Was that hot wiring? *Hold together, baby!*

Thanas's brassy voice softened. "Your Highness, unless all the Ssi-ruuk retreat, we are now specifically ordered to destroy that cruiser."

"What?" exclaimed Leia.

Prickles rose on Han's neck. Only a quartet of Ssi-ruuvi picket ships prevented Thanas from doing it. His *Dominant* had plenty of firepower. "Why?" he asked.

"Contagion, General. I wasn't told specifics, and I don't make a habit of questioning orders. The consequences aren't worth it."

Leia broke in from the lower gun turret. "Question this one. Leave it alone for now, Commander." Hah—she didn't believe that contagion line any more than Han did. Governor Nereus just wanted revenge. Han spotted a thread of smoke curling out of one bulkhead and shut down the offending circuit. Crosswired like a city map, the *Falcon* could function with several boards out.

Commander Thanas's voice hardened as he addressed someone else. "Squadrons eight through eleven, sweep up those escape pods."

Leia protested, "But they're defenseless."

"We don't know that," Thanas answered coolly. "Some cultures arm their escape pods."

"Standard Imperial procedure?" Leia challenged him. "Kill the wounded to cut medical costs?"

"You don't seem concerned about the drone ships. Those are living energies."

"Enslaved," Leia snapped. "Irrevocably. Killing them only frees their souls."

"I agree," chimed in Captain Manchisco from the *Flurry*. She was helping an Imperial patrol craft harass an alien light cruiser into range of the *Dominant*'s tractor beam.

"And the aliens, Your Highness?" Thanas's voice insisted.

Leia sounded as if she were clenching her teeth. "We are fighting for the survival of the Bakuran people—and probably others, Commander. Self-defense justifies a lot. But never a massacre of the helpless."

Thanas didn't answer. On Han's scanners, a squadron of large Ssi-ruuvi fighters converged on the *Dominant*. Its turbolasers blasted two away.

"Good try, Leia," Han muttered. He cut in the comlink override. Abruptly, a swirl of lights blinked on his computer panel and Chewie bellowed over the comlink. "Great, Chewie," Han exclaimed. "Get to a quad gun!"

"What?" cried Leia.

"Threepio's running again. Just don't ask what happened to him. He'll bless us with the whole story as soon as we let him. He gave the Empire a Flutie translation program, but now we've got one too."

Leia groaned.

"How's Luke?" Han fired into another swarm of droid ships, targeting the leader. Twice now, they'd thought they'd gotten them all. Twice, some other cruiser launched a swarm.

"Still all right," she murmured. "He just dealt with a major concentration of that . . . zombie energy." The lower quad gun fired as she spoke.

"Sweetheart, forget the drones. Concentrate on your brother. You'd better warn him what Thanas just said."

"I'm trying!"

"Get Threepio to try transmitting on their frequencies, or something." Han ground his teeth. Luke *had* walked alone into Jabba's palace. He'd singlehandedly rescued Han, Leia, and Lando, literally out of the Sarlacc's sandy maw. Despite those delusions of grandeur, maybe he did know what he was doing.

.   .   .

What am I doing? Staggering on one good leg and one that cramped every time he set weight on it, Luke finished a circuit of the *Shriwirr*'s bridge. Consoles curved inward from deck to ceiling, marked by unfamiliar symbols. Several freestanding displays marked crew stations, but there were no chairs, benches, or stools. One long curved panel served as a viewport. "Do you know how any of it works?"

"I can read you the controls. That's about all."

"It's a start," Luke muttered. Something nagged at the back of his mind. Uneasy, he stepped away from Dev and ignited his saber.

Dev whirled around. "What is it?" he whispered loudly.

"I don't know." Luke paced toward the nearest concave bulkhead, then edged toward the hatchway, ducking his head. "Probably nothing."

"I doubt that."

Dev had left the cockpit hatch open. Luke slipped forward. Behind the bulkheads, he felt—thought he felt—an alien approaching. "Dev," he called, "take cover."

A P'w'eck dashed through. Luke sliced off its foreclaw, blaster and all. Then he glimpsed a pale metal gas grenade dangling by a chain from its neck. He cut the chain, thrust out a hand, and Force-flung the canister back out the hatch before whacking the bulkhead panel to slam it shut. Behind came a muffled *whump*. Wailing, the trapped P'w'eck backed across the bridge.

"Talk to him." Luke adjusted his grip on the saber and took shallow breaths to prevent the distracting cough. "Tell him I don't want to hurt him anymore. If he'll help us, we stand a better chance of using this ship."

Dev crept out from behind a control island and burst into chirps and trilling whistles. The P'w'eck hesitated, then dove for his blaster.

Luke grabbed it out of the air. "Tell him nobody else is coming till that gas clears out of the corridor."

Dev chirped. The P'w'eck shook his head again. Luke wondered if he dared try to interrogate the alien. He wasn't sure how. The creature didn't think in Standard.

Luke tossed Dev the P'w'eck's blaster. "Is there any way to tie him up? Keep him from slowing us down any further?"

Dev frowned, leveled the blaster, and shot the alien cleanly through its skull.

"Dev!" Luke exclaimed. "Never kill when you don't need to!"

"He'd have murdered us the instant we ignored him. We've got a few minutes. Let's use them!"

"Watch it," cried a strange voice in Han's right ear. Han increased power to starboard shields. Combined Rebel and Imperial forces had almost closed an arc around two more alien cruisers, but the aliens resisted. Black space sparkled with ships, shields, and energy as the Ssi-ruuk concentrated firepower on Rebel ships that occupied key attack points—just as he'd anticipated.

"*Dominant* to *Falcon*. Close up that gap at oh-two-two."

The *Dominant* had shot away its attackers, but it drifted to low starboard. Han smiled, guessing its lateral thrusters had gone down again. Maybe Luke would be safe a little longer. He spun his own ship to face solar north. The gap in question was big enough to send a Star Destroyer through. "Got it covered," he answered Commander Thanas. "Red group, and the rest of you. Follow me." After the *Falcon* like a flock of chicks sped four X-wings and five TIE fighters. Each wing kept to its own side of the *Falcon*.

"*Dominant*," came an exclamation over the clear channel, "They're counterattacking! Too much firepower at my—"

Silence. Han cracked his knuckles. He hated it when youngsters cashed in. But as losses mounted, Ssi-ruuvi ships vanished faster. The human forces would not be taken easily.

Something hit an Imperial patrol craft. "*Falcon* to *Digit Six*. Are you all right?" The patrol craft didn't answer. Wobbling, it accelerated to ram the small alien cruiser. An hour later, Han was still dodging collision debris and approaching exhaustion. Thanas drove his pilots hard, but the battle was his.

A sensor lit. Massive communications had abruptly started to flow between Flutie ships. Han punched up Threepio's translation program on a sideboard screen. With Captison's copy of the program, Commander Thanas probably expected to know if the alien commander ordered retreat . . . but that the Allies wouldn't.

Han's sideboard screen flashed a single message, endlessly repeated by the Fluties' command ship. *Disengage, full retreat. Disengage, full retreat. Disengage* . . .

Han slapped his control board madly, cutting Imperial ships out of his transmission channels. "Rebel ships," he ordered, "the Fluties are getting out. Full shields—watch the Imperials. All squadron leaders, get your ships away from Imperial fighters. Manchisco, you're in the *Dominant*'s range. Get out of it!"

"They're retreating? What about Luke?" Leia exclaimed. "Is he still on board? We can't fire on that cruiser."

Han drained weapon power into the shields. "And we're not shooting at the Imperials first." There wasn't much future for a smuggler with a conscience. Evidently the Alliance was stuck with him. "We don't *know* who's in control of Luke's cruiser," he added. "I see four picket ships still on it, riding close." It was the only big Flutie ship not retreating. All across space, oddly shaped ships were shrinking.

The *Falcon* shuddered from beam lamps to hyperdrive. Han leaped back from momentarily ionized controls. Chewbacca snarled in his ears. Light splashed the starfield in front of him, a second blast from the *Dominant*. Han blinked. "*Flurry*?" he shouted. "Manchisco! Manchisco, are you there?"

The *Flurry* was static and debris. "They got her," Han exclaimed. *Our only cruiser. Clear skies, Manchisco.* He clenched a fist at Thanas and mentally thanked Chewie for hiring that Bakuran tech to add power to the *Falcon*'s shields. He would've taken the *Dominant* if he could've, and if his conscience, down there at the lower quad guns, would've let him shoot first.

Leia seemed to speak in the middle of his head again. "Well, General, you're in charge."

Han keyed the command frequency back on. "Thanks for nothing, Thanas," he shouted. Over to intersquad. "That's it—you all saw it. The Empire just broke off our truce. We're back at war, us against them. Remember the Death Star. Form up with the *Falcon.*"

"*Falcon*, this is Red Leader. We're about a thousand kay out from you and we've got TIE fighters on all screens."

"Dogfight it, then," Han barked. "Wedge, where are you?"

That biggest Ssi-ruuvi cruiser revolved crookedly, still defended by its pickets. He couldn't begin to guess how to protect Luke . . . or if he even dared. Luke might've scared off the whole crew, but maybe not. And he certainly didn't command those four picket ships.

Meanwhile, another big egg-shaped cruiser labored to turn. A third jumped into hyperspace too quickly to have made calculations, fleeing blindly.

"Behind the planet from you. Or I was," answered Wedge's voice. "Barely heard you on satellite relay. Wait—" After a few seconds, he spoke again. "There's a lot of TIE fighter activity over at eight-niner-two-two. You might check to see what's up."

"That's the *Dominant!*" Leia exclaimed. "Go the long way around!"

Headache turned to nightmare as Thanas destroyed Rebel squadrons and Han slowly rounded up the survivors into a loose double squadron. He eyed the wallowing Ssi-ruuvi cruiser. "Leia? Tell Luke there's trouble out here."

"I'll try!"

CHAPTER

19

G AERIEL WHOOPED AS THE SSI-RUUVI FLEET FLED, BUT WITHIN A MIN-
ute, all the silver Alliance ship dots on Governor Nereus's
projection turned red. One by one, they began darkening.
She gasped and sprang off her chair. "They're not!"

Wilek Nereus rolled his nectar goblet's stem between his heavy
fingers. "Not what, Senator?"

"Turning on—attacking—the Rebels!" Not only that, but she
had to assume that the retreating Ssi-ruuk still held Luke prisoner,
and he was dying without knowing it. She drew a deep breath,
hoping her attempt to gather her wits looked like a dramatic
pause. "Sir," she started over, "on behalf of my constituency, I wish
to lodge a formal protest over the forces' conduct, which I assume
follows your orders. The Alliance people risked their lives—some
spent their lives—helping us repel the Ssi-ruuk. Is this gratitude?"

"Your constituency?" Governor Nereus's bland smile affected
only the edges of his effeminate lips. "You've already been in contact? Have you been taking telepathy lessons from someone?"

She ignored the implied, repeated accusation of collaboration
and set her chin. "My people have been grateful for Rebel assistance. They would not wish to see us—"

A comlink beeped. "Yes?" Nereus called.

"Sir, our sensors show thirty people gathered at the intersection of Tenth Circle and High Street, with more approaching."

"What are you bothering me for? Suppress it," he snapped. Again she glimpsed a tremor in his fingers, instantly controlled. Governor Nereus cut the connection and then sipped from his goblet. "Rebel assistance is already in the past. Now we must take thought for the future. What would Bakura suffer if Imperial Command learned that we accepted aid from Rebel forces?"

She clamped her jaw shut. Eppie Belden was raising Bakura, preparing civilians for the troopers' return. She mustn't think about Luke . . . although if she'd helped instead of hindered him, Bakura might already be free of Imperial rule.

But how could Bakura have repelled the Ssi-ruuk without Rebel *and* Imperial resources? What insane trick had fate played here?

Nereus picked up his multifaceted crystal full of human teeth. "My dear, you've not tasted your nectar."

She wondered if he was threatening her. "My throat hurts."

"I understand. That must have been uncomfortable. I apologize. You were not the intended recipient."

"Is there nothing you won't—" *Stoop to,* she thought, but said, "do, for the Empire?"

"You have always supported the Imperial presence. I have heard you speak eloquently of the benefits Bakura reaps through its affiliation with the Empire."

"Yes, I spoke that way. I learned the language well." *The language of treachery.*

"You will remember that your offworld education was subsidized by the Empire."

"For which I and my family have thanked you repeatedly."

"You have not yet begun to repay that debt. Now that I've had time to consider, I am certain that there is room for you on my personal staff." He slitted his eyes.

If Eppie's revolt succeeded, that threat would be empty. If the revolution stalled, though, she might serve the Bakuran underground in Imperial uniform. What had Leia Organa endured as an Imperial senator?

Governor Nereus studied the projection of near space, smiling. Noticeably fewer red Rebel dots "menaced" the system now.

"Did you order Commander Thanas to kill them all?" she asked bitterly.

Nereus swept dust that she couldn't see off his ivory desktop. "Yes. For the safety of your people. Commander Skywalker is another matter. The larvae will be beginning to migrate again. They require a plentiful blood supply in which to pupate. The aorta is sweetly close to the bronchial tubes. He won't suffer long. He is an excellent physical specimen. It's my guess that the aliens will take him with them, as they retreat. They should preserve his body for one day, long enough for adult Trichoids to emerge and infest the Ssi-ruuk. Trichoids are short-lived, but they survive by sheer numbers. We are free from the threat of entechment, Gaeriel. You and your constituency should thank me."

Nothing—not her habit of diplomacy or her fear of Wilek Nereus or even her deliverance from entechment—could entice her to thank him for murdering Luke Skywalker this way. And Senator Leia Organa, and all the Rebels who'd come to help Bakura. Once Bakura understood what had happened, Governor Nereus would need an Imperial legion to put down the resultant uprising . . . and thanks to the Alliance, he could not call down that legion. She ought to feel victorious.

Hollow desperation made her shiver. Luke had saved her from the Ssi-ruuk and their captive human, but she couldn't help him in return. That disrupted the Balance of her life. She fingered her pendant and dared to think of the gravest extreme: civil war, long and bloody, Bakuran lives against Imperial technology, unless . . . perhaps . . . she and Eppie could rid Bakura of Wilek Nereus. She steeled herself to stay with him and hope for a chance.

•   •   •

Han didn't need a cruiser's threat board to know they were losing. He'd managed to gather several X-wings and an A-wing into a moderately effective formation, but no matter how he and his shipmates used the *Falcon*'s armaments, one arc at a time Commander Thanas closed a tight, classic globe. System patrol craft and TIE fighters hung in all directions, drawing Rebels out of the *Dominant*'s dead zone into tractor range. Though Commander Thanas's damaged flagship drifted on minimal thrusters, its turbolaser batteries had already swung toward him. The *Falcon*'s power banks were all but exhausted. He needed to shut down all systems and let them recharge.

"All right, Leia," he said over the comlink. "Admit it. That 'bad feeling' of yours was the smart side of the Force." He feinted toward a TIE fighter. Its big brother, a carbon-streaked patrol craft, matched his vector. He backed off. "We're all dead, every ship in the battle group, unless somebody comes up with something brilliant . . . and fast."

Leia answered from the lower gun turret, "There must have been something we could've done." She sprayed a weakening energy burst from her quad guns. "Some way we could have—"

"You're dealing with Imperials. Every one that's high up enough to give orders is only in it for number one."

"We're starting to leave Luke out of the equation," she insisted again.

"Maybe he *is* out," Han answered soberly. "Thanas's drift vector is going to take him right past that Flutie cruiser."

From the upper gun turret, Chewie roared angrily.

Something in the pattern in front of him sparked his memory of a gaming table long ago and far, far away. Something brilliant. . . . "But if we could take the *Dominant*, our fighters might be able to break out and scatter."

Leia's turret suddenly felt chilly. "Sure. How?"

"Look where that Imperial patrol craft's hanging, the one

about sixteen degrees north. If we dropped back about twenty degrees and rammed it, it'd squirt out of formation and hit the *Dominant* hard aft. The *Falcon*'s the only ship we've got left with enough mass to carry it off. Thanas deserves his behind cooked."

"*Carrack*-class cruisers have their generators just aft of midline."

"Exactly. Ka-boom."

Leia felt strangely detached. "Count on you to try a carom shot. Can you get nav computer confirmation on that course?"

"Just did. With full power to front shields until the last possible moment, we could do it. Of course, hitting the patrol craft that hard would finish the *Falcon*."

"Of course." Leia tapped two fingers on her firing controls. *Luke?* she pleaded toward the drifting cruiser. She sensed nothing in return but a harried flicker. Busy.

She heard a soft click. "Listen up," Han announced in a genuine general's voice. "Form up behind the *Falcon* and get ready to break for open space. Get home as best you can. Don't try hyperspace jumps unless you can pair up with somebody with nav computer capability."

That would take years, but they'd make it. Leia cleared her throat and added, "Scatter the fire of Rebellion. It will flare up everywhere the tinder is dry."

"Poetic," muttered Han.

"Inspiration is three tenths of courage." Somebody protested over the intersquad frequency. Leia didn't stay to listen. She unstrapped and climbed up/sideways out of the gunwell's artificial gravity to the main level.

"Have we nearly finished?" Threepio asked brightly as she passed the gaming table.

Leia didn't want to hear the odds of surviving this maneuver. "Yes. Nearly finished."

"Oh, *good*. My servomotors won't stand much more of this bashing about . . . Princess Leia . . . !"

She swung into the cockpit. Han glanced at her, frowned, then waved one soot-streaked hand gallantly at the copilot's seat.

Little gestures like that—not pillows or berry wine—made her love him. "Thank you."

"Chewie wants to ride it out in the turret," he explained.

"I understand."

"Only takes one to execute a ram anyway," Han muttered. "Sorry, old girl."

Leia opened her mouth to complain.

"Not you. The *Falcon*." He started shunting power away from all systems except a few: thrusters, she guessed, fore shields, and the upper gun turret. Again she tried to touch Luke. Again, the harried flicker.

"Okay," he said. "That's programmed. Now we get you to the escape pod."

"Oh-ho, no," she retorted. "Not unless there's room for two. Or three."

"You can't ram on autopilot, and we need a gunner. Kiss me for luck and get clear. The Alliance needs you."

"I'm not going anywhere without you."

"Go on, move," he said. "You're valuable."

"Valuable, schmaluable. I'm not running away. I'm a Skywalker, too. Maybe this is my destiny."

"All right, you're valuable to *me*. Chewie," Han shouted. "Get down here and get the princess into—"

Chewbacca's answer roared through her head. "He means 'no,' " Leia said primly, but she laid a hand on Han's shoulder and squeezed, thanking him without words. Wouldn't this be perfect justice—Vader's daughter, ramming an Imperial ship for the sake of the Alliance? Even if the maneuver failed, she'd achieved a victorious kind of symmetry. Finally, she could think about Darth Vader without flinching. *Watch this, Father!*

Two TIE fighters broke formation and swooped up at them. Possibly their scanners showed no power to the lower turret.

But their scanners had no way of determining this was no stock freighter. Han flipped the *Falcon* one hundred eighty degrees. Chewie snarled gleefully and picked them off.

Leia adjusted her hand on Han's shoulder. He squeezed her fingers before lunging again for the controls. As the *Falcon* approached the patrol craft from behind, the patrol craft almost doubled its rate of fire. Either it had brought another bank of laser cannon online or Commander Thanas had figured out what Han had in mind. Han added a twisting maneuver to the ram program. A display indicated seventeen seconds to impact. They had to survive that long. A massive energy bolt breezed past the *Falcon's* belly.

Chewbacca growled. "Tickles," Han translated. He switched off fore shields, so that impact would transfer more energy to the patrol craft's mass. "Look out, Thanas."

While Dev examined one freestanding bridge station, Luke finished a deep, rasping cough. If he weren't so busy, he'd try to heal himself. He glanced at the deck and twitched his right leg, still unable to shake a sense of impending disaster. Maybe the unseen future was closing in. Ever since he'd glimpsed Han and Leia's future sufferings at Bespin, he'd wondered if he would foresee his own death.

He reached out to check on Leia.

Her determination to face certain destruction caught him off guard. Hurriedly he searched her consciousness and found . . .

Ramming? In the *Falcon*? Luke tumbled down to a sitting position on the deck and ignored Dev's questions. Ignored his body, the Ssi-ruuk still on board, and everything else. He had only seconds.

His itching chest demanded another cough. He had to get out of this bad air! He sent his awareness questing across space in another direction for a presence he knew only faintly: Commander Pter Thanas, aboard the *Dominant*.

Thanas leaned over his pilot's station as Luke seized the edge of his consciousness. Thanas's thoughts, will, and worldview surrounded him. This battle was only a game, but a game he must win, or finish his life in . . . in a slave mine? That explained plenty! Luke eyed the pilot's velocity control slide. Full speed ahead would blow the *Dominant* out of offensive formation and cause heavy damage to already crippled thrusters.

Full speed would also bring him into striking range for the *Shriwirr*. Thanas wanted that.

Abruptly Luke lost contact. He doubled over, coughing, trapped by his weakening body on the hard cold deck of the *Shriwirr*.

"Sir?" Thanas's pilot looked up worriedly. "Is something wrong?"

Pter Thanas blinked. For some reason, the image of Luke Skywalker had sprung into his mind. Dismissing it, he made a difficult decision. He must destroy the threat of contagion, no matter what it cost him.

Smoothly he shoved the control slide forward.

Leia leaned toward Han. "Kiss for luck?" she asked.

"Sure." Those lips would be the last thing he felt.

He was about to touch them when she jerked back. "Luke!" she exclaimed. Chewbacca cried full-alert.

"What, Chewie?" Han spun toward the fore scanners. They claimed that the *Dominant* was plunging forward at irrational speed. "We must've taken another hit," he exclaimed. "They've ionized our scanners again."

Chewie bellowed: Change course!

Han slapped the full sensor array back on, then seized main controls. The *Falcon*'s cockpit grazed the patrol craft so close that it bent lateral antennae on both ships.

"All squadrons, follow us!" he cried. "There's a break in the blockade!" He spoke aside to Leia, "We'll get these Rebel regulars out of the danger zone, then double back to finish the *Dominant*."

She didn't answer.

Leia thrust her head against the back of her seat and concentrated on breathing. As plainly as she'd felt Luke's sudden alarm and his effort, now his exhaustion paralyzed her.

Han shouted into his microphone, "Red group, Gold group, form up on me. We've got 'em between us!"

Out the viewport, Imperial forces shifted. Farther away, four X-wings and an A-wing hadn't made it through the gap before it closed. Her eyes weren't focusing properly. "Where's that patrol craft we were going to ram?" she asked. Her hands shook.

"About ten kilometers to starboard."

Chewie's cry sounded exultant.

Luke? She gripped her armrests. *What's happening to you?*

Luke covered his watering eyes and took several shallow breaths. It irritated him to think that Thanas didn't care who won. He'd like to blast Pter Thanas and his forces out of the universe. The Ssi-ruuk, too. Yes, he was losing his temper. He no longer cared. He simply wanted to stop coughing.

The *Dominant* kept closing, growing perceptibly larger in the viewport.

"Dev, is this cruiser armed?"

"I assume so." Dev reached down a hand.

"Find the . . ." Another cough racked him. "Find the weapons station." Luke let Dev pull him up off the deck.

"Are you all right?"

Luke wasn't. He teetered dangerously close to the dark side, but he didn't care about that either. *Leave me alone, Yoda.* "I need a breath mask."

"It wouldn't fit."

"I know. I've got to try something." He had barely enough energy to focus his attention deep again and regain control. Strength flowed up to match his anger, dark and empowering.

Gasping, he flung the energy aside. In the Emperor's throne room, he'd touched the dark side's power. He could have destroyed Darth Vader . . . shared the throne, ruled the galaxy . . . and been destroyed with the second Death Star, if he hadn't thrown away his lightsaber. Would he sell himself for a lesser temptation?

He stared out the viewport. The *Dominant* blasted another X-wing. *I trusted you, Thanas. I trusted you.* He'd had such hopes for the man. Had he read the Force wrong? And Leia and Han may have escaped for the moment, but until the *Falcon*'s energy banks recharged, they couldn't go far. He had to save them.

He could save them easily, if he—

There will always be people who are strong for evil. His words to Gaeri came back to him. *The stronger you become, the more you're tempted.*

Alien presences snagged his attention from above, on another deck.

"I found weaponry!" Dev cried.

Luke cleared himself of fear and desire and relaxed again into the Force, willfully ignoring the siren call to quick strength and power. He had renounced the darkness. That, not Thanas, was the enemy; and it lived inside him. He reached Dev's side. "Can you get me a battle display?"

"I can try." Dev stepped to another station and started jabbing keys. "You've got an ion cannon on line, I think. Try aiming it with that wheel key. Hurry."

Luke glanced up at the overhead panel. The *Dominant* would be in range within minutes. "Let's try a ranging shot." He swiveled the keyboard into line with Dev's battle array. "First target." He rolled the wheel key and fired. Nothing happened on Dev's screen. He relaxed deeper into the Force and shot again.

"There!" Dev pointed at a visible trail through battle debris.

"I see it." Now a little to the left, widen the beam again, and . . .

One of the *Shriwirr*'s Ssi-ruuvi picket ships imploded. The remaining pair broke formation and shrank into distant points of light.

Now, it all came down to self-defense. A duel between crippled cruisers . . .

Something clicked overhead. Luke lunged aside and ignited his saber. Down to the deck dropped a brown Ssi-ruu and three P'w'ecks, each armed with a paddle beamer. Without pausing to think, he swung two-handed.

Dev skittered backward. "Master!" he shrieked.

Firwirrung swept away from the Jedi and brandished his crippled stump. "Traitor!" he sang. "Betrayer of all you held dear!"

Dev held the P'w'eck's blaster on target, but he couldn't shoot Firwirrung. They had shared a table. He'd slept at the edge of Firwirrung's nest, a pet at its master's feet. His eyes watered. What to do?

"Traitor!" Firwirrung bellowed. "Ungrateful beast!" Wronghanded, the Ssi-ruu swept a silver beam mercilessly and accurately through Dev's shoulders.

Dev crumpled. He fell on his back, bitterly regretting his relapse. Too late, too late. He craned his neck, almost all he could move. The Ssi-ruu spun toward Luke. "Look out!" Dev cried.

Again Luke's thoughts threatened to betray him. *Your hatred has made you powerful*, spoken in the Emperor's cracking voice, spun a web through his memory. He needed power—now. Sweeping his saber blindly, he dispatched the third and last P'w'eck. As Dev fell, the Ssi-ruu aimed his paddle at Luke.

By sheer force of will, Luke snuffed out anger and fear. Aggression, too: Quick power brought temporary triumph, but it seduced and betrayed the wielder. *I will not turn! Not if I die for it.* He leaped into a short suspended somersault and grabbed both edges of the overhead trapdoor, knowing the big Ssi-ruu would have him in another moment. He could do no more on his own. This was the end.

A simultaneous flash from all status screens almost blinded him as he dropped. Expending the dregs of his power, he hung in midair for a full second. Sheets of energy swept the bridge deck. Commander Thanas must have struck. Luke curled up and let himself fall. Bulkheads, decks, and instruments sparkled before they went dim. Then all lights failed, even status screens. He hit the deck and bounced gently upward again.

Gravitics blown too?

He sensed Dev's presence, but not the alien's. Cautiously, coughing in darkness that only the viewport illuminated, he settled back onto deck tiles. The *Shriwirr*'s forward momentum gave it some natural, directional pull. "Dev?"

"Here," croaked the boy, from the direction where artificial gravity had been.

Luke felt himself slide toward one bulkhead. He grasped something huge, hot, and scaly that reeked as if steaming. "Where?" he asked. "Dev?"

"Here. My deck shoes and clothes . . . insulated me a little."

Luke groped along the alien body and found a human form lying close by. Painfully hot, it slid toward the bulkhead with him. "My eyes," moaned Dev. "My head's hot. It's burning."

"Are you in any other pain?" Luke asked urgently.

"I can't . . . feel anything below my shoulders, where he . . . clipped me."

"There's almost no light in here," Luke said, "I don't think you're blinded."

"Bridge . . . probably hit. Shield overload."

Luke's shoulder struck a bulkhead that stopped his slide. He and Dev lodged in the corner. He reached up and found the underside of a console. At least they'd stay here for a while.

Had the Force betrayed him?

He gulped and coughed. He'd resisted the dark side. Darkness favored death. Commander Thanas's blast had killed the **V**-crested Ssi-ruu, but at what cost to Dev?

I'm tired, Yoda. I don't have time for philosophy. Let me rest. He hunched forward, coughing uncontrollably.

"Are you all right?" Dev asked.

Residual heat from the deck and bulkhead stifled him. *Leia*, he called. *Leia?* Too weak to make contact, he projected his slight, returning strength into the youngster. At first, he could only tweak Dev's pain perception. Dev sighed, relaxing tangibly.

As Luke lent power to Dev, he felt his focus strengthen. "Dev," he urged. "Open your mind to me." As he'd shown Eppie Belden how she might heal herself, he gave Dev that knowledge. "Draw on your strength," Luke insisted. "You can do it. I've got to get us off this ship—"

A horrendous cough interrupted him. Automatically, he turned the healing focus onto his chest.

Two greedy pinpoints of life gleamed with primitive instincts: Eat. Cling. Reproduce. Survive.

A blast of understanding underscored his panic. He tried to touch minds with one of the pinpoints, but it had no mind. It ate its way instinctively toward blood. It was chewing through a bronchial tube toward his heart. Reduced to a single instinct, him- self—survive!—he curled toward the bulkhead.

Leia clenched the armrests of her cockpit chair, frightened nearly numb. The star field dipped and swirled in the viewport. She stared at the Ssi-ruuvi cruiser, which drifted directionless like a huge blistered egg.

"The kid bought us breathing room," Han muttered. "I've almost got everybody out of the globe. Is he okay?"

"No! We've got to help him!"

Han's head turned sharply. "He's not dead, is he?"

"I can't feel him any more." She let him hear her desperation.

Han glanced at the sensor boards and examined the alien cruiser. "Thanas scored an awfully good hit. All power's gone. Hull's breached. She's leaking air."

"But it's *Luke*. He could be shielded by some kind of energy field or obstruction." She couldn't relinquish hope. "Can we get in close? Sneak on board?"

"Maybe." Han worked controls, stirring the stars. "I'll try to get closer. Maybe a docking bay—" He swooped at an edge of the Imperial formation. From the dorsal quad gun, Chewie scored a lucky hit on a patrol craft's energy banks. Waves of debris followed the *Falcon* away. So did the rest of the Rebel forces. "There!" he exclaimed. "Now let's get behind that cruiser, where the *Dominant* can't fire on us."

"Rogue Leader to *Falcon*," announced Wedge's voice over the intersquad link, "we're clear to run at the *Dominant*."

"Wait!" Leia exclaimed. "Bully Commander Thanas into changing course so he can't hit the Ssi-ruuvi ship again, but don't destroy him. The Rebellion could use an Imperial cruiser."

"Spoils of battle, Your Highness?" Wedge chuckled. "Will do. If possible. Somehow I doubt the Empire will let us have her."

"Yeah," muttered Han. "Nice thought, but he's certainly got a self-destruct."

"Wedge, just give Commander Thanas a clear message," Leia insisted. "We're not stooping to his tactics."

The egg-shaped cruiser loomed closer. Han steered low along its surface, looking for a place to dock the *Falcon*. *We're coming, Luke,* Leia thought. A terrifying stillness hung where his presence had been.

CHAPTER

20

GLOOM SETTLED OVER GAERIEL LIKE A STICKY GRAY RAIN CLOUD WHEN Commander Thanas's *Dominant* blasted the alien cruiser. Governor Nereus laid a heavy hand on her shoulder. "Come, Gaeriel, you knew that he could not survive. If he returned to Bakura, the plague that followed would make destruction by the Death Star look like a quick, pleasant end to civilization."

She slipped out from under his hand.

Still gloating, he sat down at his ivory desk and summoned a quartet of stormtrooper guards. "Soon, Imperial peace will reign on Bakura. A single pivotal troublemaker remains to be dealt with."

She braced herself to leap before the stormtroopers could fire, but he raised a hand. "You overestimate your importance." He touched his console and ordered, "Bring up the prime minister."

Uncle Yeorg? "No!" Gaeriel exclaimed. "He's a good man. Bakura needs him. You can't—"

"He has become a symbol. I have tried to be lenient with Bakura, and it betrays my good intentions. I give up. I must operate like any other Imperial governor, branding the terror of the Empire on Bakuran hearts. Unless—" He stroked his chin. "Unless he, or an-

other representative of the Captison family, would publicly ask
Bakura to accept me as his successor. You could save your uncle's
life, Gaeriel. Tell me you'll do so, within three minutes, and he'll
survive."

Conscience jabbed her from both sides. She couldn't allow Governor Nereus to execute Uncle Yeorg, but neither could she ask
Bakura to lie down for Wilek Nereus. Again she braced herself to
jump him. Two troopers raised blast rifles.

"Bodyguard training." Governor Nereus smiled. "They're watching you."

Gaeri stared around Governor Nereus's office, taking in plaques,
tri-Ds, and crystals. Teeth, parasites, what other loathsome inter-
ests did he keep hidden? "You say you'd let him live. But would
you? Or would you infect him with some parasite, like Eppie
Belden? That's not alive."

"Orn Belden thought so."

Another trooper entered, pushing her manacled uncle with the
business end of a blast rifle. Yeorg stood straight-shouldered, looking taller in her eyes than Nereus could, for all the governor's bulk.

"One offer, Captison, one minute to accept," Nereus announced.
"Get on the tri-D. Tell your people to lay down their weapons and
submit to Imperial rule. To me, as your designated successor. Or
die here with your niece watching."

Yeorg Captison didn't hesitate. He pulled his shoulders back,
creating dignity out of an old, torn Bakuran uniform tunic. "I'm
sorry, Gaeri. Don't watch. Remember me bravely."

"Gaeriel?" Governor Nereus licked his upper lip. "Will you make
the broadcast? Perhaps I could sweeten the pot—"

At that instant, the trooper beyond Uncle Yeorg buckled and fell.
A piercing electronic whine rose from all five troopers' helmets.
Gaeri leaped for the nearest incapacitated trooper, seized his rifle,
and waved it in Governor Nereus's general direction. Evidently
he'd hesitated. His ornamental blaster remained in his crossdraw
holster.

All five stormtroopers writhed. Even from a distance, the whine hurt her ears. What was going on? "Take off your blaster, Nereus," she said shakily. Whatever this was, it looked like her chance.

"You don't even know how to find the safety," he answered, but he kept both hands on the ivory desktop. Clumsily, Uncle Yeorg seized another helpless trooper's blast rifle with his fingertips. His wrist-bound grip looked ineffectual, but at least the trooper didn't have the rifle any more.

Governor Nereus's command console flashed and went black. The door slid open. Eppie Belden marched in with a spring in her step surprising for a woman of 132. Her round-faced caregiver, Clis, slunk behind. Eppie brandished a blaster with competent ease. "Hah," she exclaimed. "Got 'em all." She strode straight to Governor Nereus and lifted the blaster from his holster, then disarmed the other stormtroopers. "Clis," she ordered, "get a vibroknife and cut Yeorg out of those binders." Clis hustled out, pale and obviously ill at ease in a confrontation. Gaeri sympathized with Clis. It was Eppie's bravura that startled her.

"You," Eppie snarled at Governor Nereus. "If those hands move, you're dead. Do you understand?"

"Who are you, old woman?"

Eppie laughed. "Start guessing, youngster. I'm Orn Belden's revenge."

Belden: Nereus's lips formed the word. "You can't be here," he cried. "Scarring of the neocortex is permanent."

"Tell that to Commander Skywalker."

Governor Nereus's cheek twitched. "Skywalker is dead, by now! They'll eat him alive. Inside out—"

Eppie seemed to shrink. "Coward." She leveled her blaster at his chest, silencing him. He pulled a deep breath, clenching and unclenching his fists. The tableau held for several breaths, then Eppie lowered the blaster slightly. "I'm giving you to the Rebels," she growled. "I'd had it in mind to let Bakura set up a revolutionary tribunal, but if you've killed the Rebels' Jedi, I have a guess they'll take a stiffer revenge out of your lousy hide than Bakura would."

Gaeri wished Eppie'd just kill him now—obviously she had the guts to do it—but evidently Eppie had other ideas. Gaeri glanced out the office window. Another stormtrooper lay writhing on the greenway path. Still another wrenched off his lumpish white helmet and flung it aside, then knelt, covering his ears with his hands and shaking his head.

"Where were you, Eppie?" Gaeri asked.

"Close by, in the complex," she muttered. "Is it true, what he said about Skywalker?"

"We don't have any confirmation that he's dead, but Governor Nereus . . . infected him. How did you do this?" She waved a hand, taking in Nereus's command center and the limp storm-troopers.

Eppie stared at Nereus. "A couple of dozen old friends who are still in high places, with good access codes," she said. "An alien invasion force that kept most of *his* troopers too busy to watch their backs. And one new ally." She called back over her shoulder, "Come on in."

Through the doorway rolled Luke's droid, Artoo-Detoo. "When the emergency patrol took you away," said Eppie, "he got to a master terminal and called me in. I sent out a friend to fetch him. This little guy's worth his weight in reactor fuel on the master circuits."

"You took off his restraining bolt?" Nereus's hands twitched at his sides.

"You ought to lock him up," Gaeri whispered. "He's losing his grip."

Eppie flicked her blaster's safety on and off. "I almost wish he'd try something."

Curled up in the darkness, Luke could think of only one thing to try. He breathed slowly and focused his attention on the pinpoints of living instinct inside his chest. He touched one. Neurologically primitive, its only response was to flinch and go on eating. They were obviously parasites. He sensed their ravenous hunger.

As panic threatened to immobilize him, he thought of the smell of fresh blood: sweet, warm, faintly metallic. He extended the thinnest thread of a probe toward one creature.

Recognition: Some minuscule awareness understood. He imagined mouthparts pulling free and a head turning toward him. It was desperately hard to project the smell while judging its effect on a primitive, alien awareness. He brushed the second creature with the scent.

All around his point of consciousness, his own heart thudded. He swirled the scent-illusion away from them a few millimeters, tempting them to follow. One awareness dimmed out and forgot the scent. He brushed it again with the tempting odor of life. It hummed recognition. It drew closer.

He couldn't concentrate on both individuals. His body wanted to cough, and within seconds, something was definitely in the way.

He inhaled cautiously and then exploded, hacking. Something spewed out of his mouth.

One wasn't enough. Virtually exhausted, he crafted the scent-illusion again and stroked the remaining creature. Its attention flickered for an instant, then faded. He thrust again into its perception.

This time, he snagged it. Slowly, slowly, he led it along a dark bronchial tunnel. It radiated fierce hunger. He tried not to gag or choke—or swallow. Slowly he sipped a deep breath around the creature, inhaling until his aching lungs strained.

Then he let go, retching and coughing. This creature caught on his teeth. It squirmed, making a gruesome mouthful. He spit it out and then flailed blindly for it in the dark cabin. Something squashed. He couldn't find the other creature.

He lay limp on the deck tiles, too tired to feel triumphant, and shut out the external world to perform a focusing exercise. Slowly his despair lifted, then he remembered Dev. They had to find a way off the *Shriwirr*. Without power, and possibly still under attack, it could break up around them.

He couldn't. Sleep beckoned, and so did the Jedi healing trance. His eyes ached. He could shut them for a few moments. . . .

A glimmer on one bulkhead caught his eye. Was he hallucinating lights in the corridor?

"Luke?" called Leia's voice. "Luke!"

Disbelieving, he pushed up off the deck. "Here!" His throat burned. He must've scratched it bloody.

A pocket luma swept into the *Shriwirr's* bridge, followed by a slim arm. The rest of Leia wore a breath mask, shipsuit, and magnetic boots. Han and Chewie followed. Her luma shone like life itself. "How did you get on board?" Luke asked her.

Leia hurried closer. "They left the landing bays open. They're gone. The ship's dead, except for you."

"Where's—" Luke began. Then he spotted Dev.

The boy lay stretched out beside him, tangled in his long robes. His chest rose and fell slowly. Massive red energy burns traversed his exposed arms and face. His eyelids covered sunken gaps.

Beside him on the deck tiles wriggled a creature as long and thick as a finger. Short legs waved wildly at the light. Its fat, striped wet body tapered in green and black stripes toward a pointed end. Audibly disgusted, Leia squashed it flat.

"Thanks," Luke whispered.

"Relax, kid." Han knelt and raised him over one shoulder.

Luke swallowed. "Bring Dev."

"You've got to be kidding . . . *Leia!*" She was already trying to hoist the unconscious youth. Chewie pushed in and cradled Dev like a doll. "Let's move," ordered Han.

Safely on board the *Falcon*, Leia knelt beside Luke's bunk and rested her head on his shoulder. Delicately he accepted the link to her strength. He bathed himself in healing energy that felt clean, warm, and familiar. When he swallowed, his throat no longer burned. Soon, he could breathe without wanting to cough.

Where had he picked up those nauseating parasites?

He sat up. "I'll rest later," he insisted, "really rest."

"You'd better," Leia murmured, "but we haven't got time now. We've still got the *Dominant* to deal with. Its repair crews have probably been busy."

"What happened to it?" Luke gulped at the thought of Pter Thanas. Had he doomed the Imperial commander to slavery?

"It blew out its lateral thrusters again, so it can't steer. And signals coming off Bakura are crazy. There's a revolution going on."

Luke slid to his feet. The right leg still ached, but not as badly. "I'm ready," he said, but he let Leia support him. They shuffled to the cockpit together. Leia helped him fall into a seat.

"Hey, youngster," Han greeted him. "You look pretty good for a dead man." Chewbacca whuffled agreement.

Luke cleared his throat experimentally. "Thanks." He pointed at the subspace radio. "Anything on there about Gaeriel Captison?"

"Maybe," said Han. "Some groundside group claims it's got Wilek Nereus in custody. They're barricading themselves inside the Imperial offices sector of the Bakur complex." The *Dominant* appeared to sweep underneath the *Falcon*'s hull; an illusion, of course—the *Falcon*, not the *Dominant*, was maneuvering. "Threepio worked on maximizing energy bank recharge while we were on the Flutie ship. I think we can deal with Thanas the way he deserves. Then we'll worry about Nereus."

"Easy—" Leia interjected.

"Wait," Luke said a little louder. In Commander Thanas's place, he'd order the huge, valuable cruiser destroyed, rather than let it fall into Alliance hands. He couldn't spot a single TIE fighter. They'd probably scattered, afraid to be caught in the shock waves of a *Carrack*-class cruiser's final explosion. Confirming Luke's guess, a babble of Rebel voices announced that the *Dominant* had lost shield generators. *Not lost. He shut them down,* Luke guessed.

"Here goes!" Han swung the *Falcon* around to deliver a death blow.

"Wait!" Luke repeated. "We want that ship. Even damaged, it'd be a lucky catch." Luke leaned toward the pickup. "All forces," he ordered, "this is Commander Skywalker. Cease fire immediately. Alliance forces, confirm on this channel."

"What?" asked Han. Three younger pilots also protested.

Luke repeated his order, then he tried to thrust the Force across the distance to touch Commander Thanas once more. He couldn't. Even though he'd cast out the parasites before they chewed into his heart, he was too weary from using the Force. If Thanas elected to destroy the *Dominant,* Luke could do nothing.

Except . . .

Out into the Force he projected calm. Peace. Peace was possible. . . .

And this was Thanas's last chance.

Pter Thanas flinched as Skywalker's order went out over the subspace radio. During this battle something had reawakened in him, something that cared. Something he'd buried years ago, at Alzoc III.

Nereus wouldn't hesitate to send him back there, too. He glanced at a red-barred compartment. It hid a lever labeled "self-destruct." Another compartment, halfway across the bridge, held its mate. Pulled simultaneously, they would blow the *Dominant's* main generator. The blast would incinerate everything around it.

His career was over.

He turned to his aide, a stiff-backed five-year man. "Abandon ship," he ordered, "all hands." Crew members might get far enough away to escape destruction. Bridge crew, however, must remain. Such was standard Imperial discipline. Those levers had no time delay.

The young aide shifted from one foot to the other, awaiting his next order.

Thanas stared at his black boots, spotlessly polished on a polished deck. At Bakura, as at Alzoc III, he'd received unethical orders from a superior officer he did not respect. These could be his final moments, sacrificed to an uncaring Empire . . . the legacy of a dead emperor.

Or he could recant and admit that he'd misspent his entire life.

Then again, he remembered Governor Nereus's parting orders. Coolly he straightened and looked around the bridge. His crew was visibly bracing for a last act of heroism.

"Communications," he barked, "give me a channel to Skywalker. Wherever he is."

"Done, sir."

Pter Thanas faced the communications station and laid a hand on his blaster. Someone on this bridge would be watching him. "Commander Skywalker," he called, sliding off the safety. "I must warn you of something. Any contact you have with humans endangers their lives. Nereus ordered me specifically to ensure that you did not return to Bakura. He says you now carry some kind of infestation or plague."

"I've taken care of that," Skywalker's voice answered, "before it could spread. Remember, I am a Jedi."

He should have expected that. Still, Skywalker's voice sounded weak. "Truly? Or is that just for show?"

"I'm on board the *Falcon* with my closest friends. I wouldn't be here if I had any doubt."

Thanas glanced around the bridge. "Very well. If I surrendered the *Dominant* to you—"

Motion caught his peripheral vision. A crewman sprang to his feet, lunging for his belt. Thanas spun and stunned him: the Imperial Security plant, here to make certain the warship didn't fall into enemy hands.

"Commander Thanas?" asked Skywalker's voice. "Are you there?"

"Slight distraction. If I surrendered the *Dominant*, would you guarantee that you will release my crew members, who conducted this battle under my orders?"

"Yes," Skywalker said hoarsely. "We'll send all Imperial personnel to a neutral pickup point, and let them return to their homes—unless any want to defect. You must give each one that choice."

"I can't do that."

"I'll arrange it."

Thanas gripped a railing. What kind of traitor handed over Imperial property and gave Imperial personnel the chance to jump ship?

The kind of traitor who still owed Talz slave miners a debt he could never repay. Perhaps the Alliance would be more lenient than that colonel had been back at Alzoc III. "Done," said Thanas. "Take me to the Alliance and deal with me as you will."

Skywalker exhaled heavily. "I accept your ship. And, temporarily, your person. Shuttle over to my . . ."—he seemed to hesitate—"my flagship. Please bring a medical corpsman. I'll see that he's released as well."

"Are you ill?"

"I said I've taken care of that. I have another human on board who was badly burned. I think he could make it, if he got help quickly."

"Oh." Thanas narrowed his eyes and made a guess. "Sibwarra?"

Skywalker hesitated. "Yes."

"You're asking too much." What irrational, supernatural agency had raised up Luke Skywalker to judge his scruples? He paced along the bridge pit past humming banks of instruments. "But I would like to see Sibwarra brought to justice. Empire or Alliance, it doesn't matter—so long as it's a human jury. I'll see what I can do."

"I'll shuttle over a skeleton crew for the *Dominant*," said Skywalker.

Solo's voice interjected over Skywalker's, "But you'd better come over unarmed, in a survival pod. I'm making a big concession, letting you on board at all."

"Understood . . . General."

The speaker fell silent.

Thanas drew a deep breath. He had no idea what to expect next, but he wasn't taking his crew into it. He'd face the Alliance's wrath, plague risk and all, on his own. Almost. "Bridge crew, board lifeboats. Reserve a single two-man evacuation pod."

"Sir." One pivoted and loped off the deck.

"Carry him, someone." Thanas nodded at the Security man lying stunned on the deck. "Take him with you. Captain Jamer, you're in command."

"Sir." A beetle-bodied little man stalked out at rear guard. Pter Thanas rubbed his chin, then opened a line to his medical staff. Perhaps Skywalker had neutralized one threat of contagion, but Thanas wouldn't feel safe in the Jedi's presence until his own staff checked him over.

Luke glanced at Han, who maneuvered the *Falcon* toward a tiny round object. Sensors confirmed two life-forms. "You're sure you want to take him on board?" Han fidgeted.

Luke sighed, weary with arguing. "Yes. Next question?"

"Why?" Han snapped.

"We're all a little edgy," Leia said, "but this is the only place to put him. We've got to check on the rumors from Salis D'aar immediately."

"Well, even unarmed, he's not staying loose on my ship. Handcuff him to Chewie—no, to Threepio—and lock them in a cargo hold. Threepio can entertain him."

Luke smiled. "That sounds like punishment enough for anyone."

"Poor Thanas," agreed Leia.

Chewbacca delicately stroked airlock controls, keying the vacuum seal for manual release, and then Luke, Han, and Leia walked to the airlock and waited. Several minutes later, Commander Thanas stepped through with both hands raised. The posture tugged his khaki tunic askew. "I'm unarmed," he insisted. "Check me."

Leia ran a weapons scanner over him. "Looks clean," she announced. Meanwhile, Commander Thanas's small, slight companion trained a medical sensor up and down Luke's body. Luke held still, guessing Thanas had chosen the medic for his wide-eyed, soft-chinned, harmless appearance. "What's in that pack?" Leia asked sharply.

"Medical equipment. Burn treatment. Commander Skywalker asked for—"

"This way." Luke turned away from the top airlock.

The corpsman dropped his medisensor into a pocket. "Skywalker's clean, too, Commander. A preliminary scan shows severe mechanical bronchitis, but no infestation." He shrugged at Thanas.

Luke hadn't doubted, but the medic's diagnosis reassured him. He led deeper into the ship.

Threepio sat at the hologram board. Behind him, on a single bunk, Dev lay still. Threepio stood. "Greetings," he began cheerily. "I am—"

"Quiet," Leia murmured. "Take this pair of binders and attach yourself to Commander Thanas. Escort him to the aft cargo bay. You're designated security until further notice."

One binder snicked shut around Thanas's wrist, and the other clinked against Threepio's. "Very well, Your Highness. Come with me, sir. I am See-Threepio, protocol droid . . ."

Luke led the mousy little medic to Dev and gently drew a sheet off the youth's scarred, folded arms. "He's in a Jedi healing trance,"

Luke said, "and he's in no pain—for now. See what you can do for him."

"I'll try," said the medic, "but frankly, I've encountered energy-blast trauma before." He ran the pocket medisensor over Dev's stomach and chest, then shook his head. "There's little I can do. He might live a day, if he's . . . I won't say lucky. If he regains consciousness, he'll suffer. Internal damage is . . . well, there's nothing to keep him alive."

"Please try. He changed his mind about the Ssi-ruuk." And Dev had so much Force potential. He *had* to survive.

"Huh," the medic answered without enthusiasm. He reached deeper into his equipment pack.

Luke could barely keep his own body moving. Half stumbling, he rejoined Han in the cockpit. "We've got an invitation," Han announced, "from a lady named Eppie Belden. She claims to know you. She's with your friend Gaeriel at the Bakur complex. I guess there's a nasty prisoner they want the Alliance to deal with."

"Governor Nereus?" asked Leia.

"Looks that way."

He'd last seen Gaeri being dragged by Artoo from the cantina. Abruptly he remembered that meal they'd shared. This news suggested that Gaeri was safe, though. And had Eppie healed herself? Had they captured Governor Nereus? "Can you land the *Falcon* on a roof port?"

Leia laughed behind him. "Han can land the *Falcon* on an ice cube if he wants to."

Luke glanced around the cockpit, counting heads. "I assume you're calling in reinforcements?" he asked Han.

"I, uh, just ordered your new *Dominant* crew into position to fire on the Imperial garrison at Salis D'aar. It'll take a while. Our B-wing squadron's tugboating it into place. And we've got two X-wing pilots coming in to fly cover, just in case."

"Good work, Han." And Luke had his reputation as a Jedi. So

long as he didn't stumble in plain sight, the Imperials would consider him a threat. He pictured Governor Nereus's face when he walked off the *Falcon* alive.

"Your Bakuran lady friends promised to meet us at the roof port. We'll see if they manage it."

"I'm going to lie down." Luke gave one last cough. "Get me up when you're about to land."

The *Millennium Falcon* swooped through a textured blanket of clouds toward Salis D'aar. Over the city and west across one river, smoke drifted. Han brought up a remote sensor as they decelerated. Peering between Han's head and Chewie's, Luke spotted a knot of people behind a blast barricade at the complex roof port. A familiar shape waited with them. "Artoo!" he exclaimed. A swirl of long blue-green skirts, backing away from the blocked-off landing zone, was obviously Gaeriel. The *Falcon* dropped steadily on its repulsors. Gaeriel's uncle the prime minister stood near an unbound, defiant Wilek Nereus, who still wore Imperial drab with red and blue rank buttons.

"He doesn't look like a prisoner to me," Leia muttered, pointing through the viewport. "I'll make you a bet Governor Nereus doesn't intend to surrender the Salis D'aar garrison. He could hold that against all of us for a long time."

Han reached for belly gun controls.

"Don't you dare." Leia shook her head. "We're back to diplomacy."

"And we've got Commander Thanas," said Luke. "He could surrender the garrison."

The *Falcon* settled to ground with a muffled thud.

"Particularly if you told him to," Leia returned. "How are you feeling? Could you . . . ?"

"I can't push it. You'd better take charge."

"Right," she said grimly. "I've set up enough Resistance cells to know what happens if we botch this."

.   .   .

Leia clenched her seat while Han sprang up and loosened his blaster in its leg holster. "Okay, Goldenrod," Han called into the comlink. "Bring Thanas to the main ramp."

Luke stood up more slowly. Leia almost saw two Lukes: one strong, cocky, and victorious, the image he meant to project—and one withdrawn, worried, exhausted, and in pain. Tired enough to make mistakes.

She squared her shoulders. "Do you want to stay on board until it's obvious which way this is going?" she asked.

"Uh . . . sure." Luke scratched the back of his neck. "Nereus probably thinks that he killed me, anyway." He stepped to one side of the main hatch and unhooked his lightsaber. From there, he could hear without being seen. "Be careful."

Threepio appeared around the bend in the corridor. Commander Thanas matched his pace step for step. "Your droid tells interesting stories," Thanas commented drily. "Despite the fact that he insists —repeatedly—that he's not much of a storyteller."

Educating the prisoner, Threepio? Commander Thanas had probably gotten an earful of Alliance propaganda.

The main hatch hissed and then opened. Leia led down the ramp. The rooftop group filed around the blast barricade toward them, Captison in the lead, closely followed by Governor Nereus and his female escorts . . . and Artoo. Han kept one hand on his blaster. Once Leia and Han reached the rooftop, she glanced back. Threepio followed, shackled to Thanas. Chewie came last, bowcaster already fitted with a quarrel. The air smelled unpleasantly smoky.

"Artoo!" exclaimed Threepio. "You can't *imagine* what I've been through—"

"Save it," snapped Han.

Commander Thanas ignored his metallic escort and walked eyes-ahead, expressionless like a man who expected a brutal dressing down. He passed Leia at the foot of the ramp and came to attention as well as anyone could when handcuffed to a protocol droid.

"I assume you're not expecting compliments." Governor Nereus closed the distance between them, clasping both of his hands behind his back in a swaggering pose. "A few years ago, when I commanded a cruiser, a commander who surrendered his ship was stood against the nearest wall and shot."

Leia stood forward. "We brought him with us only to prove that he's in our hands, Governor. He is not your prisoner. He's ours. As I hear you are."

"I'd like to see you hold either of us."

"You have no space forces left. Surrender your garrison, and you and all your people may leave Bakura freely . . . immediately." An X-wing flying patrol tore shreds from the low smoky clouds.

Governor Nereus smiled placidly at Leia. "Perhaps you forget that I still command three thousand land-based troops. Furthermore, Imperial survivors are landing all over Bakura in lifeboats as we speak. You have had a single ship surrender to you. That is all."

"We've moved the *Dominant* into a stationary orbit, Governor," Leia countered with a grateful glance at Han. "Its armaments are locked onto the Salis D'aar garrison. I know it's not designed for planetary assault, but it'll do considerable damage if we give the order. Even if we released you, you couldn't hold Bakura forever against the will of its people."

"No? That is standard Imperial policy. It's working all over the galaxy." Governor Nereus kept his hands open and in full view. Evidently Han's blaster made him more nervous than he was showing otherwise.

Someone shoved Leia from the left. Gaeriel strode between Han and Governor Nereus, keeping just out of the line of fire. Leia had never seen her look so defiant. She'd knotted her shawl over her skirt, out of the way, and wedged a blaster rifle under one arm. It dangled, ready to use. Finally Leia guessed what Luke saw in her. "Governor," Gaeriel announced, "if nothing else is going to come of your treachery, then I shall make my own small gesture. I resign from Imperial service."

Nereus centered his hands over the side stripes of his trousers. "You cannot. You belong to the Empire."

"I think not, Excellency." She spoke calmly, but Leia saw that her unmatched eyes were puffy, as if she'd been crying. If she'd been grieving for Luke, she had a surprise in store. "Princess Leia, please accept my congratulations on your victory—" Gaeriel stiffened, turning as pale as if she'd seen a ghost. Leia pivoted back on one foot.

Luke stood at the center of the *Falcon*'s main hatch, saber in hand but not ignited, looking like a lithe gray-suited shadow against the *Falcon*'s dark interior. She would've bet his smile had something to do with Gaeriel's open mouth and wide eyes. The thin little woman standing next to her brightened and whispered, "Hello, Jedi."

Whatever Wilek Nereus had stepped forward to say, he forgot it. "No!" he exclaimed, horror twisting his heavy features. "You can't be here! Get back on board! You'll infest us all! You don't realize—"

Luke took one step down. "Gaeriel Captison belongs to Bakura, not the Empire."

Governor Nereus whirled toward Gaeri. With speed that belied his age and bulk, he yanked the blast rifle out of her hands.

Luke dropped into a crouch. Han had already drawn his blaster. Nereus fired twice. One bolt deflected off the *Falcon*'s hull. The other flashed toward Luke, intersecting a green-white blade that whipped into its path and deflected energy back along its own course.

Wilek Nereus fell blank-eyed. Luke stumbled, too. Gaeriel gasped. Leia froze in place. *Get up, Luke!*

Artoo rolled forward at top speed, beeping and whistling. Slowly Luke pressed back to his feet. He held the saber upright in front of him, its hum the only sound Leia heard over her thumping heart.

He waved the little droid back. Han leaned over the governor, blaster steady, but Nereus didn't move again.

Leia stepped around Governor Nereus's body toward the Bakuran prime minister. Captison snapped to attention, regaining poise. "Prime Minister Captison," she said, "for this moment Bakura stands alone. If your people choose to rejoin the Empire . . ." she nodded aside at Commander Thanas, "we will withdraw and leave you to conduct your own affairs. Commander Thanas may supervise your defense against the Ssi-ruuk, if they return before the Empire sends you another governor. You may continue alone, knowing the Ssi-ruuk might return. But if you choose to align yourself with the Alliance, we should negotiate a permanent truce immediately."

Captison saluted Leia, then Luke. "Your Highness—Commander —we thank you. It is not likely, however, that the Imperial garrison will surrender."

Luke walked slowly down the ramp. Leia hoped none of the others guessed that weakness, not dignity, set his pace. "We have accepted Commander Thanas's surrender," he said, "including the *Dominant,* the land-based forces, and the Imperial garrison."

Leia held her breath and waited for Commander Thanas to contradict Luke's statement. The thin Imperial frowned, but he said nothing. Was he holding his tongue, or was Luke keeping him from speaking?

"Commander Thanas," said Luke, "you are free from custody. If Bakura's citizens ask the Empire to leave, you will oversee the troops' withdrawal."

Thanas nodded and raised his wrist. Threepio's arm came with it.

"Let him go, Threepio," said Luke.

The droid produced a master chip and waved it over Thanas's binders.

Luke moved closer and looked up at Thanas. "Take charge of your men, sir. Remember, the *Dominant*'s new crew is watching."

Thanas opened his mouth as if he wanted to speak, then seemed to change his mind. A double-podded local patrol craft streaked out of the hazy sky and landed close to the *Falcon*. Two Bakuran enforcement officers sprang out, steering a repulsor litter between them. They hurried toward Nereus's body.

Commander Thanas turned on one heel, keeping his military posture painfully straight. "Detail," he called, "fall in." Nereus's stormtroopers followed Commander Thanas's long stride toward the nearest drop shaft.

"You're just going to trust him?" Leia whispered to Luke. "What did you do?"

"Nothing." Luke's eyes also tracked the commander. "He's not forgetting the *Dominant*. Even if it's not up to full capacity, we hold the high ground. And besides, I have a feeling."

"Will you excuse me?" Prime Minister Captison raised his bushy white eyebrows. "I must make an emergency broadcast. I can almost guarantee that Bakura's people will choose to join the Alliance after all that has transpired today, but I must consult them."

Leia could almost guarantee it, too. "By all means." She inclined her head respectfully. To her delight, Luke saluted and even Han came to attention. Captison strode toward a different drop shaft.

Still watching, Father? Leia glanced over one shoulder, but all she saw . . . or sensed . . . was hazy gray sky. Every world she took from the Empire was another defeat for the ghost of Darth Vader.

On the other hand, if Anakin Skywalker cared to look on, that wouldn't bother her in the future. She'd found her peace in the midst of battle.

Gaeriel pulled her elderly companion toward Luke. This, Leia guessed, had to be Eppie Belden. "Well done, young man!" The tiny woman gripped Luke's elbow, then seized his hand and pumped hard. "And thanks. If Bakura can ever do something for you, just name it."

Gaeriel glanced aside, then said to Luke with heartfelt relief, "You're alive. Did you—"

"Can we talk later? I've got a very sick . . . friend on board, being treated for burns."

Forget Dev Sibwarra, Leia wanted to shout. *He's dead. This girl has finally come around. Don't let her go, if you want her!*

"Oh," Gaeriel exclaimed, stepping back. "Go ahead. I'll wait."

Leia frowned at her brother's back. He was already halfway up the ramp, walking stiffly with his head bowed.

Gaeriel touched Leia's arm. "I've never met anyone like him, Your Highness."

"You never will again, if he leaves you here," Leia muttered. "Excuse me." She trotted after Luke.

CHAPTER

21

LUKE REJOINED LEIA AT THE HATCHWAY. "HE'S STRONG ENOUGH TO APprentice," he explained hastily. "And young enough. We've got to save him."

"I'll help if I can. But, Luke . . ."

Commander Thanas's medical corpsman held a mask and clear tubing to Dev's mouth, and he'd bandaged Dev's ruined eyes. "Bacta purge," he said briskly. "It might accomplish something. It might not. At any rate, I gave him something for pain."

Abruptly Dev lifted one arm. Luke leaned over and tried to smile encouragingly. "Dev? It's me, Luke."

Dev pulled the tube out of his mouth. "Wait!" cried the medic. Sticky fluid splashed the deck. Luke grabbed and bent the tube, stopping its flow. The sickly sweet smell evoked wretched, claustrophobic memories of a tank on icy Hoth. The corpsman seized the tubing and locked on a clamp. "Don't let him talk long, if you really want to save him."

Luke knelt. "Dev, you can start your real training even before your body heals. It'll keep you occupied."

"Oh, Luke." Dev smiled back faintly. "I could never become a

Jedi. My mind is scarred. I've been . . ." He pulled a deep breath and struggled on. ". . . controlled. By others—for too long, Luke. Thank you for letting me finish cleanly."

Luke lifted Dev's scarred hand between his own. "Alliance surgeons can do wonderful things with prosthetics. They'll treat you at Endor."

"Prosthetics?" Dev's eyebrows raised above the bandage. "Sounds like entechment." He shuddered.

"Don't let him talk any more!" The medical corpsman shoved Luke out of the way and pushed his mask back onto Dev's face. Luke tottered against the bulkhead and stretched toward Dev's presence to reassure him. Dev gleamed in the Force, fully as clean as he had claimed. Dev must have concentrated on healing his spirit, not his body, while he lay in the Jedi trance.

But he seemed to be shrinking. Luke knelt again and enveloped Dev with his own strength, trying to anchor Dev's presence more strongly to his ravaged body. Dev returned a wash of gratitude.

Abruptly, light flooded out of the Dev-spot in the Force. Luke flinched at its brilliance. "Dev?" he called, alarmed.

The flash faded. Dev Sibwarra's presence vanished with it into a vast, surging sea of light.

"Lost 'im," the corpsman growled, glaring at his medisensor. "He really didn't have a chance, Commander."

Luke stared. *Where's the justice?* he wanted to cry. *He'd made a start. He could have learned control.*

Couldn't he? Luke seemed to see Yoda standing on the *Falcon*'s gaming table, leaning on his stick and shaking his head.

"Sorry." The medic drained his tubing, coiled it, and swept his other gear back into the carry pack. "I gave it my best try with portable equipment."

"I'm sure you did," Leia murmured.

Luke covered his eyes with both hands and coughed.

"You'd better rest, sir," said the medic. Leia's voice, and the medic's, grew fainter and farther away. Luke stayed on his knees, remembering the young man who had suffered, and escaped, and died on the celebration side of victory.

Some time later, a small hand rested on his shoulder. "Leia?" he asked softly. "Did you—"

"No, Luke. Leia's down in the complex negotiating. It's me."

That was Gaeriel's voice. Had Han invited her on board? Luke struggled to stand, but his right leg wouldn't push. "Help," he muttered. Gaeriel pulled him up by one arm. To his surprise, she swept off the shawl she had tied around her waist. Delicately she shrouded Dev's face.

"Thank you," he murmured. "No one else cared."

"I did that for your sake, not his." Gaeri raised one eyebrow. "Was he really all right, in the end?"

"In his mind? Yes," he answered quietly.

"Why?" Gaeriel whispered. "Why did you want to save him of all people?"

Not wanting to meet her eyes, Luke spoke toward the *Falcon*'s deck. "He'd known suffering. I wanted him to know strength."

"I'm not sure it was just strength you showed him. You also gave him human compassion."

Control. He must control. He wanted to collapse in her arms. He tried to smile.

"Don't." She slid her hands around his waist, then up toward his shoulders. Pulling him close, she whispered, "Let it out, Luke. It hurts. I know. You'll have joy later. The Cosmos balances."

Flinging pretense aside, Luke held her and cried. She stood and took it. Maybe seeing him like this would balance her memories of his powers. Finally quieted, he led her to seats at the hologram table.

"How did you—" She faltered. "I assume—you killed the Trichoid larvae?"

"Is that what they were?" he asked. "How do you know?"

"I got one, too. Governor Nereus called in a medic for me. But you had no medic."

"I had the Force."

"You were wonderful at the cantina. I'll never forget that."

"What else could I have done?"

She stared up at him. Strands of honey-colored hair, stirred by the *Falcon*'s ventilators, drifted into her face.

"Your world is beautiful," he murmured. "I'm glad to have seen it."

"I have no desire to leave again. Ever."

"Bakura will be sending an envoy to the Alliance," he said gently, trying to mask his last hope. "You're perfectly trained for it."

"When that day comes I will nominate someone else, Luke. I have work to do here. Eppie will need me, and Uncle Yeorg. I'm a Captison. I've been trained for *this*."

"I . . . understand." Disappointed in the end, he rested his elbows on the hologram table and shifted his legs. The right one still ached where he'd wrenched it, and breathing deeply hurt. He'd spend the entire hyperspace run back to Endor in another healing trance. Either that, or Too-Onebee would dump him into a tank again. Probably both.

"Are you taking prisoners of war?" she asked quietly.

"We don't do that. It would make liars of us, and lies of our goals. Every trooper we send home will tell three or four others that the Alliance . . . well, that we had them in our power but we let them go."

"Luke?" she whispered. She laid her fingertips on his shoulder. "I'm sorry."

He felt the softening he'd hoped for, too late. He turned to her slowly and fully opened himself to the Force, hoping to make the sensation last. This time, she wouldn't raise her defenses. "What for?" he asked. "This has been a victory for humankind."

Her cheeks colored. "I want to be your ally, Luke. But from a distance."

He pushed back a quiet desolation that threatened to send him over another emotional brink. He mustn't think of spending forever alone. "From a distance," he agreed, hesitantly touching her face. "But just once, from here."

She leaned into his arms. He kissed her, letting the moment flood his perception, petal-warm lips and the deep sweet warmth of her life presence.

Before she could pull away and ruin the memory, he released her. "I'll see you off the ship," he murmured. They stood. He walked her along the corridor, careful not to limp.

The medic intercepted him at the top of the ramp. "I believe you need attention, sir. I assure you my sympathies are neutral."

"Good-bye," Gaeri murmured.

Luke squeezed her hand. *The Force will be with you, Gaeri. Always.* He stared after her until she vanished into a drop shaft with a last flicker of skirts. A breeze dropped swirls of fine ash from the rioters' fires on permacrete outside. The last stormtrooper had long vanished down the drop shaft, following Commander Thanas.

Luke faced the young Imperial medic. "Right," he said, rubbing his forehead. *Here we go again.*

"Come on, Junior." Han leaned against a bulkhead. "Let's use this doc while we've got him."

Luke let them lead him to a bunk. He drew a careful breath and lay down to have his leg and lungs scanned.

It was a good thing Thanas and his garrison didn't know that the *Dominant* was really no threat to Salis D'aar. Its new "crew" consisted of two excited Calamarian youngsters—two who hadn't come down for shore leave.

Rank by rank, a thousand Imperial personnel boarded a large but ancient Bakuran space liner under Commander Pter Thanas's eyes. Bakura wanted the Empire gone. The announcement had come yesterday, two hours after Nereus's death. Over half his men weren't even there to ship out. Some had never straggled in, dead or deserted. Others had vanished last night: Skywalker's people were keeping his promise, no doubt. Most of Thanas's ranking officers led the formation, but he noted the absence of two medical supervisors and the weather officer. All remaining Imperial war materiel—right down to the stormtroopers' armor—must be left to the Bakurans, forming the nucleus of their new home defense force. Units of that force would soon join the Rebel fleet.

There weren't many TIE fighters left for Bakura to use, though, after the Ssi-ruuk and then the Rebels decimated them. That concerned him.

Two Bakuran guards, the only armed men in sight—no, one was a woman—stood behind him. At last the final unit boarded. "Ramp, up," Thanas called in crisp military singsong.

He continued to stand on the ground, at attention. The Bakurans' stares burned his back. Inside the cockpit window, an experienced Imperial war pilot craned his head. Thanas saluted him, then signaled with one hand for liftoff. He backed away.

Engines ignited. He kept backing, as did the Bakuran guards. The shuttle lifted and began a slow turn.

Free . . . perhaps. Pter Thanas reached left-handed into his pocket. He held his salute while his hand closed on something small and hard. One Bakuran dropped to a firing crouch.

Smoothly Thanas drew out his pearl-handled folding knife. Ignoring the guard, he tucked his chin to his chest and sliced the red and blue rank insignia from his uniform. He pulled it off by one corner and dropped it into a pocket.

Then he turned to the crouching guard. "Sir," he said, "take me to Prime Minister Captison. If you mean to refit a *Carrack*-class cruiser for service, you need experienced advice. I know that cruiser."

The Bakuran lowered his Imperial blaster rifle. "Under the Alliance, sir?"

Thanas nodded. "That's right, soldier. Under the Alliance. I'm defecting."

"Uh, yessir. Follow me."

Thanas followed at a quick march to a Bakuran landspeeder.

One TIE fighter went to the Alliance as booty. Commander Luke Skywalker pulled rank and got the shuttle mission . . . with the medic's reluctant approval.

Approaching the captured Ssi-ruuvi cruiser, newly repaired and rechristened *Sibwarra* (though its small Alliance crew called it the *Flutie,* and he suspected that was the name that would stick), he gripped the controls through the gloves of a full vacuum suit. Compared with an X-wing, this was like riding an unshielded cargo box. It turned and accelerated like a terrified womp rat, but it wobbled, unstable in every vector plane.

It wasn't just his lifelong urge to fly a TIE fighter—once—that had driven him to request this mission. He must return to that Ssi-ruuvi bridge for a final glimpse. He felt as if the odor of darkness still clung to him, he'd come so close to falling. How many times must he renounce the darkness? As he grew in power and knowledge, would temptation beckon again and again?

Gingerly he docked the fighter in a vast Ssi-ruuvi hangar bay, perhaps the same one where Han had landed the *Falcon* to rescue him. The Bakuran replacement crew would surrender it to a Rebel pilot for transport to the Fleet, eventually, since Luke's carrier had been destroyed. There would be regular communications between Bakura and the Alliance, now. Admiral Ackbar might want to use the TIE fighter in some future undercover operation, although Luke would recommend shredding it for flak.

Hurriedly he made his way to the bridge, where he stood for a moment in the hatchway and watched a bustle of activity.

It looked foreign, but not hostile. It was only a place built of metals and plastics. Yet the ship's very bulkheads seemed haunted with Dev's long deception and his years of servitude, and with the slaved human energies Luke had liberated.

Light endured, and so did darkness. He would choose daily.

Luke walked the cruiser from top to bottom. When he finished, three hours later, he left with a clear conscience. No captive human energies remained.

Han pressed one finger to his ear and waved Luke to a seat behind Chewbacca. Once his hand dropped, he growled at Chewie, "I don't care what you were doing. Recording circuits ought to be on at all times."

Chewie clanged a bulkhead with his spanner. Evidently the often-modified *Falcon* was up to her old tricks.

"What is it?" Still standing, Luke waded into the argument.

"Subspace radio, relayed from maximum range. From Ackbar, too, coded. I had to decode as it came in, since Furball here disengaged the automatic—"

"Ackbar?" Leia set a hand on Luke's shoulder. He touched it, grateful for her consolation.

"Yeah," drawled Han. "Something about 'Imperial battle group,' something something 'small,' and 'quickly if we can.'"

"We scattered so many of them, back at Endor." Leia leaned forward. "Ackbar's scouts have probably found a group he thinks we could handle. The Empire is still vast. We must maintain the momentum of their downslide."

"Well, then," said Luke, "time to head back. After . . . ?" He glanced down at Han for confirmation.

"Oh, yeah. Sure, kid," Han mumbled. "Might as well strap in, Leia. Luke has business to finish. It'll just take a minute."

"Now, Mistress Leia," Threepio called over the comlink from his post with Artoo at the gaming table. "Let me tell you how I arrived at the *Falcon,* dressed in stormtrooper armor . . ."

Luke made his way to the primary airlock, where Chewbacca had carried Dev's body. Sorrowfully, he reached down and brushed Gaeri's feather-soft shawl with his fingertips. Chewbacca had wrapped it tightly around Dev's head and shoulders, after swathing the rest of him in an old blanket. He'd lost them both, Gaeriel and Dev . . . yet both had touched and taught him. Both would live in his memory. "Thanks," he whispered.

"Ready, Luke?" Leia asked softly over the comlink.

Luke backed out of the airlock. Automatically it hissed shut behind him. "Wait a minute," he told her. He hurried back to the cockpit and stared out the main viewport.

Leia clasped his hand. Han pulled the hatch release, then reversed lateral thrusters. As the *Falcon* accelerated heavenward, Dev's body plummeted toward Bakura. It finished burning, clean and brightly, down through the planet's high atmosphere.

Luke stared at the meteor, a momentary flare of brilliance . . . like all life. Nothing really, in the sweep of time. But everything, in the Force.